WASHINGTON!

The ninth exciting novel
in the WAGONS WEST series—
epic adventures of daring men and women
whose struggles fulfilled a nation's destiny
and brought the American way of life
to the brawling settlers of
the great Northwest.

WAGONS WEST

WASHINGTON!

COURAGEOUS MEN AND WOMEN EMBRACE THE SPLENDOR OF LUSH MOUNTAIN FORESTS AND BRING LAW TO A VIOLENT LAND

TOBY HOLT—
The hot-tempered son of wagonmaster
Whip Holt blazes a trail west to face the
challenge of danger and love.

ROB MARTIN—
A handsome land surveyor who is Toby Holt's
partner and best friend until fate makes him
a rival for a woman's love.

CAROLINE BRANDON HOLT—
The seductively beautiful courtesan who
has become Toby's wife . . . and
may become his ruin.

BETH BLAKE—
The vivacious, attractive young woman whose
attentions heal a war hero's wounds, but
whose affections are pledged to another man.

WHIP HOLT—
The valiant old patriarch of Wagons West
vows to fight for his son's interests, but
the rugged mountain terrain threatens to
push him to the limits of his strength.

TOM HARRISON—
A huge lumberjack who takes whatever he
wants—and he wants liquor, women and
the Holt land.

FRANK WOODS—
A powerful young blacksmith who is ready to
kill to protect a woman's honor or
to avenge a friend.

BETTINA SNOW—
The lovely New England widow who joins the
"cargo of brides" sent to marry the lonely men
of Washington, but finds a promise of happiness
shattered by an unscrupulous criminal.

CLARISSA SINCLAIR—
A handsome, sensual woman who searches for a
new life on the frontier and finds a fearless
lover who can match her strong-willed desires.

Bantam Books by Dana Fuller Ross
Ask your bookseller for the books you have missed

WAGONS WEST ★ NINTH IN A SERIES

WASHINGTON!

DANA FULLER ROSS

 Created by the producers of
White Indian, Children of the Lion,
Saga of the Southwest, and
The Kent Family Chronicles Series.

Executive Producer: Lyle Kenyon Engel

BANTAM BOOKS
TORONTO • NEW YORK • LONDON • SYDNEY • AUCKLAND

WASHINGTON!

A Bantam Book / published by arrangement with
Book Creations, Inc.

Bantam edition / September 1982
2nd printing . September 1982   4th printing . September 1982
3rd printing . September 1982   5th printing . . . . . . July 1983
6th printing . . . November 1984

Produced by Book Creations, Inc.
Chairman of the Board: Lyle Kenyon Engel

ISBN 0-553-25010-8

Published simultaneously in the United States and Canada

PRINTED IN THE UNITED STATES OF AMERICA

H   15 14 13 12 11 10 9

WASHINGTON!

This is a work of fiction. While the general outlines of history have been faithfully followed, certain details involving setting, characters, and events may have been simplified.

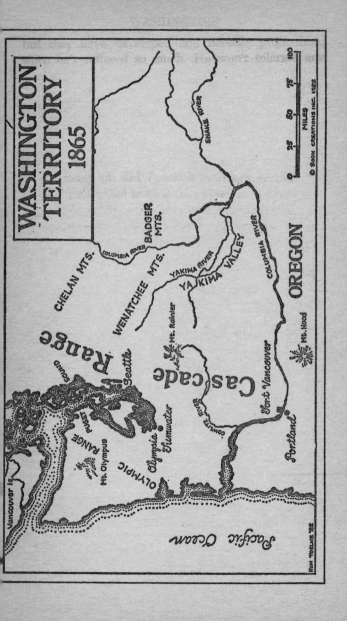

★ Lumber Camp of Holt, Martin, and Woods ★

I

Early in 1865, the Civil War was coming to an end, and the exhausted Union and the humbled, doomed Confederacy would soon be reunited once more and would begin the long, arduous task of reconstruction. That portion of the United States that lay farthest from the arena of combat, the Pacific Northwest, recovered the normal tenor of its ways more rapidly than most other sections of the nation precisely because it was so remote. Directly to the west lay the Pacific Ocean, to the north stood Canada, and to the south were Oregon and California, both of them having achieved statehood in the previous decade, and both of them prospering and growing.

The territory of Washington was indeed still a frontier wilderness, and very isolated, but the residents of the area neither knew nor cared. What they realized beyond all else was that they lived in a land of unsurpassed physical grandeur, and the residents of the small lumbering and farming community of Tumwater regarded themselves as fortunate. Tumwater lay a mile from Olympia, the territorial capital, which rested at the base of Puget Sound and was a rich source of lobsters, crabs, oysters, and other seafood. To the north were the Olympic Mountains. To the east lay the Cascade Range dominated by Mount Rainier, a mighty, perpetually snow-covered peak that soared more than fourteen thousand feet above sea level.

Tumwater's vegetables were oversized, and the salmon from Washington's lakes and streams were enormous. The trees—spruce and fir, cedar and hemlock—were some of the most magnificent of the American Far West, many of them soaring to heights of two hundred feet and more. The forests of the territory were responsible for Tumwater's primary industry, lumbering.

Rob Martin, red-haired and green-eyed, recently discharged from the Union army after four years of service, sat inconspicuously at a table in the rear of one of Tumwater's few eating and drinking establishments and was well satisfied with the town and with himself. Rob had been born and had grown to manhood only a hundred miles away, in Oregon, to which his parents, Dr. Robert Martin and the former Tonie Mell, had migrated as members of the first wagon train to the area. So he was not entirely a stranger to either the atmosphere or the scenery of Washington, for it was similar to that of Oregon in the early days, when it was still a United States territory. Indeed, Washington had at one time been part of the vast Oregon Territory, before Oregon had become a state in 1859.

Rob and his partner, Toby Holt, the son of the

great mountain man, Whip Holt, and his wife, Eulalia, had acquired a large tract of land in Tumwater, sight unseen. As soon as Rob returned to Portland, he intended to write to Toby at the army hospital in Washington City, where he was still recovering from a battle wound incurred in the war, to tell him the good news. They were very fortunate; they were the owners of choice, rich property that was bound to pay handsome dividends.

The scene was raucous, but Rob accepted the turmoil as normal and natural. This was payday for the lumberjacks, and they had turned out in force to celebrate. They were doing more drinking than eating, and on hand to help relieve them of their hard-earned dollars were a number of prostitutes, who provided one of the community's few diversions.

Rob enjoyed his vegetable soup as he watched the lumberjacks. They worked hard, but they also played hard, and there was nothing mean-spirited about them. They joked amiably, and even when two of them competed for the favors of one of the trollops, they seemed to enjoy the game.

Suddenly the atmosphere changed. Two newcomers entered the café, one of them the tallest, huskiest man Rob had ever seen, and the crowd fell silent. What Rob noticed most was the undercurrent of fear that seemed to run through the crowd. Certainly the large man was of a size to inspire fear. He was perhaps five or six inches taller than Rob—who was himself six feet tall and broad-shouldered—and he had arms and legs that resembled the stout trunks of trees. His hands were enormous, and his dark, bearded face seemed to be twisted in a perpetual scowl. His companion, surprisingly, was short and slender. He had beady eyes and a groveling air.

Rob was curious and asked the waitress, who had just brought him a platter of freshly baked bread, "Who are those fellows?"

The middle-aged woman seemed uneasy as she replied. "Everyone hereabouts knows Tom Harrison," she said. "He runs the lumber camp, and he's as ornery and mean as they come."

Rob continued to eye the man speculatively. "You mean he owns the lumber camp?" he asked, surprised that such a roughly dressed man should be a proprietor of valuable property.

The waitress shrugged. "I don't rightly know as how I can answer that question," she said. "All I know is that what he says goes around here."

"Who's his friend?"

The contempt in the woman's voice was unmistakable. "That there," she said, "is Mr. Trumbull. He's the paymaster of the lumberjack community, and he's a sure-enough jackal. He just follows Harrison around, and whatever Tom wants, Mr. Trumbull makes good and sure he gets it."

At that moment Harrison looked slowly around the large room, his black eyes gleaming, and finally he paused to study a grizzled lumberjack who was paying no attention to him. The roughly clad man had placed an arm around the waist of a heavily made-up prostitute, and drawing her onto his lap, he began speaking to her earnestly in a low tone.

For some reason Harrison was insulted. Pointing to the man, he muttered something under his breath to Mr. Trumbull, who nodded, walked closer to the table occupied by the lumberjack, and called to him,

"You there! Don't you know that Mr. Harrison demands a mite of respect when he comes into a place? The least you could do is stop talking and pawing the wench until he decides which woman he wants."

The man was startled but held his ground. "I don't know who Harrison thinks he is, but it don't matter none to me," he said loudly enough for everyone to hear. "I'll mind my own business, and let him mind his!"

Harrison emitted a roar and pointed a huge forefinger at the man who had committed lese majesty. "I reckon," he growled in a voice that sounded like a saw cutting through hardwood, "that you need to be taught a lesson, mister." He began to advance slowly toward the table, grinning sourly.

The lumberjack stood abruptly, his movements so sudden that the woman tumbled from his lap, rewarding him with a long, vulgar curse. Ignoring her, the lumberjack reached for the ax that he carried in his belt, but before he could draw and raise it, Tom Harrison was virtually on top of him. The sound of Harrison's fist striking the other man's face echoed through the café, and the lumberjack dropped to the floor, like a tall tree that had just been cut down.

Rob Martin had never seen such an exhibition of raw power; never had he encountered anyone endowed with the brutal strength of Tom Harrison.

The other customers also had watched the scene in shocked silence, and all at once they began to talk. Their conversation was obviously strained, but all had the same thought in mind: they wanted to appear busy in order not to draw Harrison's attention to them.

Rob Martin continued to be fascinated, however,

and did not lower his gaze. So, when Harrison and his companion sat down at a nearby table, the attention of the lumbering community supervisor was drawn to the young veteran. Only then did Rob look away, butter a slab of bread, and eat it with what was left of his soup.

The waitress reappeared, but instead of serving the rest of his dinner, she placed a shot glass of whiskey in front of him. "Compliments of Tom Harrison," she said in obvious disapproval, then hurried off to the kitchen before he could question her.

Rob raised his head and saw Mr. Trumbull watching him closely. Tom Harrison appeared to have no interest in him, however, for he was sitting with his chair tipped back and his booted feet on the table top as he sipped a drink.

Suddenly the giant's associate jumped up and hurriedly joined Rob. "Be you Martin or Holt?" the little man wanted to know.

Rob was stunned that anything was known about him. "I'm Robert Martin. Captain Holt, my partner, won't be discharged from the army until he's completely recovered from his wounds." Rob paused. "How did you happen to know my identity?"

Trumbull's tone became reverential. "Mr. Harrison," he said, "knows everything there is to know in Tumwater. He knows who owns every inch of property, he makes it his business to find out about every stranger who comes to town, and there ain't nothing that escapes him."

"Mr. Harrison appears to be quite a man." Rob motioned toward the victim of Harrison's assault, who slowly hauled himself up off the floor, shook his head, and then crept quietly from the café.

Trumbull nodded solemnly. "He's the boss, and Lord help anybody who wants to argue the matter with him," he said. "He likes his booze strong, his women willing, and his property productive."

Rob Martin concealed his amusement. "You work for him, do you?"

"Well now, I'm on his payroll," Trumbull said, "and I aim to please him when I can. And when I have the opportunity, I look out for myself, too."

Rob gingerly fingered the glass of whiskey Tom Harrison had sent over to him. He was not fond of strong drinks and certainly had no desire to be beholden to Harrison. "Since I never knew of Mr. Harrison's existence until a few moments ago," he said, "I wonder why he's being so kind to me?"

Trumbull smiled and sat down in a chair next to Rob's. Then he lowered his voice and said, "You and your partner got your hands on a choice piece of land, mighty choice. Matter of fact, we were wondering just the other day how you happened to acquire it."

That, Rob decided, was none of the man's business. It so happened that Whip Holt had done considerable exploration in the area, a quarter of a century earlier, after he had led the first wagon train to Oregon from the East Coast, and he had established a claim to the property. Now that the war had ended and Toby and Rob were searching for gainful occupation, he had turned the site over to them to utilize as they pleased. That, however, was not the concern of any outsider.

Trumbull did not appear to take it amiss that his question had not been answered. "Mr. Harrison," he said tentatively "has a hankering for that land. A real hankering."

Rob replied mildly, "I guess a great many people would like it. I understand that the stands of trees on it are extraordinary, even by the standards of the Washington Territory."

Trumbull nodded conspiratorially and leaned closer to Rob. "Seeing that Tom owns the property that adjoins yours," he said, "he sure would like to own your land, too. I'm sure if you made it available to him, he'd be glad to pay you a fair price for it. What do you suppose you and your partner would want for it?"

Rob took a deep breath. "That land," he said, "isn't for sale. We've had it for some time, and we're going to start lumbering there in earnest one of these days, so we're going to keep it. But thanks all the same."

Trumbull's manner changed. No longer jovial and buoyant, he looked sorrowfully at the younger man. "Mr. Martin," he said earnestly, "you be new to these parts, and I hate to see anybody get off on the wrong foot. Like I said, anything that Tom Harrison wants, Tom Harrison gets. He's a good friend, but he's a mighty bad enemy."

Rob did not raise his voice. "Are you trying to tell me," he said, "that he'd regard me as his enemy simply because I refuse to sell a valuable parcel of land to him?"

"Well, now, it all depends on the point of view and where you sit," Trumbull said. "Tom kind of considers Tumwater as his private preserve, you might say. Since he owns a number of parcels here himself and manages quite a few others, he's become accustomed to having everything nice and cozy. If you don't want to cooperate with him, you might run into all kinds of trouble."

"What is that supposed to mean?" Rob demanded, a metallic quality creeping into his voice.

Trumbull spread his hands in a helpless gesture. "You might have trouble, for one thing, in recruiting a work force of lumberjacks," he said. "For another, you might have a hard time finding someone to haul your logs away to the sawmills. There's all kinds of things that could happen."

Rob smiled slightly. "You assume," he said, "that my partner and I come from the East somewhere."

The little man nodded. "Right," he replied. "It's like Tom was saying just the other day, that a couple of war veterans from New York or Pennsylvania or somewhere saw an opportunity and bought themselves a chunk of prime forest land hereabouts."

"Toby Holt was born on his father's ranch in Oregon," Rob said, "and I hail from the town that's now called Portland. We're not greenhorns out here, and our folks came across the country in the first wagon train. I reckon we have as much reason as anybody else to call this part of the U.S.A. home. Just thought I'd mention the point in passing," he added nonchalantly.

Trumbull absorbed the news in silence and then asked, "Is your partner any relation to Whip Holt, the mountain man?"

Rob's expression remained unchanged. "He's Toby's father and my godfather. Toby and I were brought up to believe in our rights, you know. We don't scare easy, we won't be bullied, and although

9

we're peaceable enough, when we're hit, we strike back, good and hard."

"Don't get me wrong, Mr. Martin," Trumbull said piously. "I'm a law-abiding man myself. Tom Harrison now, he sometimes steps outside the bounds of the law, but only when he's dealing with unruly characters, you might say. He finds it easier to haul them into line that way."

"You can tell Mr. Harrison—or if you wish, I'll be delighted to tell him myself—that my partner and I are keeping our property in Tumwater. We have no axes to grind, but if Harrison decides that makes us his enemies, then so be it. He'll find we can take care of ourselves."

"Don't be too sure of that," Trumbull replied softly. "Maybe you know your way around the wilderness, and maybe you can handle firearms, but you've never run into the likes of Tom Harrison before. He's like a solid block of granite, and anybody who runs into him is going to crumble. He won't budge, and don't you forget it."

"It's going to be interesting," Rob answered pleasantly, "because Toby and I can be two of the most stubborn fellows you ever did meet. We don't scare easy."

"Mr. Harrison," Trumbull said plaintively, "told me to give you a message if it appeared that you were being a mite reluctant in wanting to sell to him." He reached into his belt, drew a hunting knife, and placed it on the pine table.

Rob picked up the knife, tested the point and blade with his thumb, and then suddenly, swiftly drove the steel shaft into the soft pinewood table. It remained there, quivering slightly, until Trumbull pulled it out of the wood and slipped it back into its sheath. Giving an exaggerated sigh, he rose and started back to rejoin Tom Harrison at their own table. "Don't say you ain't been warned, Martin," he declared.

Rob remained remarkably civil. "The same to you," he replied.

The mighty Columbia River, the so-called gateway to the Northwest, separated the state of Oregon from the Washington Territory. On the south bank of the river, near the community that now called itself Portland, stood the ranch where Whip Holt raised horses. His spread consisted of more than two thousand acres and was considered unique in Oregon.

The ranch house, originally built of logs, still had a rustic motif, but Eulalia Holt had constantly enlarged it over the course of a quarter of a century. With much of the structure now made of clapboard and brick, it was as comfortable as any dwelling in New York or Chicago. The rooms were furnished in good taste, and the guest quarters were almost sumptuous.

Certainly Cathy Blake, the wife of Major General Leland Blake, a distinguished commander of one of General Ulysses S. Grant's corps, had no cause for complaint. One of the oldest friends of Whip and Eulalia, who had herself played a leading role in the crossing of the continent on the first wagon train to Oregon, she was enjoying being a guest at the Holt ranch while her husband completed his tour of duty, and she was very much at home there. In fact, she surprised herself because she was so much at ease. She and Whip had enjoyed a romance during the

11

wagon train journey, but she had married Lee Blake and had lost her heart to him. Cathy thought of Eulalia Holt and smiled. Only a woman who was very sure of herself and of her husband would be more than willing to tolerate the presence under her roof of her husband's still-attractive former sweetheart.

Staring critically at her reflection in the dressing-table mirror in her bedchamber, Cathy had to admit that time had been kind to her. Her long hair was still blond and only faintly sprinkled with gray. Her blue eyes remained large and compelling, and there were remarkably few wrinkles at their corners.

A tap sounded at the door, and before Cathy could speak, it burst open and then slammed with a vengeance. Beth Blake, a younger, almost identical version of her mother, flounced into the room and petulantly threw herself into an easy chair near the dressing table.

Cathy regarded her daughter with amusement and pride. In her mid-twenties and a graduate of Antioch College, Beth had spent the last two years touring the major capitals of Europe and somehow avoiding romantic entanglements with her many European suitors. Indeed, she had almost become engaged to a dashing young Prussian nobleman, Bernhard von Hummel, who had courted her both in America and in Europe, but at the last moment she realized she had no desire to be an aristocrat's wife. Like the daughters of so many army officers, Beth had lived in all parts of the United States as well as in Europe, and she was far more worldly and sophisticated than her mother had ever been.

"That woman," she declared emphatically, "makes me positively ill."

Cathy, knowing who her daughter was referring to, said nothing and picked up a brush and applied it vigorously to her hair.

"There she is," Beth said, sitting upright and nodding toward the windows. "Have you ever seen such a disgusting sight?"

Following her daughter's gaze, Cathy looked out the window and saw Caroline Brandon Holt, Toby's wife, who was mincing on the path that led to the stables, As usual, her gleaming blond hair hung loosely to her waist, she was heavily made up, and she wore a low-necked, figure-hugging dress, which was totally inappropriate for wear on a ranch. The heels of her shoes were so high that she had difficulty in walking.

"Unbelievable, isn't it?" Beth demanded. "She shows absolutely no respect for the people she is living with and the man she's married to. The strumpet!"

"Let me remind you, dear," her mother replied gently, "that we're guests under the Holt roof. I don't think it's any too polite to call Toby Holt's wife ugly names."

Beth showed signs of impatience. "In case you've forgotten, Mother, I got to know Caroline when I went back to school and accompanied the wagon train from Nevada to the East. Almost everyone on that train knew she had been a professional prostitute in Nevada. I must admit that Caroline behaved courageously when we switched to the railroad and the Confederates temporarily gained control of the train. However, when she was seriously wounded, she used her injury to get Toby to marry her—he thought that he was giving in to her dying request! Well, you know the rest. She recovered her health completely, and the Holts have been saddled with her ever since."

"Assuming that you're right, dear, and I'm not for a moment doubting your story," Cathy replied, "I honestly don't see what anyone can do about it. Caroline is Toby's legal wife, and Whip and Eulalia feel responsible for their daughter-in-law's welfare and well-being until their son regains his health sufficiently to return here for her."

"Uncle Whip and Aunt Eulalia are being taken advantage of," Beth said, then fell silent.

"In all justice to Caroline, whom I've known since her late first husband was associated with your father as a geologist in Denver, she must be bored living such a quiet life on a secluded ranch. She's young and high-spirited and enjoys a good time, and I daresay that she dresses and makes up as she does just to give herself something of a lively feeling."

"I'm sorry to disagree with you, Mother, but you really are wonderful. You find something good to say about everyone. The reason that Caroline primps and dresses the way she does is simply to attract men."

"Are you implying that she's unfaithful to Toby?" Cathy asked, raising an eyebrow.

Beth hesitated for a moment. "No," she said at last. "But I've noticed that every man who comes here stares at her, and she loves every minute of it."

"Well," Cathy said, "it's none of our business, so dismiss her from your mind."

"I wish I could," Beth replied, "but I'm feeling sorry for Toby. He's been recovering from a serious war injury, and he's coming home to a wife who's too much for him to handle. I don't envy him."

"I thought you didn't get along any too well with Toby Holt."

Beth shrugged. "That's because you and Papa always threw me at him, and the Holts threw Toby right back at me. I came to know him, however, on the wagon train from Nevada, and he's a good person. Certainly he's too good for Caroline, and he deserves a better fate than he has in store as her husband."

The likes and dislikes of the younger generation were too confusing for Cathy to understand, so she left her daughter and wandered out to the kitchen of the ranch house, intending to get herself a cup of tea. She heard voices as she approached the room and, slowing her pace, saw Eulalia Holt and her sister-in-law, Cindy Woodling, sitting at the table conversing earnestly in low tones. Halting to look at them, Cathy had to admit that Eulalia, too, had retained her striking beauty and her svelte figure. Her dark hair had not faded, and her blue eyes were still huge and startling. Her skin was that of a much younger woman, and thanks to the care she exercised in watching her diet, she was as slender as she had been as a young woman on the wagon train that had brought them all to Oregon. Certainly she didn't look like the mother of a grown son and of an adolescent daughter.

"Come in, Cathy," Eulalia called.

"Are you sure I'm not interrupting?"

Both women shook their heads. "Certainly not!" Eulalia said.

"As a matter of fact," Cindy Woodling added, "perhaps you can make a contribution to our discussion. We're wrestling with a rather nasty little problem."

Cathy entered the kitchen, saw a pot of tea simmering on the stove, and poured herself a cup before she joined her old friends at the table.

"I'm afraid," Eulalia said, "that we're discussing my daughter-in-law again. I don't know if you've seen Caroline today, but her outfit is outlandish—it's just too much, and she's plastered her face with cosmetics, as though she were in a Denver or a San Francisco saloon."

Cathy smiled slightly. "I just caught a glimpse of her, and I know what you mean."

"The problem that faces Eulalia and Whip," Cindy said, "is how to handle such a flamboyant daughter-in-law, when they also have a daughter in her mid-teens living under the same roof. Young Cindy is growing up, and she's very susceptible now."

"I see what you mean," Cathy said, "and offhand, I'm afraid I can't make any constructive suggestions. Have you tried speaking to Caroline and urging her to alter her appearance?"

Eulalia sipped her tea, then sighed wearily. "I've talked to her until I am hoarse, and so has Whip. She agrees to everything we say. In fact, it's rather remarkable how she never disputes a word, but she pays no attention to our advice and continues to do precisely as she pleases."

"To an extent," Cathy said, "I think that's the case with the entire younger generation. They became adults during the Civil War, and it left a strong mark on all of them."

"There's more than a war that's left its mark on Caroline," Eulalia said. "Cindy, what do you think?"

Both Cathy and Eulalia turned to Cindy and were prepared to accept anything that she might say to them. They had not forgotten that many years ago Cindy had joined their wagon train in order to escape a life as a prostitute in Louisville and had successfully rehabilitated herself.

"I suppose," Cindy said, "there's no real difference in the temperament of a trollop today and the trollops of yesterday. They're alike in a great many ways. Most of them went into the work because of economic necessity, and they enjoy exercising control over men." Cindy paused a moment, scrutinizing the two other women, then plunged ahead. "You won't like this, I'm afraid," she said, "but I've never forgotten a saying we had at the house near the waterfront in Louisville where I once worked. 'A whore is a whore, and as long as she looks and acts like one, she'll be one.'"

"You're not very encouraging, I must say," Eulalia murmured.

"Are you suggesting, Cindy, that Eulalia and Whip are going to be forced to condone Caroline's appearance and her flirtatious conduct with every man who comes to the ranch?" Cathy asked.

"If you're going to keep her here, I'm afraid you have no choice. She's a grown woman, and you have no right to criticize either her appearance or her conduct."

"I've made it plain to her," Eulalia said, "that for young Cindy's sake I wish she'd be more circumspect. She seems to understand what I am talking about and agrees, but she changes nothing."

"In that case," her sister-in-law said, "you may be forced to ask her to leave."

17

Eulalia looked miserable. "I wanted to do just that," she said, "but I can't. My husband won't permit it. Almost four years ago, when he and Toby parted company in the East, Toby asked as a special favor that we look after his wife until he came for her. He's been seriously wounded in the service of his country, and he's spent the better part of a year in an army hospital. Both of you know Whip. He pledged his word to his son, and nothing on earth will persuade him to break it."

Cathy and Cindy exchanged quick glances. As Cathy well knew, honor meant everything to Whip Holt, and if his mind was made up—as it was, apparently—nothing could be done about it. "Then I'm afraid," she said, "you'll just have to grin and bear it."

"When Toby does get here," Cindy said, "perhaps he can talk some sense into his wife. In any event, the problem will be his, not yours."

Recalling her own conversation with Beth a short time earlier, Cathy added, "Cheer up, Eulalia, dear. The situation could be far worse, you know. As nearly as I can tell, Caroline is indulging in a few surface mannerisms. I'll grant you that she wears rather outrageous and revealing clothes and that her cosmetics would do credit to a dance-hall hostess, but she doesn't actually stray from the marital path, as I understand it."

Eulalia nodded slowly. "Yes, you're right there," she said. "She hasn't actually done anything worse than engage in some silly flirtations with some of the hired hands and the male visitors to the ranch. She hasn't actually engaged in any affairs."

Cindy laughed harshly. "That's because she has more common sense than you give her credit for having. She knows that if she really is guilty of infidelity to Toby, you and Whip will throw her out instantly."

"Yes," Eulalia agreed. "Such conduct would negate Whip's promise."

"Then, under the circumstances," Cathy said, the only advice that I can give you is to be patient a bit longer. Hold on tight and explain your own values often and emphatically to young Cindy. She's a sensible child, and I'm sure she'll accept your guidance and Whip's. How soon do you expect Toby to arrive?"

"We had word that he was due three months ago, and then we had another letter saying that we could expect him last month. So I honestly don't know," Eulalia said. "All I can tell you is that, as anxious as I am to see Toby again, I'm just praying that he'll be able to control the wife he so foolishly married!"

Caroline Brandon Holt entered the large horse barn, where two young ranch hands were busy leading horses into the corral. She was looking forward to chatting and flirting with them, and she knew they would respond to her and look at her as all men did. This activity didn't totally relieve the boredom of living on the ranch for the last few years, but it was better than nothing.

Leaning against the door of one of the horse stalls, she smiled provocatively at the men, enjoying the way they gazed hungrily at her superb body encased in a figure-hugging gown of yellow silk.

"Mornin', ma'am," the taller of the two young men said, and he courteously doffed his wide-brimmed hat with his free hand, the other still holding the lead rope of one of the horses.

"Good morning—ah—Tom," Caroline said in her sweetest, most enticing voice.

"This here's Tom, ma'am," the tall ranch hand said, pointing to his partner. "Me, I'm Bob."

"Oh, dear," Caroline said giggling, and moved up to them, her green eyes wide and inviting. "There are so many men on the ranch, I get their names all mixed up."

"That's all right, ma'am," Tom said. "You can mix me up all you want." He smiled broadly, well aware that his meaning was not lost on the sensuous creature, who was standing so close to him that he could smell her perfume.

Caroline, her hands on her hips, returned the smile and positioned herself so that her body grazed the man's arm.

Bob added, "Me and Tom sure like being mixed up by you." With that, he winked at Caroline and allowed himself a long, slow look at her cleavage.

Suddenly the horse the men were leading began to bridle, and they were brought back to their senses. They well knew what kind of woman they were dealing with, but they also knew that she was married to their employer's son and that they dare go no further with her or they'd be immediately discharged. So they went back to their work, leading the horses out into the corral and eyeing Caroline from time to time as she leaned against the stable door and watched them.

Caroline certainly had enough sense to avoid any further intimacies with the hired hands. She knew that the Holts and their guests, Cathy and Beth Blake, would quickly learn of any indiscretions on her part, and she had to content herself with the kind of byplay she was expert at. It was the only way she knew to bide her time.

What exactly she was biding her time for was not clear to Caroline. She knew her husband had been wounded in the war and would be home soon, but she didn't particularly look forward to his homecoming. It wasn't that she didn't find Toby attractive and virile, but the thought of being tied down with him on the ranch, constantly surrounded by the disapproving eyes of his family, made her cringe. If perhaps they were able to get a house of their own in Portland, then she would be able to do with him as she pleased and do what she wanted for herself. But every moment she had spent on the ranch had been hell for her. Sooner or later she would have to get out. How she did not know, but she would take the first opportunity offered to her.

By this time Beth Blake had come to the stables to take one of the horses out for a ride. As she saddled and bridled her favorite mare, she saw Caroline standing not far away, watching the ranch hands. She felt nothing but contempt for the other woman. Leading her horse from the stable, she mounted and, after a brief canter, paused to rest at the crest of a hill.

As Beth gazed out across the rolling hills, she saw no signs of human habitation anywhere, and she rejoiced. She had to admit to herself that of all the places she had lived, there was nothing quite like the Pacific Northwest. She could understand the love the Holt family had for their property.

Suddenly she saw something moving through the grass, and when she realized it was an animal, she reached for the pistol that she habitually carried when making an excursion alone. Then, when the creature came closer, she dropped the pistol back into its holster and laughed.

Bounding toward her was a puppy, a lively German shepherd dog, and from the looks of him, he was no more than two or three months old. His paws were still thick and only semiformed, but his tail wagged furiously, and he flattened his ears against his head as he barked in greeting.

Reacting instinctively, Beth leaped from her saddle to the ground, scooped up the puppy, and regarded him quizzically. "I think you're lost, mister," she said. "The Holts don't have any dogs, and you're right smack in the midst of their property. Where do you come from, and who are you?"

The animal licked her face, and his tail wagged even more furiously.

The sound of a man's voice behind Beth startled her. "Well, now," Whip Holt said, chuckling, "what's all this?"

Beth turned and looked up at him on his horse. Although he was approximately the same age as her father, he looked much older, perhaps because he was afflicted with such severe arthritis. But no ailment could keep the renowned Whip Holt out of a saddle. Still lean and tanned, with the whip responsible for his nickname wound around his middle, he sat in the saddle with seeming ease, ignoring the aches of his protesting body.

"Let's have a look at you, young fellow," Whip said as he dismounted, and taking the puppy from Beth, he examined him thoroughly. "He's a healthy young critter," he said.

Beth nodded. "He must belong to someone and

got lost," she said. "All I know is that here he was in the middle of the range, rushing toward me."

Whip handed the dog to her and grinned. "Well, like it or not, young lady," he said, "it appears you've acquired a dog for yourself. I'll pass the word in town that he showed up here, and we'll see if anybody claims him. If not, you have yourself quite an animal."

"I'm sure Aunt Eulalia won't be very happy when she learns that I'm taxing her hospitality."

Whip chuckled and shook his head. "Don't you believe that for a minute," he said. "Toby had a shepherd for years, and Eulalia wouldn't think of turning the dog out. She has a warm spot in her for shepherds." He paused and studied her for a minute. "Going anywhere special?"

"No," she replied. "I was just out getting some exercise."

"Good, then I'll ride with you, if you don't mind."

As Beth mounted her horse, cradling the puppy with one arm and holding the reins with the other, she realized from Whip's somber expression that something was troubling him. As they trotted along, she waited for him to speak.

"How would you like to give an old man a mite of advice?" he finally asked.

"I'd be flattered," Beth said.

"Well, you understand your generation better than I do," he declared. "It's that confounded daughter-in-law of mine." He sighed. "You crossed the continent with us when she traveled east from Nevada," he said, "so I reckon that you know her about as well as anybody knows her. What do you make of her?"

"Do you want my real opinion, or shall I be polite, Uncle Whip?"

He frowned. "You ought to know me well enough to realize I always want the truth," he said, "no matter what."

"All right!" There was a touch of defiance in her attitude. "If you really want to know, I can't stand Caroline! She's a trollop, and I say she hasn't reformed in the least. I feel sorry for Toby, but I have no idea what to advise him. He was asking for trouble when he felt sorry for her and married her because he thought she was dying. She's the kind of woman who creates havoc for everyone around her."

Whip nodded thoughtfully and stared off at the mountains in the distance. "Toby was inexperienced when he married her, and his heart was bigger than his mind," he said. "I've seen women like Caroline all my life, I've run into them in saloons and in gambling halls and even less polite places for forty years or more, and I'm damned if I know how to protect a son who has to be confused and upset and miserable after spending nearly a whole year in an army hospital. That's what I wanted to find out from you. What can I do to make Toby's burden a little lighter?"

Beth considered the question and then replied firmly. "I'm afraid, Uncle Whip, that you can't do much of anything. Toby was a college boy studying railroading when he went into the army, but that was a lifetime ago. Since then, he's come to know life and death at close quarters, and he's become a man. I'm afraid that Caroline is strictly his problem, and he'll need to handle her as he sees fit."

Whip sighed again. "You've got a solid head on your shoulders, Beth," he said. "You always have had ever since you were a little tyke. I can't help wishing that you and Toby—" He broke off suddenly. "No point wishing that the moon was made of cheese," he said, "because it isn't."

Respecting his mood, Beth remained silent for the remainder of their ride. After circling the perimeter of the ranch, they ultimately headed back toward the house.

Suddenly Whip appeared more cheerful. "Let's see what that puppy does if you put him down," he said. "I'll be interested to find out whether he comes with you or heads off somewhere else."

Beth obediently placed the dog on the ground, and to her secret delight he trotted after her mare as rapidly as his short, wobbly legs would carry him.

Whip asked, "What are you going to name him, Beth—assuming no one down in town claims him?"

"I've already decided, Uncle Whip. As long as he's adopted me, he might as well adopt my name. I'm going to call him Mr. Blake."

"Mr. Blake," Whip called to the puppy, "you've got a smart head on you. I like that."

When they arrived at the house, Eulalia Holt gave the dog her immediate approval, much to Beth's relief. Cathy, however, was embarrassed. "I think this is asking a trifle too much," Cathy said. "You not only are putting up Beth and me until Lee gets here, but now you're going to be bothered with an unruly puppy as well."

"Nonsense," Eulalia replied. "Mr. Blake is already a member of the family, so there's not much that anyone can do to persuade him otherwise."

A short time later, a young man rode into the compound, and Beth was delighted when she recognized Rob Martin. They had seen each other several times when the Blakes had visited Oregon in the past. Beth had last seen him just before he'd gone off to war in 1861. She hurried out to the corral to greet him as he dismounted.

He saw her approach, and his face lit up. "I'm in luck," he said. "I heard tell you were here, and I rode out from town to see you the minute I got home today from the Washington Territory." He dismounted and removed his hat.

Smiling broadly, Beth extended a hand to him. Rob took it and pressed it warmly.

Reacting unconsciously, she made no attempt to withdraw her hand prematurely. She was vaguely aware of the fact that it felt natural and good nestling in the palm of Rob's large, brawny hand. "You look well," she said, examining him carefully. "Older, of course, but that's to be expected. My father said in a letter that you had become a splendid infantry platoon commander."

"Nice of General Blake to say so," he replied, "but all that's behind me now. The last I heard about you, you were gallivanting around Europe."

"Europe is behind me," she replied. "I'm glad I had the opportunity to see a number of countries, but I'm even happier to be home. I never knew how much I missed this country until I left it for a time."

He studied her closely. He had always admired Beth but had been forced to agree with his parents that she had been more than a little imperious and spoiled. But it appeared, at least at first glance, as though she, too, had matured and had become the woman she had shown such promise of becoming.

They walked together into the house and went to

the formal parlor, where they chatted at great length.

Eulalia and Cathy had been intending to go into the parlor themselves, but they stopped when they heard the sound of the young couple's voices. They exchanged a swift glance; each knew what the other was thinking.

"I believe I'll wait till later to welcome Rob back," Eulalia said. "He and Beth seem thoroughly preoccupied."

Cathy smiled. "Rob has been sweet on Beth ever since they were children."

A look of pain crossed Eulalia's face and then vanished. "I know," she said. "Once I hoped that Toby would wake up to her qualities and would give Rob a battle for her hand, but things just haven't worked out that way."

Cathy, aware of Eulalia's bitter disappointment, could only reach out sympathetically and pat her on the shoulder.

"A cup of tea cures just about every ailment there is," Eulalia said, "including a sour disposition. Let's go out to the kitchen and drown ourselves in a cup or two, shall we?" They strolled away from the parlor and made their way to the rear of the house.

Sitting together in the parlor, Beth and Rob brought each other up to date on all that had happened to both of them in the years since they had last seen each other. Beth was particularly interested in his joint venture with Toby Holt in the Washington Territory, and as Rob described the scenery there, it occurred to her that she had taken Rob Martin for granted too long. He was an exceptionally attractive man, virile and straightforward, ruggedly handsome and far more direct than the European men with whom she had dealt in the past.

For his part, Rob was convinced that his initial analysis of Beth had been correct. She was no longer tart-tongued, and she was the prettiest and most wholesome woman he had ever seen. It was strange, he mused, but they had not been ready for each other when they had last met shortly after the Civil War had started. They had needed these years of hardship and rough experience to appreciate each other.

All at once, Rob realized they were not alone in the room. Looking up, he saw someone standing in the entrance to the parlor and was startled by the appearance of the most extraordinary young woman he had ever seen. Her long, straight blond hair fell almost to her slender waist. The green color of her enormous eyes was emphasized by a skillful application of eye shadow, and her scarlet mouth shone invitingly. Her figure was superb, and she did nothing to conceal it. On the contrary, the plunging neckline of her snug-fitting gown revealed the cleavage between her large, high breasts, and a daring slit in her skirt showed a length of leg, clad in a black net stocking.

Had Rob seen the young woman in a saloon frequented by Union officers, he would have known at a glance that she was a high-priced courtesan. Seeing her here, in the Holt house, confused him.

Beth followed his gaze and was annoyed but not surprised when she saw Caroline. It was obvious to her that Caroline had seen Rob arrive and had deliberately primped for his benefit before making an appearance. There was no way to get rid of her, however, and Beth tried to cope as best she could, making the necessary introductions.

Rob was stunned. While in the army, he had received letters from his parents describing the provocative woman Toby had married, but he hadn't expected to see anyone quite so provoking. Nevertheless, he was polite as he stood and said to Caroline, "I saw Toby not too long ago."

Caroline came into the room and sat down opposite the young couple, crossing her legs artfully in order to reveal still more of her thigh. "How long ago did you see him?" she asked politely.

It was clear, at least to Beth, that the other woman had no interest in her husband but was merely saying what was expected of her.

Rob explained that he had last seen his friend about nine weeks earlier. "He was making fine progress, and I'm sure he'll be heartened by my report on the property we own in the Washington Territory," he said. "I think you can expect him home at any time."

Caroline nodded, smiled, and murmured something to the effect that she found it difficult to wait for Toby to appear. However, she blatantly flirted with Rob, who didn't quite know how to react.

It soon became apparent that Caroline knew nothing about her husband's business, and in response to her questions, Rob had to explain to her that he and Toby were joint owners of a rich tract of woodland, which they hoped to develop, in the Washington Territory.

Caroline was not interested in the details of the business arrangement. Instead, she picked out what was important to her. "If you and Toby are partners," she said, her sparkling eyes widening, "then you and I

29

are certain to see a great deal of each other. I'm so glad," she added softly.

Rob was so startled that he didn't know how to react. Beth, coldly furious, came to his rescue and said she would escort him to his waiting horse. Ordinarily she would have treated Rob circumspectly after their long separation, but she realized there was only one language that Caroline was capable of understanding. Therefore, she took his arm in a gesture that was both intimate and proprietary.

Caroline knew better than to challenge the other woman, particularly when the third party was her husband's partner. Thus, she gave him her most limpid smile and bade him farewell.

Mr. Blake, the shepherd puppy, frolicked at Beth's heels as she walked with Rob to the corral. She was secretly pleased that Rob, who had been greeted warmly by Eulalia Holt and Cathy Blake as he left the house, had accepted Eulalia's invitation to supper the next day. Beth also looked forward to dining at the Martin house, as soon as Rob made arrangements with his mother.

As they stood together at the hitching post, Rob could not resist mentioning the subject that troubled him. "Toby told me the story of how he happened to get married, but he didn't go into too much detail about his wife's personality. Is she—ah—always so forward?"

"Always, I'm afraid," Beth replied unhappily.

"Toby has changed," Rob said slowly. "He was a boy filled with dreams of railroading when he went off to war, and what struck me about him most when I visited him at the army hospital was his similarity to his father. He always had those qualities, I'm sure, but they have developed and become pronounced since he's suffered so much. He won't tolerate any misconduct on his wife's part any more than his father would."

"If he's the least bit like Whip Holt," Beth replied, absently bending down to pat the puppy, "then I feel almost sorry for Caroline. There's going to be a real electrical storm when he arrives here, complete with thunder and lightning!"

II

The house, an imposing structure of red brick, stood at the crest of a hill, and from it one could see virtually all of the bustling, still-growing town of Independence, Missouri. Strangers would have known at a glance that the structure was the dwelling of important residents of Independence, and they certainly would have been right.

Sam Brentwood, one-time mountain man, friend of Whip Holt, and the original leader of the first wagon train to Oregon, had prospered enormously since he had married Cathy Blake's older sister, Claudia, and had settled with her in the then frontier town of Independence. In the past quarter of a century, the community had become the starting point for the Oregon Trail and the Santa Fe Trail, and most of the pioneers who had made the long journey to the West had purchased their supplies, firearms, and even their wagons and horses from Sam Brentwood, who had become one of the leading citizens of the state and who had devoted himself wholeheartedly to the Union cause in the war.

Now he and Claudia were enjoying a rare evening, entertaining their brother-in-law, the distinguished Major General Leland Blake. Claudia knew that she and her husband had aged a great deal; Sam, who still walked with a limp, had become white-haired and had gained considerable weight in recent years, and Claudia, herself, had developed a matronly figure. Lee Blake, however, appeared to be almost as youthful and vigorous in appearance as he had ever been. Granted that his hair was now gray and that his face was lined, but the candlelight of the dinner table was kind to him, and his voice was as rich, vibrant, and strong as it had always been.

"As you can well imagine," he said, "I'm looking forward to seeing Cathy and Beth again. I missed Beth, unfortunately, when she landed on the East Coast from Europe. I'd been given command of one of General Grant's corps, and I couldn't take the time to go up to New York to see her before she went out to join her mother in Oregon."

"I know that Cathy is marking days off her calendar until she is reunited with you," Claudia said. "She writes about almost nothing but you in every letter."

Lee grinned. "That's good to hear," he said.

Sam piled more roast beef on the guest's plate and poured him another glass of wine. "You mentioned earlier that you saw Andy recently," he said.

"Indeed I did, and you have every right to be proud of your son," Lee replied, "as proud as I am to be his uncle. As you undoubtedly know, he was made a brevet or temporary colonel about six months ago, and he's commanded his regiment so brilliantly since that time that I think it quite likely he'll be given the permanent rank of colonel when hostilities come to an end. General Grant is very impressed by him, I know, and he has good reason to be. Andy is a first-rate officer."

"Well," Claudia said, smiling, "you set the example for him. We heard in a letter from Cathy that you were given a commendation by President Lincoln himself."

As usual, Lee was embarrassed by praise. "I guess the President had nothing better to do one afternoon, so he wrote me a splendid letter, and I'm very glad that he did. I've seen combat so long in this war that Ulysses Grant has relieved me of my assignment and has had me reassigned to the overall command of the Army of the West."

"Does that mean you'll be going back to the Presidio in San Francisco or to Fort Vancouver in the Washington Territory, opposite Portland?" Sam asked.

"I'm going to continue to make my headquarters at Fort Vancouver," Lee said, "because I have my choice, and I know Cathy will be pleased. So many of our old wagon train friends are living in Oregon directly across the Columbia River from the fort, you know."

The Brentwoods nodded. "Will Beth be satisfied with life out there?" Claudia asked.

Lee smiled slightly, but there was a hard undertone in his voice as he replied. "She'll be satisfied because she has no choice in the matter," he said. "The quarters at Fort Vancouver are perfectly splendid, and her mother and I love the country."

"I think you're in for a pleasant surprise when you become reacquainted with your daughter, Lee,"

Claudia said. "She spent about ten days with us on her way out to Oregon after her return from Europe, and she's changed a great deal."

"For the better," Sam Brentwood added. "If you don't mind my saying so, she was inclined to be a trifle flighty and sharp-tongued, but she appears to have grown up now."

"I'm very glad to hear it," Lee replied. "After all that the country has undergone, I'm in no mood to cope with a temperamental daughter."

"How much longer do you suppose the war is going to last?" Sam asked.

Lee Blake sighed and shrugged. "The ability of the Confederates to hang on is little short of amazing," he said. "For all practical purposes, they've lost the war. Sherman's march destroyed the heartland of their farming country and of their principal crop, cotton. They've suffered frightful losses in manpower, far worse than the Union has sustained, and it's miraculous that they can still send armies into the field. But General Lee is a military genius second to none, and if we'd had him with us in the Union army, the war would have been ended by now. His troops are totally devoted to him and will stand with him until the bitter end. Grant has the unenviable task now of grinding down the Rebels until their high command finally realizes that the situation they face is totally hopeless. The war could end tomorrow, it could drag on for another three or four months, but no more than that, certainly. The Confederates are on their last legs, and their economy is in a state of collapse."

"I thank the Lord that Andy has survived without a scratch and has done so well. We knew that you would distinguish yourself, Lee. You've made a habit of doing just that for so many years."

Lee stirred uneasily and changed the subject from himself. "Andy made a wise decision when he chose a military career for himself," he said. "I don't think I'm revealing any military secrets when I tell you that I'm not the only member of the family who will have stars on his shoulders. Knowing what Grant and Sherman and others in the high command think of Andy, it's inevitable that he'll win a promotion ultimately to brigadier general."

Claudia beamed proudly, and Sam raised his glass. "I want to drink a toast to my boy and to you, Lee, as well as to all the other gallant officers on both sides of this terrible war. I thank God that the end is at last in sight."

The tent had been patched repeatedly, but the canvas had become so threadbare that it failed to keep out the rain. It was no ordinary rain that fell in Virginia in mid-March, 1865, however. The weather was extraordinarily cold, and the rain was icy and penetrating. Both the Union forces and the beleaguered Confederates, who were evacuating their major cities, were suffering as a result.

Two officers huddled in their greatcoats ate their usual dinner of baked beans, bacon, and hard biscuits, which they consumed by the flickering lights of cheap candles set on bits of broken dishes that stood on two small tables in the tent. Colonel Andrew Brentwood, the regimental commander, ate steadily, without relish. His second in command, Major Scott Foster, looked pensively at his plate. "As I wrote to my wife," he said quietly, "when this war is finally ended and I am reunited with her, I never want to see beans or bacon again. I know I'll never see anything like these biscuits. I think that every regimental cook in the Union army takes special instructions in how to render flour inedible."

Andy chuckled. "At least we have a roof of sorts over our heads," he said. "That's more than a great many people can say today."

"True," Scott conceded. "I tell you, Andy, my heart goes out to the Rebs. Their supply lines have been disrupted so thoroughly that they can't be getting more than a small quantity of the food they need."

Andy nodded and raised his head to listen as a cannon began to boom in the distance. "There's our nightly lullaby," he said. "General Grant is giving the Rebels no peace."

Scott listened to the roar of the cannon, too. "I find it significant," he said, "that every night that we make artillery music, the Confederate responses grow feebler. They're lacking not only food, but they're running short of ammunition as well."

"I saw a Washington newspaper of ten days ago this afternoon," Andy said, "and I read a number of quotations from the President's second inaugural address. It was apparently quite a speech. He pointed out that both we and the Rebels read the same Bible and pray to the same God, with each of us invoking His aid against the other. There's one quotation that sticks in my mind: 'It may seem strange that any men should dare to ask a just God's assistance in wringing their bread from the sweat of other men's faces; but let us judge not, that we be not judged.'"

"Trust Mr. Lincoln to sum it all up," Scott said.

"I'm going to feel lost, you know, when General Lee surrenders, as he inevitably must do in the next few weeks, and we're finally sent home."

"Are you planning on staying in the army?"

"No, there are plenty of you regulars for that. I'll go back to civilian life. What I'll do exactly, I don't know yet, but I'll want to rest and think and talk it all over with my wife before I make up my mind. In a way I envy you. Your career is all set."

"I suppose it is," Andy replied, "but I'm sick of bloodshed, and I hope I've seen the last of it for a while."

Scott finished his meal and placed his plate on the small table beside him. "We're fortunate, both of us, you know," he said, "and staying healthy from now until the war ends is about all that we can ask. I keep thinking of fellows like Toby Holt."

"Toby certainly demonstrated that he was Whip Holt's son," Andy said. "The way he and his company dug in and repulsed wave after wave of Confederate attacks was little short of miraculous. I've never seen a finer demonstration of military leadership."

"He's been promoted to captain, and he has commendations from you and from General Grant to prove that he covered himself with glory," Scott said, "but somehow I don't think that's quite enough. He's been recuperating for nearly a year now, and his health still hasn't been fully restored. I can't help wondering if he'll be disabled for the rest of his life—like so many men in both armies."

Andy sighed and shrugged. "The last time I spoke to Toby's doctors," he said, "they assured me that he'll enjoy a complete recovery—if he wants to recover. They say his only remaining trouble is mental. He's depressed and debilitated and shows no interest in leading a useful life."

"He was young, and he went through hell," Scott said. "He had the stuffing kicked out of him."

Andy nodded soberly. "Maybe his mother and father can help improve his mental outlook," he said.

Scott shook his head. "There's no finer man in this whole world than Whip Holt," he said, "and from what I hear, his wife is quite a lady. But they don't have the right medicine for Toby. He needs the right kind of encouragement from the right woman."

"And that whore, Caroline Brandon, most emphatically isn't the right woman. Is that what you're thinking?"

Scott shrugged. "I don't want to seem uncharitable," he said, "but, yes, that's more or less the drift of what was going through my mind."

"Millions of people in both the Union and in the Confederacy are going to have to make major adjustments once peace comes," Andy said. "And the test of an individual's manhood is the way he responds to the challenge. Don't you worry about Toby Holt. He has the qualities that will see him through and enable him to win an even bigger victory than he won on the battlefield."

"I hope you're right, Andy," Scott said fervently. "I hope it with all my heart!"

Rob Martin rode to the crest of the hill, where there was a break in the towering evergreens that surrounded him and loomed so high above him. There he reined in his gelding, halted, and enjoyed the view. To say the least, the scenery of Washington Territory was breathtaking. Directly ahead lay Budd

Inlet, located at the southern tip of Puget Sound. To the north rose the Olympic Mountains, and to the east was the Cascade Range, where Mount Rainier, covered with her blanket of perpetually glistening snow, stood as the symbol of all that was grand and greater than human-scale in the territory.

Rob unconsciously touched the pocket in which he carried the letter that had brought him here. Directly ahead, on the shore of Puget Sound, was a collection of log buildings. An American flag flew above one of them, so he assumed this was the office of the governor of the territory, William Pickering. Adjacent to the governor's office stood the territorial legislature, also made of logs.

Rob had lost no time in hurrying to Olympia, the capital of the territory, after he had received Governor Pickering's communication, which had said he wanted to see Mr. Martin at his earliest convenience on a matter of urgent mutual interest. His curiosity piqued, and sensing a possible business opportunity, Rob had left Oregon as soon as he had received the communication. Now, descending into the town, the thought struck him that the Olympia of 1865 was much like Portland, Oregon, of a generation earlier. The buildings were, without exception, made of logs and were located on streets that were wagon-rutted tracks that turned to seas of mud when it rained, as it frequently did in Washington.

The men, the majority of them lumberjacks or fishermen, wore open-throated shirts of heavy wool, and stout trousers that could stand the abuse of frontier living. The women were similarly dressed for comfort rather than for style, and virtually all of them were clad in floor-length dresses of thin wool. It was late March, and although there was no snow on the ground, except on the heights, the weather was raw and the wind that blew down from the Olympic Mountains was penetrating.

But Rob was accustomed to such weather after a lifetime in the Pacific Northwest, and he paid no attention to it as he made his way into the town, falling in behind a farmer's cart laden with hay.

His guess proved to be right. A militiaman armed with a rifle and bayonet, who stood outside the entrance to the building with the flag, assured him that this was indeed the governor's office. A few moments later, Rob found himself unceremoniously being ushered into the presence of the chief executive of the territory.

William Pickering resembled a lumberjack, it was said, which was why President Lincoln had appointed him. His many supporters, however, were quick to point out that he had an alert, probing mind and, above all, boundless ambition and a conviction in the future of the land that he governed.

"You're prompt, Mr. Martin. I like that," he said in a deep voice as they shook hands. "Make yourself at home."

As Rob sat down, Pickering said, "I hope I haven't taken you away from anything important, Mr. Martin, but I believe you'll find it worth your while. I note by the land records that you and Toby Holt own considerable property not far from Olympia in Tumwater."

"That's right, Governor, we do," Rob replied.

"Are you absentee owners, or are you planning on settling here?" Pickering demanded.

"I can't really answer that question until my partner is released from an army hospital in the East and joins me here, sir," Rob said. "But I'm inclined to believe, offhand, that we'll be obliged to settle in the territory. I don't see how we can either cut logs or initiate farming operations if we are living elsewhere."

Pickering smiled broadly. "Ah," he said, "I'm relieved to hear it. Now, young man, I want to know whether some information I've gleaned about you and your partner is correct. Is it true that you earned your college degree as a land surveyor?"

"Yes, I did, sir," Rob replied, "but I haven't had much opportunity to practice my profession. The war came along soon after I obtained my degree, and I've been in uniform ever since. I was just released from military service recently."

The governor nodded. "It's also true that young Mr. Holt studied the principles of railroading at the University of Michigan?"

"Your information is correct, sir," Rob said. "But Toby's situation is very similar to mine. He's had plenty of book learning but relatively little experience in actual railroading. He's been in the army for the past four years."

William Pickering leaned back in his chair and spit out a stream of tobacco juice, which landed with almost uncanny accuracy in a brass cuspidor located at the far side of his plainly decorated office. "It strikes me," he said, "that you and Holt are exactly the people I've been seeking." Although they were alone, he lowered his voice somewhat. "I hope you understand that what I say to you is in utter confidence and isn't to be repeated. I'm speaking to you now as one Washingtonian to another, and I'll be just as happy if our discussion isn't reported to anybody who lives in California or Oregon."

"You can depend on me to be discreet, Governor," Rob said, slightly perplexed by the demand for secrecy.

"Due in part to the war and also because of our physical remoteness from so much of the country," the governor said, "most Americans know very little about the Washington Territory. They know we have almost unlimited quantities of first-grade lumber here, but that's about all they do know. What they fail to realize is that our valleys—the Yakima Valley, for instance—are capable of growing magnificent vegetables and fruits. The mineral resources of our mountains are virtually untapped. We fish for our own consumption, but our waters are teeming with shellfish and salmon that can add appreciably to the supplies of the country. In order to achieve her potential, however, the territory needs people. Up to now there has been some immigration, mostly by people who had no luck in the goldfields, but these small settlements are not nearly enough. Washington desperately needs more people. She won't be able to live up to her economic promise until the population is at least four to five times what it is right this moment."

Rob whistled softly under his breath. "You're envisioning a big influx of immigrants from the East, then, similar to the migrations to Oregon and California."

The governor nodded. "Yes, I am, in a manner of speaking. But folks went to Oregon because the country was in a depression and there was free land that was offered to them. The lure of gold brought newcomers to California by the tens of thousands. Today conditions are different. The Union and the Confederacy are both exhausted, and I honestly can't see people coming to Washington in large numbers by wagon train."

Rob thought about the statement and nodded. He didn't know all that much about the subject, but the governor seemed to make sense.

Pickering leaned forward, and a gleam appeared in his eyes. "As my predecessor, Governor Stevens, well knew, the salvation of Washington is going to be the railroad," he said. "It eats up distance like no other form of transportation. I see this territory as the western terminus for a railroad that spans the continent."

Rob was deeply impressed.

"Of course, that's easier said than accomplished," the governor continued. "Oregon and California are bonafide states and have members in both the U.S. Senate and House of Representatives who are looking out for their interests. You can bet your last silver dollar that they're going to fight hard to have any railroad that spans the country end its western run on their soil.

"I believe I may have the jump on them, however. I've been in touch with various financial interests in New York, Boston, and Philadelphia, and they're very much interested in the construction of a railroad that will end here in Washington. But there's a crying need for information before any funds can be raised for the building of such a road. Reconstruction of the war-ravaged areas is going to be expensive, and money will be scarce, which means that I've got to provide the bankers of the East with hard facts to substantiate my claim that a railroad should be built through Washington."

Suddenly Pickering astonished his young visitor by laughing aloud. Rob looked at him in surprise and saw his expression was one of wry amusement.

"I'm the first to admit that my scheme is far from perfect," the governor said. "I believe I have the support of President Lincoln and Vice-President Johnson for a railroad that will come to its western end here in the territory. But as I said, Oregon and California have supporters who are already active in the Senate and House. However, political difficulties are really the least of our problems."

"I'm afraid I don't follow you, Governor," Rob declared.

Again a laugh rumbled within William Pickering's heavy frame, but he looked unhappy. "We're still a wild frontier country," he said, "and we face the problems that beset a primitive land. Two of our largest Indian tribes, the Yakima and the Nez Percé, are in rebellion against the territorial authority."

"Why, sir?" Rob demanded.

"For the simple reason that white men are moving into territory they consider their own," Pickering replied. "The Indians were here first, and they resent seeing farms and ranches occupying what they consider to be their hunting grounds. Our militia isn't strong enough to put down these rebellions, and I'm afraid we can't count on much help from the federal army. America is sick of fighting."

"It's a nasty problem, I can see that," Rob said.

The governor nodded. "I'm in hopes that by the time the issue is resolved and a railroad line is actually built, the insurrections of the Yakima and the

Nez Percé will be long settled. However, you needn't concern yourself with them. They're my problem, young man, not yours."

"May I ask what you consider to be my problem, Governor?" Rob asked, smiling.

Pickering's chuckle this time was wholehearted. "I've become so wrapped up in the subject that I haven't actually told you why I've brought you here, have I? I want to hire you and your partner, young Holt. You're the best qualified citizens in the territory for a vital job that urgently needs to be done."

The governor paused and hooked his thumbs in his waistcoat pockets. "A decade ago the army financed a number of transcontinental railroad surveys. One was done for the northwest, but it was never very enthusiastically received, mainly because the proposed railroad would have to go over some very rough terrain and actually cross two or three mountain ranges. Thus, the cost would have been enormous. What these surveyors failed to do, however, was to locate the mountain passes that would have obviated the need for the railroad to scale high mountains and to span valleys and gorges on high trestle bridges many miles in length. I want you to make a new survey for a northern transcontinental railroad line, one that will avoid as many of these obstacles as possible and that can be linked to rail lines in Montana and Dakota and all the way across these United States. Then I'll have something practical and feasible to take to the financiers of the East. I believe that you and your partner are remarkably well-suited for such an assignment, since you're a surveyor and he knows railroads. I'll pay each of you one hundred dollars a month for a period up to a year until you get the task completed."

The financial offer was dazzling, and Rob, who hadn't expected to be earning that amount of money for years to come, swallowed hard. "I'm pleased to accept, sir, on behalf of both my partner and myself," he said. "But I don't want to take any job under false pretenses."

"What do you mean by that?" Pickering demanded.

"Laying out a railroad across Washington isn't going to be easy," Rob replied. "I'm not all that familiar with the complete topography of the territory, but I know this much—we have some exceptionally rugged mountain ranges here, and it will be extremely difficult to find a track route that will not require enormous capital to build."

"You're not admitting defeat before you even start the job, I hope," the governor declared in alarm.

Rob shook his head. "Hell, no! I just thought it was fair to point out to you, Governor, that the assignment that you've given Toby and me isn't going to be easy by any stretch of the imagination. But easy or hard, we'll get the job done."

Pickering was relieved. "The twelve-month period that I cited was something of an arbitrary figure," he said. "If you can complete the assignment in less time, so much the better. If you need more than a year to do it right, take what you need. The entire future of the Washington Territory is going to depend on your efforts. So what you do has got to be sound and right!"

*　　*　　*

Whip Holt was on the range with Stalking Horse, his Cherokee friend from the wagon train days and, for the last twenty-five years, foreman of the Holt ranch. The two old friends were taking count of the livestock, the one chore Whip particularly enjoyed doing. Ignoring the arthritis in his hips that plagued him and made him so uncomfortable in the saddle, he rode for hours, occasionally pausing to make a notation in the battered, leather-covered notebook he carried.

Suddenly he saw a familiar figure approaching in the distance, in the blue and gold uniform of a Union officer. He tugged his broad-brimmed hat lower over his pale eyes, peered intently, and then immediately spurred his stallion to a gallop.

Lee Blake did the same, and they raced toward each other, reining their mounts to a halt, dismounting, and clasping hands with the warmth that only friends of a lifetime could feel for each other.

"I'll be damned," Whip said. "I always thought that major generals traveled in style. But here you are all by yourself."

"I don't need any escorts in this country," Lee answered, grinning. "I arrived at Fort Vancouver a short time ago, and I left my aides there. Believe me, I knew the way to your house."

"But why didn't you telegraph to tell us you were arriving?" Whip asked. "You know, the lines have reached us even way out here in Oregon."

Lee chuckled. "I like the element of surprise. It's something we learn in wartime." For a moment, both men became quiet at the reference to the recent, harrowing war. Then Lee, smiling again, broke the silence. "How are you, my friend, and how's everything?"

"I'm feeling about as well as can be expected for an old colonel who's been put out to pasture," Whip said. "Eulalia's fine and so is Cindy. Your wife and daughter are in good shape, too, and I'm sure they're going to be a heap happier than they've been once they set eyes on you."

"Where are they? At the house?"

"I reckon so," Whip replied, and without further ado, they started off toward the ranch house.

After proceeding a short way, Lee said quietly, "I hope you can brace yourself, Whip, but Toby is going to be arriving here tomorrow. He should have stayed longer in the hospital, but the army made the mistake of granting him his discharge and so lost authority over him. He insisted on coming home, and—well, he's not in very good shape."

"Is he going to recover?" Whip's voice was taut.

"I spoke to the commandant and a senior surgeon of the hospital. Ordinarily a patient who has been wounded as severely as Toby has may or may not recover fully. They say he'll recover all right—if he wants to."

"He's a Holt," Whip said, and to him that summed up everything. His son would regain his health because he had the willpower necessary to do so.

As they drew closer to the ranch house, they saw two females riding across the range ahead of them, and Whip waved when he recognized Beth Blake and his own daughter, Cindy.

Beth's calm deserted her, and she let loose an undignified Indian war whoop, then broke into a gallop and rode madly toward the approaching men. Cindy, grinning broadly, deliberately hung back in order to give Beth the opportunity to be reunited with her father.

Lee and Beth dismounted, and he picked her up, hugged her, and then held her at arm's length, her feet still dangling in the air. "Let me look at you!" he exclaimed. "Lordy, but you've grown up. You were still a schoolgirl when I last saw you, and now you're a woman."

"A woman," Beth added quietly, "who's capable of standing on her own feet if her father will have the courtesy to lower her to the ground."

Lee chuckled appreciatively as he set her on her feet. "You may be an adult, honey, but you still have the same sense of humor."

"It's my turn to look at you, Daddy," she said. "It's amazing, but you haven't changed in the least." She was lying. The war had taken its toll, and although Lee Blake looked fit and strong, he nevertheless had aged considerably.

They mounted their horses again and resumed their ride toward the ranch house, Whip and young Cindy diplomatically riding a dozen paces behind them in order to give the chattering father and daughter the privacy they deserved.

As they rode, Whip took advantage of the opportunity to glance over at Cindy, who, like the men in the family, had sandy-colored, wavy hair and pale blue eyes. She was able to ride a horse as well as any boy her age, and right now was at the awkward stage between adolescence and maturity, shunning dresses and other articles of female attire. But Whip knew that when Cindy was Beth's age, she would be equally as pretty and feminine.

"Would you carry on like Beth if *I* came back after being away a long time?" Whip teased his daughter.

"Oh, Pa, don't talk so," Cindy said without looking up. "You're not going anywhere."

"But if I did," Whip persisted, grinning broadly.

"Sure, Pa, I'd miss you a lot!" Cindy said emphatically, her eyes wide as she looked up at him.

"Just checking, that's all," Whip said, and reached over to give his daughter an affectionate pat on the arm.

Cathy and Eulalia were in the kitchen and happened to glance out the window at the approaching riders. When Cathy Blake saw who it was, she threw open the back door of the house and, raising her skirts so she could move more quickly, came running into the open. Tears were streaming down her face, but she was laughing, too.

A moment later she was enveloped in her husband's embrace. Whip deliberately averted his gaze. His glance met his wife's, and he was mildly surprised to see there were tears in her eyes, too. This was an occasion long to be remembered.

The Holts stayed out of the way of the reunited Blake family for the better part of an hour, and then they all sat down to a dinner of Eulalia's vegetable soup, steaks which she had barbecued over an outdoor pit located outside the kitchen, and potatoes that had been baked in the coals. Whip had asked Lee to break the news to Eulalia about Toby's homecoming, since his friend would be better able to answer her innumerable questions.

Everyone seemed to be talking simultaneously,

and only Caroline Holt remained uncharacteristically silent. General Blake, whom she had known when her late first husband had been associated with him in Denver before the outbreak of the Civil War, had greeted her with a measure of reserve; she had felt his rebuff and sulked accordingly.

Now Lee looked at her briefly, then directed his full attention to Eulalia. Without raising his voice, he revealed that Toby would be coming home the following day, and he repeated what he had told Whip, that Toby's health left a great deal to be desired.

Beth noted that Caroline's expression remained unchanged, which convinced her more than ever that Toby's wife was indifferent to him.

The color drained from Eulalia's face, and she inadvertently raised a protective hand to her mouth, as though warding off a blow. "How do you know that Toby will be here tomorrow, Lee?" she asked in a voice that trembled slightly. "How do you know he won't be here the next day or even the day after that?"

Lee Blake took a deep breath. "As it happens," he said, "Toby arrived with a trainload of other convalescents in Independence the day before I was scheduled to leave, and my troops accompanied them for the rest of the journey. Toby's across the river at Fort Vancouver right now, and he'll be home in the morning."

The revelation stunned everyone present, and only Whip reacted with seeming calm. He blinked rapidly several times, but his expression remained Indian-like, and he showed none of his feelings. Eulalia, however, rose slowly to her feet. "Toby is actually here?" she demanded. "He's really at Fort Vancouver this very minute?"

Lee did his best to soothe her. "At the urgent request of the post physician," he said, "he's resting. He's had a long, arduous journey across the continent, and he needs a breathing spell before he's reunited with those whom he loves. Believe me, Eulalia, he would have come with me this afternoon if it would have been possible for him to do so."

She looked at the officer, then at her husband. "Is it possible for us to go to Fort Vancouver to see him?"

"If you insist," Lee said.

Whip spoke for the first time. "But you don't advise it, I take it."

"No, I do not," Lee Blake replied flatly. "Toby has spent nearly a year convalescing from wounds that almost took his life. He's had a rough time—a very rough time. He needs this respite to compose himself. I realize how anxious all of you are to see him again, but for his sake, I urge you to wait and let him follow his original plan and come to you here tomorrow."

The sun rose higher over Mount Hood, its rays glistening on the snows of the glacier that capped the great peak. Although it was not yet April, there was a strong hint of spring in the air, and the scent of the sea mingled with the smells of earth, forest, and herbs.

Eulalia Holt stood stiffly erect, her hand tightly clasping her husband's, and she unconsciously leaned against him for support as she stood at the ferry slip that was the terminal for boats crossing the Columbia River.

On Whip's other side, his daughter, Cindy, echoed her mother's attitude. She, too, was tense, and she, too, was relying on Whip for support in this time of crisis.

Only Caroline Brandon Holt stood apart from the family group, seemingly aloof and indifferent. She was wearing one of her more provocative gowns, and as always, she was heavily made up. She presented a picture of what Lee Blake thought of as seductive calm.

Neither he nor anyone else could have guessed the state of Caroline's inner turmoil. After years of separation, she was about to be reunited with the husband who was almost a complete stranger to her. Looking back on the events that had led to her marriage, she could scarcely believe them herself. She had flirted with Toby Holt on the long journey from Nevada to New York, it was true, but she had been motivated only by boredom. He had been good-looking and was so obviously interested in her, susceptible to her charms, that she had been unable to resist taking advantage of him.

Little did she then realize that she would become his wife, that in her fright and confusion over being shot and severely wounded, she would reach out for the security of marriage before she died.

Then, by some miracle, she had lived and had recovered her health. Before he had gone off to the warfront, they had slept together only a few nights. They had enjoyed a token relationship at best. Caroline had to admit to herself that she could recall no significant details of those occasions. She had bedded so many men that the experiences all ran together in her mind and became meaningless. But this man who was about to rejoin her was nevertheless her husband, and her future depended on him. She was prepared for any eventuality and was ready to act accordingly.

Lee Blake, studying the north shore of the Columbia River through the new, powerful binoculars that were issued only to Union generals, lowered the glasses and said quietly, "The boat that is carrying Toby across the river is just shoving off now."

The tension became so great that it seemed like a living force. Only Whip appeared to be calm. Eulalia knew, of course, that he was going through an inner turmoil as great as her own, but no one else on earth would have guessed it.

The gig, manned by a crew of six soldiers from the Fort Vancouver garrison, was rowed steadily across the river, and the sergeant in charge negotiated the swift currents with practiced ease. As the long, low vessel neared the south bank, it became possible for them to see the occupants of the gig clearly, and they searched eagerly for Toby. He sat erect, amidships, supporting himself with walking sticks that he held in each of his hands.

His mother, who hadn't quite known what to expect, was relieved. Her son was intact and, at first glance, appeared to be in good health. For that, she uttered a silent prayer of thanks to God.

On closer examination, however, the changes that the war had made in Toby Holt became apparent to those who knew and loved him. It was obvious to everyone awaiting him that he had matured, but the most startling change, which surprised even Eulalia, was the strong resemblance he now bore to his father. Toby was no longer husky. He had grown lean and angular in precisely the way that Whip was lean. No spare flesh covered his bones, and he appeared to be made only of sinews and muscles. In spite of the fact that he was still suffering from his wounds, he looked as though he could leap into a saddle and ride one hundred miles or more without any difficulty.

It was Toby's face, however, that truly marked his similarity to his father. His eyes, as pale and as searching as Whip's, had acquired the same strong characteristics: they were hard and unyielding, the eyes of a man who had seen death frequently and had come to terms with it, the eyes of a man who was totally unafraid of what any other human being could do to him. At the same time, however, behind his steellike façade, there lurked the hint of other qualities, the qualities that had so long made Whip attractive to the opposite sex.

Eulalia, loving her husband with all her heart and soul, recognized his twin in her son. She knew that beneath the hard crust that protected Toby from the world was a very human young man, who was sweet and loving and vulnerable. She wanted to take him in her arms and cradle him as she had done when he had been a baby, but she knew she had forfeited that right, having lost it to his wife.

Whip looked at his son and was relieved beyond measure. He knew that no matter what wounds Toby had suffered or how long a convalescence might stretch ahead of him, he would survive and, more than that, would overcome his problems.

Young Cindy recognized the similarity between her father and her brother as clearly as did anyone else present. She had been rather young, to be sure, when Toby had gone off to war, and she couldn't recall him too clearly. So it was something of a surprise to her to see that he looked as much like Whip as did Whip himself.

Caroline was mildly surprised by her initial failure to react to Toby's appearance at all. She had to admit to herself that with his penetrating eyes and his firm expression, he didn't resemble the young man who had gone off to command an infantry platoon against the Confederates. Although she wouldn't have admitted as much to anyone, she was uncertain whether she would have recognized him had she passed him in the street. She had said good-bye to a good-looking and personable youth, and now in his place, a man with what appeared to be a granitelike resolve and a backbone of steel was coming home to her. Her instincts told her that she faced serious problems.

She reacted as she always did and turned on the charm, gazing at him with all the seductive appeal that she was capable of assuming. She felt she had been slapped in the face when Toby stared at her briefly and then averted his eyes and looked at his parents, smiling and raising a hand in greeting to them.

Caroline was convinced he had served notice on her that she was an outsider, a stranger, and that she had no place in his inner family circle. Very well, she thought, if that was the game he wanted to play, she would play it to the hilt.

Toby's actual reaction to his wife was one of shock. The strongest memory of her that lingered in his mind was that of a pale-faced, frightened young woman who had been fighting for her life. He was stunned to see a healthy, robust Caroline, whose erotic appeal to any man was overwhelming. This lovely, desirable creature was his wife! He would need time to acclimate to that fact. Until then, he couldn't help but feel more than a trifle shy and inadequate.

The rowers propelled the gig onto the grassy bank of the river, and several of them jumped ashore and hauled the craft higher onto the land. Toby stood and, steadying himself with his walking sticks, moved stiffly and somewhat awkwardly ashore. Then, determined to make light of his injuries, he tucked the two canes under an arm and walked slowly forward, showing no sign of a limp.

Eulalia curbed her strong urge to rush forward and embrace her son. He had a wife now, and it was her prerogative to greet him first. The cautioning hand that Whip put on his wife's arm was actually unnecessary.

Caroline knew the Holts were holding back, giving her the opportunity to be the first to greet her husband. She took a deep breath and started toward him, her hips swaying seductively, as was her custom.

Toby halted and awaited her. Their eyes met, and there was no recognition, no warmth that either displayed. Two strangers were about to greet each other after a wartime separation that felt as though it had lasted for decades. Caroline walked up to Toby, halted, and raised her face to his. He bent to her and brushed her lips with his. Their kiss was a mere gesture, a token, an acknowledgment on the part of two strangers that there was a tenuous relationship of some sort between them.

Eulalia's heart sank. For her son's sake, she wanted to intervene to end the painful incident as soon as possible. But before she had a chance to move, young Cindy could control herself no longer. Overjoyed by her brother's return, she raced toward him and threw her arms around his neck with such gusto that she almost knocked him off his balance. Toby's booming laugh filled the air and mingled with the tinkling, joyous merriment of his sister.

He sounded, Whip thought, as though he had not laughed for a very long time.

III

Dr. Robert Martin had brought Toby Holt into the world and had taken care of him since birth, and the young, retired army officer submitted with relatively good grace to the physician's exhaustive examination. When he was finished, the doctor nodded and smiled. "You can put your shirt on again, Toby," he said, "and then sit down."

"What's the good word, Doctor, or is it good?"

"My findings," Dr. Martin replied, "corroborate those of the physicians in the army hospital. You've completely recovered from your wounds, which is something of a miracle. Your problem now is one of regaining your strength. That means you'll have to get plenty of exercise and lots of rest."

Toby nodded and grinned.

Dr. Martin knew the younger man's temperament all too well. "You're going to want to be totally recovered in a day, Toby, and that's impossible," he said. "Let me warn you right now that if you indulge in too heavy a rehabilitation program, you'll do yourself more harm than good, and you'll actually set yourself back. I'd like to prescribe a regimen for you, and I urge you to follow it."

Toby waited expectantly.

"Sleep late every morning," the doctor told him, "that is, relatively speaking. I know that everyone is up at around six in the morning here, but I urge you to stay in bed until seven or eight. Do the exercises that you were taught at the army hospital in the morning, and after you eat a light lunch, climb into the saddle and get out to the range. I know of no better exercise for you than horseback riding in the fresh air, and I'd say that two or three hours a day are just what you need. But, again, I warn you. You'll note I said two or three hours a day, I didn't say five or six."

"I understand, sir," Toby replied.

"To be on the safe side, I'm going to take no chances," Dr. Martin said. "I'm going to repeat the instructions I've given you to your parents, and I'll also spell them out to your wife. Where is she?"

Toby had no wish to admit that in the forty-eight hours he'd spent at home, he had seen very little of Caroline, who, for whatever reasons, spent as little time as possible in his bedchamber. He had had only one interview with his wife, who had sat in the armchair by the bed and had talked desultorily about life on the ranch in the last few years, then had left him alone, without even an attempt at a parting kiss. "She's somewhere around the ranch, I reckon," he said vaguely.

Although the physician heard something in Toby's tone, something that the young man himself perhaps failed to realize was there, he didn't pursue the matter. He took his leave after suggesting that his patient return to bed. "I can imagine you're rather sick of bed after all the months you were forced to spend on your back in the hospital," he said, "but just keep in mind that it's the best of all possible places for you."

Toby had just donned his shirt, but he removed it again and reached for the pajamas that were hanging on a wall peg in his bedchamber. He intended to follow the doctor's orders to the letter; there was so much to be done, so much lost time to be made up that he knew the first thing he had to do was to recover his health. It was true that after the icy meeting with Caroline, he had been engulfed with waves of self-pity and depression, the kind he had suffered so badly while recuperating in the army hospital. But just being back at his family's ranch had rejuvenated him considerably, and he was determined to recover from both his mental and physical ailments, Caroline or no.

"A letter came to Tonie and me today from Rob, who's still up in Washington," Dr. Martin said as he took his leave. "He asked me to tell you that as soon as he comes home in a few days, he'll be over to the ranch to see you."

Toby had to exert great self-discipline in order to force himself to return to his bed. He had received letters from Rob telling all about the exciting prospects in Washington, and he couldn't wait to get started. He quickly settled down, however, with a newly published book on railroading that would bring him up to date on developments that he had missed during the war years.

He soon became immersed in the text, and a tap

on the door had to be repeated before he heard it and responded.

Caroline, looking more seductive than ever, came into the room and struck a pose. "I waited until I was sure the doctor had gone," she said, "before I came in."

"He was looking for you," Toby said. "He wanted to tell you about my condition." He repeated what Dr. Martin had told him.

The details bored Caroline, and she made no attempt to conceal her lack of interest in them. Toby became aware of her disinterest, and his voice trailed away. He realized that this meeting was going to be no better than the others, and he willed himself not to get depressed.

There was an uncomfortable silence as they looked at each other. Then Caroline asked awkwardly, "May I sit down?"

He nodded, thinking it strange that his relationship with this woman who had become his wife should be so formal.

She lowered herself into the armchair beside his bed. Certainly it was not accidental that she revealed a long expanse of leg. "I don't quite know how to say this to you, Toby," she said, "but I just want you to know that I'm grateful to you. You took a chance on me, marrying me when we didn't know whether I'd live or die, and I—well, I appreciate your effort."

Toby, embarrassed, muttered, "There's no need for any gratitude."

Caroline braced herself, for she had decided that today she would once and for all speak her mind and try to make the most of the difficult situation. "Anyway," she said, "here we are, and I guess we're going to be starting a new life together."

"It looks that way," he replied.

"I feel like I've been living on this ranch forever," she said. "How soon will we be moving to our own place?"

Her question surprised—even shocked—him. The last thing on earth he wanted to do now was to leave the comfortable and friendly environment of the ranch. "We're lucky," he said, "that my parents are being so hospitable. It's going to take us quite a while to get a house of our own. For one thing, Rob and I haven't even started to develop our property up in Washington yet, and for another, he and I have to conduct a survey together for the governor of the territory, and that's going to take us quite a spell to complete. You'll be much safer and happier right here than you'd be in some temporary quarters in a frontier town in Washington."

Caroline pouted. "I don't want to sound like I'm complaining," she said, "but your mother disapproves of me, I think. She's been prejudiced against me by Cathy Blake. I knew the Blakes in Denver, and she disliked me even then."

Toby shook his head quietly. Cathy Blake was open-minded and lacking in prejudice, and he couldn't imagine her taking an active dislike to Caroline or anyone else without good cause. However, he didn't want to argue the point with this stranger who was his wife. "Ma isn't shy about expressing her likes and dislikes, and she hasn't said a word about you since I've been home," he said, "so I think you must be mistaken. Anyway, you'll have to be patient. I need time to get my strength back, and then Rob and

I will need time to get our business dealings organized. That means this place is going to be our home for some time to come. Let's just be glad we have a comfortable, pleasant roof over our heads."

It was obvious that Caroline was badly disappointed. She'd been certain she could persuade Toby to move away from his parents' dwelling and take a place of their own where she would feel freer to do as she pleased. Definitely out of sorts, she rose swiftly and left the chamber, slamming the door behind her.

Within moments, Toby could hear her moving around in the room that adjoined his. He had to admit to himself privately that he was relieved his mother had given him a separate room, apart from Caroline, so that he would be undisturbed when he decided to rest. The truth of the matter was that he wasn't yet prepared to face the prospect of sexual intimacies with his wife. Her erotic appeal was so strong that it overwhelmed him, and he felt the great need to become better acquainted with her before they went to bed together.

Perhaps he was just procrastinating, making excuses for being unwilling to bed her, but he didn't think so. He had not really known Caroline all that well before their marriage and their subsequent, abrupt separation, and he truly didn't know what he had in common with her. He knew he wanted her, but he had the good sense to realize that that desire, in and of itself, was an insufficient base for a sound marriage.

Toby returned to his reading but found he could no longer concentrate, and he was annoyed because his mind wandered. So he welcomed the interruption of another tap at the door.

He grinned at Beth Blake and her inseparable companion, Mr. Blake. Whip had indeed located the owner of the puppy in Portland, but the man said he had all he could do with the remaining five puppies from the litter, and he was only too glad to give up one of them.

"I hope I'm not disturbing you," Beth said cheerfully.

"Not at all. Please come in," he replied.

"Is there anything I can do for you? Could I bring you some tea or something to eat, perhaps?"

"Don't pamper me," he replied, still smiling. "I'm not an invalid, and I don't want to be treated like one." In spite of his words, he couldn't help contrasting Beth's generous attitude with the selfishness that Caroline had just displayed.

"I eavesdropped when Dr. Martin explained your situation to your parents," she said, laughing, "so you don't need to tell me that you're doing all right."

Toby well knew that Caroline had no interest in horseback riding, and the thought occurred to him that he would very much enjoy Beth's company if she cared to accompany him. He drew in his breath sharply and said, "I guess you also overheard that I've been ordered to ride for two or three hours every afternoon. If you have nothing better to do, maybe you'd like to come with me today."

She surprised herself by replying promptly, "I'd love it."

It was strange, Beth thought, that she and Toby had developed a rapport. All through their childhood and adolescent years they had quietly loathed each other; however, now she could see the good qualities in him, and she knew from the expression in his eyes that he appreciated and liked her, too. She warned herself, however, not to become too close to him, which would be very easy to do. Under no circumstances could she allow herself to forget that he was a married man.

Chatting easily with Beth, which he had never been able to do before he had gone off to the war, Toby quietly marveled at how well they got along together, and he couldn't help wishing that he could establish a similar easy camaraderie with Caroline.

The shepherd puppy, bored by the conversation of the young couple, drew attention to himself by coming to Toby's bed, putting his front paws up on it, and wagging his tail.

Chuckling, Toby reached out and scratched the dog behind the ears.

"Mr. Blake likes you," Beth said.

"Is that so surprising?" Toby demanded, still petting the dog.

"Yes," she said. "He's paid no attention to anyone else, including people who make a fuss over him, like your father and mine. You're the first person to whom he's responded."

"I'm flattered," he said.

When Beth took her leave, agreeing to ride with him immediately after lunch, the dog lagged behind and was reluctant to accompany her.

"Whatever has gotten into you, Mr. Blake?" she demanded.

"You dumb dog," Toby said. "Go with your mistress."

The shepherd responded by jumping onto the bed, his tail wagging furiously, and curling up beside Toby.

"You've acquired a special friend, it seems," Beth told him.

"I'll throw him onto the floor," he replied, "and you can get a length of rawhide from the kitchen to use as a leash."

She shook her head. "Oh, no," she said. "That wouldn't be fair."

Toby was amused by the puppy's intransigence. "Go on, Mr. Blake. Your place is with your mistress."

The dog wagged his tail and nestled still closer to Toby.

Beth looked at the man, then at the dog, and laughed aloud. "Mr. Blake," she said, "appears to have made a choice. I thought he was my dog, but obviously I was mistaken. He belongs to you, Toby."

"Under no circumstances could I take him from you," he protested.

"You aren't doing a thing about it," she said. "He's clearly made his own choice."

"Then I'll have to persuade him to change his mind."

Beth shook her head. "No. I often think that dogs are like people and their wishes ought to be respected. I'll be far happier—truly I will—if you'll keep him."

He didn't want to argue the point. "Well," he said, "I'll let him stay with me for the time being, but when you and your parents move across the river to Fort Vancouver in the next couple of days, Mr. Blake will go with you."

Beth knew better but said nothing. It was clear to her that the dog had indeed claimed Toby as his master, and she was completely reconciled to the relationship. In fact, she was pleased to think that she had been able to contribute something to the well-being of a war hero who had done so much for his country and had suffered so greatly.

That was the beginning of the extraordinary bond that grew between Toby Holt and the shepherd dog. The animal remained friendly with Beth but became closely attached to Toby, following him everywhere. When he and Beth rode on the range, the dog trotted at the heels of his stallion. At meals, to the amusement of Whip and Eulalia, the puppy stretched out on the floor beside Toby's place, and he made it clear that he considered the foot of Toby's bed his own. In almost no time, or so it seemed, the dog rarely allowed his new master out of his sight.

Only Caroline seemed impervious to the new relationship of man and dog. She made no comment on the puppy's presence, and it appeared as though she were actually unaware of it. All Toby could think was that she was so occupied with thoughts about herself that no one else entered her mind.

"I insist that you keep Mr. Blake," Beth said two days later as she and her parents made plans to move across the Columbia River to Fort Vancouver the following morning. "He prefers you, and although we'll always be friends, he's definitely your dog."

Nothing that Toby could say would change her mind.

That afternoon Toby challenged Beth to a race, giving her mare a considerable head start, and she promptly accepted the challenge. He demonstrated that his recuperation was well under way when he beat her handily, without unduly exerting himself. After they returned to the ranch house, however, both laughing and out of breath, he discovered that he was more tired than he had realized. At Beth's gentle but firm insistence, he obeyed Dr. Martin's instructions and went off to bed to rest for an hour or two before supper.

Toby dozed for about an hour and then awakened when he heard the sound of voices outside his bedroom window. Propping himself on one elbow, he saw Beth strolling in the yard with Rob Martin, who had just returned from Washington and had come to the ranch for supper to discuss surveying plans with his partner. The first thought that entered Toby's mind was that he would need to dress quickly so he wouldn't keep his friend waiting. But then he realized there was no need to rush.

Beth and Rob were deeply engrossed in conversation and appeared to be fully occupied with each other. It would be an intrusion, actually, to interrupt them, Toby thought.

Absently stroking Mr. Blake's head, Toby was stunned to realize that he was almost overcome by a deep wave of jealousy. He had no claim of any kind on the affections of Beth Blake. On the contrary, he was himself a married man, and his own obligations lay elsewhere.

He knew to his deep and lasting chagrin that he had made a terrible mistake when he had married Caroline Brandon, but he faced the unexpected dilemma squarely. He realized that as an honorable man he had to put Beth Blake out of his mind for all time. If he had erred when he had married Caroline, he would pay the penalty for his mistake, but under no circumstances could he reveal his real feelings to Beth. Not only was he not free to pursue her, but it was plain to see that she and his partner were very much taken with each other.

Rising, he poured water from a pitcher into a large basin, then splashed it on his hands, face, and neck. Drying himself, he began to dress for supper, his mind still whirling.

A tap sounded at the door, and his father came in. Whip looked uncharacteristically uncomfortable. "You got a minute or two for a mite of talk?" he asked.

"Sure, Pa." Toby gestured toward the armchair. His father elected instead to sit on a plain chair of pine, which would offer him greater support and create less of a problem for his arthritis.

"Your mother has been after me to have a few words with you," he said, clearing his throat. "You know how she is when she sets her mind to something. She's like that puppy resting on your bed who worries at a bone until he can't see straight."

Toby buttoned his shirt, tucked it into his trousers, and donned his boots.

"Your ma," Whip said, speaking succinctly, "thinks it isn't right and natural for a married man to be living apart from his wife." He was so embarrassed that he averted his gaze.

Toby turned red. "My marriage is unusual, I reckon," he said. "I'm sure you remember the circumstances."

Whip nodded, relieved that the conversation was easier than he had anticipated. "I know," he said, "and I reminded your ma of them."

"I don't feel at ease with Caroline," Toby said. "Maybe there's something the matter with me, Pa, because she sure is an attractive woman. But I don't quite know what to say when I'm with her."

Whip took a deep breath and shook his head. "I don't know what experiences you've had in the army," he said, "but until you went off to war, you never knew a woman as—ah—worldly as Caroline."

Toby appreciated his delicacy. "You're right, Pa," he said, "and now I'm married to such a woman. I keep hoping that she'll change, use less cosmetics, and—well—dress more like a lady."

"You're her husband, Toby," Whip said bluntly. "You could tell her to tone down her appearance, and she'll blame well have to do what you say."

Toby shrugged and spread his hands. "Meaning no disrespect, Pa," he said, "that's the old-fashioned way of handling a woman. I don't see relationships that way."

Whip slowly pulled himself to his feet and jammed his thumbs beneath his belt, striking a pose that was familiar to all who knew him. "Your ma," he said, "is a heap smarter than I've given her credit for being, as usual. She's right, and I'm wrong."

Mystified, his son could only look at him.

"Your ma says," Whip declared somewhat harshly, "that you're not going to control your wife until you master her in bed, and there's the truth. Either you move into her room or move her here into yours. After you've slept with her, it will be easy enough for you to get her to act properly and show you the respect you deserve." He turned away abruptly and started for the door.

Toby realized how much the effort had cost him. "Thanks, Pa," he said, "and thank Ma for me, too."

Whip paused, one hand on the latch. "I made myself clear enough?"

Toby nodded and smiled in spite of himself. "Very clear," he said.

His parents were right, as they always were, he reflected. He had no right to criticize Caroline's flamboyant dress or heavy use of cosmetics while he stayed apart from her. Once they became intimate, then he could exert his influence as her husband.

There was no time like the present, he knew. Making love to Caroline would not only create marital equilibrium, but he hoped it would also kill his unexpected desire for Beth.

The gong sounded soon thereafter, summoning the household to supper, and Caroline, the last to appear, was surprised by her husband's attentiveness. He was more conscious of her than he had been at any time since his return from the East, and Caroline told herself smugly that her appeal was as strong as it had always been. She had been on the verge of amusing herself by flirting with Rob Martin, but instead she directed her attentions to Toby.

Conversation was lively throughout the meal, and Toby participated freely but with some difficulty, caused by the boldness of his wife. Caroline, sitting next to him, pressed her calf and thigh against him, inflaming him and making it difficult for him to think clearly. She appeared to enjoy the hold she had over him.

The ladies retired to the parlor at the end of the meal, while the men remained at the table to share a bottle of port. Toby and Rob immediately plunged into a business discussion. "I don't see any good reason why you have to wait for me to begin your survey for Governor Pickering," Toby said. "You can get started without me."

Rob shook his head. "You're wrong," he said. "Sure, I could survey the land, but I totally lack your knowledge of railroads and route suitabilities. What's more, you've traveled extensively in the territory, so you know the entire region well. Since I don't, we'll save time and effort, and we'll avoid making mistakes if I wait for you and we go together."

"It may be as long as another month before I can really spend the time that's needed on the trail," Toby told him.

Rob shrugged. "Waiting for a month will suit me just fine," he said. "Besides, by that time, you'll be strong enough for us to kill two birds with one stone. We'll go to Tumwater, too, and begin work on our property there. In the meantime, we can decide on the way we're going to develop our land."

Both of the young men were satisfied with the agreement they had reached, and they walked together to the parlor, where the ladies awaited them. Beth, her voice filled with laughter and her eyes shining brightly, seemed to come alive when she saw Rob; and he reacted as though he hadn't seen her in months instead of mere minutes.

Again Toby felt a deep stab of jealousy and hastily turned toward Caroline. She rewarded him with a blinding smile.

The occasion was a festive one, as it marked the last night the Blakes would spend under the Holt roof. Whip served drinks in honor of the occasion, and Lee Blake raised his glass in a toast.

"Here's to the closest friends we have in all the world," he said. "To Whip and Eulalia, who know

Cathy and me as well as or better than we know ourselves. May our friendship continue to flourish."

"Amen to that," Whip added emphatically.

Everyone present sipped a drink. But Toby, looking forward to what was ahead that night for him, felt the need to fortify himself and consumed his whole drink in several gulps. His father needed no explanation and completely understood his son's mood. Taking Toby's glass, Whip refilled it without comment and made his fresh drink even stronger than the first had been.

Caroline, too, was conscious of what her husband was doing, and she guessed the reasons. She had known many men in her day who were awed by her beauty and needed to fortify themselves before summoning the courage to make love to her. She could ease the path for Toby, to be sure, and sitting on the sofa beside him, she inched closer to him, rubbing her thigh against his and squeezing his hand.

He was unable to think straight, and the rest of the evening was forever blurred in his memory. He could recall nothing of significance that was said, and all he did remember was that when Beth finally retired, he felt a sense of loss. That was absurd, of course; she was moving just across the river and had already arranged to ride with him several afternoons a week. He needed the strong medicine of Caroline's lovemaking even more than he had realized.

That medicine was administered before he had to wait too long. No sooner had he invited her to spend the night with him than she pushed him inside his room, slammed the door behind them, and took him in her arms.

Neither then nor later did Toby realize that Car-

oline was actually in charge of their lovemaking. It
was she who determined the length and nature of
their kiss, just as it was she who pressed close to him,
rubbing her body against his in order to further
arouse him. She disengaged herself at the appropriate
moment, then prettily and seductively guided him as
he undressed her.

Ignoring his clumsiness and obvious lack of experience, she helped him remove his clothes, too, and
as they moved with one accord to the bed, she turned
the wick low on the oil lamp that stood on his night
table, but she did not extinguish it. She was too aware
of her ravishing appearance, with her long blond hair
streaming down her nude back and her scarlet lips
glistening in the dim light cast by the oil lamp.

Toby's lovemaking was fervent—and far too
rapid. Caroline automatically slowed his pace and
pretended to enjoy all that he did to her. Again, he
neither knew nor had any way of knowing that she
was the perfect courtesan, feigning pleasure when she
felt nothing. The fact that the young man stretched
out beside her on the bed was her legal husband
meant nothing to her—his touch left her cold. She had
been in a similar situation far too often with far too
many men to feel anything.

Toby, who had been without a woman for so
long, was incapable of coherent thought. Conscious of
the proximity of this luscious creature who was his
wife, inhaling the aroma of her perfume as his hands
roamed freely over her body, he gave in completely
to the experience.

When Toby's desire for her soared to its peak,
Caroline feigned a climax. Then the couple drew
apart, and Caroline opened her eyes long enough to

smile lazily at her husband before dropping off into a sound sleep.

Somehow Toby knew that his wife had been untouched emotionally. But he did not dwell on that aspect of their relationship. What struck him as he extinguished the oil lamp and tried to make himself as comfortable as he could with this woman was a realization that shocked him to the core.

His desire for Caroline having been satisfied, he knew that his deeper, more lasting yearning for Beth persisted and was in no way diminished.

IV

On April 15, 1865, the telegraph line at Fort Vancouver, which connected the Army of the West with the East and had been installed the previous year, brought the shocking word that President Abraham Lincoln had been assassinated. The message, signed by General Grant, the chief of staff, indicated uncertainty as to whether the murder had been a Confederate plot.

General Blake immediately placed all army posts, forts, and other installations under his command on full alert. Not until seventy-two hours later, when word was received from Washington that the assassination had been the act of a demented actor, John Wilkes Booth, was the alert finally rescinded. By that time, Andrew Johnson of Tennessee, a once-illiterate tailor who had been taught to read and write by his wife, had been inaugurated as the seventeenth President of the United States.

The abrupt departure of Abraham Lincoln from

the national scene at a time when he was most desperately needed to reconcile the differences between the North and the South cast a pall over the entire nation. Countless social events were canceled, and people everywhere mourned the loss of the one man who was capable of restoring harmony.

President Johnson was recognized as a staunch Union advocate whose loyalty was unquestioned, but it remained to be seen whether he had the tact necessary to guide the recently warring factions down the road of peace.

"We're fortunate that we live so far from the scenes of the war activities," said Rob Martin, a frequent guest at the dinner table in the house of the commandant at Fort Vancouver. "We're going to be spared a great deal of the bitterness bound to afflict most of the country."

Lee Blake, sitting at the head of the table, nodded. "I won't say we'll get off completely free," he said, "but there's no doubt that conditions here are infinitely better than they are in the East."

"Did you happen to read the speech that Governor Pickering made in Olympia when he received news of the assassination?" Rob asked. "He was very firm in his insistence that he's going to push ahead for the progress and rapid development of the Washington Territory."

"I must say the governor is full of ideas," Cathy said. "I was mildly astonished by one scheme that he announced, his intention of importing what he called several trainloads of brides."

"I'll grant you that at first glance the idea seems rather crude," Beth said, "but the more one thinks about it, the more sense it makes. There are men by the thousands in the territory, and they're living without women. In the meantime, in the East, there are large numbers of single women pining for husbands they'll never get in that part of the country. It's sensible as well as courageous to bring them out to Washington and let nature take her course."

"I'm forced to agree with you, Beth," Lee said, smiling. "A great many of these young women are war widows, and their choice is to struggle by themselves in the East or to find husbands out here and lead useful, productive lives. I'm all in favor of what the governor is doing."

Beth couldn't resist teasing Rob. "Will you be on hand to greet the first load of brides when they arrive?"

He replied solemnly and deliberately. "No," he said, "there's no need for me to find a bride for myself in those who are going to be heading this way from the East. I've already found the woman I want."

His response was so swift, so sure, that Beth didn't know what to reply and felt as though the breath had been kicked out of her.

Cathy, while approving of Rob as a suitor for her daughter's hand, nevertheless felt compelled to come to Beth's assistance, and she changed the subject slightly by saying, "I understand that you're going on a surveying trip tomorrow, Rob."

"Yes, ma'am, I am," he replied. "I'm heading for Puget Sound, and I plan to work my way north from Olympia. Toby knows every inch of the territory, of course, having traveled all over it with his father more times than anybody can count, but I thought while I'm waiting for him to join me, I'd see for myself whether there is a good and solid potential western terminus for a railroad somewhere on the Sound. While I'm about it, I'll have another look at our property in Tumwater, and by that time I reckon Toby will be well enough to meet me in Washington and start making surveying trips with me in earnest."

Lee grinned. "I suspect that by now Toby is rather eager to get to work."

"Eager, sir?" Rob laughed aloud. "That's putting it mildly. I think that Whip has to lasso him and Eulalia has to hog-tie him to his bed to prevent him from plunging into work right now."

"You and Toby make a first-rate team, Rob," Beth remarked.

Rob shrugged. "Maybe we do, and maybe we don't," he said. "It all depends on the results we get."

Cathy and Lee were struck by his earnestness.

"General," he continued, "you and Mrs. Blake can understand this better than most. My generation grew up here in Oregon on stories of the wagon train that brought all of you across the continent to this land. We're familiar with the hardships and the quarrels and the Indian fights and the foreign agents and all the rest. What was most important and what strikes us the hardest is that you persevered and you won. Well, my generation faces a similar type of challenge in the Washington Territory. There's a vast, untamed wilderness to conquer, and many of the settlers who've come to Washington aren't all that wholesome. A good many of them are greedy opportunists who will suck the land dry without putting anything into it. I see a future for Washington—a glorious future—and I want to do all I can to make that dream come true. So does Toby. So do all of us who grew up on stories of your wagon train."

Beth nodded somberly. "I know precisely the feeling that you're describing, Rob," she said. "I grew up on those wagon train stories, too, and I want what you want. Call on me for any help that I can render to make Washington a more secure and productive country!"

A week after Rob departed on his journey, Caroline Brandon Holt was returning to the ranch house shortly after noon from one of her innumerable shopping expeditions in town. She bought very little, thinking that the stocks were dreadfully inadequate, but she had discovered that shopping was a way of passing time and getting away from the ranch.

She rode slowly, daintily, never having quite overcome her fear of horses, even though her mare was a gentle creature, and she held a parasol over her head to shield her skin from the powerful rays of the sun. She heard hoofbeats behind her but did not look around until a man asked her in a deep baritone, "Excuse me, ma'am, but is this the way to the Holt ranch?"

Caroline turned and was secretly elated to see a tall, heavy-set giant of a man mounted on a stallion. She knew at a glance that this stranger was her type of man. She had no need to analyze him or herself, but she recognized in him a potentially exciting lover, probably because he appeared to be the sort of man who would ride roughshod over people to get what he wanted. So she favored him with a broad, flirtatious smile as she replied, "Indeed it is the right road, sir. As a matter of fact, I'm Mrs. Toby Holt—Caroline Brandon Holt—and if you care to ride with me, I'll show you the way."

"That's right nice of you, ma'am. I'm Tom Harrison of the Washington Territory, and I've come down here to see Captain Holt on business." He studied her surreptitiously and recognized her type at once. Harrison prided himself on his knowledge of women, and he was positive that this stunningly attractive blond creature, who was Toby Holt's wife, was available to the man who played his cards right. He allowed his gaze to linger on her until he had exceeded the bounds of good taste and had become insolent.

But Caroline did not take offense. On the contrary, she blossomed under his scrutiny and began to enjoy herself thoroughly. No man had looked at her with such raw desire in his eyes since she had come to Oregon.

"Is Captain Holt home?" he inquired, still ogling her.

Her shrug indicated her contempt for Toby. "I can't imagine where else he'd be," she said. "He never goes anywhere or does anything."

Harrison began to understand the young woman's situation. Here was a luscious, lively wife, who was fretting because she was compelled to spend her days and nights in a quiet backwater. Harrison felt certain he could seduce her in a short time, given the right circumstances.

They soon came to the ranch house, and Caroline, neither knowing nor caring that her tardiness had caused her to miss dinner, went off in search of Toby. She found him about to depart for his afternoon's exercise, riding the range, and she hastily told him that he had a visitor.

Toby vaguely recalled Rob Martin mentioning

Tom Harrison, but the name didn't quite jell, and he was polite and amicable as he entered the parlor. It was a tradition in the West to accept a stranger at face value, and only when a man proved himself unworthy of friendship was he rejected. "You're looking for me, Mr. Harrison?" he asked pleasantly.

Harrison was surprised by his appearance. He had heard that young Holt was convalescing from serious wounds incurred in the war, and he had assumed that the former officer was an invalid. Instead, he found a lean figure of a man, more than six feet tall, whose tanned face, rugged build, and sinewy arms and legs indicated a surprising degree of good health. "I'm Tom Harrison, a neighbor of yours in Tumwater. I reckon you've heard of me."

Now Toby knew the man and remembered what Rob had told him. "My partner may have mentioned you," he said, giving away no information.

Harrison felt his host's cordiality dissipate, and knowing he would need to act quickly, he decided to dispense with formality. He had come all the way down to Oregon for only one thing, and he was determined to get it. "I know you're a busy man, Captain Holt," Harrison said, "so I won't waste your time. Your claim in Tumwater is a choice piece of land. In fact, added to the property I already have there, it makes a mighty attractive package. I'll be honest with you, Captain Holt, I want that land of yours, and I'm willing to pay solid dollars for it. Gold or silver, take your choice."

Toby's eyes narrowed, but his voice remained pleasant, although there was no warmth in it. "As I believe my partner, Rob Martin, told you when you offered to buy it from him, Mr. Harrison, that land is not for sale. The Holts have owned the claim for a long time, since before the war, as a matter of fact, My partner and I are very much aware of the property's worth, and we intend to develop it ourselves." He smiled as he added, "Naturally, we plan to be good neighbors, and we'll cooperate with you to the fullest in putting in roads that will service both your property and ours, and in any other way that we can both benefit."

Tom Harrison had anticipated overwhelming a wounded war veteran with an attractive financial offer. Instead, he was being left out in the cold, and he hastened to improve his position as best he could. "I urge you to listen carefully to my offer before you turn it down, sight unseen, Captain Holt," he said. "Money don't grow on trees, leastwise not the kind of money that I'm prepared to offer you. The claim didn't cost a red cent. Well, maybe it cost a dollar or two to register it, but that's about the size of it. Now I'm willing to offer you one hundred dollars an acre, and I believe you own around one thousand acres, so what I'm offering you is a fortune, more money than most people ever see in their whole lives."

Toby was startled by the size of the man's offer. However, he put temptation behind him and smiled regretfully. His voice was firm as he said, "I appreciate your offer, Mr. Harrison, and I sure won't forget it. It isn't every day that a man is offered that amount of money, but as I said, Rob and I have our hearts set on developing that property ourselves, and we want to see what we can do with it."

Harrison scowled, and unconsciously a harsh note crept into his voice. "I know logging, Captain Holt, and you don't. I have the crews and the equipment to cut down trees and ship them off to the sawmills. All I ask is that you think about my offer for a spell. Don't be so awful-fired fast to turn it down."

Toby planted his feet apart and hooked his thumbs in his belt. "You may be right in everything you say, Mr. Harrison. I wouldn't doubt it, but the way I feel, frankly, is that if the property is worth one hundred thousand dollars to you, then it must be worth every penny as much to Rob and me. So we'll keep it, and if I'm wrong, if I'm making a mistake in judgment, I'm sure we'll ultimately pay the full consequences for it."

Harrison could no longer contain his wrath. "You're not only a know-it-all, Holt," he exploded, "but you're also a damn fool! You're going to regret this!"

Toby remained calm, the other's anger convincing him that he was right in taking a firm stand. "Maybe so," he replied. "That's one of the risks a man takes in business."

Harrison came closer to him and glowered. "I give you my word that you're going to regret this," he said. "I guarantee it."

Toby's manner changed subtly. His voice hardened and his face became expressionless. "I hope you're not making the mistake of threatening me, Mr. Harrison," he said. "I don't take kindly to threats, and I actively resent them when they're delivered under my roof."

"You can resent anything you damn well please," the huge man snarled, holding his ground.

"I think that we've exhausted our ability to hold a mutually profitable conversation, Mr. Harrison,"

Toby said. "It would grieve me to have to be inhospitable and run you off this property."

Harrison looked at him in amazement and was so amused that someone would physically challenge him that he laughed boisterously.

All at once, Toby produced a snub-nosed Colt six-shooter from beneath his coat. "I don't talk to hear my own words, Mr. Harrison," he said. "After three years of fighting the Rebels, I give you my word that I've learned how to handle this gun. I advise you to take yourself somewhere else, to be quick about it, and not to come back here."

Harrison opened his mouth, studied his adversary, and changed his mind. He knew that Captain Toby Holt meant every word he said and that no jury in Oregon would find a Holt guilty of shooting a trespasser. He bowed abruptly, then marched out of the ranch house and stalked to the hitching post where he had left his stallion.

Toby followed him as far as the door and leaned against the frame, watching until the big man rode off down the path that led to the public road. What Toby failed to realize was that Caroline, overcome by curiosity, had eavesdropped on the conversation. Tom Harrison excited her, and she was thrilled by the boldness of his demand, by the ruthless attitude he displayed under the Holt roof.

Before the conversation in the parlor had come to an end, she had slipped away, mounted her mare again, and had ridden hastily to a point beyond a clump of birch and evergreen trees that blocked a view of the public road from the Holt property. There she waited for Tom Harrison to appear.

She had no idea what she was going to say to

him, nor did she have any specific plan in mind. All she knew was that she had to see him again and that she thoroughly enjoyed taking the risk that she would be discovered in the company of the stranger whom Toby had been forced to expel from the house.

Glad she was wearing a gown of plum-colored silk with a plunging neckline, she sat sidesaddle, then carefully crossed her legs and hoisted her skirts to reveal her thighs. She was sorry she hadn't had the opportunity to freshen her makeup, but there was no point in regretting what couldn't be helped. She already knew that Harrison was interested in her, and that knowledge gave her the confidence she needed.

Tom Harrison, fuming impotently, wondering just how he would get even with Holt, rounded the bend and halted in astonishment when he saw the enticing blond creature obviously waiting for him. "Well, now," he said as he tried to collect his wits. "Well, now."

Caroline favored him with the full power of her most alluring smile. "I couldn't help overhearing your conversation with Toby," she said glibly, "and I couldn't let you leave without apologizing to you on behalf of all the Holts. His attitude was typical, you know. The men in this family are outrageously independent and think they can do everything unaided. They'd run the world if they could."

Harrison recovered his wits. "Does Captain Holt know that you've ridden out here to have a word with me?" he asked. "Does his father know it?"

A mischievous expression came into her sparkling eyes. "Hardly," she murmured.

"I see," Harrison said, and saw a great deal more than the young woman suspected. He realized she was not only bored but was aching for an opportunity to rebel against the Holt family. Very well, he would give her that chance—and in the same way would get back at Toby Holt.

"I appreciate the trouble you've taken on my behalf, Miss Caroline," he said. "I'm always grateful when somebody makes an extra effort for me, and I'm not one to forget that kind of favor."

Caroline eyed him boldly. "I've done nothing really, Tom," she murmured. "I'm no hypocrite, and I believe in expressing my feelings."

She was making them clear enough to him, he thought, and smiled inwardly. "You've got to allow me to return this favor," he said. "Maybe you'd come into town and have supper with me at the Oregon Inn?"

She laughed lightly. "I'd love it, you know," she replied, "I really would. But the inn is located in a small town, and the Holts are regarded hereabouts as special, very special. We wouldn't be finished with our soup before Toby learned that I was dining with you, and his honor—Holts are always worried about their confounded honor—would demand that he ride into town and create a scene."

"I see," he said.

"So, though I regret the need to refuse your kind invitation, I'm afraid I must."

"There's a way around your objections," he said when she made no move to ride off toward the house.

"Oh?" Caroline raised an eyebrow, and it was apparent that her interest was sparked.

"We could have supper served in my room," he said.

She knew she was being invited to participate in an assignation, but she did not flinch. "If Toby finds out what I've done," she said, "that will be the end of our marriage. His parents will insist that he throw me out."

Harrison stirred uncomfortably in his saddle. "I don't want to cause you to lose the food you eat and the roof over your head," he said.

She waved it off disdainfully. "As if that mattered. I have a considerable nest egg of my own, and I don't need the Holts to support me." That much was true. She had earned large sums as a courtesan in Nevada, and before that in Denver, and she'd been able to save a great deal of money. She had known what it was like to be destitute, and never again would she be in that position.

Seeing Harrison brighten, Caroline said, "But don't think for a minute that you're going to get your hands on a penny of my money. On the contrary. I expect to be paid for any favors I grant." There! She had made her positon very plain.

There was no longer any doubt in Tom Harrison's mind as to their future relationship. She had made it clear, and he could take it or leave it. He chose to take it. She showed far more spunk than any of the prostitutes in Tumwater, and she was infinitely better looking. What was more, he would be repaying Toby Holt immediately for his discourtesy, and he would even the score in a way that the young veteran had not anticipated. That prospect appealed to him enormously. "Your terms sound fine to me," he said. "Now I'm waiting for your answer."

"Where's your room?" she demanded.

"Second floor, front," he replied.

"I'll be there as soon after sundown as I can manage. I'll have my valise with me. There really isn't that much I'll need to pack—just a few of my favorite dresses. I'm certainly not going to bring along the clothes my mother-in-law has been buying for my wardrobe."

Harrison inched his horse closer to hers, and reaching out with a huge, powerful hand, he gripped her thigh with it. "I'll be waiting for you," he said.

Caroline knew full well that she was burning her bridges behind her, that she was terminating her relationship with Toby and was severing her ties with respectability. But she no longer cared. For month after month she had lived a life of respectability, and she couldn't remember a time when she had been so bored.

Tom Harrison was the sort of brute who excited her, and although she'd be abandoning security by running away with him, life wouldn't be dull. Most of all, she could be herself. She wasn't made to play the role of the law-abiding housewife. She had discovered that fact during her first marriage in Boston, and the free life that she had led in Colorado and in Nevada had convinced her that she was happy only when she behaved as she wanted and gave in to her impulses of any given moment.

"You won't regret the wait, honey," she told him in a low tone, her voice filled with promise.

"Where in tarnation is Caroline?" Whip demanded as the Holt family went to the dining room for supper. "She missed dinner this noon, and now she's late again."

"The last I knew she was in town, shopping,"

Toby said. "No, wait a minute, she came home in time to tell me that that lummox, Harrison, was here to see me."

"Yes," Eulalia said, "I saw her briefly this afternoon and again this evening. But we didn't stop to talk. She seemed rather preoccupied."

Whip was a patient man, but only up to a point. "Damnation," he said, "she ought to know by now that this is a private home, not a hotel. Cindy, do all of us a favor, will you?"

The teenage girl nodded.

"Before I lose my temper and say things that I'll regret," Whip said, "go off to Caroline's room and fetch her. Don't get into a discussion with her, just tell her that supper's on the table."

Cindy hastened to do his bidding, and the rest of the family sat at the table, where Whip helped himself from a platter of breaded veal cutlets and Eulalia passed a platter of dumplings.

They were still serving themselves when Cindy returned, looking mystified. "Caroline isn't in her room," she said, "but her closet door is open, and I think some of her clothes are missing."

Toby looked at his father, then at his mother. "Excuse me for a minute," he said. "I'll be right back."

He left the table, and the others began to eat without comment. He soon rejoined them, and he, too, began to eat.

"It looks," he said at last, "as if Caroline is gone."

"Gone?" his mother demanded. "Where?"

He shrugged. "Some of her flashier dresses are missing, and so are her high-heeled slippers, her cosmetics, and both of her silk capes. She appears to have decided to take herself elsewhere."

Eulalia marveled at her son's calm and was struck anew by his remarkable similarity to his father.

"When did you last see her?" Whip asked his wife.

"Less than an hour ago," she replied.

"In that case, she's gone no farther than town," her husband said. "Since she's too unsure of herself on horseback to make a long journey at night, she undoubtedly is finding shelter with someone in town."

"I'll eat my supper first, and then I reckon I'll have to do my duty and try to locate her," Toby said quietly.

His parents looked at him, then at each other. There was no need for them to communicate. Each knew what the other was thinking: Toby's love for Caroline was, to put it mildly, strictly limited. Eulalia was relieved that he would not grieve for a young woman who was unworthy of him, while Whip was quietly pleased that his son was showing an adult attitude and had too much good sense to mourn the loss of a trollop whom he had married because he had felt sorry for her.

Cindy gaped at her elders as she looked at each of them in turn. A score of questions crossed her mind, but she had the good sense not to ask any of them. She knew she would find out more by observing silently and listening intently.

Toby ate a second slab of fresh peach pie, which he topped with a slice of homemade cheese. Then he pushed back his chair. "If you don't mind, Ma," he said, "maybe you could keep a cup of coffee hot for me. I think I should get this mystery solved before it gets too late in the night."

His mother nodded, as did his father, and they said

nothing as he left the room and headed toward the stable to saddle his stallion.

Eulalia sighed. As Whip commented to her later that same night, it was not an unhappy sound.

Toby returned alone after an absence of no more than an hour and a half. "Where's Cindy?" he asked as he joined his parents in front of the parlor hearth, where a hickory log was burning.

"She's in her room doing her schoolwork," Eulalia told him.

"Good," he said, and squatting, rested the weight of his legs on the heels of his boots.

His mother smiled. He appeared to have acquired all of his father's habits, the bad as well as the good.

"I followed a couple of false leads," Toby said calmly, "and then I had a hunch, so I stopped in at the inn to see the Woodses."

Ted and Olga Woods, the parents of one of his close friends, had, like the Holts, been among the original settlers in Oregon. The owners of the Oregon Inn, they were successful, completely trustworthy, and had the best interests of Toby at heart.

"Caroline is there," he said. "She's having supper with Tom Harrison in his room. In addition to their meal, they ordered a bottle of whiskey, and Uncle Ted told me that she arrived with a valise."

"You didn't bang on the door and invite yourself to the party?" Whip inquired.

Toby grinned wryly. "No, I don't enjoy nasty scenes any more than you do, Pa. I wouldn't avoid a scene if it would do some good, but I see nothing to gain by breaking in on them."

Events were moving too rapidly for Eulalia.

"What will become of Caroline?" she wanted to know.

Her son shrugged. "I assume she'll be going up to Tumwater with Harrison, but maybe she has other plans. Whatever they are, they're her business, not mine." He spoke emphatically, his tone and facial expression indicating clearly that he was finished with Caroline.

"Good riddance," Whip said.

Eulalia nodded. "Good riddance," she echoed.

Whip spent a restless night. Eulalia could hear and feel him thrashing on his side of the bed, and in the small hours of the morning he climbed out of bed, donned the shabby dressing gown that he steadfastly refused to replace, and went to the windows. There he sat motionless for at least an hour, staring at Mount Hood, which was bathed in moonlight. Then he crept out of the room.

Eulalia knew that he had gone to the kitchen to drink a cup of leftover coffee, which was still in the pot. Dr. Martin had told him repeatedly that such coffee was too strong and hence bad for him, but his wife made no attempt to follow him tonight. He needed this time by himself. She knew better than to ask him what was troubling him. When he was ready, he'd reveal it to her.

At breakfast Whip was composed and appeared ready to talk. He waited until Cindy gulped her meal and hurried off to school. Then, eating his eggs and bacon with enjoyment, he turned to his wife and son. "Last night," he said, "when Toby brought us the news about Caroline, I was mighty relieved. Then I got to thinking, and it was like I had some burrs under my saddle."

"I've been thinking, too, Pa," Toby told him. "It strikes me that Caroline and Harrison are getting off too easy. I could follow them and shoot him, and I'd be acquitted by any court. But the way I see it, I can't blame Harrison alone for being a wife stealer. It strikes me that a fellow's wife can't be stolen unless she's willing. At least half the blame goes to Caroline. But whether they're getting off easy or not, I'm washing my hands of Caroline and want nothing more to do with her. I just hope that my path doesn't cross Harrison's when I go up to Tumwater to start developing our property. I have pretty strong feelings against him, and there's no telling what I might do."

Whip had listened carefully, and he consumed a slab of toasted fresh bread before he replied. "I know how you feel, son, but I'm prepared to go a step farther. She's still your legal wife, and even if you'd like to wash your hands of her, as you put it, you're still married to her. The way I see it, the mistake has already been made, by you and by her. The best thing for both of you is to try to make the best of it. I think she should be given the chance to come back and make her life with her husband."

His wife stared at him aghast.

Whip turned to his son. "Would you have her back if she was genuinely sorry and repented?"

Toby was silent for a time and rubbed his chin reflectively. "That's not an easy question to answer," he said. "I suppose if Caroline's regrets were real and if she made an honest, all-out effort to be a good wife, I'd be inclined to forgive and forget. But to be honest with you, I don't see her reacting that way. I don't know her all that well, I'm sorry to say, but I can't see her as the sort of woman who realizes she's made a mistake and tries to compensate for it."

"Neither do I," Eulalia said emphatically. "She's a complete strumpet with a strumpet's mind and lack of responsibility and contempt for law-abiding folk!"

"You may be right," Whip conceded, sighing. "You usually are. But I feel a sense of responsibility in this business that I've got to get rid of. I brought her to Oregon from New York, and I need to be satisfied in my own mind that her cause is hopeless, that she has no intention and no desire to live the life of a decent wife and mother."

"What do you have in mind?" Eulalia demanded.

"By now," he said, "Caroline and this Harrison are undoubtedly on the trail to Tumwater. I aim to give them a headstart, and then I'm going to follow them there within the week."

Eulalia drew her breath in sharply.

"I want to see her and speak to her," Whip said. "I want to find out for myself whether she's willing and able to come back to Oregon and reform. If she is, I'll bring her back here, and my duty will be done. If not, if she tells me to mind my own business and sends me away empty-handed—well, I'll be satisfied that I've fulfilled my responsibility."

Toby looked straight at his father. "If you ask me, Pa, you're wasting your time. You're going off on a fool's errand."

"That well could be," Whip agreed. "I'm not going to argue the point with you. I simply say that I have to do it. I'm being selfish, you understand. I'm doing this simply for the sake of my own conscience."

❊   ❊   ❊

Ted Woods, the proprietor of the Oregon Inn, heard the sound of chopping and wandered to the windows of the second-floor suite that he and his family occupied. He still strongly resembled the blacksmith he had once been. His shoulders were powerful, muscles still rippled in his arms, and his powerful hands were huge. All at once he chuckled.

His wife, Olga, joined him at the windows and, standing beside him, slipped her arm through his. She still bore vestiges of the pretty young woman she had once been, although like her husband, she enjoyed eating and, like him, too, had gained considerable weight.

"Tell me what is funny," she said. "I've been depressed ever since Toby Holt's wife ran off with that lumberjack. And to think they used our hotel for their rendezvous!"

Ted put his arm around his wife's ample waist and gestured toward the yard. "I'm watching Frank," he said. "What a man he is!"

Frank Woods, their son, had survived his twin brother, who had died at an early age of pneumonia. Now as big and brawny as his father, Frank was busy with an ax in the side yard, chopping down an oak tree.

"Must he cut down a fine old tree?" Olga asked, frowning.

"We're following our usual practice of planting two young oaks to replace it," Ted said. "If you look carefully, you'll see it stands right in the middle of the plot where the new wing is someday going to go. In order to increase the size of the inn, we are obliged to get rid of the tree."

As he spoke, the oak toppled to the ground.

Frank quickly and efficiently severed it from the stump with several quick blows of his ax, then trimmed off the small branches with speed and efficiency.

"I marvel at Frank's familiarity with wood," his mother said. "Watching him work makes me realize the advantages of his having been born and reared in the Pacific Northwest."

Frank bent down, picked up the trunk of the tree, which had a girth equal to that of an adult man, and carted it off to the rear of the inn, where he would split it and chop it into firewood.

Ted chuckled again. "Look at that," he said. "God knows I was strong when I was his age, but my son is infinitely stronger. He handles that heavy oak as though it were young pine. He's truly amazing."

Olga had to agree with that estimation. Their son, in spite of his great physical prowess, was a surprisingly gentle man and, like his father, slow to anger. Ted had fought hard all his life to control a violent temper. His son, seeing only the results, was known among his peers for his ability to stay calm under the most trying conditions. Only those who knew him well realized that when he did lose his temper, it was best to give him a very wide berth. On such occasions, he became ferocious, and his tremendous strength made him dangerous.

"The physical activity is good for him," Olga said. "It helps him get rid of his frustrations."

"What frustrations?" Ted demanded.

She sighed, and her gray curls bobbed up and down when she shook her head. "I don't know, but he was very sour and withdrawn at breakfast this morning. I decided it was best not to question him. He's a man now, not a boy, and he's entitled to his moods."

"Maybe I can find out," Ted said.

"Without being obvious and without prying," his wife told him.

He laughed as he went off to join his son. He and Frank had a close rapport that no woman, not even the young man's mother, could quite understand.

He found Frank behind the inn, where he had already quartered the tree and was now splitting it into small logs for the fireplaces of the guests. Ted picked up an ax, and wielding it with the same powerful ease that his son displayed, joined Frank in the task.

"Thanks, Pa," Frank said, then fell silent.

Ted worked side by side with him for some time, making no attempt to speak. "Something's bothering you," he said at last.

Frank nodded but did not express himself.

"Can I help?"

Frank neatly severed a length of firewood, then rested on his ax. "I'm feeling sorry for Toby," he said. "Before his wife and that lumberjack left the inn, I don't mind telling you, Pa, I had to control myself from going to their room, beating him to a pulp, and dragging her back to the ranch by her hair. I had to warn myself repeatedly that what Caroline was doing was none of my business and to steer clear of it."

"That was wise," Ted said. "Toby has license to do blame near anything he wants, but that privilege doesn't extend to his friends."

"I think that woman's plain crazy," Frank said. "Toby suffered enough with his wounds. He sure doesn't need this humiliation."

"I know how you feel, and I sympathize with

that position," his father said, "but if I've learned anything in life, it's not to question actions that appear to be inevitable. Although we can't see it now, maybe it's all for the best that Caroline Holt revealed her true nature and cleared out before she and Toby settled down on their own to make a joint life for themselves."

"How could it be for the best?" Frank demanded indignantly.

Ted Woods's massive shoulders rose and fell in a silent shrug. There was no way he could pass his own vast experience on to his son. Frank would have to accept or reject what he was told, and to accept it was asking too much of any young man.

Frank picked up his ax and, in a sudden burst of energy, let fly with it, reducing a length of timber to firewood. "I'd like to discuss something with you, Pa," he said. "Just between us."

"Sure, what's on your mind?" Ted asked.

"You may laugh at this, but I've kind of been looking forward to the arrival of that cargo of brides in Washington, as the newspapers keep referring to the young women who are heading out this way. I guess it's no secret to you and Ma that I haven't met anybody hereabouts who interests me, and I've been wondering—and hoping in a way—that there would be someone suitable in the cargo. I've kept telling myself that a woman needs a lot of courage to join a group like that, and I admire that kind of spunk."

Ted grinned at him. "As you know," he said, "your mother came here all the way from Russia, and you can imagine the courage that took. I'm all in favor of the cargo of brides, and although I haven't discussed them with her, I'm sure she is, too."

"I reckon I'll find out soon enough," Frank said. "I had a couple of talks with Rob Martin before he headed up to Puget Sound on the possibility of joining him and Toby in their Tumwater venture, and I've got to go out to the ranch and discuss it further with Toby this morning, much as I hate facing him on the morning after his wife ran away."

When he finished his chore of chopping firewood and clearing away the brush of smaller branches, Frank had no further excuse to linger in town, so he steeled himself, mounted his gelding, and rode out to the Holt ranch.

Toby was in his room, reading, his mother said.

The embarrassed Frank didn't quite know how to behave, and he became overly boisterous. "What are you doing indoors on a beautiful spring morning like this?" he roared as he opened the door of Toby's bed-chamber.

The young former officer looked up from the book he was reading and grinned. "You wouldn't understand this," he said, "but I'm engaged in a pursuit called improving my mind. You might try it sometime."

Looking reflective, Frank studied him for a few moments, then silently picked up Toby and his chair with no visible effort and carried them easily into the corridor.

"Are you crazy?" Toby shouted. "Put me down."

Both of them were laughing so boisterously that Eulalia appeared from the kitchen to learn the cause of their mirth. She had to laugh, too, as she watched Frank carry her son in his armchair through the kitchen and deposit him in the yard outside.

"This is more like it," Frank said as he gently put

the chair down on the grass. "Now breathe in some of this good, fresh air."

Toby never failed to be awed by his friend's physical strength. Frank had not only undergone no strain but was not even breathing hard. "Now," Frank said, hoisting himself to the corral fence and perching there, "how do you really feel?"

Toby knew the reason for his friend's anxiety. "I'm fine," he said. "I won't pretend I'm not shocked by Caroline's conduct, but there's nothing I can do about it, and I refuse to cry over spilled milk. I have a score to settle with Tom Harrison, but that can wait. I'm in no rush."

Frank clenched and unclenched his huge fists. "I'll be glad to give you a hand," he said. "All you've got to do is say the word."

Toby shook his head. "Thanks, but when a chore is this personal, a man has to attend to it himself. I'm in no rush, though; it will keep." He changed the subject abruptly. "Have you given any more thought to the proposal that Rob and I made to you?"

Frank nodded. "That's why I'm here," he said. "I'd feel a heap better if you let me pay for my share in the partnership."

Toby shook his head firmly. "The claim cost us nothing; there's no need for us to make a profit at your expense. We wanted you with us for two reasons, Frank. First off, you know a great deal more about lumbering than Rob and I do, and that means we can get started cutting logs practically immediately. The other reason is a bit more subtle. I've recovered enough to spend my full day in the saddle surveying for a new railroad, but my actual strength is questionable, and it may be a good many months before I'm back to where I was before I encountered those Rebel shells with my name on them. The development of the Tumwater property requires brawn, and you're just the man to supply it."

"If you and Rob are satisfied," Frank said simply, "it's a deal."

Toby rose from the chair, walked to the fence, and shook hands with him. "We're going to make a whale of a team," he said. "Can you leave for Washington within the week?"

"You bet," Frank said. "I've already mentioned this to Pa, and he says the inn can get along just fine without me. My time will be my own."

"I expect Rob will be back in Tumwater then," Toby said, "and he'll meet us there."

All at once, Frank's beefy face was creased by a broad grin. "We'll be getting there," he said, "just about the time that the cargo of brides arrives. That should prove interesting."

Toby's shrug indicated his indifference to the prospect. His separation from Caroline was too new, too raw, for him to feel even the slightest tremor of excitement over the pending arrival of a large number of strange young women from the East.

The Grand Hotel Tumwater was far less grand than its name indicated. A ramshackle, two-story log building, it had been used most recently as a dormitory for lumberjacks. The public rooms consisted of a dining room, a small lobby almost empty of furniture, and a saloon that was a favorite drinking place for men who wanted to kill an hour or two in the company of their friends.

The most that could be said for the hostelry was

that it had a large number of rooms, each of them equipped with a brass bed. For that reason it was selected by the harried officials of the Washington Territory to accommodate the first group of brides to arrive by wagon train from Independence, Missouri.

The twenty-five women, many of them accompanied by small children, were tired from their exhausting journey across the Great Plains and the endless ranges of mountains.

Bettina Snow, of Massachusetts, stood uncertainly just inside the entrance to the hotel and felt very forlorn. Brown-haired and dark-eyed, she was uncommonly pretty, a fact that not even the strains of the journey nor her simple linsey-woolsey dress could conceal. Anyone looking at her—and a group of men in the saloon were already ogling her—could see that she was thoroughly confused. The scenery, the climate, the barren hotel, the overly hearty welcoming speech by one of Governor Pickering's subordinates—all were alien to the life she had known in Fall River. Uncertain of herself and of her future, Bettina bitterly regretted having joined the group of women so blatantly searching for husbands.

Unfortunately, however, she had no choice. Her husband, a sergeant in General William T. Sherman's army, had been killed during the latter days of the war. The textile mills in Fall River no longer had army uniforms to turn out and were closing their doors, so there was no work available for her, and she had herself to support, along with five-year-old Lucy, her daughter. When a decent woman became desperate, she would try almost anything.

"Lucy!" Bettina had allowed her mind to wander for a moment, and now the child had vanished again.

She scanned the lobby frantically, then peered into the saloon, where Tom Harrison, who was drinking with his crony Mr. Trumbull, caught a glimpse of her full face and admired her inordinately.

A young woman of about the same age materialized out of the milling throng and stood beside her. Clarissa Sinclair, a widow from Philadelphia, had become friendly with Bettina on their wagon train journey. At least a head taller than the New Englander, with her red hair worn in a topknot that made her appear even bigger, Clarissa was broad-shouldered and raw-boned, towering above every other woman in the group.

"What's wrong?" Clarissa asked.

"It's Lucy," Bettina answered, uncertain whether to laugh or cry. "She's disappeared again. I swear to goodness, I take my eyes off that child for one second, and she's gone."

"We'll find her," Clarissa replied soothingly. "We always have. Where were you when you last saw her?"

"Right here, standing on this very spot!"

"Very well, then," Clarissa said, taking charge, "you wait right where you are. Don't budge, just in case she shows up. I'll go hunt for her." In spite of her bulk, the woman moved gracefully and swiftly as she made her way into the dining room.

Bettina remained where she was and nervously plucked at a handkerchief. She was too distraught to note that some of the men in the bar, particularly the huge man sitting at one end, were eyeing her and talking about her with considerable anticipatory pleasure.

After a short wait, Clarissa Sinclair reappeared,

triumphantly carrying Lucy Snow. Not surprisingly, in the child's arms was a small kitten that obviously was the cause of her disappearance.

"Look, Mama!" the little girl cried rapturously. "Look what I found!"

"I see." Bettina exchanged a despairing glance with Clarissa. Her daughter was enamored of every dog and cat she encountered.

"Can we keep him, Mama? Please. Please!"

Bettina shook her head slowly. "He seems like a dear little kitten, and I wish we could keep him, Lucy," she said, "but our own situation is too precarious. We're being quartered in this—ah—hotel for the present, and the government is providing the very food that we eat."

Clarissa quickly intervened. "The government is spending enough money on its cargo of brides project that I don't think Washington will run out of funds by feeding one small kitten. I can think of better places to keep an animal than a hotel room, but if we can stand it, so can the kitten."

As usual, her new friend made good sense, so Bettina ultimately relented. "All right, Lucy," she said. "For the present, at least, you may keep the kitten."

The little girl squealed ecstatically.

Crossing the lobby at that moment were the recently arrived Frank Woods and Toby Holt, the latter accompanied by his dog; they were quartered in the one section of the hotel not being utilized for the cargo of brides.

Seeing the kitten in the little girl's arms, Toby snapped his fingers. "Heel, Mr. Blake," he told the dog. "Steady, boy. We don't want to upset a little girl

107

or hurt her kitty." The dog obeyed and paid no attention to the kitten.

Something in Bettina Snow's appearance attracted Frank Woods, but he didn't want to embarrass her by staring as he and Toby proceeded together to the far side of the lobby. "I'll go out to the property and collect Rob," Toby said. "Then we'll all meet back here and have ourselves a good meal."

Ordinarily Tom Harrison would have known better than to intervene in the cargo of brides when the territorial officials were still on hand. But he had consumed just enough liquor to make him reckless, and ignoring the suggestions of Mr. Trumbull that he stay where he was, he insisted on coming into the lobby.

"Well, little lady," he said, "you're new to Washington, I take it."

His tone was oily, his bulk frightening, and Bettina instinctively shrank from him. Her obvious fear amused Harrison, who chuckled and reached out a large hand to grasp her arm. "I don't eat ladies for breakfast," he said, "and I sure wouldn't hurt somebody as pretty as you."

He was just a cheap masher, she thought, and jerked her arm away from him.

Ordinarily Clarissa Sinclair would have come to her friend's rescue, but on this occasion, even Clarissa hesitated. In spite of her size, the man who loomed in front of her was infinitely larger, and she recognized the fact that she was no match for him.

Sensing trouble brewing, Mr. Trumbull tried to persuade his patron to leave. "It's getting late, Tom," he said, running up to him as fast as his spindly legs could take him. "You told me not half an hour ago that you've got to get home."

Harrison shook him off impatiently. "I'm waiting," he said, "for the lady to speak to me." He bared his teeth in what looked like a caricature of a smile.

Frank Woods, alone after Toby's departure, observed the scene across the lobby. Certainly he needed no explanation. Not only did he recognize Harrison, whom he hated as his friend's enemy, but he was aware that the attractive young mother found his attentions annoying. Before he could stop himself, Frank crossed the lobby in a very few strides.

Suddenly his bulk squeezed into the space that separated Tom Harrison and Bettina Snow. "The lady is busy," he announced flatly.

It was a rare experience for Harrison to meet someone else at eye-level. He hadn't seen the young giant on his trip to Oregon—Frank having been off in the distance when he noticed Harrison at the inn—but he knew that here was an antagonist worthy of respectful attention. "If she's occupied," he said, "she can tell me so herself."

The peace-loving Frank, who rarely lost his temper, astonished himself by feeling a blinding rage well up within him. "I'm telling you on the lady's behalf," he said, and thrust his face closer to that of the other man.

"Come along, Tom," Mr. Trumbull begged. "You don't want to start something here."

There was a moment of electric silence. Frank Woods was ready to fight, and Harrison recognized that fact. Sizing up his antagonist, he knew he would become involved in a brawl in which he could be seriously hurt.

"Come on, Tom, come on now," Mr. Trumbull wheedled.

Frank stood his ground, his fists clenched, ready for instant combat.

Harrison laughed harshly. "We'll meet again, ma'am," he said, and turning on his heel, stalked away.

Frank took off his hat and bowed awkwardly to Bettina. "I reckon he won't bother you anymore, ma'am."

Bettina recognized the gentleness that was the essence of this man and said, "I'm very grateful to you, sir. You saved me from an embarrassing predicament."

Frank shuffled his feet and was unable to meet her gaze. "I know the cook," he said to little Lucy. "Maybe your ma will let you come with me, and we'll get some milk for your kitten."

Lucy instantly attached herself to this thoughtful new friend, and Bettina smiled and watched as Frank guided the child toward the kitchen.

"You seem," Clarissa said, speaking without envy, "to have found an interesting protector."

Bettina nodded. "Thank goodness he came along when he did. That horrid man is a real brute."

Frank soon returned with the little girl, the kitten, and a dish of cream, which he placed on the lobby floor.

"Shouldn't the cat be fed outdoors?" Bettina asked.

Frank grinned at her. "No, ma'am. Folks are mighty informal in these parts, as you'll find out after you've been here for a spell."

Clarissa took charge introducing her friend and herself and learning Frank's name.

"I want to thank you again, Mr. Woods," Bettina

said, "for saving me from a very embarrassing situation."

Frank turned his hat in his hand. "Don't think about it, ma'am," he said. "I have a score to settle with that one, in any event. He did dirt to a friend of mine, and I'm not forgetting it."

She had come, Bettina reflected, to a land far more violent than Massachusetts.

"Do I take it you're going to be in Tumwater for a spell?" he asked.

"Indefinitely, to the best of my knowledge," she replied. "It's been a long journey, but I believe this is the end of the road for us."

"They're putting you up here?" There was a hint of incredulity in his tone.

Bettina shrugged. "It's a solid roof over our heads, and it doesn't move or bounce. That makes it better than the wagon that's been the only home we've known for several months."

Clarissa couldn't help laughing. "I was late following you into the lobby, Bettina," she said, "because I just learned from a man who's on the governor's staff that we're only making our temporary quarters in this hotel."

Bettina was relieved, and her large brown eyes shone with pleasure.

"Where they intend to move us from here, I don't know, but we'll have more comfortable quarters, I was assured of that."

Prodding himself, Frank summoned all of his courage. "I aim to be in Tumwater myself for a spell," he said. "I've come here with my partners to look at some property we own and to start developing it. Someday, when you and your little girl have nothing better to do, maybe you'd ride out there with me and have a look at the place."

Equally overcome by shyness, Bettina could only nod.

Clarissa Sinclair lost patience with both of them. "Bettina will be just delighted to ride out to your property with you, Mr. Woods," she said, "and you can be sure Lucy will love the outing, too."

The tongue-tied Bettina looked at her friend gratefully.

"The day after tomorrow is Sunday," Clarissa continued briskly. "Am I mistaken in assuming that the Lord's day is observed here?"

Frank liked the sense of humor of this breezy, candid young woman. "Yes, ma'am," he said. "We're a God-fearing territory of the United States."

"Good," Clarissa replied briskly. "Then there are bound to be some churches in Tumwater, and that means that we can get to services, Bettina, for the first time since we've left Denver." She turned back to Frank. "Suppose you pick up Bettina and Lucy after church on Sunday morning," she said, then amended herself by adding, "if that's convenient with you, of course."

"Yes, ma'am," he said, "that will be just fine." He grinned at Bettina and patted Lucy on the head. "I'll see you Sunday, then," he said. "Meantime, Lucy, you take good care of your kitten." He backed off, then made his way through the lobby and went outside to await Toby and Rob's arrival.

"There's—there's nothing like forcing a social engagement on a man," Bettina said, laughing helplessly.

"It was plain he wanted to ask you," her friend

replied, "and equally plain that it would have taken him an hour to get around to it, just as it would have taken you another hour to accept the date. I don't have the patience anymore, so I simply speeded the whole process. They say that God helps those who help themselves, but those who don't can rely on their friends."

V

Caroline Brandon Holt looked at her reflection in the full-length pier glass in the bedchamber of Tom Harrison's house and was eminently satisfied with what she saw. Her "good-luck dress" had seen her through a variety of experiences in Denver, and she had had it copied precisely by a seamstress in Nevada. Seldom worn since she had left the silver country, she had nevertheless taken care to carry it with her always. Made of shimmering black satin, it was a backless, halter gown with a neckline low enough to entice those who were fascinated by her full, round breasts. The dress—or what there was of it—fitted her snugly, like a glove, and a thigh-high slit on one side of the floor-length skirt not only made it possible for her to move about but had the added advantage of showing off one of her shapely legs. As she well knew, no man could be impervious to her beauty when she wore that dress. Tom Harrison stood no chance of winning the battle that she intended to wage with him.

Nor had he won a battle with her yet, though Caroline sometimes let him think he had. She could control him totally, and as far as having any regrets about leaving Toby—well, she simply never allowed herself to think about him.

She had been in Washington for a week now, and she felt like a queen. She was constantly surrounded by men—and they made no secret of their desire for her when she strolled around Harrison's lumber camp or when she went the few miles down the road into Tumwater to do her shopping. Not that there really was anything to shop for in the pitiful excuse of a general store, but she got enough satisfaction from knowing she could have any man she wanted simply by crooking her little finger.

Hearing Tom fumbling with the front door lock, she quickly walked into the parlor, where she stood, in order to insure that he would feel the full impact of her appearance. As he came into the living room, she saw at a glance that his eyes were slightly glazed. He was at least partly intoxicated, but not too drunk to know what was going on around him, and that, too, suited her perfectly.

Giving him no chance to speak first, Caroline simulated a cold rage. "For your information, Mr. Harrison," she said, "you're more than two hours late. You told me when you left this morning that you intended to return no later than noon, and it's now half past two in the afternoon."

"I don't live by keeping my eye on a clock," he muttered defensively.

"When you're dealing with me," she told him firmly, "you'll be on time. You set the hour when you'd come back, I didn't. If you had no intention of being here at noon, you should have said so. I'm not trying to govern your comings and goings, but I insist that you be punctual in your appointments with me."

"I was delayed," he said.

"Yes, I assume as much," she replied haughtily, "but that's no excuse." She was goading him into losing his temper, and at last her effort succeeded.

"I'm not beholden to anybody, including you, for where I go and what time I show up," he said, "and don't you forget it."

"There are a great many things both of us should keep in mind," she replied, thrusting out her breasts and standing proudly. "You proposed marriage to me—assuming I could find a court somewhere that would give me a divorce from Toby—and I turned you down for the simple reason that my money would become your money, and there's no way on earth that I'm going to share what I've earned with any man. That's lesson number one. Lesson number two is that I'm free to do as I please when I please to do it. You claim that freedom for yourself, and I claim the same freedom."

"What the hell does that mean?" he demanded, his eyes glittering dangerously.

She inched closer to him, her body almost touching his. "I have no ties to you, and I'm no more responsible to you than you are to me," she said slowly. "Keep me waiting for hours and I'll simply pack my belongings and leave."

His exasperation increased. "It strikes me," he said, "that you need to be taught a lesson. If there's only one way I can persuade you to respect me, I'll beat you until you do."

Measuring him shrewdly, Caroline knew he

wanted her and that, consequently, she already had the battle won. She was too experienced to be in the least perturbed by his threats; she had known too many men, men of all natures, rich and poor, emotional and phlegmatic, courageous and cowardly. There had been a time when Tom Harrison's threat would have caused her to cringe, but she well knew that that was the one thing she could not afford to do. She was in control, as always, and she fully intended to maintain her mastery.

"You won't beat me," she said, "because you don't dare touch me. I'm unique here in Tumwater. This town has never seen anyone like me, and if I show up with bruises on my face and body, everybody will know you for the bully that you are. What's more, I'll walk out on you. You've had the whole town buzzing because you took Toby Holt's wife away from him. Well, folks will buzz all the harder because you weren't man enough to keep her here. I guarantee you I'll see to that. I'll spread the word good and proper before I clear out of town."

He raised a clenched fist, then let his hand fall to his side again. "You wouldn't do that to me," he said. "You wouldn't make me a laughingstock with the people in my own town."

"I wouldn't?" she demanded, taunting him. "Just try me and see. Hit me once, and folks will laugh you out of town."

He glowered at her but wisely decided to make the best of the situation. "Get us a drink, will you?" he demanded. "There's something I want to discuss with you."

She smiled sweetly, but instead of going to the table where he kept his liquor, she sat on the nearest chair, carefully revealing a long expanse of leg. "You've had quite enough to drink for the present," she said. "If you have something you want to discuss, I'm willing to listen."

He made his capitulation complete as he sank heavily into a chair opposite her. "Whatever you say," he muttered, and waited for her to gloat.

Instead, Caroline's expression was demure but provocative.

"I felt insulted," Harrison said, "when you turned down my proposal of marriage—but I've come to see the point you were making, and I guess you were right. There's no reason you should have to share money you've earned with any man. At the same time, though, I hate to see money lying fallow, going to waste, if you know what I mean."

"No, I don't." The one topic that could get her mind off herself was money.

"If you lock a silver dollar away in a strongbox, at the end of a year or even ten years, what you'll have in that box will be exactly one dollar. I believe in investing money, watching dollars multiply."

Now he was talking her language. "We're in total agreement," she murmured.

"You ought to go into business," he said, "and as near as I can tell, there's only one business you know real good. What's more, if you agree to my offer, I'll match your investment dollar for dollar. We'll be partners."

"What have you got in mind?" she asked coolly.

He was all business now, and the glaze disappeared from his eyes as he spoke; apparently he was willing himself to be sober. "This is a frontier community with a vengeance," he said. "There are men in

Tumwater by the hundreds. Half of them are on my own payroll. I say the area is right for a trollop who knows her business."

Caroline's smile was superior and slightly glacial as she shook her head. "There's no way on earth I'd be interested," she said. "In Denver and in Nevada, miners came to me with their pockets bulging with gold and silver. Any lumberjack here who empties his pockets will be lucky to find wood chips and sawdust in them. They couldn't afford an evening with me no matter how well you paid them."

"I wasn't suggesting that you make yourself available to them," Harrison said. "My idea is that we open a house. I have just the property in town, and it's big enough for about a dozen girls. With your experience you could run the place, and we'd split the profits. I'm telling you, Caroline, the men in this area are hungry for women, and we'll make a fortune."

She thought about the idea for a time and decided that she liked it: the plan was sound. "I can see some problems," she said. "Where will we get the girls? I certainly wouldn't want to hire any of the riff-raff who work in the local brothel."

"I've been thinking about that," he replied, "and I reckon we can recruit some of the women from the cargo of brides."

Caroline shook her head emphatically. "That's a terrible idea," she said. "Forget it."

Harrison challenged her. "Why is it so awful?"

"Because those girls are amateurs, and it would take months of training and experience to turn them into professionals. The only way an enterprise like this is going to make money is if it's thoroughly professional from the outset."

119

He nodded. "You have a valid point," he said. "I suppose I'll have to send Trumbull down to San Francisco and hire some recruits there."

She nodded and smiled. "That makes a great deal of sense," she told him. "We'll inspect the property later today. How soon can you send Mr. Trumbull to San Francisco?"

Harrison chuckled. "You're not letting any grass grow under your feet, I see."

"Certainly not," she replied. "When I come across a sound business idea, I want immediate action. I'll go into details with you later as to the types of girls I'll want Trumbull to hire, and I can guarantee you what I guarantee myself, a very large return on your investment."

"Right about now," he said, "it's time to seal our partnership with a drink." Not waiting for her reply, he rose, went to the cabinet in the corner, and poured generous quantities of whiskey into two glasses.

Caroline knew he would become unmanageable if he drank too much. She raised the glass that he handed her, stretched voluptuously, and said, "I believe I know a far better way to seal our relationship."

Harrison looked her up and down slowly. Then, placing his untouched glass on the table, he sauntered toward her. "You have the right idea," he said huskily.

She allowed his hands to roam over her body wherever he pleased. With luck, she, too, might become aroused, for any man who treated her with physical contempt was more attractive to her than one who regarded her as a lady. But that was unimportant to her now. What mattered was that she was going to be active again, earning large sums of money, and the prospect delighted her.

Whip Holt arrived in Tumwater late in the morning and encountered no difficulty in being directed to Tom Harrison's house. He had set out from Oregon the day after his son and Frank Woods had left. Toby had made it clear that he wanted no part in this attempt to get Caroline to return to the ranch, but he agreed that if she did return, he would come home after finishing his business in Washington and fulfill his marital obligations. Thus, Whip did not see Toby and Frank while he was in Tumwater, but rather went right to Harrison's house, which was, at most, one mile from the property Toby and Rob Martin owned. Uncertain of his reception, he nevertheless left his stallion at the hitching post and went to the front door.

Harrison was out, having gone off on an errand concerned with his lumber business, and Caroline was alone in the place. Wearing a frilly negligee, a gift from Harrison, she opened the door, and when she recognized her visitor, she clutched her neckline, drawing it more closely around her.

Whip spoke easily. "Sorry to come barging in on you like this," he said pleasantly, "but I have a need to see you. Can you spare a few minutes?"

Completely rattled by his totally unexpected appearance, Caroline froze and didn't know what to reply. Finally, however, she nodded.

Whip followed her into the living room. The place was sparsely furnished, obviously the home of a man. He looked around, taking in the atmosphere, but made no comment as he seated himself.

121

Taking a chair opposite him, Caroline made certain that her negligee covered her legs.

"You know me fairly well," he said, "so I'm sure you realize I haven't come here to lecture you or to deliver any sermon."

She finally found her voice and nodded. "That's good," she murmured.

"We're kind of proud of the name Holt," Whip said. "We've accomplished a lot under that name, my son and I, and we don't like seeing it dragged in dirt. That's as good a reason as any for my coming to see you, Caroline. I want to give you the opportunity to change your mind about leaving and to come back to Oregon with me."

"Really?" she asked, astonished.

He nodded. "It wasn't easy for Toby to agree to my coming to see you, I'll tell you that much, and he's a bigger man because of it." Whip stopped short. "Anyway, I'm not one for making speeches. You know what Toby has to offer you, and you have a pretty fair notion of the kind of life you'd lead with him. Your decision is up to you."

Before she could reply, the front door opened, and Tom Harrison came into the house, stopping short when he saw the visitor in the parlor.

Suddenly apprehensive, Caroline said, "This is my father-in-law, Tom. He wants me to go back to Oregon with him."

Harrison's eyes narrowed. Like everyone else in the Pacific Northwest, he well knew the name of Whip Holt and was familiar with his exploits as a guide and trapper, as an Indian fighter, and as an explorer. He was particularly conscious of the reputation that Whip had acquired for preserving the law.

But scrutinizing the legendary character, Harrison saw that he was an old man. It was true that around his middle he carried the whip that had given him his nickname, but before he could unwrap it and make use of it, it would be a simple matter to knock him unconscious. By the same token, if he tried to draw either of the revolvers that he carried in his belt, it would be easy for Harrison, some decades his junior, to disarm him.

Therefore, Tom Harrison was neither awed nor impressed. Whip Holt was, like so many others, a man who could be overcome by threats of brute force.

Acknowledging the introduction with a curt nod, Harrison asked, "What have you told him?"

Caroline smiled. "You came in before I had a chance."

"Go ahead; I'll listen," Harrison told her.

She turned to Whip, her smile totally lacking in warmth. "I'm sorry," she said, "but your offer doesn't interest me. I must refuse it."

Whip sighed gently and wondered whether to let the matter drop or whether to try harder. An inner voice told him that he was wasting his time, but he hated to admit defeat.

Filled with confidence, Harrison smiled broadly, nastily, showing two rows of uneven, yellowed teeth. "Holt," he said roughly, "why don't you get the hell out of here before I'm forced to throw you out?"

Caroline gasped inaudibly. Never, to her knowledge, had anyone shown Whip Holt such a lack of respect.

Whip himself was stunned. The insult was deliberate, and Harrison was demanding a confrontation.

But Whip was still able to examine himself and others with lightning speed, analyzing and probing faster than could most men. He quickly recognized the fact that the man's confidence was not ill-placed. Harrison had the advantages of youth and size, and no matter how much an arthritic, elderly man might resent him, it would be the height of folly to fight him.

There had been a time, not so many years in the past, when a single stroke of the expertly wielded whip or a prod from a loaded gun would have brought the bully to his knees. Now, however, the tables were turned. Though Whip was tempted to pit his vast experience against the other man's brawn, he deliberately desisted. It was senseless to create a scandal at his age and to have it whispered in every city, town, and hamlet on the Pacific that he had engaged in a brawl with a young bully over a courtesan—who happened to be his daughter-in-law. It was best to take his leave at once.

Sorry he had given in to the impulse that had brought him to Washington, Whip rose to his feet, nodded impersonally to Caroline, and took his leave. Not glancing again in the direction of the triumphant Tom Harrison, whose boisterous, mocking laugh followed him into the yard, Whip felt a sense of humiliation unlike any sensation he had ever before known.

Bettina Snow, her little daughter, and Clarissa Sinclair, using funds provided for the purpose by the government of the Washington Territory, moved out of the Hotel Tumwater and rented a small house just outside of town. Lucy was promptly enrolled in the local school, which was the territory's first, and the two women settled down to an uncertain future.

One aspect of their lives, however, proved to be highly predictable. Every Sunday, immediately after church, Frank Woods came calling on Bettina. He had taken charge of his partners' property and was beginning to cut lumber. For all practical purposes, he had become a Tumwater settler.

On the fourth Sunday after their arrival, Frank announced when he showed up that he had some special treats in store for Lucy. The little girl became wildly excited and, jumping up and down, wanted to know more. He told her she would have to let the surprises unfold.

The first of them readily became apparent. Awaiting them in the street outside was a handsome open carriage, pulled by a team of horses. Bettina halted in astonishment.

"This is my carriage," Frank told her. "I made it myself in my folks' stable a couple of years ago, and my pa forwarded it to me when I wrote him for it."

He helped Bettina to a seat and then lifted the little girl to a place beside her.

"I don't believe I've ever ridden in a real carriage before," Bettina murmured.

"You deserve it and a great deal more," Frank told her. Then, afraid he had spoken too freely, he was overcome by embarrassment. She, too, became shy and looked away from him.

They rode into central Tumwater in silence, and Bettina was again surprised when Frank pulled to a stop in front of a long, large saloon. She looked at him questioningly.

He merely laughed and, perching Lucy on one shoulder, said, "Come along."

They entered the saloon, in which only a few

lumberjacks were drinking because the hour was still quite early.

Walking partway down the length of the bar, Frank halted and introduced Bettina and Lucy to Cargill, the proprietor, a grizzled man in a colorful shirt, who was busily washing glasses in a pan filled with soapy water. Then Frank proudly pointed to a parrot sitting on a perch that appeared to be made of gold. The bird, who had a hooked bill and brilliant, multicolored plumage, regarded the newcomers through unblinking, dark eyes.

"Hector," Frank said solemnly, "this is Lucy."

"I'm glad to know you, Hector," the little girl said politely.

The bird stared at her but made no sound.

Cargill shook his head. "Just because you're a hero, Hector, doesn't give you the right to be spoiled. Remember your manners and greet the lady properly!"

"How do!" the bird croaked shrilly. "How do, Lucy!"

The child burst into laughter and clapped her hands.

Bettina was highly amused, too. "You say he's a hero?" she inquired.

"You tell them the story, Mr. Cargill," Frank suggested.

Cargill beamed and, drying his hands, handed the parrot a small biscuit. "One night about a week ago," he said, "I was held up by a no-good rogue who enjoys Tom Harrison's patronage. But Hector fooled him right good and got him off his guard, and a couple of my pals in the saloon were able to snatch the man's gun and run him out of town without a shot

126

being fired. I don't mind telling you I was so grateful to Hector that I took some of my life savings and invested it in a solid gold perch for him."

"I think that's wonderful," Bettina said. "What did Hector do?"

"Face me," Frank told her, "and turn your back to the parrot."

She did as she was bid.

"Now," he instructed her, "order me to raise my hands."

"Put up your hands!" she said dutifully.

Then she flinched as she heard the distinct, unmistakable sound of a gun being cocked directly behind her. She turned but saw only Hector sitting on his perch.

Lucy laughed so hard that tears came to her eyes.

"Say the words again." Cargill was grinning.

Once more Bettina said, "Put up your hands!"

To her astonishment, the sound of a gun being cocked was heard again, and this time there was no way to mistake its source. The sound was made by the parrot, whose imitation was perfect.

The surprised Bettina shook her head in wonder.

"It's a little trick that I taught Hector just for the fun of it a couple of years ago," Cargill said. "I had no idea it would come in so useful."

"How do, Lucy," the parrot squawked. "Cargill, I'm hungry. Lucy is hungry."

Laughing, the man went to a wooden box behind the bar and produced two cookies, one for the child and the other for the parrot.

"Harrison, the man who annoyed you in the hotel lobby," Frank said to Bettina, "is hated by so many people hereabouts that Hector has become the most popular figure in town."

Cargill chuckled as he nodded agreement. "No two ways about that, ma'am," he said. "My business has just about doubled since Harrison's crony was run out of town, thanks to Hector. The only trouble is that the blame bird is spoiled."

"I think he's wonderful!" Lucy exclaimed, clasping her hands together.

The parrot made no secret of his agreement with her. "Hector is wonderful!" he screamed.

"We'd better be on our way," Frank said, "before that bird's head gets too big for his body."

"Come back anytime, ma'am, and bring your little girl to see Hector," Cargill said. "You don't have to order a drink, and you'll be as safe here as you are in church. Any friend of Frank Woods and Toby Holt is a friend of mine!"

"Now we're going out to my woodland for a picnic," Frank said, "and when we get there, I'm going to show you a young raccoon I've been taming."

Lucy squealed with delight as she sat between her mother and Frank on the seat of the carriage.

It was only a short ride to the mountaintop property.

As the carriage bounced over the thickly rutted dirt road—the road having been carved out of the forest by Frank Woods's own two hands—they passed some rough-looking lumberjacks, who heckled them as they passed. They were Harrison's men, and what they were doing on this road was a mystery to Frank. Though it was true Harrison's lumber camp was nearby, he had his own road leading to it, and Frank just hoped his underlings weren't up to something.

But there was nothing he could do about them, since lumbering roads were not considered private property. Frank spurred his horses on, and the carriage jostled uncomfortably, but he was anxious to get Bettina and Lucy away from these men.

Frank had already built a small cabin for himself on the property, and he had begun hiring lumberjacks, who were now in the process of constructing a bunkhouse for themselves. When they arrived, Frank unhitched the team of horses and showed Lucy and Bettina around. The little girl was entranced with the raccoon Frank had tamed, and which was living in a little house Frank had constructed for it. Indeed, Frank had built a zoo for all the animals he had caught, most of which were the offspring of animals that had been killed by hunters. There was a fox cub and a pair of otters and even a fawn that gamboled about in the enclosure Frank had made. Lucy fed all these animals nuts and pieces of apple, and she squealed in delight as the little animals took the food from her with their paws or licked her with their tongues.

Then Frank took from the carriage a picnic basket that Cargill had packed for him, and he, Lucy, and Bettina sat in a clearing among pine trees to have their lunch. Bettina smiled as Frank gave the little girl all the best pieces of chicken and then for dessert gave her a big chunk of maple candy.

"You're too good to her, Frank," Bettina said, shaking her head.

"Rubbish!" he replied, and exchanged a grin with the little girl. "Lucy is my friend, and what are friends for if it isn't to have fun together?"

There were tears suspiciously close to the surface

behind Bettina's laugh. Frank Woods, she reflected, was almost too good to be real. It was difficult for her to realize that perhaps her fortunes had changed dramatically for the better. To have found a young man, rugged and good-looking, obviously able to support a family, who had established a close rapport with her daughter and seemed to be strongly drawn to her, was too much for Bettina Snow to contemplate.

One person who was not in the least surprised by the consistency and growth of Frank's interest in Bettina was Clarissa Sinclair. A shrewd judge of human nature, Clarissa had predicted Frank's reactions from the outset.

Now, alone in their little house on the outskirts of town, Clarissa methodically cleaned the interior, scrubbing floors, dusting every surface, and making certain that the entire place was immaculate. It did not matter to her that neither she nor Bettina owned the furniture they were using, which had come with the house. Cleanliness for its own sake was of paramount importance to her.

She worked steadily, without a break, and eventually had the satisfaction of knowing she was gaining the upper hand. She wished, not for the first time, that she could find gainful employment of some sort during this awkward interim period when she was waiting to be discovered by the right man. Had she realized how embarrassing it would be to become a member of a cargo of brides, she would not have volunteered. But it was too late to back out now. She had come all the way from Philadelphia, and she was obligated to stay here until she and some local bachelor struck a sufficient rapport for them to marry.

An unexpected tap sounded at the front door. Clarissa peered out through a window and saw a slender, beady-eyed little man waiting. She didn't recognize him, even though she had seen him with Harrison at the Hotel Tumwater the day she had arrived in Washington.

She quickly removed her apron and tore the bandanna from her head, letting her dark red hair fall freely before she answered the summons.

"How do, ma'am?" he said politely. "My name is Trumbull."

Clarissa was pleasant. "What can I do for you, Mr. Trumbull?"

"I wonder if I could come in for a minute. I want to speak to you about something personal, you might say, and I don't think this outside door is quite the place to do it."

Standing aside, she waved him in. He entered the living room and sat gingerly on the edge of a chair, turning his broad-brimmed hat in his hands. "If my information is correct, ma'am, you're Mrs. Sinclair, and you came here with the cargo of brides."

She nodded. "That's correct."

"If you've found a husband and are planning on settling down in the immediate future, you would be wasting your time talking to me," he said. "If, on the other hand, your future plans are still up in the air and you wouldn't mind picking up some spending money, maybe a great deal of money, then I think it would be worth your while if we have a little chat."

"I never object to income, Mr. Trumbull," she said.

He drew in a deep breath, privately wishing that Tom Harrison would stop giving him all the unsavory assignments. He was scheduled to travel on the next steamship leaving Puget Sound for San Francisco, where he had been instructed to hire prostitutes for the new brothel. But first he thought he would approach Clarissa Sinclair, who he was sure would be a notable addition to the house. "You—ah—you aren't like most women, Mrs. Sinclair," Mr. Trumbull said, seeming very ill at ease.

Clarissa was privately amused. "If you mean I'm a head or two taller and forty or fifty pounds heavier than most women, you're quite right, Mr. Trumbull. I'm not the least bashful about my size. I've been taller and heavier and stronger than most women all of my life, and I've learned to stop being shy about my appearance."

He looked relieved. "Good," he said. "That makes it much easier to talk freely."

"By all means," she said.

Trumbull shifted his weight uneasily in his chair, but his smile was bland. "As I'm sure you realize, Mrs. Sinclair, the population of the territory is made up mostly of men these days, and seeing that you're such a striking-looking woman, I'm sure you are getting, and will continue to get, more than your due share of attention. That's why my boss is interested in you."

"Your boss, Mr. Trumbull?"

"Yes, ma'am," he said. "Tom Harrison, and in this case, his partner is involved, too. A lady by the name of Caroline Brandon Holt."

Neither name meant anything to her.

"They're opening a new place here in Tumwater,"

he said, "a very classy house. There won't be another place like it in the whole of the territory."

She nodded complacently, not understanding what he was saying.

"We expect it to do three or four times the business of the ordinary establishment, and everybody connected with it will clean up. So you have opportunity to get in on the ground floor, you might say. You'll be paid well, too. You'll get to keep three out of every four dollars that you make. You'll get a day off every other week, and you can set your own work schedule."

There was a brief silence as comprehension at last dawned. Speaking slowly and distinctly, Clarissa said, "Let there be no mistake, Mr. Trumbull. You're offering me a position in a brothel?"

"This new house that Tom and Miss Caroline are opening," he said, "is too high-class to be called a brothel."

She nodded slowly, and a faint smile appeared at the corners of her mouth, although her eyes remained serious. "Was it your idea or this Mr. Harrison's idea that I might be a suitable recruit for this new establishment?"

"Tom noticed you, of course, as has just about every man in the territory," he said. "But the idea of offering you a job—well, to be honest, it was mine. Miss Caroline says she don't want to hire any amateurs, but I convinced her that a girl who looks the way you do can't possibly be an amateur."

"I gather," she said genially, "that you intended that remark as a compliment."

"Sure," he agreed, and grinned.

Clarissa stood, laughed softly, and wiping her

133

hands on the sides of her housedress, she quickly crossed the room and lifted the man bodily out of his chair. The startled Trumbull spluttered in protest.

Clarissa carried him up the staircase with almost no effort and, going into the bedroom and opening the window, shoved him head-first out of it. Terror-stricken, Trumbull squirmed and tried in vain to free himself, but Clarissa managed to retain her hold on him and shoved his upper body through the open window.

"If I do what you deserve, Mr. Trumbull," she said, "I'll let you drop to the ground below. It isn't far enough to kill you, I don't think, although I'll grant you that you might break an arm or a leg."

"You're mad!" he panted. "For God's sake, let me go!"

"I don't enjoy being compared to a trollop," Clarissa said severely, "and I very much resent your offer of employment."

"If I made a mistake, I'm sorry and I apologize," he told her hastily, babbling in fright. "Everybody makes mistakes, and I happen to be wrong, that's all. It's an error I won't repeat."

Clarissa's large, competent hand closed over the back of his collar, and she hauled the frightened man back into the bedroom, where he collapsed in a quivering heap on the floor. She looked at him, her eyes expressionless. "You're fortunate, Mr. Trumbull, that I was in a good mood today," she said. "If I were you, I'd take myself elsewhere before my mood changes and I lose my temper."

Trumbull hastily scrambled to his feet.

All at once, Clarissa's expression changed. She caught hold of the front of his shirt and held him at arm's length in a tight grasp. "Take a word of advice from me," she said, "and stay out of my sight for all time. The same goes for your friend, Harrison."

Then she shoved him backward with such force that he stumbled as he struck the bedroom wall. He managed to regain his balance quickly, however, and hastened out of the bedroom. Grabbing the banister, he ran down the staircase as fast as his little legs would take him.

Clarissa stood at the top of the stairs as he raced out the front door without even closing it behind him. "Remember, Mr. Trumbull," she called, "when I say I don't want to see you anywhere, I mean anywhere. Anytime I show up someplace, you clear out!"

Having heard of his father's humiliation at the hands of Tom Harrison, Toby Holt was glad that he himself did not encounter Harrison before leaving Tumwater to begin surveying, and he was even more pleased that he didn't see Caroline. No good would have come from an accidental meeting with either, and he was afraid that he would have become embroiled in a nasty fight with Harrison if their paths had crossed. As for Caroline, he had no desire to see her again—and he was privately relieved she had not returned to Oregon with his father.

It was far better to travel across the uncharted mountains with his dog at his stallion's heels. He breathed the pure air of the heights, he relished the absence of other human beings in the vast expanses, and although he failed to realize it, he regained his health far more rapidly than he had done on lower ground.

Rob, who knew and loved the mountains, feeling

completely at home in them, nevertheless marveled at Toby's expertise. As nearly as Rob could judge, Toby had inherited Whip Holt's talent for existence in the wilds.

Toby had no idea how he did it, but he always knew when game was near, and his cocked rifle was ready in his hand even before Mr. Blake warned him with a low growl of the proximity of game. He had an instinct for the presence of streams in lands where water was scarce, and he always knew where to find comfortable bivouac areas with ample patches of grass so the horses could graze.

Like his father, he had a sixth sense, too, for the proximity of other human beings in the area. One afternoon, as he and Rob were riding single file, with Toby in the lead and the shepherd dog about halfway between them, Toby suddenly raised a hand, halted, and cocking his head to one side, listened intently. Then he turned in his saddle and silently mouthed a single word. "Men," he said. He cocked his rifle, and Rob did the same.

Again relying on instinct, Toby dismounted, and holding his reins looped around one wrist, he advanced on foot. Rob promptly followed his example.

Mr. Blake moved closer to his master, but the dog also sensed the need for quiet and neither barked nor growled.

All at once an arrow whizzed past and landed with a thud in a tree. Toby immediately raised his rifle to his shoulder, and the sound of his shot echoed and reechoed across the mountains. An Indian clad in buckskins, his face smeared with vermilion paint, toppled from an unseen horse and sprawled on the hard, unyielding, rocky ground between two boulders.

Toby and Rob instinctively took refuge behind the nearer of the boulders, which was large enough to protect them and their horses. The dog remained in the open, his ears upraised, his tail standing out behind him. But Toby snapped his fingers sharply, and the animal knew what was expected of him. He took cover, too, and gave a low, menacing growl.

By this time, Toby had reloaded and fired again.

Now, for the first time, Rob could see a band of eight or ten warriors mounted on horses. All were armed, all wearing buckskins, and the war paint on their faces identified them as Nez Percé.

"They saw us coming," Toby said, and Rob had to agree with him. The Indians were on higher ground.

"This is a deliberate ambush then," Rob said.

Toby nodded. "They need a lesson," he said, "or these mountains will be too dangerous for us." His rifle spoke again, and a brave toppled from the saddle.

Now Rob fired, but his shot missed its target by inches, barely grazing the feathers on a warrior's headgear. Toby, however, was endowed with almost miraculous marksmanship. He fired his rifle twice more, then reverted to the brace of revolvers that he carried in his belt, and each of his shots struck home. Their band badly decimated, the braves broke into an undignified, hasty retreat, taking their mounts and their wounded with them.

Toby could have harassed them further and killed several of the braves, since their retreat across the difficult, broken ground was slow. But after making his weapons ready for combat again, he did not fire them. Instead, he sat with his rifle across his lap as he watched the Indians putting more and more ground between them and the enemy who had bested them.

Rob was mystified. "How come you've broken off the engagement?" he asked. "You're letting them get away free!"

Toby shrugged. "I don't believe in shedding blood needlessly," he said. "The Nez Percé thought they could overwhelm us because they outnumbered us so heavily, but we've taught them something they won't forget in a hurry, and I see no reason to kill when a wound is just as effective."

Rob, watching the Indians retreat, nodded quietly.

Although the incident lingered in Rob Martin's mind for a long time, Toby appeared to forget it. He made no mention of the Nez Percé again, and on their daily rides through the uncharted wilderness, he was always alert but did not appear to be particularly searching for Indians. He assumed that the Nez Percé had learned a lesson they would remember, and he was right.

Much to Rob's astonishment and pleasure, his friend appeared to thrive on the rugged life they were compelled to live in the desolate land of the heights. Displaying infinite patience, Toby caught a number of trout in swift-flowing mountain streams, and when he brought down an elk that had made its way through a mountain pass, their supply of meat was assured. Thereafter, for several weeks, they ate only meat and fish, and Toby swore that they were subsisting on the healthiest diet in the world. "It's like my pa has always said," he declared. "We have plenty of meat and all the fresh mountain water we want. We're living like kings."

His ability to stay alert in the saddle for hours on end increased noticeably, and his stamina improved steadily. The mountains completed the long task of rehabilitation that had begun in an army hospital so many months earlier.

Not only was Toby's health restored, but his energy for the task at hand was boundless. Although his knowledge of surveying was limited, he knew railroading well enough to distinguish which passes were feasible for the building of tracks and which offered too many difficulties to be practical.

Rob seemed to be working incessantly with his maps and charts, making notations on them, and sketching the route that the proposed railroad should take. "I'm glad I'm not charting this line alone, Toby," he said. "It would be hopeless, far too much for me. But you actually make it seem easy."

"As you well know," Toby replied, "it's anything but easy. However, I love this life up here, and you seem to thrive on it, too. It's too bad that the days of the mountain men are ended."

Rob laughed. "When you and I spend week after week surveying these heights, I'm blamed if I can see that the days of mountain men have come to an end."

Toby grinned and shook his head. "It's sad to say, but they really have, you know," he said. "I'm thinking of men like my father and Kit Carson, who could spend entire winters above timberline, shooting the game they needed for their food and living on the pelts they trapped. Those days are gone, and they'll never return. It's too bad for America, I think, because the mountain men contributed something precious to our national heritage. Something that we won't see the likes of again. No, Rob, you and I could never earn our living up here. There isn't that much game, and there aren't that many furs any more. We need subsidies like the pay that we're getting from Governor Pickering in order to earn our living."

"I don't think the spirit of the mountains is dead, not by a damn sight," Rob said. "Not when a man gets along in this wilderness the way you do."

Toby chuckled and made no reply. He was content with life on the heights, and his unfaithful wife and the man who had disappeared with her seemed very far away.

They came down below timberline into the forests, and late one afternoon when they paused to make camp, Mr. Blake was suddenly alert when he saw or heard a rabbit in the underbrush. He darted after it, and when the rabbit took off, he followed.

Afraid the dog was venturing too far from camp, Toby called to him to return. But Mr. Blake paid no attention. The dog followed the scent of the rabbit for a long time and then suddenly came up short. There was another smell far more potent and infinitely more sinister that suddenly assailed his nostrils, and his hair bristled when he realized that directly ahead of him was a pack of wolves, including females and their cubs. One large gray male, lean and apparently a leader of the pack, separated himself from the throng and moved forward cautiously. Stopping short of the dog, the wolf halted and snarled in challenge.

Mr. Blake unhesitatingly accepted the call to combat. An instant later, the dog hurled himself at his foe, his powerful jaws working as he sought his opponent's throat.

The two animals were fairly evenly matched, but the shepherd was endowed with a quality that was lacking in the wolf, a quality of courage that enabled the domesticated animal to triumph. The wolf was not lacking in strength, power, or stamina, but he was fearful, a trait that was unknown to Mr. Blake, and the dog soon gained the upper hand. Both animals were bleeding, but the wolf was the first to desist, and he slunk off into the underbrush, tacitly admitting defeat. The shepherd stopped short and began to lick his wounds.

The wolf pack promptly accepted the victor. Two of the males came forward, their ears flattened against their heads, and their lack of hostility showed their willingness to accept the dog as one of them. He had defeated a champion of the pack in a fair fight.

When the entire pack began to move off through the underbrush, Mr. Blake joined them as though this were the most natural thing in the world to do. His wounds forgotten, he was at peace with the wolves and quickly became one of them.

That night, Toby and Rob sat at their campfire, neither saying very much. They had tried as best they could in the growing darkness to find the shepherd, but to no avail. Now it was late at night, and Toby was disconsolate. Suddenly the young men heard wolves howling in the distance. "Damnation," Toby said, "there's another obstacle to the return of the dog."

"Surely he has enough sense to avoid a pack of wolves in order to get back to us."

"I'm not sure what he has sense for and how

much sense he may lack," Toby replied unhappily. "All I know is that we can't go searching through these highland forests for him. It would be like looking for the proverbial needle in a haystack. All I can do is hope he comes back. If he doesn't, I don't know how I can face Beth again."

Rob nodded glumly. "I know what you mean," he said. "She was mighty fond of that dog when he was a little puppy."

"She was more than fond of him," Toby replied. "She made me responsible for him, and I feel that I've let her down."

"Now that's a pile of rubbish," Rob said. "It was hardly your fault that the dog ran off."

"I should have had enough control over him so that he wouldn't have gone in the first place," Toby replied. "But there's no sense in beating myself for what might have been. I just hope that somehow the dog will show up before we break camp in the morning."

Mr. Blake, having cast his lot with the wolf pack, did not reappear, much to Toby's bitter disappointment. He only wished he wouldn't have to tell Beth the news.

The loss of the dog was bad enough, but it also reminded Toby of how badly he missed Beth Blake. Just thinking about her caused a deep, persistent ache within Toby, and he realized how fortunate Rob Martin was. He knew that Rob, too, had developed a deep interest in Beth, and he realized that his friend was free to pursue her, free to pay court to her, free to use every means at his disposal to persuade her to marry him.

Too late, Toby had seen her as the woman he

should have married. But like it or not, Caroline was his lawful wife, and regardless of whether they were together or she was off somewhere with Tom Harrison or some other man, the ties that bound her to Toby were still legal and present, and it was unlikely he could do anything to break them.

VI

Frank Woods promptly demonstrated to his crew of newly hired lumberjacks just how capable he himself was at felling and trimming trees and just how hard he was willing to work. Watching him chop down a large fir tree, deftly trim off the branches, and haul the trunk single-handedly to the logging road, they were vastly impressed with their new boss and were willing to work hard for him. Thus, within a remarkably short time, the lumber camp grew and prospered. The forest owned by the partners, Holt, Martin, and Woods was gradually thinned, and enormous piles of logs sprang up next to the logging road and were hauled by mule team to the sawmills on Puget Sound.

Even Tom Harrison's henchmen couldn't stop the logs from being brought to the mills, some of which were as far away as Portland, but that didn't mean Harrison wasn't going to try to make life miserable for the partners. He still hadn't given up on getting the property for himself, and he certainly had no intention of letting the partners prosper. Tom Harrison was dictator in Tumwater, and he did what he wanted.

One night while he was sleeping, Frank Woods heard a commotion in the woods outside the bunkhouse, and throwing on his flannel robe and shuffling into his slippers, he ran out into the night to see what was amiss. He was joined by some of his loggers, and they all went to the spot where they heard the noise. There, lying in a little clearing and writhing in agony, was a man who worked for Frank.

"That there's Clark," one of the lumberjacks said to Frank. "I thought I seen him missin' from his bunk."

Sure enough, while the others had been sleeping, Clark had been dragged from his bed by three of Harrison's henchmen. According to Clark, who told the other men the whole story as soon as he was brought back to his bed and given a drink of whiskey, he was accused of breaking his contract with Harrison, and as a result the three henchmen beat him up soundly.

"I never had no contract with Harrison," Clark bawled. "Loggers never needed no contracts before Harrison came along. We worked where we chose and for whoever we chose."

Realizing something needed to be done, Frank went into Tumwater to speak with the territory-appointed sheriff. There a rude shock awaited him. Finding the sheriff in his office, feet up on his desk and drinking from a jug of hard cider, Frank explained what had happened up at his logging camp and said he wanted to press charges.

"Cain't," was all the sheriff said, without so much as a glance at Frank.

"Why can't you?" the big man asked, incredulous.

"Ain't got no proof."

Frank Woods was never very good at arguments, but he knew well enough when he had a good case, and he had one now. "I got the proof of the man who was beat up."

"Don't mean nothin'." The sheriff still didn't look at his visitor but took another swig from his jug. "Coulda been he just had too much to drink and fell and hurt hisself."

With this last remark, two of the sheriff's deputies, who were playing cards in the back of the room, let out a long laugh. Frank looked at them and was shocked to realize that he had often seen these two men in the company of Harrison, usually at the saloon. Frank quickly realized these were Harrison's henchmen and that the sheriff was no doubt also in his "employ."

The sheriff was looking at Frank now. "Why don't you be a good boy and go back to that loggin' camp of your'n, an' just be glad nothin' worse happened." The deputies let out another raucous laugh, and the sheriff went back to his jug.

Frank realized that short of having a showdown with Harrison, there was nothing he could do, and he was enough of a believer in law and order to want to see justice done, not more violence. He decided he would wait until Rob and Toby returned to Tumwater, tell them the whole story, and see what they could do.

*　　*　　*

Toby Holt and Rob Martin came down from the mountains, arriving in Tumwater late on a Saturday afternoon. They saw no point in going on to Olympia to report to Governor Pickering until Monday, so they arranged to stay at their property with Frank Woods.

When they arrived, Frank was shaving and changing into clean clothes, much to their amusement, and they looked first at him, then at each other. "Something special in the wind, Frank?" Toby asked.

The big man nodded. "This is Saturday, and Bettina Snow has agreed to have supper with me tonight," he said. "Come along and meet her and say hello to her friend Clarissa, too."

"You seem to have made yourself right at home in Tumwater," Rob observed, laughing.

Knowing he was being teased, Frank refused to rise to the bait. "Clarissa Sinclair," he said, "got a big lump sum of money from the federal government for some kind of heroism that her late husband performed during the war," he said. "So, blamed if she didn't go out and buy the biggest building in town. She's turned it into a rooming house now, and not only are Bettina and her little girl living there, but so are a number of lumberjacks, as well as some of the other women from the cargo of brides who want decent quarters for decent prices."

In spite of himself, Toby was impressed. "Mrs. Sinclair," he said, "sounds like quite a woman."

Frank nodded, then crossed the room and sat on his bed, which creaked and sagged under his weight. His tone serious, he told the other men what had taken place behind the bunkhouse and how he had gone into town only to learn that the sheriff and his deputies were on Harrison's payroll. "There doesn't seem to be anything we can do about it, either," Frank said, pulling on his massive boots. "Harrison has this town in a stranglehold."

"There is one thing we can do," Rob said. "Toby and I are going to Olympia on Monday morning in order to file a preliminary report on the railroad. At that time we can tell the governor just what's going on here."

"Do you think he'll be able to do something?" Frank asked hopefully.

"He *has* to do something," Toby said from where he stood, leaning against the wall of the room, arms folded across his chest. "Washington doesn't have much of a future if men like Harrison are allowed to do whatever they want, without any respect for law and order."

"The first thing the governor better do," Frank said, "is appoint a new sheriff for the area, one who won't take Harrison's bribes." He sighed, then rose from the bed. "Well, are you two coming into town with me or not?"

They knew he was anxious for them to meet Bettina Snow, so they finally agreed to accompany him, and after bathing in a swift-running stream, which only frontiersmen accustomed to the mountains would have done, they, too, donned clean shirts and pants for the evening. Then they accompanied Frank to Clarissa's new boardinghouse.

They gathered in the main parlor, a cheerful room with many substantial-looking armchairs, a sofa, and a big, stone fireplace. Bettina Snow was delighted to meet Frank's two partners, about whom she had heard so much, and at her insistence, Clarissa agreed to go with them to the Hotel Tumwater for supper.

Lucy, who was already in bed, would be looked after by one of the young women living in the boarding-house.

Clarissa would have invited Toby and Rob to stay with her for supper, but having just met them, she didn't want them to think she was too forward or too eager to please. Consequently, she accompanied them to the restaurant instead.

As they walked the short distance to the hotel, Toby told Clarissa, "I'm afraid they won't have much to offer other than Irish stew, but at least we won't have to cook it ourselves."

"Do you do much of your own cooking, Captain Holt?" Clarissa asked.

"I've fixed every meal that I've eaten in the past month," he replied, grinning, "and to be honest with you, I'm sick of my own handiwork."

A large crowd was gathered at the hostelry, the bar was filled, and the newcomers were fortunate to occupy one of the last available tables in the dining room.

Toby didn't like the atmosphere this particular evening, but he kept his thoughts to himself. Many of the lumberjacks had been drinking, and the presence of harlots in their midst hinted at the possibility that trouble might erupt at some point during the evening. But he told himself he was being unduly apprehensive. He, Rob, and Frank could handle any emergency that might arise and would encounter no difficulty in providing the two ladies they were escorting with ample protection.

The first surprise that greeted Toby was a pleasant one. On the menu for the night were large, freshly caught shrimp and oysters from Puget Sound, beefsteak, baked potatoes, and blueberry pie.

"It appears," Clarissa told him, "that you were wrong, Captain Holt."

"I take it all back, ma'am, and I just hope that the meal tastes half as good as its promise."

They were served with platters of cooked, cooled shrimp and raw oysters, which they ate with gusto, and Toby noted that Clarissa Sinclair was eating her fair share.

"There's nothing as delicious as Pacific shellfish," he told her.

She laughed. "You know, we have pretty good shrimp and oysters in Philadelphia too," she said. "As a matter of fact, we also have lobsters from the North Atlantic and shad from our Pennsylvania rivers— seafood that you can't get out here."

"Well," he replied quickly, "I guess you'll just have to make do with the fresh salmon that's a specialty hereabouts."

"Very neat, Captain Holt," Clarissa said. "I'm already learning it isn't wise to duel with you."

Bettina and Frank were deeply immersed in conversation when suddenly she broke off, fell silent, and stiffened. Following the direction of her gaze, Frank saw Tom Harrison standing in the doorway to the dining room, staring at Bettina. Harrison had been drinking, and he was conscious only of the presence of the pretty, young woman.

For the first time since Caroline had gone off with the man, Toby set eyes on him and was engulfed by a wave of deep, bitter hatred.

"Don't you worry," Frank told Bettina, "I'll get

rid of him." In spite of his bulk, he rose quickly and gracefully to his feet.

Seeing Frank, Harrison drew his woodman's ax from his belt and smiled wickedly. Then he started to move across the room.

Not hesitating for an instant, Frank reached out and snatched an ax from its resting place on the floor beside a party of lumberjacks.

It appeared certain that there would be bloodshed. Neither of the two burly, broad-shouldered men, who were about to come face to face, was willing to yield.

The sentiment of the crowd ran strongly against Harrison, but he was too drunk to know or care what people thought. His only thought was that Frank Woods was standing between him and this woman whom he wanted.

Toby Holt studied Frank's face for a long moment and knew that his friend's patience had run its course. It was obvious that Frank was exasperated and that he intended to engage in a vicious duel with Harrison, regardless of the outcome.

Rob Martin apprehensively reached for the guns in his belt, and Toby said softly, "Don't touch your firearms. Otherwise, every man in the place will start shooting, and there will be even worse casualties than otherwise." Realizing his friend was right, Rob left his guns in his belt.

Clarissa Sinclair's calm deserted her. "They'll kill each other," she murmured in alarm.

"Not if I can help it," Toby replied, and rising slowly to his feet, he hitched up his belt.

People in the restaurant hastily rose from their tables and cleared to one side of the dining room.

There was no sound now in the room other than the footsteps of the two giants as they slowly approached each other, each of them grasping a heavy ax, each of them determined to see this fight through to its end.

Suddenly Toby materialized between the two combatants. He carried his revolvers in his belt, but he did not draw them. "Frank," he commanded quietly, "sit down and cool off!" He did not raise his voice, but he spoke with a ring of sincerity, an air of command that could not be denied.

Frank Woods had no idea why he was obeying his friend; all he knew was that he had to do what he was told. He meekly resumed his seat, somewhat confused, still gripping the ax in his large, brawny hand.

Toby was somewhat relieved, but his expression remained unchanged. "Harrison," he said, in the same even tone, "you're making an exhibition of yourself. Go to your table, sit down, and behave like a gentleman!"

A sneer on his face, Tom Harrison continued to advance, ax in hand. Well aware of the danger he faced, Toby nevertheless did not flinch. "There's nothing wrong with your hearing, Harrison," he said. "Do as I tell you, and be quick about it."

Harrison slowed his pace, although he continued to advance. "Why the hell should I do what you tell me, Holt?" he demanded.

Toby smiled thinly. "There isn't a jury in this territory," he said, "that would convict me if I put a bullet into your heart, and you ought to have the good sense to realize it." Slowly, his motions almost exaggerated, he drew one of his guns, and when he cocked it, the clicking sound was heard throughout the room.

"I've killed a good many men in war," Toby said. "Most of them fine, upstanding fellows—who happened to be my country's enemy. This situation is different. You're my personal enemy, Harrison, and I'll exterminate you with no more feeling than I'd squash a bug." He raised his voice, and it echoed through the crowded room. "For the last time, sit down!"

Harrison found himself staring into the muzzle of a loaded, cocked Colt six-shooter. He halted.

"Do what he says, Tom," one of Harrison's cronies called from the doorway. "He means business!"

Harrison's eyes met Toby's, and all at once the big man sobered. He could read certain death in the calm, pale blue eyes that bored into him. He needed no other persuasion. His bravado crumbled, and he turned away, his lips moving as he cursed silently.

Toby made no move until Harrison had walked disgustedly out of the dining room. Only then did he uncock his gun and return quietly to his seat.

Frank Woods's temper cooled, and he thanked his friend profusely for his intervention. Toby shrugged. The incident was ended, and he preferred to put the entire matter out of his mind.

Clarissa Sinclair couldn't help staring at this tall, sinewy man. Never had she encountered anyone with such nerves of steel. Overcome by curiosity, she could not resist saying, "You looked positively tranquil while you were facing that brute. Weren't you frightened?"

Toby grinned at her and shook his head.

"I'd have been scared stiff," she confessed.

He continued to smile. "Fear is a good and healthy thing to feel," he said. "It makes folks cautious and prevents them from behaving as they shouldn't. As it happens, though, I had nothing to be afraid of, and I knew it. I was in complete command of the situation, you see, and if he had as much as started to raise the ax, I would have put a bullet into him."

"You really would have shot and killed him," Clarissa said in surprise.

Toby's eyes hardened, and he spoke without expression. "Harrison," he said, "is my personal enemy. I'd get rid of him without feeling a qualm."

Clarissa marveled at the strength and the purpose of this rugged, very attractive man, and she was fascinated. "If you feel that way about him," she said, "how could you have refrained from killing him just now when you had the chance?"

"As I said, I'd have had no qualms about killing Harrison if he came any nearer to me with that ax. But it's one thing to kill a man in self-defense, another to kill him in cold blood. Even though Harrison's a criminal and a scoundrel, I refuse to take the law into my own hands. If people did that, there would be total chaos, and this country wouldn't be much of a place to live in. I didn't almost get myself killed in the Civil War just to see the United States fall apart at the hands of people with no regard for the law!"

Frank Woods confided in Bettina Snow and told her that Caroline, Toby's runaway wife, was living in Tumwater and was actively engaged in establishing a brothel with Tom Harrison as her partner. "She's living with Harrison at his house," he said.

"Does Toby intend to do anything about it?" the perplexed Bettina asked.

He shook his head. "I don't think so," he said. "If you ask me, he's trying to pretend the whole situation doesn't exist. Maybe he feels that if he doesn't think about it, it will go away, just like a bad dream."

Bettina thought about the matter when she was alone, and she was unable to understand how Toby could just ignore his wife, no matter what kind of person she was. She discussed the matter with Clarissa Sinclair. "It strikes me," Bettina said, "it's a person's duty to tell Toby that his problem won't just go away by pretending it doesn't exist. I can think of all sorts of new problems that would come up if he doesn't face the issue squarely." Bettina was never as emphatic in her views as her friend, so she added, "I just don't know what's right and what's wrong."

"All I can do," Clarissa replied, "is to put myself in Toby Holt's place, and even if he has no more use for his wife—for which I certainly couldn't blame him—there's a matter of principle at stake."

Bettina nodded in agreement.

Clarissa could not dismiss the matter from her mind, and two evenings later when Toby took her to supper, she steeled herself, then told him what she thought about his indifference to the fact that his wife was in town, living with another man.

As she had anticipated, he accepted her statements without comment, and his expression did not change. This reaction, more than anything else, convinced her that her opinion had made a deep impression on him, and she was glad she had given in to the impulse to tell him what she felt.

Toby wrestled with the problem in private for the rest of the night and slept very little. Certainly he was not fooling himself. He was relieved to be rid of

Caroline and had no desire to resume a relationship with her. He had been quietly pleased when his father had failed to convince Caroline to return, and Toby knew he would be content if his path and Caroline's never crossed again. On the other hand, she was still his legal wife, and no matter how much he disliked her, he could not erase that fact.

He was beginning to enjoy himself again, even though Beth Blake appeared lost to him for all time. He had to admit that he was interested in Clarissa Sinclair, whose candor he enjoyed and whose unusual appearance he found attractive. He could not, in all justice to her, continue to see her, however, if he remained a married man.

There was one possible solution to his problem, although it appeared fairly unlikely. Until the war, divorces were rarely granted by the courts of any state in the Union. But that situation was changing; veterans everywhere were returning home from military service to find that their marriages had soured, and as a result, the courts in some states were adopting a more lenient attitude toward the granting of divorces. As far as Toby knew, the courts in Oregon might prove sympathetic, provided a husband and wife both testified that they found themselves incompatible.

Certainly the matter was worth discussing with Caroline. It would be to her advantage, as well as to his, for her to be free to marry again if she chose to do so. He wanted to have a frank discussion with her, and if she agreed, perhaps they could issue a joint appeal to a state court in Portland. At least the effort was worth making.

The next morning Toby decided he would go to

Caroline at once and would discuss the problem with her frankly and honestly. He felt confident of his ability to persuade her to see the matter as he saw it and to join with him in appealing to the court for a divorce.

As it happened, Caroline was also thinking about a meeting with Toby, but she felt far less self-assured. She had heard that he was in town—and, indeed, had encountered Tom Harrison in the hotel. But as far as Caroline was concerned, she was sure Toby was in Tumwater to make her go back to the life she hated at his parents' ranch in Oregon. In fact, she was so sure of it that she was afraid to go out for fear of running into Toby, and she kept inside the house, growing more and more restless, for she also was afraid that at any minute Toby might show up at her door.

The fact of the matter was that Caroline Brandon Holt could never face Toby again. He had been so good to her, treating her with a respect and courtesy that she had never been shown before by any man. If she were to meet him now, after all she had done, she didn't know what she would do.

Caroline was becoming so distraught that one day, as Harrison was about to leave the house for a trip into town, she halted him. "You didn't tell me," she said, "about the run-in you had with Toby the other day."

Harrison had no desire to discuss the matter. "What was there to tell?" he asked solemnly. "We exchanged a few words, and that was the end of the matter. We didn't come to blows, more's the pity."

Caroline failed to see through his bravado because her mind was on other matters. "I don't believe Toby wants to fight with you," she said. "As a matter of fact, he's just using you as a means of getting at me."

The suggestion surprised Harrison, who grinned cynically. "I didn't see him come chasing after you when you left Oregon with me," he said. "What makes you think that he's the least bit interested in you?"

"You don't understand," she replied. "Toby is a Holt. They not only own the biggest ranch in Oregon, but if you listen to them, you'd think the whole of the Pacific Northwest was their private property. They're very proud people, and they're stuck on themselves."

"I still don't see what that has to do with you," Harrison replied brutally.

Caroline sniffed disdainfully. "Toby's father came all the way to Tumwater just to see me," she said, "and I don't regard it as accidental that Toby is here, himself, right now."

"He owns an extensive property here that I've been trying to get for myself," Harrison said. "He and his partners have hired a dozen hands, and they're beginning to cut timber. The logs are hauled to the sawmills on Puget Sound, and already their lumber camp is showing a profit. I don't think Toby Holt's presence has any connection with you."

"You're completely mistaken," Caroline declared impatiently, shaking her head so that her long, blond hair swayed back and forth. "I walked out on Toby; I disappeared. One simply doesn't treat a Holt in that cavalier a manner. Remember, the family likes to think they're invincible. That means he's going to want me back, even though he may secretly loathe me. That doesn't matter; it's the façade of respectability that the Holts present to the world that really counts. So he'll come after me, and if necessary, I'm sure he's prepared to drag me back to Oregon by the hair."

Harrison chuckled dryly. He was convinced that she was exaggerating, that Toby Holt wanted nothing more to do with her. But there was little to be gained by arguing the point with her. Caroline had become his business partner in a venture that promised to be highly profitable, and until the organization of the brothel was completed and the place had begun to function smoothly, he knew he would be wise to stay in her good graces. She had far too mercurial a temper for his taste, and although he subsequently would be able to drop her, he realized that for the time being, he would be wise not to upset their relationship. He opened the front door, intending to leave the house, but something that he saw outside caused him to change his mind, and he quickly slammed it again. Going to the nearest window, Harrison concealed himself behind the curtains and pointed.

Caroline looked in the direction that he indicated and gasped. Riding up the steep hill toward the Harrison house at the crest was Toby Holt.

"Just as I told you!" she gasped. "He's coming after me!"

Tom Harrison thought it far more likely that young Holt was coming in search of him. They had unfinished business to be settled, and that, he concluded, was undoubtedly the reason for his impending visit.

Caroline gave in to a complete sense of panic.

"Hold him off, Tom!" she exclaimed. "Don't let him come near the house yet! I've got to have time to get away!"

The man stared at her. He had never seen her this agitated, and he began to wonder if she was in her right mind.

"Please!" she begged. "I need time to saddle my mare and put some distance between me and this place."

Harrison refused to believe she was in any danger at all, but he was willing to humor her, chiefly because it suited his own purposes. Toby Holt was riding alone, and no other riders or pedestrians were within sight. Regardless of what the young Oregonian's mission might be, this appeared to be a perfect opportunity to be rid of him for all time. Harrison was not forgetting the humiliation he had suffered at Holt's hands. Taking his rifle from its resting place on a pair of wall pegs, Harrison hastily loaded it and took careful aim out the window.

By now Caroline was gone. It was enough for her that he intended to keep Toby Holt occupied. She had no interest in what threatened to become a gun duel. All she knew was that she had to escape before meeting Toby.

Never had she moved so swiftly. She saddled her horse in record time, mounted the animal, and rode out into the open. She had no idea where she was going, and although she failed to realize it, she chose the most difficult of paths for herself when she turned her mare toward the mountains.

In the meantime, Harrison took aim and fired. The sound echoed and reechoed across the hills, and the man was bitterly disappointed when he saw his enemy continue to advance toward the house. Hastily reloading, Harrison fired a second shot. Due to his carelessness and speed, he missed his target by an even greater margin.

Toby Holt realized that someone in the house—presumably Tom Harrison—was trying to kill him, and a feeling of deep anger replaced his original sense of shock. He was stunned by the man's cold-blooded attempt to murder him in broad daylight.

As he quickly realized, Toby had two choices. He could continue to ride toward the house and could engage in an all-out battle with Harrison, or he could behave more sensibly, withdraw, and await a more opportune time to try to make contact with Caroline. Common sense prevailed, and Toby drew back, prudently riding behind a pair of twin oaks that offered him a measure of shelter.

As he sat his mount, he was astonished to see Caroline, her hair streaming behind her, spurring her mare to a gallop as she headed toward the mountains.

All that crossed his mind was taking advantage of the chance to see his wife alone, in order to reach agreement on a divorce. Realizing that he would be drawing farther from the house, and hence moving out of the range of the gunman lurking inside, he turned his stallion and followed Caroline.

After riding the better part of a mile and a half, Caroline made the mistake of glancing back across her shoulder and was horrified when she caught a glimpse of Toby following her. To Toby's vast annoyance, she increased her pace and rode as though she were being pursued by the devil.

Caroline's mind was seething, and she was no longer capable of coherent thought. Her guilt about her shabby treatment of Toby threatened to over-whelm her, and she was convinced that he was intend-ing to force her to return with him to Oregon. There could be no other reason, she told herself repeatedly, that he could be following her.

The tensions of the chase, added to the strains she had been undergoing for weeks, were too much for her to bear. For the first time in her life, she found herself in a situation that she was completely incapable of handling. She was at the mercy of a man, something that she had sworn she would never allow, and her feeling of helplessness compounded her fright and drove her, at least temporarily, over the brink of sanity.

Scarcely aware of her location and of where she was heading, Caroline directed her mare onto higher, rockier ground. The glacial snowfields loomed ahead, but she was not aware of them.

Toby's sense of irritation increased moment by moment. Ordinarily Caroline was a very cautious rider, and more often than not, she was timid on horseback. But today she was breathtakingly reckless, taking risks that even the most experienced riders would hesitate to attempt. In spite of his own su-perior abilities, Toby found it impossible to gain on her. No matter how rapidly he rode, Caroline rode faster, and every time he found a shortcut, she took even more hazardous chances and maintained her lead.

He had no idea where she was going or why she was fleeing as though the devil himself were breath-ing down the back of her neck. Perhaps she didn't re-alize, Toby thought, that he was trying to catch up to her in order to have a discussion with her that would be of mutual benefit. Cupping his hands, he shouted to her. Caroline gave no sign that she heard him; if anything, she increased her speed still more.

Growing weary of this wild-goose chase, Toby ultimately drew one of his revolvers and fired it into the air. There, he thought. Caroline was certain to hear that sound!

The distraught young woman not only heard the shot but immediately assumed that Toby was firing at her. The few shreds of sanity she had retained promptly deserted her.

They had come to a region of high cliffs, narrow valleys, and even narrower defiles. Using all his skill to keep his stallion pushing forward, Toby was half convinced that he should abandon the chase. Because Caroline was acting like one who was demented was no reason he had to follow her example. But his stubborn streak asserted itself and kept him going. It would be a blow to his pride, he knew, if he allowed an inexperienced rider to beat him at horsemanship.

Suddenly, as he rounded a sharp bend in the trail, he was astonished to see that Caroline and her mare had both vanished from sight. He was afraid that his vision was playing tricks on him, but he could find no trace of them anywhere, and he sat very still in the saddle, reconstructing the scene as he best recalled it and searching the higher ground ahead. People did not disappear into thin air—there had to be some logical explanation. Determined to find her, Toby moved forward cautiously onto higher ground, then paused beside a raging torrent, a mountain stream that churned furiously as it descended over sharp rocks to lower ground.

Although Toby didn't know it, Caroline had seen

a large crevice in the side of the mountain, and on impulse, she had spurred forward, driving her mare into it.

Suddenly the animal stopped short, and the young woman stared ahead in astonishment. She seemed to see her reflection and that of her mount everywhere. Scores of Caroline Brandon Holts returned her scrutiny. She saw them directly ahead; they were on the roof of the cave and on the floor; and when she realized that there were some behind her, she was gripped by a terror more intense than any feeling she had ever known.

Losing control of herself, Caroline emitted a bloodcurdling scream. The sound bounced from one wall of the cavern to another, and the optical illusion contributed to the strange, mysterious situation in which she found herself: all of the Carolines who were staring at her seemed to scream simultaneously.

Caroline had no idea that she had wandered into an ice cavern. Water from the rushing stream, beside which Toby was currently sitting, dripped into the interior of the cave through tiny openings in the roof, and the bitter cold turned the water to ice. The walls, ceilings, and floor of the cavern were coated with sheets of clear ice that were perhaps a half-inch to an inch thick in places, and what Caroline actually saw in the dim light that came in through the entrance was her own shadowy reflection repeated endlessly on the slick surface.

The mare pawed the ground nervously, almost slipping on the ice, and neighed. To Caroline, it seemed as though dozens of horses were neighing. Her reason had totally deserted her, and the experience had become a living nightmare. Divine justice was at work, she told herself, and she was being punished for her cool and inconsiderate treatment of Toby, who had deserved far better at her hands.

She was sorry for him, sorry for all whom she had abused in the past, but most of all, she was sorry for herself, and that sense of pity so overwhelmed her that she had no room left in her for any other feeling. The nightmare, she knew, had to come to an end, but unlike a dream, it went on, and she was powerless to break its spell. Her fears surged still higher, and she became convinced that the Caroline Brandon Holts whom she saw everywhere were sitting in judgment on her.

Perhaps they intended to surround and suffocate her in order to make her pay for her sins. That was it! She had to escape—quickly—before they killed her!

In spite of the chill in the ice cavern, perspiration soaked Caroline's hair and streamed down her back. Dismounting, she slipped on the ice. Her feet shot out from under her, and she landed flat on her back. A score of Carolines peered down at her from the ceiling. Again she screamed, and again the other Carolines answered her, the sound of their voices so precisely like hers that she was certain they were mocking her.

Her panic wild, her terror unreasoning, Caroline scrambled to her feet, and slipping repeatedly, she abandoned her mount and started toward the mouth of the cave.

Another nasty spill sent her sprawling, and when she regained her feet, she saw that her skirt was bloody from a cut on one knee. Blood also was dripping from one hand, which she had injured on sharp stones. But she felt no pain, and the sight of her own blood spurred her to an even greater frenzy. Her enemies were closing in on her!

Toby, who was sitting on his horse no more than fifty feet from the entrance to the cave, was astonished when Caroline suddenly emerged from the cavern, running madly, her long hair tangled and streaming behind her, her skirt torn and bloody. He had no idea why she was fleeing, but he did recognize the fact that she was badly frightened. Her eyes were wide, and he had never seen such complete, overwhelming terror in the face of another human being. He reacted instantly and called to her. "Caroline!"

She heard the sound of Toby's voice, recognized it, and then saw him on his stallion only a short distance away. Her nightmare was not yet ended. She had escaped from the other Carolines only to fall again into the hands of the vindictive Toby, who was demanding vengeance for her treatment of him. Sobbing as she tried in vain to catch her breath, she turned and ran blindly away from him.

Before Toby could dismount and stop her, she tumbled down a steep incline, rolling over several times before she landed with full force in the mountain stream at a point where it was whipped to a froth by the sharp rocks over which it was descending.

As Toby watched in horror, Caroline landed facedown in the water. The jagged rocks slashed her mercilessly, and for a few moments the seething, white water turned scarlet. Toby flung himself from his saddle and raced to the bank of the river in order to help her.

Mustering all her remaining strength, Caroline

reached for the supple trunk of a young evergreen
that stood on the bank downstream. Her reach, however, was too short, and her fingers closed around the
stem of a brilliant scarlet and yellow wildflower. She
plucked it, and then suddenly it fell to the ground
from her nerveless fingers as her grip relaxed.

The rush of water was too powerful to be
resisted. Bouncing and jolting her on the rocks as it
carried her downstream, the river flipped Caroline
onto her back, and she gazed with sightless eyes at
the blue sky high above the mountains.

Toby realized that there was nothing he could do
to save her. Nature had taken her own revenge, in her
own way, and had rendered him a widower.

He gazed at Caroline for a long time as the river
carried her body lower and lower down the mountain
into Puget Sound below. Somewhere she would be
washed ashore, and there he would bury her.

Bending down, Toby picked up the scarlet and
yellow wildflower that she had plucked with her last
remaining strength before she had died. He would
bury it with her, he thought. It was the least he could
do for the beautiful, misguided young woman who
had been his wife. Finding her horse, Toby led the
animal behind his own mount as he rode slowly down
the mountainside.

Toby Holt was inconsolable. For days he stayed
inside the cabin on the Tumwater property, either lying on his bunk, looking up at the ceiling, or else
standing by the window, staring out at the forest beyond. He left the cabin only once—to go out and find
Caroline's body and give her a proper burial. This he

did, burying with her the wildflower she had plucked but removing from her finger the wedding band that his father had given Caroline at the last-minute marriage ceremony, when Toby had suddenly realized he didn't have a ring. This ring was Whip Holt's own wedding band, and Toby intended to return it to his father.

Coming back to the little cabin, he continued to brood and conversed only with Rob and Frank, repeating the same things over and over.

"I don't know whether Caroline was deliberately trying to kill herself or was just trying to get away from me," he said for the thousandth time. "I'm afraid I'll never know."

Rob and Frank looked at each other briefly. Finally Rob cleared his throat. "Toby," he said, "you're torturing yourself needlessly. You're quite right when you say we don't know and we'll never know why Caroline behaved as she did. All we do know is that the Lord God Almighty works in strange and mysterious ways. Caroline deserved her fate, and I can't weep for her."

"I can't, either," Toby said, as he walked to the fireplace, where the cooking fire burned low. "But I can't help thinking what a waste her death was. She was young and beautiful, and she had every reason in the world to live."

"That's where you're wrong, my friend," Frank told him. "She *should* have had every reason to live and to be happy. As you say, she was a heap prettier than most, and a lot of women would have given years of their lives to look like her."

"But Caroline had a rotten streak that ran deep

inside her," Rob said, picking up the narrative. "She made herself miserable, and she created misery for everyone around her. You've got to snap out of this depression, Toby. You can't spend your days and nights beating at yourself for what might have been."

Frank stood. "There's only one way to break out of it that I know," he said, "and that's to do something about it. The three of us are heading for Cargill's saloon, right now."

"I don't much feel like drinking," Toby said, but his friends ignored his protest. Frank grabbed Toby's broad-brimmed hat from its peg on the wall, Rob threw him a clean plaid shirt, and they stood waiting as he reluctantly donned his garb.

They rode into Tumwater together, with Rob and Frank flanking Toby, both of them prepared to block his return to the cabin in the event that he changed his mind. As they drew near to the saloon, they heard the raucous voice of Hector, and it was evident from the sound that the parrot was holding court.

"Hector is hungry!" the bird screeched.

As they entered the establishment, they saw the parrot sitting on his golden perch. Several patrons were offering him biscuits. One held out a bunch of grapes, which Hector disdainfully ignored, and another was slicing an apple for the parrot's possible consumption.

In spite of himself, Toby laughed. It was the first time he had laughed in the week that had passed since Caroline's death. All at once, he looked up, saw where his companions were leading him, and stopped short. Bettina Snow and Clarissa Sinclair, both in attractive party dresses, were sitting at a table, and it was obvious that the men were expected.

"You set this up deliberately," Toby said in a low tone.

Frank grinned at him. "I can't say as how you can blame me for that," he replied. "I figured you needed to see people other than Rob and me."

Bettina was somewhat embarrassed when she saw Toby, but Clarissa came right to the point. "I'm sorry to hear about your loss," she said.

Toby shook his head as he sat beside her and discovered that it was a relief to discuss the problem that had been weighing on him. "I don't feel a sense of loss," he said. "I've been feeling depressed because I feel so sorry for her. She had such a wonderful potential, and she never lived up to it."

Cargill brought them schooners of beer, and as Clarissa sipped her brew, she spoke thoughtfully. "I never knew your wife," she said, "and I wouldn't have recognized her if I had seen her, but I do know one thing. Most people in this world have a marvelous potential, and very few of them ever live up to it. The others fail and have only themselves to blame."

Toby thought about her remark and was compelled to agree with it. "You're right," he said. "We're all our own worst enemies."

"I gather," Clarissa said gently, "that you're including yourself in that company."

He was surprised by her candor and involuntarily looked at her.

"You have two partners," she said, "who are your very good friends. They've both been worried about you. They say you've just recovered your health and your strength after a long year of convalescence and that you're making yourself ill now by grieving over the death of your wife, even though she deserted you."

Toby shook his head. "When you put it that way," he said, "you make me sound like a fool, which I hope I'm not. I can't pretend that I loved Caroline any more than I can pretend that I missed her after she went off with Harrison. If anything, I was very much relieved that she was going on a separate path. What's been bothering me, I think, is the fear that I drove her into killing herself."

"Suicide," Clarissa told him, "is a desperate act, and I'm convinced that anyone who commits it is at least temporarily insane. I don't see how you can blame yourself for what your wife did, and I think you're suffering needless guilt. Have you tried looking at the other side of the coin?"

"What's that?"

Clarissa smiled. "As you know, I'm a widow. My husband belonged to an infantry regiment in Mead's army and died at Gettysburg. When people commiserate with me and tell me that I was married to a hero, I always agree with them. But I'll tell you the truth, Toby. My husband was the meanest man in the world, and liquor, which he regularly consumed in large quantities, made him even meaner. I led a miserable existence before the war, and I was very much relieved when he went off to fight. I'll be completely honest with you and say that I'm glad that he didn't come back from the war. For his sake, I'm sorry that he didn't live. For my sake, however, I can't help but be relieved, and there isn't a day that passes that I don't realize how much better off I am that Otto Sinclair isn't here with me. Well, you're better off now, too."

Her candor was as refreshing as it was astonish-ing, and it left him defenseless.

"I'm not advocating that you rush out and marry again in the near future," Clarissa said. "In fact, I be-lieve you'd be very foolish if you did. You ought to let a long period of time elapse. Long enough for all your wounds to heal. But in the meantime, you're free."

He smiled at her and replied shyly, "I reckon I am!"

"It's no secret that you like me," she said. "I can see it myself when you look at me and when we talk. It should also be no secret to you that I like you equally as much. But I know that every time we've seen each other in the past, you've been troubled be-cause the specter of your marriage has been hanging over you and made you feel guilty. Well, look at the bright side of your situation now, Toby. The shadows are gone, and you're free to do whatever you wish, however and whenever you wish to do it."

This blunt, plain-talking woman was right in all that she said. Toby felt a rush of gratitude and grinned at her as he raised his beer mug. "If you don't mind," he said, "I'm going to drink to you, Clar-issa Sinclair."

She inclined her head gracefully, then lifted her own mug in return. "Here's to you, Toby Holt," she said.

Rob, sitting across the table, was aware of the byplay and exchanged swift glances with Frank and Bettina. There was no need for words, but he knew now, as they did, that Toby would recover from the blow caused by Caroline's untimely, tragic death. His whole life lay before him, and he would make of it and of himself what he would. Knowing his ambition, drive, and self-discipline, Rob was certain that Toby's future was bright.

VII

Though Washington was mostly wilderness and was slow to be settled, there were some individuals who regarded the territory as a promising frontier. They came from nearby Oregon and California, which were experiencing rapid growth, to find in the Washington Territory the vast tracts of unclaimed land where they could raise crops and make their homes. But like all the settlers who came to the remote territories of the West, these people found they were not welcomed by the Indians.

Ishmael Wilkins and his brother Matthew had settled with their families on a choice piece of land in the eastern section of the Washington Territory. The land was fertile, they grew crops and raised beef to sustain themselves, and they were soon joined by additional settlers from other parts of the West, who were looking for good land in abundance.

The settlers, however, were a source of great concern to the Nez Percé Indians of the region. Years earlier these Indians had been content to make peace with the white men coming into their land and had even signed treaties to keep the peace. But they now felt these treaties were being ignored and that the whites were invading their hunting grounds. Thus, some of the Nez Percé braves went on the warpath to teach the whites a lesson.

Ishmael Wilkins and his wife, Sarah, were eating dinner in their little house on the land they had claimed and cleared. A fire was blazing in the hearth, and as they sat at their oak table, heads bowed in grace, a wild shrieking and a thundering of horses' hooves could be heard.

Ishmael and Sarah broke off in mid-prayer and looked at one another, fear in their eyes. The shrieking they heard could be only one thing: Indians on the warpath. Up to this point there had been no encounter with hostile Indians, and indeed, as far as they understood, the Indians of this region were peaceful. But for some reason, it looked as if all that had changed.

"You get down under the table," Ishmael commanded his wife, and he quickly rose from his chair and went for his rifle leaning in the corner. Sarah did as she was told, as Ishmael went to the shuttered windows and opened them a crack to peek outside.

What he saw caused his blood to freeze. Indians had galloped into the clearing where their little settlement was located and were beginning to burn down the houses of the other settlers. Perhaps a thousand feet away, where his brother's house was located, Ishmael could see flames and many Indians on horseback surrounding the house. Some of the Indians had dismounted and had entered the burning house, pulling out Matthew and his wife. Even from this distance, Ishmael could see the man and woman being tomahawked and scalped.

He knew there was no hope for Sarah and him. He stuck his rifle through the crack in the shutters, prepared to fire when the Indians drew nearer but well aware that at best he'd be able to kill only one or two of them before the rest descended upon their house. Perhaps, he thought, he would be better off praying.

Kneeling at the window, he began to recite the Lord's Prayer as more than a dozen Indians galloped toward the house. Suddenly his wife joined him at his side, clutched him tightly, and recited the prayer in unison with him. There was a crack of rifle fire as he shot and killed one of the Indians, but by then it was too late. Three braves in war paint crashed through the door, and two others leaped through one of the other windows. In a moment Ishmael and his wife were dead.

Many Americans believed that President Andrew Johnson had an impossible assignment. The South disliked him because its people felt that he had been a traitor to the Confederate cause during the war, while the North looked askance at him because it regarded him as a Southerner. Radicals in Congress were infuriated because he blocked their efforts to punish the South so severely that the entire country would have suffered, and a good many moderates and liberals felt that he was being overly soft on the former Confederate states. "No matter what I do, somebody is going to criticize it," he said to his wife. "So I'm just going to keep doing what I consider best for the whole country. I am President of the entire United States, not just the North or the South, and the sooner the country realizes it, the better off we'll all be."

Perspicacious and sensitive government officials soon came to recognize Andrew Johnson's sense of dedication to the welfare of the entire nation, and no one was more aware of it than William Pickering, who was visiting the capital on official business. In his first private meeting at the White House with the President, he was astonished by the breadth of Andrew Johnson's knowledge of the Pacific Northwest.

"Your section of the country, Governor," President Johnson told him, "is vital to the future development of the entire nation. Not only do you have countless raw materials, but Washington, Montana, and Dakota offer settlers something that's been a precious American heritage since the foundations of this nation were laid. I'm speaking about the accessibility of free land. As long as there is such land, we can continue to expand."

Pickering nodded. "That's quite true, Mr. President," he said, "and that's why we consider the building of a railroad to the Pacific Northwest so vitally important."

"It's important for far more reasons than are obvious, Governor," the President replied forcibly. "It's true, construction has already begun on the central route, and there is no underestimating the importance of this, the first transcontinental railroad. But work on the Northern Pacific Railroad must also begin soon. For one thing, with Puget Sound as a terminus for the railroad, our Oriental trade can be as important and as lucrative as our trade with Europe is to the East Coast."

Pickering was delighted with his grasp of the situation.

"What's more," the President went on, "this administration is in the process of negotiating with Russia for the purchase of Alaska. Once the American flag is flying there, the so-called Pacific Northwest will assume an even more vital role in the progress and expansion of the country. I'll appreciate it, by the way, if you'll keep the information about the coming purchase of Alaska confidential. We're not ready to announce it until Secretary Seward completes his negotiations with the czar's representatives."

"You can rely on me, Mr. President," the governor declared.

"You can begin to understand," Andrew Johnson said, "why we feel the building of a railroad into your area is so all-important. But unless these Indian rebellions come to a halt, we're going to have the devil's own time building that railroad. I sent a personal letter to General Blake, the army commander in the Pacific Northwest, asking him if he needed additional troops to put down the Indian uprisings in Washington and Montana, but he assures me he has enough men to do the job. Do you agree with that estimate?"

Pickering stroked his beard thoughtfully. "Lee Blake is a military expert, which is far more than I can say for myself, Mr. President. If he says he has sufficient troops, I'd automatically take his word for it. From where I sit, I feel he's undoubtedly correct. I'm thoroughly familiar with the uprisings in Washington, of course, and although the Yakima and the Nez Percé are troublesome, they can and will be brought under control. I'm less familiar with the situation in Montana, but I assume the tribal uprisings there, nasty though they may be, are also somewhat limited in nature."

Andrew Johnson leaned back in his chair. "I'm relieved to hear your reply, Governor," he said. "The mere mention of an Indian uprising fills people with horror these days, when everyone is so sick of warfare. It's good to know that you concur with General Blake's estimate that these rebellions can be controlled."

"They *must* be controlled," Pickering said. "We cannot have any more bloodshed and destruction." He had already told the President what he had learned just before he had left Washington: that a group of settlers had been massacred by Nez Percé braves.

The President was frowning. "The deaths of those settlers were needless, outrageous, and I'm counting on General Blake to make sure there is never a repeat of such a tragedy. I'm also counting on him to prevent Indian flare-ups that will delay the building of the railroad."

Pickering shook his head. "Under no circumstances, Mr. President, will Indian troubles or any other difficulties interfere with the building of a railroad into the Northwest. I consider the construction of such a line as a top priority."

"Good!" the President said forcefully. "Then we're in complete agreement as to what needs to be done."

"As rapidly as our surveyors finish their work—and the job is being done by a couple of young fellows who know railroads and know the terrain, too—we're hoping to hire crews and start laying tracks. I feel as you do, Mr. President. The future of my section of the country is virtually limitless. And the building of a railroad is definitely the first step in the right direction!"

Toby and Rob made rapid, substantial progress in surveying for the route of the future Northern Pacific Railroad, and they were pleased to discover that they were far ahead of schedule. They had already covered most of the ground with which Toby was familiar, which made it necessary for him to return to Oregon to pick up his father's maps and charts of the more remote mountain areas. He arrived at the ranch one afternoon and, picking up his mother, held her in the air as he embraced her.

"Put me down this instant, Toby Holt," she commanded. "You know how I hate to be held with my feet dangling in the air."

Her son chuckled as he lowered her to the ground, and Whip joined in the laugh as he shook Toby's hand. "There's no need to ask how you're feeling, son," he said. "Obviously you've regained your strength if you can lift your mother like that."

"Meaning, I suppose, that I've gained weight," Eulalia said. Her response was what her husband and her son expected, and both laughed again.

Then Eulalia took a deep breath and spoke quickly. "We were shocked when we received your letter about Caroline's death," she said, "but on reflection, we decided that perhaps it's just as well that things have worked out as they have."

Toby nodded. "I tried to look at it that same way," he said.

"She must have been a very unhappy girl," Whip said somberly.

"If there's life after death," his wife added, "I hope she's found peace in it."

"Amen to that," Whip declared.

Looking very serious, Toby reached into the pocket of his buckskin jacket and pulled out the wedding band he carried with him. "I guess I can give this back to you now, Pa."

"Your ma has already given me a new ring, Toby. You keep that one. Someday you'll find someone to give it to."

Suddenly Cindy appeared, greeting her brother with adolescent boisterousness, and that ended the subject.

At supper that night, Eulalia remarked casually—almost too casually, "By the way, Toby, I was visiting with Cathy and Beth Blake a couple of days ago, and they were asking after you."

Toby smiled inwardly. He realized that his mother still entertained the hope that he and Beth would get together someday, and the passing of Caroline apparently had fanned the flames of that hope. What he would not tell her just yet was that his own interest in Beth Blake had also been rekindled, and perhaps, after all, his mother's dream of their marriage might indeed come true. "I plan to call on the Blakes while I'm here," Toby said cheerfully. "How are they?"

"The general has his hands full," Whip said, and told his son about the massacre of white settlers in the eastern part of Washington. "He's now making plans for a campaign against the Nez Percé and the Yakima, as well as against a couple of tribes in Montana. He's rooted out a nest of diehard Confederates in San Francisco who were planning to sabotage our shipping there, and I understand that he's also had to dispatch some troops to squash some minor disturbances in southern California."

Toby whistled under his breath. "I'd say he really has his hands full."

"His situation is looking up," Whip said. "Colonel Andy Brentwood has just arrived to join Lee's command."

Toby was overjoyed. "Andy is here? At Fort Vancouver?"

Whip nodded. "Not only is Andy here, but so is his wife."

"I haven't seen Susanna since we crossed the country together on the silver train," Toby said. "How is she?"

"As feisty as ever," Whip replied, chuckling.

"That's both unkind and unfair," Eulalia said severely. "Susanna Brentwood is a perfectly charming, intelligent young woman. She is a credit to the family, and I can't blame Cathy for showing her off."

"Did you know she writes newspaper articles?" Cindy interrupted, looking wide-eyed as she turned to her brother.

"You bet," he said. "She was one of the best-known lady newswriters in the whole country. I didn't know she was still active."

"I don't believe she'll ever retire," Eulalia said. "I've never seen any woman who approaches her work with such enthusiasm."

That, Toby thought, sounded precisely like Susanna Brentwood.

He was so anxious to be reunited with his former army commander, or so he thought, that he took the ferry across the Columbia River to Fort Vancouver the following day. The fact that he knew Beth would be there was coincidental, he tried to tell himself, and had nothing to do with the speed of his visit.

Lee Blake was engaged in a staff meeting when Toby arrived at the post, but Colonel Andrew Brentwood, looking even more gaunt and hollow-eyed than usual, came to the door of his temporary office.

Toby had to restrain himself from standing at attention and saluting. Reminding himself forcefully that he was a civilian now, he shook Andy's hand vigorously.

"Let me look at you," Andy said. "I guess it's true—you really have recovered, Toby. You sure look better than you did when I visited you in the hospital."

"I'm feeling better, I can tell you that much," Toby said, grinning. "Are you being stationed here at Fort Vancouver?"

Andy shook his head. "As a matter of fact, I've been given an assignment that my colleagues are going to attribute to the fact that I'm related to General Blake. Well, if they knew him, they'd know he'd be the last officer on earth to play favorites." He smiled a trifle self-consciously. "I'm in luck," he said. "I've been made commander of Fort Shaw in Montana. There are about three tribes of Indians kicking up their heels in the vicinity, and it looks like I'm going to have my hands full. I'm being given a reinforced regiment to restore order in the territory."

Toby was impressed. "That's a tall order," he said.

"Not too tall, I hope," Andy replied. "Anyway, Sue is delighted, as you can imagine. It's going to be that much more grist for her mill, and she expects to write a whole series of articles on what the army does there."

Toby joined in his laugh. "I'd say she's lucky to be married to such an active officer."

"She's even luckier than you know," Andy replied, still chuckling. "Since General Blake is now her uncle by marriage, he was in no position to refuse her formal request for an interview. So he did what he refused to do all through the war, and he granted her an interview that she turned into a really first-rate article. You'll see her back at the house, of course. I assume that you're going to join us for dinner at the Blakes?"

When Toby hesitated briefly, Andy slapped him on the back. "Never fear," he said. "I've been told to make myself at home, and that includes the right to invite guests to the commandant's house for meals. Besides, the whole Blake family would court-martial me and have me shot on sight if I didn't ask you to come and have a meal with us."

Toby accompanied him back to the Blake house, where Cathy welcomed him warmly. So did Susanna, who came in from the garden. In all the time Toby had known her, traveling with her on the wagon train from Nevada, the pixieish, brown-haired Susanna had elected to wear boy's shirts and trousers, and now she looked lovely in her pink dress with a lace collar.

After greeting Toby, Susanna said mischievously, "Beth will be along shortly. We were digging some plant trenches together when we heard you were here, but she decided she wasn't presentable."

Cathy laughed. The significance of the exchange did not pass over Toby's head. If Beth had wanted to make herself more presentable before she saw him, he reasoned, that was a hopeful sign that she might be interested in him.

She came into the room in a rush, extending both hands to him. She looked even more beautiful than Toby had remembered, with her blue eyes sparkling and her blond hair gleaming. "I'm so very glad to see you again, Toby!" she exclaimed.

Perhaps it was accidental, Toby thought, but she clung to both his hands longer than was necessary. They sat in the parlor, quickly bringing each other up to date on all the news. Beth listened sympathetically as Toby explained about the loss of Mr. Blake, and after he told her how terrible he felt, she said, "Don't worry, Toby; we'll find another puppy."

Was Toby mistaken, or was the glint in Beth's eye and the tone of her voice a promise of good things to come for them together?

When Lee Blake arrived home, he, too, was highly pleased to see Toby, and when they went into the dining room for dinner, he took the lead in asking questions about Washington.

Beth was not far behind him, and her questions indicated that she was well-informed on the state of affairs in the territory; in fact, she already knew so much that it finally dawned on Toby that Rob must have been writing her letters from Tumwater. That struck Toby as slightly odd, for in all the time the partners had spent together surveying the Washington wilderness, talking about every subject under the sun, Rob had not once mentioned Beth Blake.

As he conversed, one corner of Toby's mind remained busy, weighing, analyzing, and comparing Beth with Clarissa Sinclair. It was difficult to imagine two such dissimilar young women. Beth was dainty and feminine in every way, while Clarissa seemed overwhelmingly large. Like her mother, Beth was a complete lady in every sense of the word. Clarissa, having been on her own in the world, was far more independent and free-spirited. Toby was attracted to Clarissa and realized that he also had a physical desire for her. Beth, however, almost literally overwhelmed him. He found it difficult to think straight in her presence. He was conscious of every move, every gesture, every nuance of expression, and he realized that his desire for her was so acute that he had to exercise constant self-control in her presence.

The conclusion that he reached was inescapable: he was in love with Beth Blake. He had no idea how long he had felt as he did. Perhaps he had always loved her but hadn't admitted his feelings to himself. Now, however, there was no denying that just being in her presence made him giddy and light-headed.

After dinner, General Blake had to return to his office without delay, and Andy Brentwood went with him. Toby was on the verge of taking his leave and returning to his family's ranch across the river in Oregon, but Beth made a point of stopping him. "Don't be in such a hurry to run off," she said.

Toby found it easy to allow himself to be persuaded to stay. Perhaps it was accidental, but Cathy Blake was busy elsewhere in the house, and Susanna Brentwood went to look for her, leaving Beth alone in the parlor with Toby.

"I realize," she said, "that you already answered all sorts of questions about the progress in the development of your land, but you haven't really talked about your partner."

"Frank is taking hold nicely," Toby said. "He's

established himself as the gang boss, and our hired hands realize that he understands lumbering."

Beth stared at him, saw that he wasn't teasing her, and said demurely, "I wasn't thinking of Frank. I meant Rob Martin."

Toby felt unaccountably foolish. He talked at length about Rob, extolling his skills as a surveyor.

"Rob writes me," she said, "that your only entertainment is visiting various saloons, which doesn't sound terribly appetizing to me."

Toby gently corrected her, telling her in detail about Cargill and his remarkable parrot, Hector. Then he talked about Bettina Snow and the fact that she and Frank Woods seemed to be drawn to each other, which he and Rob approved. "Frank is a lonely sort of a fellow," he said, "and I think Bettina Snow is good for him. So is her little girl. Frank is going to be a wonderful father, although he doesn't realize it. He and the child are very close already."

"Isn't that nice," Beth said.

Somewhat to his own surprise, he found himself telling her about Clarissa Sinclair, praising her virtues of candor and efficiency.

Beth studied his face carefully as he talked, saying very little. When he finished speaking, she spoke quietly. "I don't know quite how to say this, Toby, but please accept my condolences on the passing of your wife."

Embarrassed, he inclined his head and muttered his thanks.

"I won't dwell on the subject," she said. "I came to know Caroline fairly well on the silver train, and I won't pretend that I approved of her, or of anything that she stood for. We had different philosophies of life and different approaches. I'll go a step farther and say that I think you're fortunate she's no longer with us. She would have ruined your life if you'd stayed married to her, Toby."

He wiped his perspiring hands on the sides of his trousers. "I guess you're right," he muttered.

"Fortunately," Beth said, "the better part of your life lies ahead of you, and I know you don't need me to deliver any lectures or to say that the next time you marry, be careful."

He forced a smile. "I intend to be very careful," he told her.

Perhaps, Toby reflected, this was the right occasion to tell her of his love for her. It might not be appropriate so soon after Caroline's death, but he would be careful to explain that he was sure he had fallen in love with Beth long before Caroline's tragedy. He would await the right moment in the conversation and then summon his courage to speak freely.

"Even though I've traveled a lot, I'm really not all that worldly-wise," Beth said, "but I have learned a great deal from my own experience. I thought I was in love with someone—never mind who he was—and I almost made the mistake of accepting his proposal. What a mess my life would have been, when I woke up to the fact that I didn't in the least love him, that I was merely dazzled by his European title and his manners."

He nodded sympathetically.

"And how awful it would have been for me," she went on, "when I did fall in love, as I've now done."

He was so shocked that he felt numb. Surely she wasn't telling him that she cared for him!

"I would have ruined my own life and probably would have wrecked Rob's as well," she continued.

So that was it! Beth loved Rob Martin.

Hating himself for being so obtuse, Toby reflected that he had been blind to the situation because he had not wanted to see it. Now, however, his sense of perspective had been rudely and abruptly restored. Beth Blake loved Rob Martin, and Rob loved her. He was glad for both of them, pleased that they had found each other without their lives becoming overly complicated. The fact that he himself was left in the cold, alone, was irrelevant. At least he was relieved beyond measure that he had not blurted out the state of his own feelings to Beth. Inasmuch as Rob was his closest friend, he would, of necessity, keep the state of his own feelings very much to himself, now and for all time. Never could he reveal that he, too, loved Beth.

He took his leave soon thereafter, saying that he was expected back at the ranch, and as he left Fort Vancouver and rode his stallion down the slope to the waiting ferry, he could swear that he heard Caroline's taunting, mocking laugh. He tried to close his ears to the sound, but not even the rush of water in the torrent of the Columbia River could erase it from his mind.

Thanks, at least in part, to Beth Blake's proximity, life at the Holt ranch in Oregon had lost its savor for Toby. He picked up the maps, charts, and notes on the mountain wilderness that had brought him home, and then headed back to the Washington Territory.

Gradually he acclimated himself to the indisputable fact that his best friend was going to marry the woman he loved. He would have to live with that fact for the rest of his life. But Toby was more of a realist than he was a romantic, and he knew it would serve no useful purpose for him to pine for a lost love. That which was beyond his ability to alter would have to remain unchanged, and he would not brood about it.

He arrived in Tumwater late the following day and found that Frank, who had finished his day's work, had taken Bettina out for the evening. Rob had left a note for Toby, explaining that he was absent on a brief surveying trip in order to check some of the details on their maps, but that he would return to meet his partner in Tumwater in a few days.

At loose ends for the evening, Toby bathed in the stream, changed his clothes, and somewhat to his surprise, found himself calling on Clarissa Sinclair, who occupied a suite of rooms in the boardinghouse she owned. She made no secret of her pleasure at seeing him again.

"I realize this is short notice," Toby said, "but maybe you'll come out to supper with me?"

"I have a much better idea," Clarissa said. "Why don't you stay right here and let me cook supper for us? I went fishing today for the first time in more years than I care to remember, and I caught a marvelous salmon that I've been baking in clay. Since it's far too large for me to eat alone, you'll be doing me a favor if you'll stay."

Readily agreeing, he accompanied Clarissa to the little kitchen in her apartment, where she promptly set two places at the table.

The fresh salmon was delicious, as were the boiled new potatoes and fresh string beans that Clarissa had cooked with it. For dessert, she produced a peach pie hot from the oven.

"I must admit," Toby said, laughing, "that I didn't expect to eat treats like this tonight."

"I don't always eat this way myself," Clarissa told him. "Usually I eat in the big dining room with my boarders, and our cook prepares our meals for us. This is the first time that I've fixed salmon, and the peaches for this pie came from the backyard. The cook had extra fruit and didn't want to see it spoil, so he gave me the peaches, and I made the pie."

"I'm glad you did," he said, eating with enjoyment.

The weather was cool, although it was summer. Toby lighted a fire, and they sat together in Clarissa's parlor in front of the hearth, where he mixed them a rum drink that was one of his family's favorites; it consisted of rum, cloves, and sugar, into which a poker was plunged after it became red hot in the fire.

"This is delicious," Clarissa said as she sipped her drink.

"It would be more suitable in a snowstorm," Toby said, laughing.

They leaned back against the cushions piled on the floor in front of the hearth and looked at the flames as they sipped their drinks. All at once, Toby became aware of his desire for Clarissa. Their eyes met and held, and he knew that she was hoping he would make love to her. Not realizing what he was doing, Toby sighed.

Clarissa's eyes looked very wise as a half-smile appeared on her full lips. "You're afraid," she said, "and I can't blame you. Most women, these days, use situations like this to trap a man."

Toby didn't know quite what to reply. But Clarissa gave him no opportunity to speak, and as always, she was completely candid. "We're both adults," she said, "and neither of us has any ties. That makes us free to do what we please without hurting anyone—including ourselves."

Her meaning was clear, but Toby continued to hesitate. "You're a lady," he said, "and I don't want to take unfair advantage of you."

"It's because I know that you regard me as a lady," she replied, "that you wouldn't be taking advantage of me. Knowing that I'm amenable, you would have treated me unfairly had you made love to me without preamble. But you're showing me great respect, and I must admit I like it."

Both of them moved without quite being aware of what they were doing, and their shoulders, bodies, and thighs touched as they continued to sit side by side and finish their drinks.

"I don't know what I want permanently," Toby said.

"I figured as much," Clarissa told him.

"Wait, let me finish," he said. "I want you, but I have no way of even guessing whether I'm in love with you. That's as honest as I know how to be, and I hope you're not insulted."

Clarissa laughed softly. "I want you, Toby Holt, and to the best of my knowledge, I'm not in love with you. I'm very fond of you, it's true, but I don't know you well enough as yet to determine whether I love you. So I'd say we're in the same boat."

He looked at her, she met his gaze, and neither wanted to turn away. Toby reached out and covered her hand with his.

Suddenly she giggled.

"What's so funny?" he demanded.

"I've never known any two people to take such pains assuring each other they mean no harm," she said. "Can't we just admit that we're both adults and that neither of us is going to be hurt?"

"Are you sure of that?" he demanded.

"Quite sure," she said firmly.

They moved toward each other simultaneously and in an instant were locked in a fervent embrace.

All that Toby had experienced in recent weeks had added to his tensions, and he found that his desire for this woman was overwhelming. Clarissa, too, had been starved for affection for a very long time, and her passion matched his. Without thinking about it, they shed their clothes, and they began to make love before the roaring, crackling fire.

Toby soon realized that he had met his match in Clarissa. In spite of her size, she was agile and quick, and having committed herself to an affair, she shed all her inhibitions. He was determined to master her, and she, playfully, tried to assume the upper hand. Their contest was spirited, and ultimately Toby took control.

Neither then nor at any later time did he know whether Clarissa had succumbed to him deliberately or whether he actually overpowered her; not that it mattered. What was important was that the sense of loneliness that had haunted him ever since he had been wounded in battle vanished, never to return.

It dawned on him that Clarissa, too, obtained deep satisfaction from their relationship. She had been married, and her sexual abstinence after the death of her husband had seemed somewhat abnormal to her. Now, she, too, could be herself and was fulfilled.

What made their relationship so pleasant was their mutual recognition of the indisputable fact that neither would hurt the other in any way. Each of them felt safe with the other, and it was that trust, more than anything else, that bound them together.

Eventually they drifted off to sleep, and when they awakened early in the morning, they made love again. Then they talked at length, and Toby was not quite aware of what he was saying when he revealed that he was in love with Beth Blake but had no chance to win her because his best friend had a prior claim. "I've decided," he said, "to keep busy. It's the one sure guarantee I have of retaining my sanity."

"You can count on me for help anytime," Clarissa told him.

"I know," he replied, "and I'm grateful. I just wish there were some way I could solve the problems we face at our property here. That man Harrison is too much for us."

"What's going on, Toby?" Clarissa asked, leaning forward and looking into his eyes.

"What's *not* going on?" Toby replied. "When Frank is alone in Tumwater, in charge of the property, he's harassed constantly. Lumber disappears after it's been cut, hired hands are either assaulted or else are offered more money by Harrison and leave us, and we run into countless snags trying to have the lumber carted off to market. And there doesn't seem to be any recourse. Tom Harrison runs this town like he owns it—and in a way he does. He pays off the sheriff, the deputies, everybody, and there's absolutely no respect for law here. We've been up to Governor

Pickering to explain the situation here in Tumwater, and he appointed another sheriff—the best man he could find among the available candidates. Well, the pickings were pretty slim, and the new sheriff appears to be as crooked as the first. He's already made it clear to us that we have no proof that Harrison has been sabotaging our logging camp."

"It's a bad situation," Clarissa said.

Toby nodded. "Short of taking the law into my own hands and going after him myself, I'm not too sure how to handle a situation like this."

"I'll put on my thinking cap, too," Clarissa said, "and I'll see if I can come up with something. Tom Harrison has never done me any direct harm, although he's been terribly annoying to Bettina, but it would give me a great deal of satisfaction to see him put in his place once and for all."

The next day Toby rode high into the mountains to a property that he and his father owned jointly, just below the timberline. It was a wonderful spot, just a half-day's journey southeast from Tumwater but remote from civilization. In addition, it overlooked a valley where Toby and Rob anticipated the railroad would eventually run. The forward-looking Toby realized that a great city might someday be built in this valley, and his mountaintop property would greatly increase in value.

As he rode ever higher, his senses alerted him to the presence of someone else up here in the mountains. There was no smell of a cooking fire, no sign of horse tracks, but Toby, with the Indian-like instinct of his father, was certain there was another human being in the vicinity.

It didn't take him long to find the trail. Someone on horseback had come from the other direction and had veered off through a thicket of scrub pines to an even higher elevation. It was so unusual for someone else to be up so high in the mountains that Toby decided to follow the tracks and see where—and to whom—they led. Tying his stallion to a stunted pine tree, Toby proceeded by foot, making his way cautiously in the event that the stranger up on the higher elevation was hostile.

After climbing a rocky slope, he came out on a little ridge. There he saw a rugged-looking horse, untied and snorting and shuffling the ground. Toby quickly recognized the spotted, multicolored horse as an Appaloosa, the breed developed by the Nez Percé Indians.

Toby was no longer concerned for his safety, even though he knew one of the Nez Percé was in the immediate vicinity. He could certainly defend himself against a lone brave.

He advanced a few yards and then saw that in the rocky wall surrounding the ledge was a cave. He assumed that the Indian had gone inside, but rather than pursue him in the cave, Toby decided to wait outside for a time, knowing that the brave would soon come out for his horse. Sitting on his haunches, he was like an Indian himself as he remained motionless, waiting for the other person to appear. As it turned out, he did not have long to wait before a tall, broad-shouldered Indian with shoulder-length blond hair appeared outside the opening of the cave. If the brave was surprised to see another person on the ridge high in the mountains, he did not show it. Instead, he walked directly up to Toby, who had risen, and raised his hand, palm upward, in a sign of peace. Toby also raised his hand and waited for the brave to speak.

"Greetings," the Indian said in English, which amazed Toby. "You are surprised I speak your tongue," he continued. "I was taught by my mother, a white woman. She had been the slave of my father, a noted war chief, and they were married. Thus, I speak your language and have been given the English name of David Corn Tassel because of my yellow hair."

"My name is Toby Holt," Toby said in the tongue of the Nez Percé, which he had learned as a boy. The brave was as amazed as Toby had been to hear the other speak in his own tongue. "My father is also a noted man—Whip Holt."

"There is no one among my people who does not know of your father," David Corn Tassel said. "He has visited our lands in peace and traded with us."

The two young men continued to exchange greetings, then David Corn Tassel explained he had come to the cave high in the mountains in order to pray.

"It is here in the mountains that I feel closest to our creator," he said. "Though I am not Christian like my mother, I still believe there is one creator for all people, and that was why I was praying to him to stop the hostilities between your people and mine.

"Our tribe is not warlike. We have honored the treaties we signed with your government. But your government has not honored those treaties. Too many white people are allowed to come onto the lands that were supposed to be reserved for us, and your government does nothing to stop them. That is why some of our braves have gone on the warpath. Still, the killing of innocent people is no way to solve this problem, and my heart grieves."

"I understand what you are saying, friend. My father has told me of his life with the Indians, with whom he has traded when he lived in the mountains. In those days there was peace; now there is only fighting. Yet the white man must have a place to live, too."

"Yes, it is sad we cannot live side by side, in peace. Here you and I are in peace, but it may be that one day we, too, will fight against one another."

"I hope that day does not come," Toby said solemnly.

"And what is it you do high in the mountains, my friend?" David Corn Tassel asked.

Toby told about the property the Holts had claimed here years earlier and that he was thinking of building a dwelling on this land.

"To show you that white man and Indian can work side by side," David Corn Tassel announced, "I will help you build your house."

It was already late in the day, so they set up camp and got a good night's sleep before beginning work the next morning. Using axes Toby had brought with him, they started to fell the trees and carve them up for logs. David Corn Tassel showed himself to be adept at timbering, and his energy was boundless. Toby, too, worked tirelessly, and the physical exertion did him immense good. Only after working twelve hours that day did they finally rest and make a campfire. They boiled water for a soup, and Toby again surprised his friend with his knowledge of the wild plants to be used for a broth.

For the next few days, they continued to clear

the land on the mountaintop property. Finally, they decided to take a respite from their labors and go out hunting. David Corn Tassel was a superb bowman and brought down a large elk, which they cleaned and skinned. That night they had elk steaks for dinner.

After working nearly a week, they had made a large clearing and had stockpiled a great number of logs, enough for a house and one or two outbuildings. As they sat, resting on their blankets and admiring their handiwork, David Corn Tassel turned to Toby and said, "Now that I have proved that white man and Indian can work together and be good friends, I must return to my people."

"I hope we will always continue to work together, David Corn Tassel," Toby said as the Indian rose and gathered his things. "Someday you and I will show our people what friends can accomplish together."

"I hope you are right, Toby Holt." The two men clasped forearms in a gesture of farewell, then David Corn Tassel mounted his horse and galloped away down the mountain trail.

When Rob Martin made his appearance the following day, Toby having left a note for him in Tumwater telling of his whereabouts, he was astonished to see that a large rectangle of relatively level ground had been cleared.

"What's all this?" Rob demanded.

Toby explained about his meeting with David Corn Tassel and how the Indian had helped him cut down trees. "If our surveys are accepted," Toby told Rob, "the railroad will be running almost directly below us here. This land is valuable now, and it's going to be worth a great deal more. Thanks to David's help, I've been able to develop it and will be able to build a lodge here."

Rob nodded in agreement. "You're absolutely right," he said, "and I'm going to help you."

"Only if you'll accept part ownership of the lodge," Toby told him.

Rob demurred, but Toby was insistent. "It strikes me the joint ownership of a lodge is the least I can offer you after you've helped me to build it."

Under the circumstances, Rob had to accept, and did so with as good grace as he could muster.

They worked hard on the lodge for the next forty-eight hours, thereafter riding out into the eastern part of Washington to return to their surveying activities. By now, the route they had plotted traversed more than half the territory, and it would be only a matter of time before the entire Washington portion of the Northern Pacific Railroad was completely mapped out.

A few weeks later, Toby and Rob returned to the property and resumed their construction work. They were unexpectedly joined by Frank Woods, who threw himself into the project with such zeal that they made remarkable progress. At Frank's suggestion, they made plans for two weekends later, by which time the lodge would be sufficiently completed to offer comfortable shelter. He invited Bettina and little Lucy to join him for the weekend, and Toby enthusiastically asked Clarissa. He was somewhat nonplussed when Rob revealed that he intended to ride down to Oregon and ask Beth to come, too.

The date of the weekend arrived, and Rob showed up with Beth.

The men escorted the women from Tumwater to the mountaintop lodge, Lucy riding with Frank on his horse. When Toby had told Clarissa about the lodge, she had insisted on donating some furniture she had no use for at the boardinghouse, and so they brought with them to the property as many beds, chairs, and linens as could fit in a small wagon.

Although Toby was somewhat apprehensive, the weekend went off without a hitch. Beth got along well with both Clarissa and Bettina, and Clarissa, the only member of the party who knew Toby's secret, did not betray him. He found it painful to be in Beth's presence and to observe that she and Rob were obviously in love, going off by themselves on walks and sharing secrets and jokes together. Only Clarissa's presence somehow made the burden easier for him to bear. Her lighthearted good humor was infectious, and the entire group had a splendid time. What was more, the men continued to make rapid progress on the building of the lodge.

"I don't know why you call it a lodge," Clarissa said as they sat outside on the porch. "It's really a house, and the rooms are perfectly enormous. Bigger than those in any house that I've ever seen."

"That's quite true," Beth agreed, "and I keep thinking what a wonderful place it will be to hold a party. The view from the porch is just breathtaking. How soon do you suppose you'll have the place finished?"

The men conferred, and Rob and Frank were inclined to agree with Toby's estimate that if the good weather held and they could work on it for another week or so, they would have it done.

Beth promptly spoke to Rob in a low tone.

"Beth wants us to announce our engagement here in a month," he said, "and to invite our families up. How does that strike you, Toby?"

It was ironic, Toby thought, that he had plunged into work on the site in order to put Beth out of his mind, and now she wanted to use this spot to announce her engagement. He promptly agreed to the request, of course, because he had no choice, and Clarissa rewarded him with silent applause. They agreed to meet again in a month's time, and Beth said she would extend invitations to her parents, to Rob's, and to Whip and Eulalia Holt.

They rode down to Tumwater together, and after Toby, Rob, and Frank had seen the women to the boardinghouse, where Beth was spending the night, they rode on to their lumber camp. There a shock awaited them.

"When I left here before the weekend to escort the women up to the mountain lodge," Frank said, "we had the results of a week's work right here where we're standing. There was a mighty pile of trimmed logs, five feet high and several hundred feet long, all of them arranged according to size, and I assigned one of my best men to guard it. Now, both the guard and the lumber are gone."

"Maybe the head of the mule-team company you hired to pick up the lumber has already showed up for it," Rob suggested.

Frank shook his head emphatically. "That's impossible," he said. "I hadn't even settled on a price with him yet. We'd arranged that he'd show up first thing Monday morning and that he'd begin to move the lumber as soon as we agreed on a price. And what about the man guarding it?"

"The man and the lumber couldn't just disappear without a trace," Toby said.

"Except that's what they've done," Rob commented.

All three exchanged quick glances. Without speaking a word, it was clear to each of them who the culprit was. This was the last straw, and they had no choice now but to take the law into their own hands. With one accord they checked their firearms, remounted their horses, and headed in the direction of Tom Harrison's house.

It soon became apparent that Harrison was expecting uninvited guests. As the trio approached the base of the hill on which his house was located, two mounted figures appeared from behind the covering of foliage. "Where do you think you're headed?" one of the men called.

Toby noted, as did his partners, that the pair carried cocked rifles. "Not that it's any of your concern," he said, "but we're intending to pay a visit on Harrison."

"Is he expecting you?" the second guard demanded.

"Well, now," Toby drawled, "I might say that he is, I might say that he's not, but what I will say is that our relationship with him is nobody's business but our own. I think you lads have already earned your pay, and that's all to the good. Just move back away now and let us pass peaceably, and there won't be any problems."

"Suppose we don't want to move an inch?" the burlier guard demanded. "What then?"

The trio regarded him mildly, and Rob's reply was soft, almost gentle. "In that case," he said, "even though we have no quarrel with you boys, we'd feel obliged to pump some bullets between your eyes."

"With regret," Toby added, "because we're peaceably inclined."

The pair had long experience with men of all types, and they knew these strangers were not joking. The quiet ones, who spoke softly, were by far the most dangerous.

"Never fear," Toby said. "Although we'd sure enjoy it, we don't intend to kill and scalp Tom Harrison. Washington is part of the United States, and in this country we have laws against killing. So unfortunately, we'll leave him in much the same state as we find him. But we're going to see justice done, and no man is going to stand in our way."

He took the lead and spurred forward, closely followed by his two partners. All three held cocked revolvers lightly in their hands, and it was plain they planned to use them instantly if trouble developed. The two guards decided they had been given good advice. They had already earned their salary, so they were wise to let these strangers ride on.

The shutters and drapes that covered the windows of Harrison's house were all closed as the three partners reached the crest of the hill. Then the sound of a woman's laughter floated out of the house on the night air.

Toby froze. He was uncertain whether the voice he had just heard had been Caroline's. Then he remembered that Caroline was dead. He reminded himself forcibly that he was allowing his imagination to get the better of him.

The door opened a few inches. The oversized, broad-shouldered man inside peered out, and then the door slammed shut. "I'll give you five seconds to clear the hell off my property," the muffled voice of Harrison roared.

"As much as we'd like to shoot you," Toby replied, "we haven't come here for that purpose. As we told your guards at the bottom of the hill, we just want a few words with you, very few."

There was no reply, no sound from within.

"Unless, of course," Toby went on, "you're too yellow to meet us face to face."

That challenge did the trick, and the door opened again to reveal Harrison standing in the frame, a revolver in each hand. Toby instantly took a firmer grip on his own revolver.

Frank Woods acted as spokesman for the partners. "Harrison," he said, "we had a week's supply of trimmed lumber on our property when we left before the weekend."

"Why tell that to me?" Harrison replied.

"Because it disappeared, along with the man guarding it," Frank said. "I've never heard tell of lumber waltzing away under its own power, and that means somebody paid off the guard and took it."

"I'm not the constabulary of Tumwater," Tom Harrison told him. "Go see the sheriff."

"It's no secret hereabouts," Frank said stridently, "that the sheriff's office is on your payroll. The lumberjacks of the town sure didn't steal that lumber. They don't have the funds to have it hauled away, and they blame well know they'd be found out in almost no time at all."

"So that leaves just one person in the area who could have bought off the guard and taken our lumber," Rob declared.

"You, Harrison," Toby told him. There was a moment of electric silence.

"Nobody accuses me of being a thief," Harrison declared angrily. "I'll shoot you down for this, Holt."

"You're just full of talk, Harrison," Toby replied quietly. "You know that if you shot me, my partners would gun you down, and I'm sure you don't want to die that way. So why don't you just give us back our lumber, and we'll leave you alone."

A defensive note crept into Tom Harrison's voice. "You can't prove that I took your rotten lumber," he said. "You're cutting down trees in your part of the forest that stand right next to trees that I'm cutting in my part of the forest. They look exactly alike, and you haven't identified your property with any kind of mark or seal."

"How do you know we haven't?" Toby demanded. "How do you know that we haven't burned our partnership name into every last one of those logs?"

Harrison had come close to being caught, and now he had to extricate himself, which he did cleverly. "I don't know whether you have or haven't done any such thing," he said, "but if you haven't marked your lumber, you're damn fools. You can look as much as you like through all the lumber here on my property, and all you'll see is a bunch of indistinguishable trees—*my* trees, because they're on my property." Enormously pleased with himself, Harrison smiled and even relaxed his grip on the revolvers. "The three of you," he said, "are nice enough lads, I suppose, but you know nothing about the lumbering business, and you're making nuisances of yourselves.

Go back to Oregon where you belong, and leave lumbering to men who know what they're doing."

Toby knew that he and his partners had been outbluffed. Harrison was right: they had no way of proving beyond any reasonable doubt that he had stolen their lumber. He could claim any logs found on his property as his, and he could substantiate that claim sufficiently to render them powerless.

He signaled to Rob and Frank, and the three partners reluctantly withdrew.

Harrison watched them for a time as they retreated slowly down the hill. His laugh, gloating and triumphant, floated after them and seemed to hang in the night air.

VIII

Major General Lee Blake sat behind his desk at Fort Vancouver and examined the communication that Governor Pickering had just handed to him. The governor, returning from his recent visit to Washington City, had made a point of stopping in Oregon to give Lee the letter personally.

The envelope bore the seal of Andrew Johnson, President of the United States, and the message inside was succinct. *The forces of law are being placed in grave jeopardy in the Washington Territory, and I have promised Governor Pickering that you will help him to the fullest extent possible. If this makes it necessary for you to delay your overall plans for deployment of troops in Montana, as well as in Washington, you may consider this letter to be an order that rescinds all previous communications on this subject.*

"The President is pretty plain, Governor," Lee

said. "It looks as if he wants me to engage in a full-scale campaign against the Indians."

"I regret to say, General, that this appears to be the only way to show the Indians that the United States intends to put an end to the hostilities once and for all."

Lee nodded as he considered what measures he would take to set up the campaign he had already begun to organize.

"The Indian uprisings continue to disturb the peace," Pickering said. "It appears as though the Yakima are going to be reasonable and make their peace with us soon, but the Nez Percé really have their dander up, and we're going to have to teach them a firm lesson before they'll subside."

Lee leaned back in his chair. "Naturally, I've been watching the actions of the Nez Percé myself," he said. "Their recent behavior is intolerable, and you—and the President—can rest assured that I'll do everything in my power to stop the destruction of life and property."

"I knew we could count on you, General," Governor Pickering replied. "But there's something else bothering me, too." He sighed. "It's the absence of order in some of the frontier communities. The worst of them is Tumwater, which should be something of a model town because the brides from the East are all living there, at least temporarily. Tumwater is a lawless place, General. The town is in the hands of a brute by the name of Tom Harrison, who does as he pleases and terrorizes decent citizens. Even the sheriff is in Harrison's thrall, accepting his bribes and letting him do as he pleases."

"You're sure of the facts, Governor?" Lee persisted. "If I'm to send U.S. infantry and U.S. cavalry into action against U.S. citizens, I've got to be dead certain of my facts."

"The situation is precisely what I've outlined to you, General, but to make doubly sure, I suggest you conduct your own investigation in any manner you see fit. Don't take any action until you've acquired facts that corroborate my findings."

"That's very fair," Lee agreed, and was relieved. The entire nation was sensitive so soon after the close of the Civil War to actions taken by government troops against civilians. "If the situation should warrant it, would you be willing to give me a directive ordering me to make Tumwater and any other towns that you suggest safe places to live?"

"By all means," Governor Pickering replied. "In fact, I'll forward such a communication to you immediately in advance of your own investigation. In that way, you'll lose no time once you agree with me that it's needful to take firm and prompt action."

Soon thereafter, the governor took his leave with a troop of cavalry provided to escort him to his own official home in Olympia.

Lee pondered their conversation, and when he came home for dinner at noon, he was silent and distracted. Cathy knew better than to ask him any questions, and she avoided controversial subjects during the meal.

Lee went back to work, and after he had finished writing a short document, he sent his sergeant major to summon Colonel Andrew Brentwood.

Andy, who was in his own office working on his tables of organization for his coming command at

Fort Shaw, immediately dropped what he was doing and hurried to the office of the commander.

"Sit down, Andy," Lee said as he returned his nephew's salute. "I need to have a little chat with you."

"This sounds serious, General," Andy said, smiling slightly.

Lee looked at him quizzically. "Oh?"

"I've been in this army long enough," Andy said, "that I immediately become defensive when a general invites me to sit down for a chat."

Lee couldn't help laughing. "And you're quite right, too." He became serious. "How much does the command at Fort Shaw mean to you, Andy?"

The young colonel put his fingertips together and studied them intently. "I realize, sir, that I'll be functioning as a subunit of the Army of the West. Nevertheless, the fort is sufficiently isolated, and for all practical purposes, I'll be on my own. I needn't tell you, General, how every officer looks forward to having an independent command. I reckon I'm just as excited by the prospect as you've been in your own day."

Lee nodded. "That's more or less what I expected. Let me assure you that I'm not going to deprive you of the Fort Shaw command. However, there will be a delay in your taking it over. The infantry battalion that's already stationed there will remain in order to do what it can to keep the Indians of the region under control. You and the rest of your troops, including both infantry and cavalry, along with some additional battalions that I intend to give you, are going to be deployed on special duty. How long it will be before you proceed to Shaw will depend in large part on how well you fare in your temporary assignment."

Only one reply was possible, and Andy Brentwood swallowed his disappointment. "Yes, sir," he said.

"I owe you my deep apologies, and I hope you'll accept them, Andy," Lee said. "I wouldn't create this delay for you if it could be avoided. But I've been given a nasty task by President Johnson, and you're the only colonel in my command who can carry it out while walking a tightrope. Susanna will be welcome to stay with us, of course, while you're occupied, and we'll do our best to continue to make her feel at home with us. Here." He thrust at his subordinate the one-page document he had written. "These are your orders. I'll answer any questions you may have."

Andy picked up the sheet of paper, read rapidly, and was mystified. Shaking his head, he said, "I do need some clarification, General. You say here that you want me to seek out the Nez Percé Indians and cause them to desist in their rebellion against the United States government. At the same time, however, you urge me to take specific measures that will spare the life and property of the Nez Percé wherever possible."

"That's correct," Lee said, "and that's one of the things that is going to make this assignment so difficult for you. The Indians are being given large tracts of land as reservations. They're going to be our neighbors for generations to come, and we're going to have to work together if the territory is to reach its potential as a state. The Nez Percé won't feel much like cooperating with us if you kill their warriors and burn and destroy their property."

"Do you seriously expect me to end their rebellion by patting them on the back?"

Lee nodded. "Something of the sort," he said. "In this situation, you'll have to be a superior diplomat, as well as a skilled officer."

Andy sighed but made no reply. He went on to the next paragraph of his orders, and then he frowned. "You say, sir, that you want me to establish the laws of the United States in various frontier communities, most importantly Tumwater, and that you wish me to conduct my own investigation before I take any action. Just what is it that I am to investigate, General?"

"I want you to decide for yourself just how bad conditions are in a town before you move in. If need be, you have authority to take any action you see fit. Establish martial law if you must. Bloody a few heads if it's absolutely necessary. If you find there are men who are breaking the law and are refusing to cooperate with the establishment of a just and orderly system, you're free to sentence them to death or send them to prison or do whatever you feel is right and necessary. But I took the precaution of requesting an investigation ahead of time because if we're forced to take action against civilians, I can see a public outcry that will end with Congress entering the disputes, and I want us to be on very safe ground. I hardly need tell you that I'll stand behind you all the way in all things, Andy."

"I know you will, General, and I'm grateful to you." Andy was silent for a moment, fingering one of the brass buttons on his tunic. "You prefaced your remarks, General, by saying that I'm the only officer in

213

your command who you think is capable of carrying out these directives."

"I do, indeed," Lee replied, grinning.

Andy tried to smile, too, but failed. "I'm grateful to you for your confidence in me, sir," he said, "but at the same time, I can't help wishing that you had a dozen other officers who could fill this very difficult bill."

The message that Toby Holt received via an army scout was direct and to the point: Colonel Andrew Brentwood wanted to confer with him on a matter of the gravest urgency and hoped that Captain Holt could meet him in Tumwater in seventy-two hours' time.

Toby and Rob had returned to their Tumwater property from a surveying trip on the eastern slopes of the mountains when the message was received, and they immediately dropped what they were doing and hurried into town.

They arrived shortly after the augmented regiment had set up its bivouac there. The presence of the troops—one thousand of them infantrymen and almost five hundred of them cavalrymen—left a strong impression on Tumwater. The girls in the brothels, including Tom Harrison's new, exclusive establishment that was now in full operation, completely forgot their civilian clientele and devoted their attention to the military. Local farmers increased the prices of vegetables by fifty percent and doubled what they were charging for meats and fish.

The harassed citizens of Tumwater wanted to call on the regimental commander to complain but were turned away. Tom Harrison, however, was received by Colonel Andrew Brentwood and remained with him for the better part of an hour.

Frank Woods, whose acquaintance with the colonel was slight, was indignant and expressed his anger freely when his partners joined him in town.

Toby listened to him in silence and then grinned. "If you knew the colonel as I do," he said, "you wouldn't worry. You can bet your last nickel that he's seeing through Harrison like a pane of glass."

A very short time later, Toby reported to the headquarters of the regiment and was immediately admitted to the commanding officer's private tent.

"I appreciate your dropping everything to get together with me, Toby," Andy said. "I knew I could depend on you."

"What can I do for you?" Toby asked.

"Where are the Nez Percé?"

Toby sighed. "I'm afraid they're still on the warpath."

"Can you locate them for me?"

"I'm sure I can, Andy."

"Well, then, I want you to find them, and the sooner the better. The one thing I want to avoid is having them hear rumors that the commander of a large body of U.S. troops is searching for them."

"You want to take them by surprise, then?"

"In a manner of speaking, I do," Andy said. "If possible, I prefer to parley with them and reach a peaceful understanding."

Toby whistled under his breath. "That'll be a neat trick if you can accomplish it."

"So I understand."

"I have a pretty good idea of the part of the territory where they are functioning," Toby said. "I would think I could locate them in about three days, and then I'd need that much more time, of course, to notify you."

Andy shook his head. "Suppose I send a couple of scouts out with you, Toby," he said. "In that way they can report back to me the moment you spot the Nez Percé, and you can keep an eye on them until I arrive."

"That's fine with me," Toby said.

"Will it be convenient for you to start out tomorrow morning? If so, I'd like to ask you and Rob to have dinner with me tonight. My chef isn't the best, but we'll make do."

Toby grinned at him. "If it's all the same to you, Colonel, why don't you allow me to invite you for dinner? I know a really wonderful cook, and you can show up in an hour or so, whenever it's convenient for you, and she'll have everything waiting."

Andy looked at him and raised an eyebrow. "You're sure the lady won't mind?"

"Not this lady!" Toby assured him emphatically.

So the arrangements were made accordingly, and Clarissa Sinclair was delighted to entertain Toby, Rob, and Colonel Brentwood at her house.

Andy was in a jovial mood when he arrived for supper and was unprepared for the sharp blast that Rob Martin delivered. "Your popularity in this town dropped all the way to zero today, Colonel," Rob told him. "You inadvertently or otherwise made a bad mistake."

"What did I do?" Andy asked.

"You spent almost an hour with Tom Harrison, and people in Tumwater can't get over it."

Andy glanced uncertainly at Clarissa, and Toby

understood the reason for his hesitation. "You can say anything in front of Clarissa," he declared, "that you can say to Rob or to me."

Andy, guessing that Toby and Clarissa had been intimate, trusted the judgment of his friend, and nodded. "One of the reasons that I wanted to get together with you and Rob this evening was to get a line on this fellow Harrison. What do you know about him?"

"Enough," Toby replied bitterly, "to burn him in hell for a long, long time. He's a thief, he's a woman molester, he's a bully who beats innocent people, he cheats, and he's totally unreliable in every sense of the word."

"He ran off with Toby's wife," Clarissa said, "and certainly has a share in the responsibility for the mental condition that led to her death."

"He stole a week's supply of lumber from our property, which unfortunately adjoins his, and then he dared us to prove it," Rob said.

"I neglected to mention," Toby said dryly, "that he has the local sheriff and his deputies in his hip pocket. We understand he bribes them regularly, which is one reason that some of his followers commit robberies and other unlawful acts so freely."

Andy Brentwood nodded. "This explains a great deal about Harrison's attitude toward me," he said. "He promised me just about anything I wanted. Listening to him, you would have thought that he owned the town."

"I'm afraid he does," Toby said.

"The big question," Clarissa declared, "is what can be done about him? We've had endless talks about him, and I mean just about everybody who lives in Tumwater has entered the discussion, but nobody can suggest anything except resorting to the tactics that Harrison himself uses."

"We've been reluctant to use force on him," Rob said, "simply because there's a matter of principle involved. But if people are desperate enough, they're liable to form a lynching party and go after him themselves."

Andy nodded and devoted himself to his meal, which he was enjoying thoroughly. "Now that I have a much clearer picture of the situation," he said, "I believe I may know how to deal with it. We'll sit tight for a spell. In fact, when the regiment goes off to meet the Nez Percé, I'll leave one company-size unit here in Tumwater as a means of guaranteeing the peace. Sooner or later Harrison will step out of line, and when he does, I'll take action against him."

"I hope you're right, and that your idea is effective," Toby replied dubiously, "but I think you're neglecting one aspect of the situation, Colonel."

"What's that?"

"Tom Harrison is smart," Toby said. "He's as smart as they come. He's undoubtedly figured out by now that you're waiting for him to make a mistake, and it would be just like him to give you no chance whatever to pounce on him."

The Cascade Mountains, a range of rugged, high peaks, divided the Washington Territory into two sections. To the west lay the most fertile timberlands in the United States, while to the east, particularly in some of the valleys, lay lands that settlers were already finding remarkably well suited to the growing of fruits and vegetables.

Mount Rainier was an anchor and a guidepost. In the valleys to the west, the Yakima Indians roamed the lands that lay south of the mighty peak, and the Nez Percé used the hunting and fishing grounds to the north and the east.

Toby Holt and Rob Martin, accompanied by three scouts from the army regiment, made excellent time as they traced the route of the Cowlitz River onto ever higher ground, and finally, after reaching its source in the high Cascades, they came to Indian Pass and descended to lower ground. Here they found themselves in a vast valley bounded on the north by the Chelan Range, and on the south by the Wenatchee Mountains, both of which traveled from west to east. This huge, natural amphitheater was bounded on the east by the Columbia River, which wound its way northward, past the Badger Mountains.

As Toby well knew from his travels both with his father and with Rob, this area comprised one of the favorite hunting grounds of the Nez Percé, and he had to admit that the Indians had chosen well. The whole region abounded in game. There were deer and antelope, moose and elk, and frequently because the grass was so rich and lush, buffalo came into the area, too.

It was a temptation to stop and devote a day or two to the hunt, but Toby resisted the urge since he was under instructions to find the Nez Percé as soon as possible.

He went about his task methodically, using every means at his disposal to help him achieve his end in the shortest possible time. As he, Rob, and the scouts headed into the thick, almost impenetrable forest, he traveled in a zigzag pattern, constantly moving back and forth in order to leave no approach to the wooded section untouched. This system was unique, and certainly took more time than a direct plunge into the forest, but in this way, he was reducing his risks to a minimum.

A few hours after Toby initiated his careful search, he and the others came out of the forest into a large, grassy plain, and his patience was rewarded. He halted his stallion, dismounted, and dropping to one knee, examined the tall grass with great care. Then he turned to Rob, who was watching him, and said, "We've found them!"

Rob was not surprised. Toby had shown him time and again what a superb tracker he was.

"The Nez Percé were here some hours ago," Toby said. "There were a number of mounted men in this vicinity."

After months of surveying the Washington wilderness, Rob also was somewhat familiar with the habits of the Nez Percé. "I assume that the purpose of these riders was to keep any game from escaping from the forest, as the main body of Indians approached."

"Exactly," Toby said. "If you look at the way these trampled blades of grass are bent, you can literally follow the trail taken by the Indians." He pointed in the direction that the column had gone.

Mounting his horse again, he set off in pursuit, advancing cautiously so that he didn't run the risk of making direct contact with the Indians. For several hours he continued to follow the trail of grass that had been bent under the hooves of the horses, and it appeared that he would not reach his quarry that day.

Toby persisted, however, even though the trail gradually led him onto higher ground. Then, about an hour before sundown, he suddenly gestured for silence, halted, and pointed.

The others, looking in the direction he had indicated, made out a vast encampment spread in a wooded valley that lay below them. Approximately one thousand Indians were assembled, all of them with Appaloosa horses, which they had turned loose to graze. At the far side of the bivouac area, the braves had built their cooking fires. They had chosen their site wisely, for the winds coming down from the mountains behind them were strong, and the smoke dissipated rapidly as it rose into the air.

Toby immediately summoned two of the scouts and sent them back across the Cascade Range to Tumwater, instructing them to report to the colonel as rapidly as they could. Meanwhile, he, Rob, and the third scout, a sergeant named Anders, would keep watch on the Nez Percé and would be able to lead the regiment to them after the troops crossed the mountain barrier.

The two scouts started off at once, and those who remained behind settled into their vigil. Thanks to the site that Toby had chosen as an observation post, the task of the next few days was not too difficult. The trio remained far beyond the perimeter of the area that the Nez Percé's sentries patrolled, and as long as they didn't reveal their proximity by lighting cooking fires, the chances that they would be discovered by the Indians were slight. Thus they subsisted on jerked venison and parched corn. Toby and his companions were never filled, never quite satisfied, but they didn't go hungry, either.

The task of keeping watch on the Indians proved to be simple, and, in fact, was boring. Each morning the Nez Percé sent out large parties of braves to scour the wilderness in every direction for game, while the rest of the Indians remained in camp and took their ease there. The only danger that Toby, Rob, and Sergeant Anders faced was the possibility that an Indian hunting party might stumble onto their own small bivouac area. But good fortune attended Toby, and the warriors at no time discovered his proximity to them.

He was fortunate, too, that the Nez Percé had chosen this particular time to stage a major hunting expedition. He estimated that they planned to remain in their encampment for at least ten days to two weeks. Toby just prayed that when Andy arrived, the problems between the Indians and the whites could be worked out by peaceful means, without any more bloodshed.

Within a week, Andy Brentwood showed up, and he and several members of his staff followed one of the scouts into Toby's camp.

"You made great time, Colonel," Toby said.

"I sacrificed manpower for speed," Andy told him as they shook hands. "I left all of my infantry units behind in Tumwater, and I moved forward with only half my cavalry."

Toby exchanged a quick glance with Rob, and in spite of his efforts to appear bland, his face fell. "How many men do you have with you?"

"About two hundred and fifty, more or less," Andy replied.

"Then you certainly will want to avoid a direct confrontation with the Nez Percé. You're outnumbered by approximately four to one, and the odds against you would be too great in actual combat."

"I am indeed hoping that a fight can be avoided," Andy said. "In any event, we'll soon find out. It's rather astonishing that the Indians haven't discovered your presence in the past week, but it would be expecting too much to hope that two hundred and fifty armed men and their horses could escape detection. I'm going to move the cavalry troops forward, and then we'll find out where we stand."

The cavalry soon started out and formed a semicircle on the heights, with the mounted soldiers facing in the direction of the Indian encampment below.

Watching the maneuver, Andy Brentwood spoke quietly. "Do I assume correctly that you're willing to go down there with me and face the warriors, Toby?"

"Sure, Colonel," Toby replied promptly, "if that's what you want."

"It is," Andy said. "Do I assume correctly that you can speak the language of the Nez Percé?"

Toby smiled. "I can make myself understood well enough."

Andy summoned the captains of his four cavalry troops for consultation, and Toby, who sat his mount some distance from them, noticed that all four captains were arguing vehemently with Andy, as was the major who was second in command of the regiment.

But the colonel paid no attention to their protests, and attaching a white handkerchief to the tip of his saber, he moved forward and joined Toby. "We'll be heading down yonder any moment now," he said.

To the astonishment of Toby and of Rob Martin,

the colonel signaled to his regimental bugler, who sounded assembly on his instrument. The shrill, piercing bugle call echoed and reechoed through the forest.

The Nez Percé were stunned by the totally unexpected proximity of U.S. Army troops. The warriors leaped to their feet, snatching up their weapons, and the air was suddenly filled with the harsh cries of their war chiefs trying to assemble them in some form of battle order.

Andy Brentwood seemed well pleased with his efforts so far. "I reckon we can go on down now," he said, and started down the steep slope on his gelding.

Toby quickly drew up beside him, and his stallion, pawing the ground nervously, matched the gelding stride for stride. Making no effort to conceal himself, the colonel brandished the sword with the white handkerchief fluttering from its tip. When they reached the floor of the valley, they were surrounded by several hundred braves, on foot and mounted, as they continued to advance.

Andy had to force himself to refrain from reaching for his rifle or a revolver. "What happens next?" he muttered.

"Something good, I hope," Toby replied, "or you and I are going to be in serious trouble."

A wizened warrior in his forties, clad in a garment fashioned of animal skins, materialized on his horse in front of the two white men, his face so heavily smeared with paints of various bright colors that it resembled the stylized faces seen on an Indian totem pole in the regions to the north. He flung his left arm high into the air and loudly demanded to know the meaning of the white men's intrusion.

Toby hastily translated the demand, at the same time halting and diplomatically extending greetings to the Nez Percé.

Andy Brentwood, ordinarily the most unassuming of men, struck a belligerent pose that in no way resembled him. "Tell them," he said, "that I am the chief of a mighty army of soldiers sent into these mountains and forests by President Johnson to keep the peace in the name of the United States of America."

Toby did as he was told, even though he doubted the wisdom of adopting such an antagonistic stand, and his fears soon were justified when the growing throng of warriors began to mutter restlessly. He hoped that Andy knew what he was doing, and he wanted to warn the colonel that it was unwise in the extreme to threaten the braves of the Nez Percé.

"I come in peace," Andy declared firmly, "but if the Nez Percé prefer war, I am prepared for it." Raising his sword high above his head, he whipped it downward in an abrupt gesture.

That was a signal that the troops on the heights awaited, and suddenly the hilltops came alive. A rifle cracked at one end of the long, semicircular line, then another and yet another. Each trooper in turn fired his rifle an instant after the man on his left had done the same.

The effect the maneuver created was startling. Gunfire rippled through the forest, beginning at the left end of the calvary line and continuing without a pause through the last trooper on the right end. In all, more than two hundred shots were fired, but the cumulative effect seemed much greater, and it appeared as though several times that many rifles were actually discharged.

The Nez Percé braves stood very still, watching the demonstration in slack-jawed wonder.

Toby had to admit that the effect was spectacular and that Colonel Brentwood had known precisely what he was doing.

"It is my wish," Andy said, "to negotiate peace between the Nez Percé and the government I represent in Washington City. It is my devout hope that this peace will be established between these brothers and will last for all time."

The wizened Nez Percé leader stared at him, studying him intently and listening for some clue as to his own future behavior. Experience with white men had taught him that he would be expected to pay a penalty for permanent peace, and he was hoping that this time, at least, the price would not be too high.

Andy Brentwood, however, well knew the mind of the Indian and was prepared to deal with it. "It is the wish of the Nez Percé," he said, "to keep the hunting grounds that they, like their ancestors before them, have used for so many generations. They wish to hunt where game is fat and plentiful and where the streams are filled with salmon and trout. It is right that they should keep that which is theirs.

"Many white-skinned brothers of the Nez Percé," Andy continued, "are already coming to this land to share in its riches. They, too, want the profits to be earned from the great trees of these forests. They have already learned that their vegetables and fruits will grow in the rich soil of this land as they will grow nowhere else in all of America. So, they, too, clamor for land, and they, too, have the right to share it and use it."

This was so like the refrain to which the Nez Percé had long been accustomed that they became far warier.

"It is right and just," Andy declared firmly, "for our Indian brothers to have that which they wish and to protect their rights. In the same way, it is right that our white brothers also have that which is theirs. These forests, these hunting grounds, these rivers are almost boundless. There is no need for brothers to make war upon each other in order to gain possession of that which they already possess. Let us sit down together in peace and let us determine together which land shall belong to the Nez Percé and which land shall belong to their white brothers. This is the only solution to the problem. I do not want to shed the blood of the warriors of the Nez Percé, and I do not want to see my own soldiers lose their blood. Let us work together for the good of all!"

As Toby translated the address into the tongue of the Nez Percé, it occurred to him that he had never heard a more moving plea for peace. Obviously the Indians were influenced by what Andy said to them, and several of the older men withdrew into the forest to confer with the wizened leader who had been acting as their spokesman.

Andy had expected a prompt reply and was nonplussed by the warrior's lack of communication with him. "What happens now?" he demanded.

"Be patient, Colonel," Toby told him. "This is very unusual, and I'm sure something good will come out of it in the immediate future, too. Just hold tight for a spell."

They sat their mounts silently, staring straight ahead and trying to appear unconcerned.

At last the painted leader of the Indians rode forward again on his horse. "Many times," he said, "we have made peace with our white-skinned brothers, only to have them double and then again double their demands as soon as we agree to lay down our arms. The Nez Percé do not seek combat. They are a peace-loving people, and it is their greatest wish that once they negotiate terms of peace, their white brothers will abide by those terms, too."

"I can promise you that we, too, will honor the terms of an agreement and that we will keep the peace," Andy said. "I speak to you on the authority of President Johnson and of his representative, Governor Pickering."

The names of the highest-ranking American authorities meant nothing to the Nez Percé. "What guarantee do you give us?"

Translating the demand into English, Toby couldn't help thinking that it was eminently reasonable. Apparently Andy Brentwood also thought so. "What guarantees do you want?" he replied. "Name them and you shall have them."

A pair of eyes gleamed in the masklike face. "Let him who is the champion of the white men meet the champion of the Nez Percé in an honorable contest," he said. "The winner will give his side the right to make the first demands in our peace negotiations. Each man—whether winner or loser—will also act as a hostage, and he will agree to forfeit his life if his side does not keep its vow of peace."

Andy did not appear to be prepared for anything quite so drastic.

The Indian leader took his silence for assent. "Let the champions of the two people stand forward," he said. "The champion of the Nez Percé is David Corn Tassel."

Toby was startled to see the broad-shouldered young man whom he had befriended in the mountains proudly ride forward. But if David Corn Tassel recognized Toby, he did not show it. He reined in his mount and stared straight ahead.

"Where is the champion of the white men?" the Nez Percé leader demanded.

Colonel Brentwood shifted uneasily in his saddle. He had no idea what kind of contest the braves had in mind and who among his own cavalrymen would be willing to compete with one of the Nez Percé. The idea that perhaps he would be a hostage whose life depended on the goodwill demonstrated by the United States government would daunt even the bravest soldier, and it was unlikely any of the colonel's men would readily volunteer.

Toby was well aware of Andy's predicament, and he realized there was only one solution. Despite the fact that he and David Corn Tassel had pledged their friendship for one another, Toby would have to compete with him. There simply was no one else who would. Moving his stallion forward several paces, he called, "I, Toby Holt, will challenge the Nez Percé champion."

The wizened Nez Percé studied him intently. David Corn Tassel's expression did not change; he continued to sit stolidly on his horse.

Andy Brentwood realized it was too late for him to intervene. Whether he liked it or not, Toby had stepped into the role.

The old Indian squinted at him. "Are you not the son of Holt, man of the mountains?" he demanded.

"I am his son," Toby replied proudly.

"Do you also use a whip with such skill that it appears to be a part of your body itself?"

Toby smiled and shook his head. "No," he said. "Only my father uses a whip in that fashion."

The leader seemed satisfied, and there was another delay while he again conferred with his subordinates, including David Corn Tassel. Then he turned and smiled. "The fair contest," he said, "will consist of the discharge of three shots at a target to be placed not less than fifty paces from the contestants. He who more nearly strikes the core of the target will be the winner, and his side may make the first demands in the peace negotiations."

"Agreed," said Toby, thinking the terms very fair.

"And if your countrymen dishonor the terms, you will surrender yourself to the Nez Percé," the painted brave said. "Just as David Corn Tassel will surrender to your people if the men of the Nez Percé do not keep their vows."

"It is agreed," Toby said, eyeing his opponent, who did not return his gaze.

Andy Brentwood frowned, thinking he'd gone too far, but there was nothing he could do to halt the agreement.

The immediate contest was far more difficult than either Andy or Toby had assumed. The Indians found a knob on a white birch tree about one hundred and fifty feet from the spot where Toby sat his mount. This imperfection in the bark of the tree was no more than a half-inch wide and perhaps a quarter of an inch high. In fact, it was difficult even to see it from the point where the two contestants would be stationed.

Andy started to protest, but Toby cut him off. "Don't worry about me," he said. "I like these terms just fine."

Andy assumed that David Corn Tassel would use firearms and was upset when the Nez Percé champion elected to utilize a bow and arrow. Toby, however, remained unperturbed. Never letting on that his opponent was a friend of his, he told Andy, "I think he's smart. He's more familiar with the weapon of his people than he is with our kind of weapons. As for me, I'll use my Colt."

The response of the warriors was immediate and emphatic when Toby announced his selection. They grinned broadly, some of them laughing aloud, and from the high-pitched babble of their conversation, it was apparent that they were highly pleased.

"Why the celebration?" Andy asked. "They act as though you've made an awful mistake by choosing to fire a six-shooter."

"Exactly so, Colonel," Toby replied. "Remember, they've been using cast-off firearms for many years. They're notoriously inaccurate, so they can't imagine anyone shooting a gun accurately."

"I sincerely hope," Andy replied, "that you prove them wrong."

Toby chuckled but did not answer. Without acknowledging each other in any way, he and David Corn Tassel both dismounted, went to the birch tree, and examined the eye-level target together. Then David solemnly walked a measured fifty paces in the clearing, while Toby strode beside him.

Both men declared they were satisfied. Then to

the surprise of everyone—no one more so than David Corn Tassel—Toby clasped the warrior's wrist in a sign of friendship. For the first time, the two men looked at each other, and both smiled, enjoying the secret they alone shared. David Corn Tassel now returned the gesture of friendship by clasping Toby's wrist, and then the two men separated and took up their positions.

For some reason that was never made clear, the Nez Percé champion was granted the right to fire at the target first. David Corn Tassel looked confident, almost ferocious, as he stepped to a line that he had drawn with the heel of his moccasin in the soft ground. Using a short Nez Percé bow that was not more than four feet long, he notched an arrow into it, took aim, and fired. It was so quiet in the clearing that the twang of the bowstring and the whispering rush of the arrow could be plainly heard. Gauging the effect of his shot with surprising speed, the warrior fired a second arrow and then a third.

Everyone peered at the tree, and even Andy Brentwood was impressed. One of the arrows had vanished and was nowhere to be seen, but two of them protruded from the trunk of the tree. Toby, staring at the arrows, saw that one of them had cut cleanly into the heart of the target and had penetrated deeply into the wood.

The partisan throng of braves cheered wildly.

Toby had already learned that David Corn Tassel was a superb shot. He grinned at the warrior in congratulations, then took his place at the firing line.

The old warrior wanted to remove the arrow from the target, but Toby waved him away, preferring to handle the matter in his own way.

Gradually, the onlookers became calmer, and quiet settled over them.

Toby drew his revolver and removed the safety catch. He peered hard at the target, squinting slightly, then he raised his extended arm to shoulder level. Three shots rang out in quick succession, as rapidly as Toby could squeeze the trigger three times.

A single, swift glance at the target was sufficient to assure him that he had achieved his goal. The old warrior and David Corn Tassel raced to the birch tree, and numerous other braves crowded behind them. Their babble soon became an uproar.

As Toby calmly fitted three more cartridges into the chamber of his gun, Andy looked at him incredulously. "As near as I make out," he said, his voice barely audible above the babble of Indian voices, "you knocked the living daylights out of the target. The arrow that the warrior fired into the tree is gone, and unless my eyes are playing tricks on me, you've landed three shots right next to each other, one after another. I've never seen an exhibition of shooting quite like it."

Toby was pleased with his efforts but could not think of them as extraordinary. For many long years, as far back as he could remember, his father had taken him to a range behind the house and had drilled him in the use of firearms. His training, and ultimately his battle experience during the war, had raised his proficiency level to that of a highly polished art.

The leader of the Nez Percé pushed through the crowd of his subordinates and stood facing Toby, his expression awe-stricken. "That which the father does with a leather whip," he declared, "the son does with a firestick."

His subordinates nodded. They, too, had never seen such magnificently accurate shooting.

Not even consulting the colonel, Toby reached a decision and, knowing he was right, decided to act on it without delay. "It has come to pass," he said, "that the son of Whip Holt has won the contest. But it is not fair that one who is so proficient with firearms should be declared the victor over him who does so well with the bow and arrow. Therefore, the white brothers of the Nez Percé waive their privilege of making their demands first, and grant that right in the coming negotiations to their Indian brothers."

The gesture was so startling, so unexpected, and so unprecedented that the braves, after a moment of stunned silence, cheered so lustily that Toby's stallion, tied to the low branch of a pine tree, became nervous and began to paw the ground.

As Toby translated what he had just said, Andy Brentwood grinned. He reflected that young Holt was a talented negotiator and should sit in on the forthcoming meetings. The settlers had lost nothing by giving the initial advantage to the Nez Percé, and the Indians, at the same time, were delighted because they had concrete proof that white men were no longer trying to take advantage of them.

Andy promptly compounded this new era of good feeling by inviting the older warrior, several of his subordinates, and David Corn Tassel to eat supper with him at his own campfire. The Indians promptly accepted, and Toby knew that the negotiations would begin that very evening.

Indeed they did, and at that time Toby told the

assemblage about his earlier meeting with David Corn Tassel and their pledge of friendship. The braves cheered in approval, and Andy smiled broadly as Toby and David clasped arms with their hands and renewed their pledges.

The talks continued steadily for the next two days, and at the end of that time, an eminently fair accord had been hammered out. Four thousand square miles of prime Washington land would be reserved for the sole use of the Indians, to hunt, fish, and live. United States Army troops would patrol the region to assure that the boundaries were protected, and in return, the Indians would not harass any settlers in outlying areas.

Colonel Andrew Brentwood signed the treaty on behalf of the United States Army, and although Toby Holt's signature had no legal bearing, he nevertheless signed on behalf of the Washington Territory settlers.

As he rode back to Tumwater at the head of the column of cavalry beside Andrew Brentwood, he had good reason to be satisfied with his labors of the past two weeks. "I just hope now," he said, "that the treaty is going to be honored. I'd hate to be forced to forfeit my life if it isn't."

Andy grinned and shook his head. "You'll be safe no matter what happens," he said. "You so impressed the Nez Percé with your shooting that they wouldn't kill you. At the worst, they would make a god out of you and worship you."

Toby was quite serious when he replied, "I'm not sure which would be worse—being killed or being worshiped."

IX

Dr. Martin and his wife were the first members of the older generation to arrive at the lodge high in the mountains, and were escorted by their son. The journey on horseback from Oregon had taken three days—twice as long as it would have been for Rob riding alone—and it had been arduous for the elderly doctor. But as one of the early settlers in the West, Dr. Robert Martin was determined to keep the pioneer spirit alive. And, indeed, when he and Tonie arrived at the lodge and were shown to their room by Rob, they felt totally rejuvenated and as robust as they had in their earlier years.

A few hours after the Martins arrived, Whip and Eulalia Holt reached the lodge, bringing Cindy with them. They had stopped off in Tumwater to pick up Clarissa Sinclair, whom Toby was eager for his parents to meet. In truth, as highly as he regarded Clarissa, Toby had ulterior motives in inviting her to the lodge. He hoped that with her present, he would be able to insulate himself from the pangs he knew he would feel when Rob and Beth formally announced their betrothal. Whip acted as his own guide for the occasion, and Eulalia was much impressed by Clarissa, finding from the outset that she and the younger woman had a great deal in common.

Late the following morning, the Blake family arrived, escorted by a half-troop of cavalry, which was automatically provided Lee as commander of a major military district. Susanna Brentwood, who had announced to the delight of all that she was pregnant, decided the trip would be too taxing and thus remained behind at the Blake home in Oregon.

Shortly after the Blakes' arrival, Toby also appeared, having gone with Andy to Olympia to report to the governor on the peace negotiations that had been successfully concluded with the Nez Percé. Andy, overjoyed to learn that he was going to be a father, could not attend the party, since it was necessary that he return to Tumwater to see about conditions there.

By that afternoon, the party was in full swing. Everyone raved about the spectacular view, and Cathy Blake announced, "I could stay here forever." The others had reason to remember her comment.

The next morning, the females amused themselves fishing for trout in one of the swift-moving streams on the property. Lee Blake, enjoying the respite from his command of the western army, and in excellent spirits because of the successful peace negotiations with the Indians, relaxed on the veranda, reading a book. This was a luxury he hadn't enjoyed in more years than he could remember. As he sat in a rocking chair, frequently chuckling at passages in

Dickens's *Pickwick Papers,* Rob Martin and his father were engrossed in a game of chess.

Meanwhile, Toby and his father mounted their stallions and went hunting. They rode in silence for a time, and then Whip spoke tentatively. "I am going to shoot off my face, Toby," he said, "but if I make you uncomfortable, just tell me to mind my own business."

"I wouldn't do that, Pa," Toby said. "You know I always listen to you."

"I was keeping my eye on you last night, boy," Whip said, "and I was a mite surprised when I realized that you're in love with Beth Blake."

Toby flushed beneath his tan. "Was I that obvious?"

Whip shook his head. "Only to me, and I reckon your ma guessed, too. But nobody else has any idea."

Toby sighed. "It's one of those unfortunate circumstances that developed totally beyond my control," he said. "By the time I realized that I cared for Beth, it was too late. She was already deeply involved with Rob."

Whip glanced at him obliquely. "This Clarissa Sinclair is quite a nice woman," he said. "Your ma gets along with her just fine, and so do I. We like her."

"I'm glad," Toby replied. "I'm pretty fond of her myself."

"In fact," Whip added gently, "we like her so much we'd hate to see her get hurt, and we'd sure be mighty sorrowful if our son was responsible for inflicting pain on her."

"That won't happen," Toby assured him. "Clarissa and I have an understanding, and neither of us is going to be hurt. We're both free to come and go as we please."

"She knows how you feel about Beth?" Whip demanded bluntly.

"Yes, sir," Toby said.

Whip shrugged, keeping his thoughts to himself. It was apparent to him that his son and Clarissa were engaging in an affair, and he thought it odd that any woman would so indulge herself when she knew that the man was pining away for someone else. But he didn't pretend to understand the younger generation.

Toby felt the need to say something more. "Whether what Clarissa and I are building together will ever amount to anything remains to be seen, Pa. I'm not capable of looking that far into the future, and I don't think she's that interested."

Whip sucked in his breath. "I'll tell you something, boy, that I've never mentioned to you or to any other living soul. But I hope it will stand you in good stead. When I led the wagon train out this way all the way from Long Island, I fell in love with Cathy—Cathy van Ayl as she was then. She was the only girl in the world for me, and I guess I rated pretty high with her, too. Well, Lee Blake came along. He was a young officer assigned to us by the War Department, and the next thing I knew, he and Cathy were getting married. I thought that was the end of everything."

His son stared at him, listening intently.

"I'd known your ma for quite a spell," Whip said, "and I was more attracted to her than I knew. First thing you know, there I was, married to her. I didn't go after her deliberately. It was just one of those things that happened. But I was scared that I was still secretly in love with Cathy."

"You don't have to say anything you don't want to, Pa," Toby told him.

Whip silenced him with a gesture. "I'm telling you this because I want you to know it. Things worked out the way they should, and it wasn't terribly long before I knew that your ma meant more to me than any woman I've ever known. It's been like that for me ever since. I've been completely happy with her—more contented than I could have been with Cathy or anyone else."

Toby nodded, not quite knowing what to say.

"You keep all this under your hat, boy," Whip directed. "I've told you for a reason. You may think that you love Beth, but it may be that you have a deeper and higher regard for Clarissa than you know. Let life develop on its own terms, and you'll be astonished at how things work out."

"Thanks, Pa," Toby replied. "I appreciate your advice and your confidence, and I'll do my damnedest to live accordingly."

Whip brought down a large elk, and Toby shot three deer. They hadn't planned on such a large kill on this hunting foray, but at least they were assured of ample meat supplies during the holiday at the lodge. They butchered the meat immediately, discarding what they could not use, in order to make it easier to transport. They returned to camp with more than half of what they had killed, leaving the rest, which they would return for, strung up high off the ground on a tree limb.

Whip was tired, so Toby rode back out to the wilderness alone to fetch the remaining meat, leading a packhorse and anticipating no troubles.

As he drew near the site where they had left the strung-up carcasses, he became aware of movement in the underbrush, and both his stallion and the pack-horse began to react strangely, pawing the ground and snorting. Not until he had dismounted, however, and taken several steps toward the meat, did he realize what was happening. A pack of wolves had discovered the discarded parts of elk and deer and was edging in toward the plunder.

As every frontier dweller well knew, wolves were not considered particularly dangerous to human beings provided that one seized and held the initiative with them. So Toby immediately drew his pistol and fired a single shot into the air over his head.

But the wolves merely retreated a few paces and did not slink off. Instead, they held their ground with uncharacteristic boldness and began to move closer again.

The realization dawned on Toby that he had seriously underestimated his foes. A rapid head count told him there were at least fifteen full-grown males in the wolf pack, and perhaps more. They had formed themselves into a rough circle around him and were gradually closing in. Toby knew that he and the two horses made a tempting target.

Engaging in some rapid calculations, he realized that he stood the risk of being overwhelmed. He carried two Colt six-shooters, both of them loaded, which gave him a dozen shots, minus the one that he had squandered by firing into the air. He knew he had a number of loose cartridges in his buckskin jacket pocket, but he had no opportunity now to count them, and he felt certain he didn't have enough in the event that the wolves held their ground and refused to retreat.

One idea that came to his mind was to mount his stallion and, leaving the packhorse behind as a sacrifice, make a wild dash for freedom. But he immediately rejected the plan, since such an attempt would be extremely risky. Wolves were like bullies and immediately knew when they had achieved the upper hand. If he tried to mount his stallion and ride off, it was unlikely that he would be able to fight off successfully the long, lean, gray figures that would hurl themselves through the air at him and his horse. He decided he had to take his stand there and then. He drew his revolvers, spinning both cylinders to reassure himself that they were loaded, and then, bracing himself, he stood with his feet apart, intending to shoot the first wolf that dared to approach him.

A long, gray shape tentatively crept toward him, advancing scant inches at a time. Steadying himself, Toby raised the gun in his right hand. Before he could fire it, however, he was astonished to see that the animal suddenly stood upright, flattened its ears, and slowly moved its long, bushy tail from side to side.

Toby swallowed hard, unable to believe the evidence of his own eyes. "Good Lord," he murmured aloud. "Is it possible? Mr. Blake?"

The long-missing dog bounded toward Toby when he heard his voice. Scarcely recognizing the scruffy creature with the tangled fur, Toby hastily jammed one gun into his belt and stroked the dog's head. Mr. Blake's tail thumped vigorously from side to side.

Suddenly, however, there was work to be done.

The wolves were taking advantage of their enemy's distraction and were beginning to move closer.

A low, menacing growl rumbled up from deep within Mr. Blake and erupted on the surface. His long teeth bared in a snarl, the dog prepared to launch himself at any wolf that dared to come closer to Toby. The wolves long had accepted the shepherd dog as one of them but nevertheless always knew that he was different.

Had they acted in concert, the creatures could have overwhelmed the shepherd. But that was not the way of wolves. Not one of them wanted to risk losing its life in combat with a dog prepared to fight to the bitter end. The potential combatants froze and remained motionless for what seemed like an eternity.

One of the wolves, bolder and stronger than his fellows, snarled, baring his fangs, and braced himself, ready to spring. Mr. Blake was totally prepared for just such a move, and another menacing, low-pitched growl rose within him.

Toby was thunderstruck. It was miraculous enough that the dog actually remembered him. To take a stand beside him, however, and defy a whole pack of wolves, was more than any man could expect.

But the shepherd's loyalty did not waver. He moved forward slowly on his powerful haunches, still growling.

The wolf apparently realized that he would be forced to fight single-handedly if he fought at all. Changing his mind abruptly, he started to back off. Mr. Blake halted and watched him closely as he made his way into the cover of much deeper grass. The dog, however, was not yet satisfied. Still only inches from the man who had raised him from the time he had been a small puppy, he barked loudly and clearly, challenging to combat any creature who dared to face him.

The wolves had lost all desire to become embroiled with this ferocious animal who had been one of them. One by one the leaders of the pack slunk away. The others, realizing they had been deserted, moved more rapidly, and soon the entire pack had put a considerable distance between itself and the shepherd.

Ordinarily the smell of raw meat would have attracted the wolves sufficiently that they would have remained in the neighborhood. But the adamant, unyielding stand taken by Mr. Blake discouraged them, and they made off through the forest, taking themselves elsewhere.

Toby looked down at the shepherd and shook his head. "I'm in your debt, Mr. Blake," he said. "If you'll just stick around and don't go vanishing again, I'll try to repay my obligations to you." He cut down the carcasses, then cutting off a slab of elk meat with his hunting knife, he threw it to the grateful dog.

While Mr. Blake feasted, Toby tied the rest of the meat to the saddle of the packhorse. Then, when he mounted his stallion for the ride back to the lodge, he was delighted to note that the dog responded with no urging whatsoever and trotted alongside the stallion.

The animal was still there, holding his place in the column, when Toby finally reached his destination.

The others were astonished by Toby's story, and Beth Blake was delighted beyond measure. She had secretly grieved when the dog had vanished, and now, in her joy, she dropped to her knees and hugged him while Mr. Blake responded by wagging his tail energetically and licking her profusely. She insisted on bathing the dog while others began to prepare the evening meal, and she succeeded, although she became so wet herself that she had to change her clothes before dinner. Then she joined her mother at the outdoor cooking fire, where the meat was being roasted. Cathy looked at her daughter but made no comment.

Beth picked up a large spoon and began to baste the potatoes, carrots, and onions that were being roasted with the meat.

"I think," Cathy said, speaking softly so that the women on the far side of the fire would not hear her, "that you're a confused young woman right now."

Beth took refuge in innocence and contrived to look blank.

"You've become formally engaged to marry Rob Martin," her mother said gently. "I wondered last night—every time I saw you looking at Toby Holt— whether you knew what you were doing, and I wondered it even more today when Toby appeared with that shepherd dog in tow."

"I was delighted to see Mr. Blake, that's all, and I was thrilled by his loyalty to Toby," Beth protested.

Cathy shook her head. "You can fool some people with that kind of talk, including your father, but I'm your mother, Beth, and all I can say is that you don't seem very sure that you want to marry Rob."

The young woman's confidence seemed to drain out of her, and her voice became uncertain as she replied. "You—you're right, Mother. I thought I knew my own mind. In fact, I could have sworn on a stack

245

of Bibles that I did. Then when Toby's wife died and he was suddenly free, I realized that maybe, after all, I had chosen Rob only because I couldn't have Toby at the time. But I can't back out of my agreement with Rob without losing my reputation."

Cathy nodded. "It's not the easiest position in the world to be in, and I don't envy you. But maybe if I share with you some of my own experiences, it will help you."

"What do you mean by that?" Beth asked.

Cathy hesitated, and turning a large roast over on the spit with two forks, she moved somewhat closer to her daughter. "I'm sure I can trust you to keep a confidence, Beth."

"Of course, Mother."

"As you know, my father married me off when I was very young to a much older man named van Ayl. He died soon after we left our home in Long Island and started our wagon train journey across the continent. I was young and giddy, but I was also a widow and had to act with the dignity of someone who had been married. To make a long story short, I fell in love with Whip Holt."

Beth was astonished. "You did? Really?"

"Hush," Cathy told her, "just listen. Whip also fell in love with me. He never said it in so many words, but words weren't necessary. I knew, as he knew, and that was all that mattered to us."

Beth shook her head as though she were unable to believe what she was hearing.

Paying no attention to her daughter's reaction, Cathy continued. "We had a falling out, a misunderstanding that caused us to go in separate directions. What it was no longer matters. Let's just say that I still believe I was right, at least in principle, although today I'd be far more forgiving than I was inclined to be when I was young and headstrong."

Beth nodded as she listened avidly to every word.

"Colonel Lee Blake had been interested in me for quite some time on our journey," Cathy said, "and he chose this particular time, when Whip and I were on the outs, to propose marriage to me. I accepted him, and we were married very soon thereafter."

"I thought you were going to tell me something very dramatic," the disappointed Beth said.

"The real drama of my relationship with Whip Holt is that nothing happened between us," Cathy said. "On my wedding day itself, I was uncertain that I was doing the right thing. Whip and Eulalia were married soon thereafter, and a short time later we arrived in Oregon. Subsequently, Whip and I saw a lot of each other, but I'm sure he is happy with the life he has chosen, just as I am happy with mine. I had to grow up before I realized that I loved your father with all my heart, as I love him still," she added firmly.

"I see," Beth murmured.

"I wonder if you do?" Cathy asked. "I hope so. I wasn't trying to relive my past when I told you this story, Beth. I told it to you for a purpose."

"Would you care to explain?"

Cathy nodded. "If you're at all like me, and I know you are, I urge you to have patience, as I did. My instinct told me that I could love your father in spite of the temptations that Whip offered to me. I suspect—at least I hope with all my heart—that you love Rob Martin. If you do, hold on to that love with all your might. Resist whatever temptation you may feel to have a relationship with Toby. His mother and I tried hard to get the two of you together, goodness knows, but you both resisted. Well, you're paying the price of that resistance now, and what's been done can't be undone. You have a responsibility to Rob. Toby is free of entanglements now that his wife is no longer with us, but it wouldn't surprise me if he's taking on new responsibilities in his relations with this Clarissa Sinclair, who appears to be a fine young woman. What they have, or don't have together, is strictly their business. However, your concern is, and must be, exclusively Rob Martin."

Beth drew in her breath. "I'm glad you feel that way, Mother," she said, "because I've been telling myself the same thing."

"You won't regret it," Cathy told her. "If I'm sure of anything in this world, I know that I did what was right, as well as good and proper, when I was faithful to the vows that I made to your father. There's been just one man in my life, and that man is Lee Blake. It hasn't been easy to live the life of an army officer's wife, you know. We've been separated for long periods—for years at a time. We've had no permanent home, and we've had to live wherever we've been stationed at one time or another. In spite of these handicaps, however, we've had a wonderful life together, and I've relished every moment of it."

"Thank you for telling me all of this, Mother," Beth said.

Cathy smiled at her. "If you can be as firm in your resolves as I was in mine, I'm sure that you'll find the happiness with Rob that I've found with your father." She patted her daughter on the shoulder, then gripped her hard and turned away, busying herself at the fire.

Beth couldn't be sure, but she thought she caught a glimpse of tears in her mother's eyes.

The night was cool as it always was high in the mountains, but the next day the temperature began to rise as soon as the sun rose in a cloudless sky. By the time the older members of the party had gathered on the spacious veranda of the lodge to drink coffee in the open, they knew the weather would be both glorious and warm.

The younger people drifted out to the veranda for breakfast, and Toby, the last to show up, appeared with a panting Mr. Blake at his heels. He and the dog, he explained, had just been exercising in the forest.

The party was unexpectedly lethargic that morning, due in part to the balmy weather. Some of the men discussed setting up a shooting range behind the lodge and practicing their marksmanship, but they did nothing about it. Some of the ladies discussed quilts they were making, but none bothered to go off to her private quarters to fetch a sample. At Beth's suggestion, heartily endorsed by Rob, it was agreed that they would eat a noon dinner of cold meats and other leftovers on the veranda.

The day was astonishingly clear, with a view for miles visible from the veranda, and the older people, visiting the lodge for the first time, were able to appreciate the reasons that Toby had chosen this site for the building. Cathy proved to be the most curious about the geography. "Is that the Washington Territory as far as you can see?"

"Every last inch of it," Whip replied, as he glanced up from his self-imposed chore of whittling a doll for little Lucy Snow, whom he had met during his stopover in Tumwater. "Most folks don't realize the size of this territory. You could set all of New England down in the middle of it, and there would be some of Washington to spare."

Cathy went to the railing at the edge of the veranda and peered out at the snow-capped peaks all around them. "I'd love to take a walk out there. It looks so cool and refreshing."

The others just sat in their chairs, saying nothing.

"I want to take a walk," she said. "I really do." She looked at each of the men in turn, but no one stirred.

Whip sighed gently, slid his knife into his belt, and rose, putting the half-completed doll on his chair. "Come along," he said. "I'll walk out yonder with you to the edge of the slope, and from there you can look up at the snow-covered peaks all you want."

They walked to the ground by way of the outdoor staircase and went forward beyond the lodge along the cliff on which it was built. Just before reaching the edge, they made a sharp left turn and moved beneath the overhang of another, even steeper cliff.

Others on the veranda continued to chat lazily. Tonie Martin came out with a fruit punch she had concocted, and Eulalia tasted it, as did Clarissa, and pronounced it perfect. Lee read his book, and Dr. Martin dozed. Toby became engaged in a long, lazy conversation with Rob on the subject of whether he should teach Mr. Blake to fetch, with Cindy enthusiastically endorsing the idea. Beth ended the talk by saying that the dog had been through enough lately, besides which, he had already proved his worth.

Suddenly a low, rumbling noise, like the sound of thunder, filled the air. Several members of the party were mystified.

"Good Lord," Toby said distinctly. "It sounds like an avalanche."

As if to emphasize his words, the sound was repeated and was prolonged, extending for ten to fifteen seconds. Even that short span of time seemed like an eternity.

Eulalia saw Whip and Cathy standing side by side several hundred yards from the lodge. They were looking up in the direction of the noise, the sun shimmering on Cathy's blond hair.

Eulalia looked in the same direction and a half-gasp, half-scream escaped her lips.

All at once everyone on the veranda was standing, staring in horror. Tons of rocks and shale were on the move and were sliding down the precipitous cliff headed directly for the spot where Whip and Cathy were standing. Dr. Martin shouted, and Clarissa started to run forward, but Toby, far more experienced in mountain living than any of the others, knew there was no hope for his father and for Cathy Blake. The descending tons of rocks were speeding at far too rapid a rate to permit them to escape.

Instinctively, Toby started to move toward his mother, wanting to protect her from the horrible sight of things to come. His sister, Cindy, sensed the impending tragedy and threw herself into her mother's arms. Eulalia stood erect, holding her daughter close, unable to tear her eyes from the scene.

Major General Lee Blake, no stranger to death

through his long, illustrious army career, stood at rigid attention as though reviewing the troops of his army corps. Beth moved up beside him, and without seeming to become aware of her presence, he put an arm around her slender shoulders. Rob Martin stood on her other side watching in helpless anguish as the scene unfolded with the grim certainty of a great tragedy.

Tonie Martin looked up at her husband, her eyes imploring. Dr. Robert Martin had performed medical miracles so often and for so many years that his patients, and his wife in particular, took them for granted, but in this situation, he knew there was nothing he could do. A single shake of his head told her that he was helpless, unable to intervene.

Toby willed the avalanche to halt, but it did not. Clarissa Sinclair now came up beside him, her strong hand digging hard into his shoulder. But he was unaware of her hand, unaware of the pain that she caused. His whole being was riveted on his father and on Cathy.

Whip Holt, the living legend, the embodiment of the American West, could not tear his eyes from the avalanche of rocks and rubble speeding toward the very spot where he and Cathy were standing. It was impossible for him to speak, as the thunderlike roar had become so loud, so penetrating, that the very earth underfoot shook. He had estimated their chances of escape and knew that flight was impossible. So rather than come to an undignified end, fleeing in vain from his destiny, he stood very still and faced it, his shoulders squared, his chin outthrust.

Cathy Blake, equally mesmerized by the tons of rocks and earth that were crashing down toward her, seemed to know without being told that the end was near and there was no escape possible. She, too, faced this abrupt finish of her life with both courage and dignity. Fear struck at her heart, but there was no sign of fear on her face, and like Whip, she made no attempt to run away.

With one accord, Cathy and Whip reached toward each other. Their hands touched, then clasped.

In spite of all their mixed emotions for each other over the decades, they had never pledged their love, and both had been true to their marriage vows. Now, however, they were prepared to die together, and they faced the certain end with a fatalistic calm that would leave its mark for all time on those who witnessed the tragedy.

Whip and Cathy were comforted by the life they felt in each other's hands, by the warmth and the pulses that throbbed for the last time.

The suspense seemed to last forever, but in reality, the entire scene took place in a very few seconds. As the avalanche neared its targets, inevitably drawn toward Whip and Cathy as though by a giant magnet, Eulalia closed her eyes.

The booming, crashing, crunching sounds of tons of boulders and earth on the move filled the air and blotted everything else from the consciousness of those who were witnessing the unforgettable scene. Whip and Cathy stood very still, their entwined hands firmly clutching each other.

One moment the couple was visible, resembling two unmoving statues, and the next instant they vanished from sight for all time, obliterated by the debris of the centuries that poured down on them and built a mound higher and higher, creating, in effect, a new mountain on the precipice, a new, sharply defined hill where there had been none.

The avalanche settled, and the sounds gradually died away. Particles of dust danced in the sunshine, and in a treetop, a bird resumed its interrupted song.

At the lodge, there was stunned silence for a very long time. Finally Toby spoke up. "The avalanche," he said in a leaden tone, "formed its own memorial for my father and Cathy Blake. If it was their destiny to be taken from us, at least nature has left us with a permanent memorial larger and more grand than any that man could make."

X

On the surface, life at the Holt ranch appeared to be normal. Toby, now always accompanied by the eager Mr. Blake, came home for a visit and found that the ranch was being ably managed under his mother's supervision. The hired hands, who knew what was expected of them, were doing their jobs well, and Stalking Horse, who reacted stoically to the news that his old friend and blood brother was dead, went about overseeing the activities of the hands, never letting on to his grief. Cindy had returned to school after her summer recess and was concentrating on her studies.

He hadn't known what to expect, but his mother's appearance and attitude surprised him. She continued to wear her usual wardrobe and shied away from the black dresses of a recently bereaved widow. She appeared to be busy from early morning until night, and she celebrated her son's return home by preparing broiled lamb chops, fresh salmon steaks, and his other favorite foods for him. He was vastly relieved, but wisely asked no questions.

He gained an insight into his mother's thinking, however, on his second night at home when General Lee Blake crossed the Columbia River from Fort Vancouver for supper at the ranch and was accompanied by Beth. The difference between the older woman and the younger was marked. Beth was somber, dressed in black, and her face looked haggard.

"You're looking well, Eulalia," Lee Blake commented. He, too, appeared healthy, although there were faint smudges beneath his eyes.

"I do my best to keep occupied, Lee," she replied. "I know the last thing on earth Whip would want would be for me to mope about, mourning him. So I keep busy and try to face each day as it comes."

"I don't see how you manage it," Beth told her.

Eulalia shrugged. "I'll admit it isn't easy," she said. "It takes a great deal of concentration and a tremendous effort, but I believe it's worth it. I don't think of Whip as having passed away. The living testimonials to him are too great."

Beth didn't know what she meant. Neither did Cindy, judging by her perplexed expression.

"For one thing," Eulalia said, "there's the ranch itself. It continues to be prosperous, as it was when Whip was here managing it, and I see no reason why business should slacken off. He left me rather well off, but I see no reason to give up a profitable business enterprise. Until something happens to convince me to sell the ranch—which is a very remote possibility—I intend to keep operating it."

"Good for you," Lee said heartily.

Toby agreed and grinned at his mother. Never had he felt so proud of her.

"Even more important than the ranch," Eulalia continued, "my son and daughter are testimonials to the influence of their father. Toby hasn't for one instant faltered in his surveying work for Governor Pickering, nor has he slackened in his work on his Tumwater property. As for Cindy, she continues to earn top grades in her class."

"I admire all of you—especially you, Eulalia," Lee said, and turned to his daughter. "You see, Beth, life does go on."

Beth's nod was noncommittal.

"I guess I've been fortunate," Lee said. "I've been far busier than usual trying to reorganize my entire command. That's taken up so much of my time and effort that I've had very little opportunity to brood, and as I'm sure you know, each day the pain of the sense of loss we suffer lessens."

"I know what you mean," Eulalia said. "The loss itself doesn't lessen. It remains a constant factor, but the misery that one feels does dissipate."

"I don't agree," Beth said, her voice suddenly strident. "My mother and Uncle Whip were taken from us in the prime of life in a senseless tragedy, and I'll never be able to accept it!"

Her father, who had obviously spoken to her at length on the subject, merely sighed. Eulalia started to speak but thought better of it.

Toby, however, could not remain silent. "There's nothing harder to accept than the finality of death," he said. "But we've got to accept it because we have no real choice. It may be cruel, and it may be senseless, but we do no favors for the dead by overindulging our grief for them, and we must keep in mind that life is to be lived by and for the living."

"Well said, Toby," Eulalia told him. "You've expressed my sentiments exactly."

"And mine," Lee added.

Beth seemed to draw farther into her shell and remained unmollified.

"By the way, Eulalia," Lee said, "since the last time I saw you, we've had telegrams of condolence from President Johnson and General Grant. I must show them to you after supper."

"By all means," she said. "And I'll show you all the newspaper articles written about Whip."

Toby glanced at Beth, and his heart went out to her. It was evident that unlike their parents, she was unable to reconcile herself to what had happened. She was disconsolate, and there was nothing that Toby or anyone else could do to help her. Beth would have to achieve inner peace on her own.

The grieving Beth Blake postponed her wedding to Rob Martin, who accepted her decision with understanding and sympathy. He threw himself into his surveying work with a vengeance, and this suited Toby Holt perfectly. The two young men immediately returned to the eastern ranges of Washington and worked from daybreak until sunset, seven days a week. Every so often, they returned to Tumwater for a few days to help Frank Woods with the lumbering operation at their property.

Thanks to their unremitting efforts, their master plan for the construction of a railroad that would span the territory began to take definite shape, and they knew that they could soon give Governor Pickering the detailed report that he required. Meanwhile, the state of affairs in Tumwater was just as Toby had predicted. With Colonel Andrew Brentwood and his troops stationed there, Tom Harrison kept out of the way, and there was little crime and lawlessness in the town. Thus, Andy had no choice but to withdraw his troops.

No sooner had the army gone, however, than trouble developed swiftly. The lumberjacks employed by Frank suddenly proved unreliable and frequently did not show up for work. It became evident that Tom Harrison was offering them far more pay to enter his employ instead. The companies that Frank engaged to haul the cut lumber to the sawmills frequently disappointed him, too, breaking their word to him and leaving the lumber untouched on his property, where it was sure to rot if exposed to the elements for any length of time. Here, too, it was plain to see the fine hand of Harrison, who interfered deliberately in order to create as many difficulties as he could for the partners.

To make matters still worse, Harrison went out of his way to harass and annoy Bettina Snow. Always choosing occasions when she was unaccompanied, he or one of the men in his employ accosted her on the street and insulted her. Indeed, the tearful Bettina told Frank how Harrison's paymaster, Mr. Trumbull, who had returned from his trip to San Francisco, had sidled up to her in the general store and had asked her to come to work in Harrison's house of prostitution.

This harassment of Bettina was intended as a challenge to Frank Woods, daring him to act. But as Frank told his partners, "There isn't a blame thing I can do to stop Harrison from annoying Bettina, just as there's no way that I can prevent him from interfering with our lumbering operation. He has the sheriff and his deputies in his hip pocket. I've just found out that the representative for Tumwater in the territorial legislature is one of Harrison's henchmen. That new brothel that he opened is a gold mine, and he has all the cash he needs or wants. In fact, the whole town is turning into his private property."

The lawless elements were so much in control of the community that even Cargill thought of moving his saloon elsewhere. "All I want," he said, "is to run a friendly little place where Hector and I can live in peace. I don't want to be forced to let Harrison's strumpets solicit business in my saloon, and I'm damned if I want to pay protection to the sheriff so I'm not robbed by Harrison's strong-arm hoodlums. This is a fine community, and there are some grand people living here, but the atmosphere is getting to be more than I can bear."

Having done everything he could think of to control Harrison, Toby once again discussed the problem with Clarissa Sinclair, whose advice he respected.

"I've thought and thought about it, and I'm afraid you can't do a blessed thing, Toby," she said. "Harrison has made himself a king in this corner of the territory. He takes what he pleases, and his word is law. He'll avoid a direct confrontation with you, I'm sure, because the one language he knows and respects is that of violent action."

"I suppose," Toby said softly, "that all we can do is to ask Andy Brentwood to come back here with his troops."

Clarissa shook her head. "The presence of the regiment," she said, "will provide Tumwater with temporary relief, nothing else. It's no solution to the problem. I honestly don't know how Tom Harrison can be curbed. All I say, and I take what solace I can from this, is that as his confidence grows, he becomes bolder and more demanding, and one of these days he's going to go too far. When that happens, we can clip his wings—I hope. Until then we can only watch him as he flies high."

Toby and Rob obtained an appointment to meet with Governor Pickering regarding the railroad survey, and they decided they would take advantage of the opportunity to appeal to the governor once again for help in controlling Harrison.

A few days later, when they finally sat down with Governor Pickering, they spread a large map on the governor's desk, and there Rob traced a route in red from the eastern end of the territory to the west. "This is the route we've selected, Governor," he said. "It's subject to some modification, of course, although on the higher levels of ground there isn't going to be too much room for give and take."

Pickering studied the map in silence for a time. "Let's keep to fundamentals for the moment," he said. "Do I gather correctly, gentlemen, that you definitely think it feasible to construct a railroad to the east that will span the breadth of the Washington Territory?"

"We do, sir," Toby said. "There's never been any question of that in our minds."

Rob grinned. "That's right, Governor. We decided right off that one way or another we'd do a survey that would make the building of a railroad line feasible."

Pickering looked at the western terminus of the red line with infinitely greater care. "As nearly as I can gather," he remarked, "the terminal point of your railroad is a little lumbering and fishing town at the opposite end of Puget Sound from Olympia, called Seattle."

Toby nodded. "That's correct," he said. "We found the access route over the mountains was the most accessible and least expensive, if we selected Seattle as the western anchor."

"I'm surprised," Pickering said, "because I wasn't expecting any such conclusion. When the railroad is built, gentlemen, I predict the growth of Seattle will be phenomenal. I'd urge you to invest in some property there, but I'm afraid you'd end up in trouble with the federal government."

Toby and Rob joined in the governor's laugh, and on sudden impulse, Rob decided it was time to refer to the explosive Tumwater situation. "I don't think we'd want any trouble with the federal government, Governor," he said. "We already have our hands full in Tumwater."

Pickering frowned, and his face darkened. "I had forgotten that you lads own property there. I can imagine the troubles you're having."

"They're not unique, sir," Toby said, "not in that area."

Governor Pickering sighed heavily. "I sympathize with you, and I wish I could do something more for you," he said. "But to be perfectly honest with you gentlemen, my situation is not an easy one. I represent only the executive branch of government in the territory. I'm not a law enforcement officer, and in order to take effective action against that rascal, Tom Harrison, who's making a mockery of justice there, I'd need an official complaint from the sheriff. But it's no secret to anyone that the new sheriff I appointed is on

Harrison's payroll, just like his predecessor. I could appoint still another man, but as you and I well know, Harrison would most likely find a way to get around him, too."

"We know only too well," Toby said.

"No doubt your lumberjacks are still being harassed by Harrison," the governor said.

"Not only that, but now we're having trouble hiring and holding lumberjacks and transporting our cut wood to market," Rob said. "The situation is getting worse every day."

"Well, be of stout heart," Governor Pickering told them. "I'm not completely defeated by this situation, nor should you be. At the moment I'm appealing to the territorial legislature to provide funds for a constabulary force in Tumwater. Now, the wheels of government move slowly, and we'll need the approval of Congress, but I think I can promise you that sooner or later there will be a police force in the town to provide law and order. In the meantime, I want you young gentlemen to have clear minds for a much larger and more important venture than any business of your own that you may be engaged in. I'm going to pass along your survey report to Washington City with the firmest endorsement that I can possibly give. Furthermore, gentlemen," he added, "I'm going to request another sacrifice from you. I want you to complete the task that you've initiated so brilliantly—I want you to continue laying out a railroad route in the Montana Territory."

Toby and Rob were flattered, and they grinned as they exchanged pleased looks. "I hope we can live up to your good opinion of us, Governor," Toby said.

"You'll accept a call, then, to continue your survey in Montana?" the governor asked.

"Indeed we will, sir," Rob replied. "It's a wonderful feeling to know that we have a major hand in a venture this big and this important."

"I was hoping you'd feel that way," Governor Pickering told them, "and I'm reasonably confident that the President, the Congress, and the private interests that are planning the development of railroads to the West Coast will leap at the opportunity to avail themselves of your further services for the creation of the Northern Pacific!"

It was inevitable that Lee Blake should learn of the excesses resumed by Tom Harrison as soon as Andy Brentwood and his troops departed. Rob Martin corresponded with Beth, and his letters were filled with his indignant comments on the latest efforts of Harrison to intimidate and cheat the community.

Lee kept the information to himself and, listening to his daughter's remarks in silence, did not mention the subject to anyone—not even to Andy Brentwood, who, with Susanna, was still residing at Fort Vancouver, waiting for his orders to take command of Fort Shaw in Montana. Not until he appeared at the Holt dinner table on Toby's next visit to his mother did Lee broach the subject.

"I understand," Lee said quietly, "that people in Tumwater are still suffering from all kinds of ailments created by that bully and criminal named Tom Harrison."

Toby quickly figured the general's source of information but preferred not to dwell on the subject in his mother's presence. Eulalia had enough on her mind without being given cause to worry about her son's welfare.

So Toby merely nodded and remarked casually, "I'm sure there have been a lot of rotten men in the relatively brief history of the West, General. It's inevitable that in a new land where might makes right and violence is commonplace, the strong—particularly the bullies—should try to take advantage of ordinary, decent people."

Lee nodded. "People like this fellow Harrison make my blood boil," he said, "but I'm afraid there's nothing I can do about him at the moment. I could once again send Andy Brentwood in with his regiment to maintain law and order, but as we know from the last time, as soon as the troops withdraw, Harrison will act up again."

Lee turned to Eulalia. "I won't bore you with the details of this situation," he said, "and I certainly don't want you to be upset by what I'm going to say, but I'll tell you frankly that it's times like this that I miss Whip sorely. This is a situation that was made to order for Whip Holt."

Whip's widow forced a smile. "How so?" she asked.

"An entire community is being terrorized," Lee told her, "by a bully who's using his own physical prowess, the support of his hired hands, and the connivance of the law enforcement officers of his community to have his own way."

"The territory can't do anything to help?"

Toby intervened and told them about his interview with Governor Pickering the previous week. "He's doing all he can," Toby said, "but it will still be a while—too long a while—before the territory will be able to do anything to curb the excesses that this man Harrison is guilty of."

Lee looked at Eulalia, and his smile was significant. "You begin to see what I mean, I'm sure. What a situation this would have been for Whip!"

"And how irresistible he would have found it!" she added. "I can just see him rising to the challenge and refusing to be distracted."

"Exactly," Lee said, chuckling. "He would have gone into that town armed only with his rifle, pistols, and whip, and one way or another, he'd have found the means to stop the bully."

Eulalia became wistful. "You're right, Lee," she said. "Whip was unique in that way. There's no question about it."

"There was nobody else like him," Lee replied. Then afraid that he might drive his hostess to tears, he changed the subject.

Toby heard very little of what was said during the rest of the evening. He appeared distracted and thoughtful, and Beth, respecting his desire for privacy, made no attempt to draw him into conversation.

He made an effort for his mother's sake to be more convivial before he left for Washington the following morning, and Eulalia did not guess what was troubling him.

Instead of going directly to Tumwater, Toby made a detour, and with Mr. Blake taking the lead, he rode his stallion along the trail that led to the lodge high in the mountains. He spent a restless night there, and in the morning he was awake early, staring at the high, avalanche-made hill that had become the tomb for Whip Holt and Cathy Blake. As he stared at the huge mound of rubble, his mother's words and

Lee Blake's comments rolled around and around in his mind. There was only one Whip Holt, they had agreed. Had Whip been alive, the situation there would have been made to order for him. He would have ridden into the town, and somehow he would have forced Tom Harrison to comply with the law.

I am Whip Holt's only son, Toby thought. I've been in training since the day I was born to replace my father. Now that he's no longer here, the time has come when I am needed and wanted. But how can I force Tom Harrison to behave when I have no idea what my father would have done?

No matter how hard he pondered the question, he could find no answer. Out of his torment, however, there grew a solid conviction: he—and he alone— would somehow have to stop the excesses of Tom Harrison. He had waited far too long for others to intervene in the name of law and order. Circumstances had prevented that intervention, and Harrison had grown too powerful for ordinary citizens to oppose him. Therefore, Toby knew that as the son of Whip Holt the responsibility was his.

Strangely, Toby felt at peace within himself as he guided his stallion onto the now-familiar trail that led down to Tumwater. Without thinking, he rode straight to Clarissa's.

Certain he heard her moving about inside her apartment, Toby tapped lightly at the door. There was no response. He knocked on the wooden partition again. "Are you in there, Clarissa?" he called. "It's Toby."

The movements inside the apartment accelerated, and at last the door opened. Toby stared in astonishment at a disheveled, badly upset Clarissa. She, who was always calm, composed, and in control of herself, obviously had been weeping. Her face was tearstained, her ordinarily immaculately coiffed hair was messy, and she was far more nervous than he had ever seen her.

"What's wrong?" he demanded.

Clarissa drew a deep breath. "I—I'll try to tell you," she said.

Without further ado, Toby went to the kitchen, knowing she kept a bottle of whiskey in her cupboard. He poured a generous quantity into a glass, added water to it, and returned to her parlor. "Drink this first," he commanded.

Clarissa obeyed, coughing and spluttering. "Now then," he said, "tell me what's wrong and don't be in any hurry, take your time."

She nodded, folded her hands in her lap, and spoke with comparative calm. "Do you remember the fellow to whom I rented the rooms next door to mine?" she asked. "Name of Dunlop. He was a one-time miner who got married in California and turned to farming. He couldn't earn a living at it, so he became a lumberjack and came up here. He was hoping to send for his wife."

"I remember him," Toby said, and had a mental picture of a large man in his mid to late thirties who had a gentle manner and smile.

"He came to me this afternoon—not an hour ago—and asked for my help," Clarissa said.

"What kind of help?" Toby demanded.

She made a great effort to control herself and be coherent. "It seems," she said, "that Tom Harrison wanted him to quit his job as a lumberjack without bothering to give notice. He was working for somebody of whom Harrison obviously disapproved. Well, Mr. Dunlop refused, and in front of a whole gang of lumberjacks, he told Harrison to go to the devil. The next thing he knew, Harrison and several hoodlums came here searching for him, and all of them were heavily armed."

"Did they threaten him in any way?" Toby asked.

"I'm coming to that," Clarissa replied. "Mr. Dunlop saw them from a window and hurried to me, asking me to give him refuge and hide him until they left. He knew they were up to no good. I agreed, but before I could do anything, Harrison and his men came here to my door and burst in. They grabbed hold of Mr. Dunlop, and he was so badly outnumbered that even though he tried to put up a fight, it didn't do him any good.

She was speaking with increasing difficulty, and Toby, feeling somewhat ill, could guess what was coming next.

"Harrison told him that he didn't allow anybody to shame or mock him and that he intended to make an example of Mr. Dunlop. Then they marched him out into the road, and as calm as you please, they plunged a knife into his heart. Just like that. They killed him in cold blood without giving him a chance to defend himself. And all because he refused to agree to do a dirty trick on Harrison's behalf."

She tried to steady herself but was on the verge of breaking down again. Taking her in his arms, Toby stroked her hair and tried to calm her. "Is there any more to the story?"

Clarissa nodded. "I gathered from the talk of Harrison and his men that they were going to take poor Mr. Dunlop's body and throw it onto the ground where he would be seen by the whole crowd who had heard Mr. Dunlop insulting Harrison. And then that horrid little man who works for Harrison—that Mr. Trumbull—came back here as cool as you please and told me that I'd be smart to forget that I'd heard or seen anything, and with that he waltzed off. If I hadn't been in such a state, I would have thrashed him."

The story was the worst that Toby had heard so far. What was more, this was the first time that someone with whom he was close had been directly threatened so severely by Harrison.

"It was dreadful," Clarissa said, "not just because they killed an innocent man without a real cause, but they were so cold-blooded about it. They put a knife into a fellow human being with less feeling than you'd show when carving a turkey."

Soothing and calming her as best he was able, Toby fried some bacon, scrambled some eggs, and made some tea and toast, then succeeded in persuading Clarissa to eat some supper.

After she had consumed at least a part of the meal, she had grown sufficiently calm to respond to Toby's tender lovemaking, and thereafter she fell into a deep, exhausted sleep in his arms.

Toby, however, remained wide awake, and donning a robe that Clarissa kept for him, he wandered into the parlor where Mr. Blake greeted him with a wagging tail. He patted the dog and stared out into the dark night.

The issues were even more clear-cut now, and there was no longer any question in his mind regarding what he would do next. He would declare open war on Tom Harrison with all that that declaration entailed.

Such a move was not without risks, as he well realized, but he faced them with remarkable calm. For one thing, the many hours he had spent in combat during the war had given him a fatalistic approach to life. Either he would be killed in action or he would survive.

Looking at his situation realistically, Toby told himself he was responsible to no wife and no children. His mother and his sister had inherited enough from his father to take care of them for life. He wasn't needed that badly by anyone, and only he would be taking risks.

His mind made up, Toby returned to bed and slept soundly, his sleep untroubled by dreams or doubts.

At breakfast the following day, he told Clarissa his decision. She listened closely and made no comment until he was through speaking. "You don't need me to tell you that you're taking chances," she said. "Harrison is ruthless, and he'll quickly attempt to end your menace to his future."

"He can't act too fast to suit me," Toby replied. "The quicker there's a showdown, the sooner the decent folks of Washington can live in peace."

She was curious why he felt so strongly that it was his duty to halt Harrison, and she couldn't help asking, "Why you, Toby?"

He shrugged. "I can handle firearms better than most," he said, "and I know how to take care of myself in a crisis. That's more than most men can say. I've been trained all my life for just this sort of an emergency, and my conscience would give me no rest if I didn't step in and accept my responsibility."

Toby Holt, Clarissa reflected, belonged to a breed apart. He was totally unlike any man she had ever met in Philadelphia or elsewhere in the East. He was a true Westerner in the finest sense of the term.

"Are you going to tackle Harrison single-handedly, or are you going to seek help?" Clarissa asked.

"If I must," Toby said, "I'll campaign against him alone, but I don't think that will happen. I'll be surprised if others don't rally to the cause. In this part of the country, you can endanger a man's freedom just so much—and then, watch out! I think Harrison may have bitten off more than he can chew."

Knowing he would not appreciate rhetoric, Clarissa reacted as though his mission were an everyday occurrence. When he left her apartment, sliding his Colt revolvers beneath his belt, she raised her face for his kiss and then simply said, "Good luck."

With Mr. Blake trotting beside him, Toby rode to Cargill's saloon. At this time of day, at the hour before noon, it was the custom for Harrison's supporters and henchmen to gather for social drinking before spreading out to do their superior's bidding. So Toby hoped that luck would be with him.

When he entered the establishment, he heard the squawking of Hector, who was holding court, and looking around the saloon, he was satisfied. He recognized at least a half-dozen men who were said to be close to Tom Harrison.

Cargill greeted Toby cordially, and Toby made it clear from the outset that he had not come here to drink. Taking a silver dollar from his pocket, he rapped on the bar with it to gain the attention of the crowd, and then he spoke in a loud voice. "This town," he said, "has a potential unequaled anywhere in the territory. We're well on our way to being a lumbering capital. Our soil is so rich that almost anything will grow in it. The salmon in our rivers and the shellfish in Puget Sound can make fortunes. But there's one thing wrong with the whole area. It suffers from a rotten odor."

His listeners were surprised, and gradually those who had continued to talk fell silent.

"It doesn't take any special investigating to find out the cause of that stench," Toby declared. "It's caused by just one source—Tom Harrison." The air suddenly seemed to become charged with electricity. "I'm not going to make any long speech about Harrison and what's wrong with him," Toby went on. "Everybody in town has suffered and just about everybody would have a different story to tell. I've decided that the time has come to put an end to the nonsense that Harrison has been perpetrating."

Toby knew that Harrison's men would lose no time in giving their employer a verbatim report on what he said.

"I declare war on Tom Harrison!" Toby boomed out. "Here and now! This town isn't big enough for both of us, and one of us will have to get out. I don't mind telling you that I've put down my roots here, and I have every intention of staying."

With that, Toby smiled at Cargill and left the saloon. As he departed, he heard Hector raucously mimicking some of his words and thereby giving them even greater emphasis. He grinned to himself and thought that the parrot unwittingly was doing him—and Tumwater—a great favor. Mounting his stallion, Toby headed for his own property.

Meanwhile, no fewer than seven of the men who had been present in his audience—including Mr. Trumbull—went without delay to Tom Harrison's house, where they excitedly gave a word-for-word account of what had been said. Harrison listened carefully, his expression blank except for the smoldering look in his dark eyes.

When his subordinates had finished, they expected a temper tantrum at the least, but Harrison surprised them by smiling and speaking quietly. "Holt is entitled to his opinion, just as I have a right to mine," he said. "He's put a chip on my shoulder and knocked it off. We'll see which of us stays in town and which of us is carried off with his body full of bullets. I don't mind telling you, boys, I've lived here for quite a spell, and I aim to be here a heap longer."

In the meantime, Toby reached his property, where Frank Woods and a crew of half a dozen lumberjacks were hard at work. He didn't want to interrupt their productive efforts, so as Frank wielded an ax, Toby told him about his challenge.

Frank continued to swing his ax rhythmically, the sharp blade biting into the wood of the cedar tree that he was felling. "I heard tell," he said, "that during the war you made a habit out of leading your platoon against superior forces. I was told that in at least two battles, you deliberately faced a company, and on at least one occasion, you picked a fight with a full battalion of Rebs."

Toby failed to see the significance of his friend's comment. "It just happened that my platoon was outnumbered on occasion," he said.

"Half the men in town are on Harrison's payroll already," Frank declared, "and most of the other half are on his side because they're afraid to oppose him. It strikes me that you can stand a little help. Since you've declared war on him, I enlist in the fight with you, and I'm with you all the way, no matter what the consequences."

Toby was touched. "You're being generous, Frank," he said, "and courageous, but I can't expect all that much from you. You and Bettina have gotten quite serious lately, it strikes me, and you have an obligation to her and to her little girl."

"It's because I've become obligated to her," Frank replied forcibly, "that I'm joining you. The time has come when every man in the area has got to declare sides. There's no room in Tumwater for neutrals!"

The tree toppled with a thud, and Frank watched it as it fell. Then, before he severed the limbs from the upper portion, he leaned his ax against the tree, wiped his hand on his shirt, and extended it to his friend. As Toby grasped it, he was reassured. With Frank Woods as his ally, he would not be going into battle alone.

In the next few hours, to his surprise, other volunteers also came to him. Some were property owners who had been deprived of their rights by Harrison, while others were lumberjacks who were tired of being intimidated by Harrison's hirelings. In all, a dozen men came to Toby, and he accepted all of them, making it clear to them that he could promise them neither victory nor safety. The struggle that lay ahead was certain to be vicious at the very least.

Late in the afternoon, Rob Martin returned to

town after visiting Beth in Oregon and heard of his friend's challenge before he actually saw Toby. He grinned broadly, a gleam of excitement in his eyes, as he rode to the property that he shared with his partners. "I was wondering how long it would be before you'd declare war on Tom Harrison," he said, "and I've won a little bet that I've made with myself. When do we start the campaign?"

"Hold on," Toby told him. "I don't know that you're taking part in any campaign. You're engaged to marry Beth, and you'd be subjecting yourself to real danger if you come with us."

Rob gestured angrily. "What the hell kind of a man do you think I am, Toby Holt?" he demanded. "I could never look Beth in the face, much less marry her, if I let you and Frank carry the burden. We agree that Harrison is a menace to the development of civilization in the territory and that he's got to be stopped—now, and for all time! If I didn't take my share of the risks and do my share in squashing him, I couldn't live with myself, much less with Beth. Count me in right now, and I don't want to hear one word of argument from you."

In spite of his private misgivings, Toby was compelled to give in to his friend's wishes.

Toby's followers agreed with him that the sooner he had a showdown with Harrison, the better the situation would be. So he set out at once for Harrison's house, flanked by Rob and Frank and with the other volunteers strung out behind them. All were armed.

What they did not anticipate, however, was that Tom Harrison had foreseen their moves and had outsmarted them. None of his followers were anywhere to be found on the approaches to his house, and the domicile itself proved to be unoccupied.

Slightly bewildered but in no way discouraged by this unexpected development, Toby and his party rode into the center of town. There he told them, "Spread out and talk to everybody you know. I can't imagine that Harrison would run away and avoid this deliberate challenge to his authority. He's probably holed up somewhere in the area, and maybe you can get some leads."

The little band did as he requested. Frank Woods, highly agitated, was the first member of the group to return to the rendezvous that Toby had designated. "Toby," he cried, "Harrison has gone too far. He's abducted Lucy Snow and ridden off into the mountains with her."

Toby stared at him in openmouthed disbelief and then saw that a weeping Bettina was directly behind Frank. Gently, carefully, he calmed her sufficiently so she could tell her story.

"It—it happened so suddenly," Bettina said. "Clarissa and I were sitting in the kitchen of the boardinghouse having a cup of tea, and Lucy was outside in the swing that Frank put on the limb of the oak tree for her. We could see her plainly, and it never crossed our minds that she might be in any danger. The first thing we knew, we heard Lucy scream, and when we jumped to our feet, Harrison was riding off with her. He had two or three men with him, but he was handling Lucy himself. She's only a little girl, of course, so he had no trouble subduing her." She wept quietly.

"Where did Harrison take her?" Toby asked.

"I have no idea," Bettina replied, and began to become hysterical again.

Excusing himself, Toby rode quickly to Clarissa's apartment and found her waiting for him. She spoke concisely and succinctly. "Harrison," she said, "headed toward the mountains with Lucy. It's clear that he abducted her deliberately in order to make certain that you'd follow him."

"That undoubtedly means he's set an ambush for me somewhere," Toby replied soberly.

She nodded, and her expression was grim. "That was part of his motivation, I'm sure. But it was only part."

"What do you mean?" he demanded.

"Harrison has achieved his success by reducing his risks to a minimum," Clarissa replied. "He's shrewd, and he has the wits of a wild animal at bay. When you challenged him today, he had two choices. He could have met you in an open field and taken his chances, or he could have done what he has done. The reason he's been successful in the world is because he's always weighted the odds in his favor, and that's exactly what he's done in this situation. He would have been taking a great risk had he met you in open combat. He's not forgetting—nor is anyone else—that your name is Holt."

Admiring her analytical ability, Toby nodded. "I think I see what you mean," he said. "By kidnapping Lucy, he not only is forcing me to follow him and to fight him on his terms in territory that he selects, but he's greatly increased his own chances of winning because he can use Lucy as a hostage."

"Exactly," Clarissa said. "He's met your challenge, and he's now making his own rules. He's like a poker player who cheats and who starts the game with four aces in his hand."

Toby's expression became grim. "The key is that he cheats," he said. "I was brought up to believe that the cheater always loses, and in this case, I think I'm in a position to prove it."

"Just be careful," Clarissa told him, "not only for your own sake, but for Lucy's."

"Don't you worry," Toby said, "and do your best to calm Bettina. I'm holding Harrison personally responsible for Lucy Snow's welfare, and may God help him if anything happens to her."

In spite of Frank Woods's insistence that something had to be done at once, Toby demurred and ruled that he and his companions would wait until morning before following Tom Harrison and his cohorts into the mountains. "The opportunities for setting an ambush are pretty extensive in the mountains," Toby explained. "The chances of setting a trap, and of leading your enemies into it, are sufficiently great that we'll have to be very careful and watch our step every moment. At night, however, our situation becomes impossible. Under no circumstances can we go searching for a murderer at night in the mountains."

"What about Lucy Snow?" Frank demanded. "My God, Harrison actually has that little girl in his possession."

"And he's counting on that fact," Toby replied, "to cause us to go rushing to our downfall. If I understand Harrison correctly, and I believe I do, he's not going to let anything happen to Lucy. Her continued good health and well-being is his guarantee of safety."

"So you're saying we'll have to wait until morning to follow him," Frank said hotly.

"I'm afraid so," Toby replied.

"Suppose you're wrong?" Frank argued, clenching his huge fists. "Suppose you're not interpreting Harrison correctly? In that case, we'll have the death of Lucy on our souls for the rest of our lives."

Realizing that Frank was deeply in love with Bettina and had a firm attachment to little Lucy as well, Toby felt sorry for him. At the same time, however, he recognized the need to hold firm. "I don't believe that my interpretation of Harrison is wrong," he said, "and I certainly don't intend to place Lucy in unnecessary jeopardy. All the same, I'm saying that we don't head up into the mountains until morning!"

Frank flushed angrily. "Suppose I tell you to go to hell, Toby, and I go after Lucy tonight myself. What then?"

Toby knew that the state of affairs had reached a critical juncture. If he lost control of his subordinates, the rescue effort would become confused, and any advantages they might otherwise gain certainly would be lost. He had served in the Union army long enough to recognize the importance of discipline to any operation.

Therefore, he replied with deliberate, stern vigor. "If you decide to leave the group and go alone, Frank," he said, "I can't stop you, and I certainly won't try. Just keep in mind that you're going to be completely on your own. Not only will you be risking your own neck, but you'll be placing Lucy in far greater jeopardy, too. I leave the decision entirely in your hands."

He turned away quickly, without waiting for an answer. Frank hesitated, and as his friend had hoped, his temper cooled. He gradually realized that Toby was right and agreed to place himself under his friend's command without further objection.

No member of the party slept well during the few hours of the night that they tried to obtain rest. The knowledge that the showdown with Tom Harrison at last was at hand was present in every mind and was compounded by the realization that a little, helpless child had become Harrison's pawn.

Rob Martin expressed the sentiments of the entire group when, sitting before the campfire, he said, "Toby, if I see Harrison and can get him in my sights, I intend to shoot him down at once. There'll be no parleying, no talk, no compromise."

Toby smiled grimly and shook his head. "I appreciate your sentiments, Rob, and ordinarily I'd applaud them. In this instance, however, let me serve notice on you and on Frank and on everyone else that I have a prior claim to Harrison. What's more, since we're acting without legal authority as a vigilante band, I'm the only member of this party who has a foolproof reason that will stand up in any court in the country. Harrison ran off with my wife, who killed herself while she was living with him. No judge and no jury in the United States would convict me of having committed a crime, even if I put a bullet directly between his eyes, which I fully intend to do."

The group stirred long before daybreak, and two of the men cooked the usual frontier breakfast of biscuits and bacon. They ate heartily, washing down the meal with bitter, strong coffee that jarred awake even the sleepiest members.

Then, when the first gray streaks of dawn appeared over the mountains in the east, they saddled their horses and prepared to leave. Before they departed, however, a tearful, deeply worried Bettina Snow appeared at the campsite, escorted by Clarissa Sinclair. Frank went to Bettina immediately and, holding her tenderly in his arms, tried to soothe and console her.

In the meantime, Clarissa said to Toby, "I'm sorry to inflict this burden on you, but Bettina was like a woman possessed by demons. She insisted she had to come and see you off."

"That's understandable," he replied. "She must be half-mad with worry."

"She is," Clarissa replied.

"I'll have a word with her myself before we go," he said.

Trusting his competence, she asked no questions. Clarissa's confidence went farther than that. She could have lectured Toby at length, urging him to be careful in his search for Harrison and warning him to watch out for dangers and pitfalls. Instead, she smiled and said lightly, "Happy hunting."

Toby was strongly reminded of his mother on countless occasions when she had seen his father off on some dangerous, difficult mission. Eulalia had gone to extremes to avoid being emotional and had seemed to take it for granted that her husband would be successful.

Now Clarissa was treating Toby in precisely the same way. There seemed to be no question in her mind that he would find Tom Harrison and dispose of the man successfully, while suffering no serious harm himself. What impressed him most was that this attitude was not feigned. Clarissa obviously had supreme confidence in him.

That confidence, in turn, inevitably made him feel more sure of himself. He grinned at her, and she smiled at him in return. When their eyes met, they both felt a rapport and closeness that made further words unnecessary.

Frank materialized beside him, one arm around the slender shoulders of Bettina Snow, whom he had managed to calm sufficiently that she was no longer weeping.

"I never make promises unless I know I can keep them," Toby told her. "So all I'm going to say to you is that we aim to do our very best for you and Lucy. I'm very fond of that little girl, and I want her to come to no harm. So trust me—trust all of us."

"I do," Bettina replied. "I pray with all my heart that you'll bring her back to me safely and in good health."

Toby grinned at her reassuringly as he vaulted into the saddle. The dirty gray smudges to the east were spreading across the sky, and daylight was increasing rapidly. "I reckon we'll be on our way now, boys," he said. "Keep your eyes open, and your powder dry!"

The pursuers had two natural advantages that stood them in good stead. First was the intimate knowledge that Toby and Rob had acquired of the terrain through which they were traveling, thanks to their surveying efforts. They knew every inch of the mountains, every turn and twist in the trail, every hidden valley, every possible site for an ambush.

Second was Toby's ability to get along in the wilderness, a quality that he had acquired from his father. He rode at the head of the single-file column, several paces in advance of Rob Martin, who was second in the line, and his dog trotted near him.

Not until that afternoon, however, did they encounter their first sign of Harrison and his cohorts. They crossed the top of a peak almost nine thousand feet above sea level, and as they began to descend the eastern slope, Toby turned to Rob, who was riding behind him. "You better pass along the word," he said. "We're heading toward Blind Alley Valley, and it strikes me that would be a natural place for Harrison to set a trap for us."

Rob thought for a brief moment, then nodded. "I hadn't thought of it," he said, "but the valley is a perfect place for an ambush. We'll come on to it without warning, and thanks to the double hairpin we'll have to make before we descend from the heights, we won't be able to see whether there's anybody lying in wait for us." He turned to Frank Woods and repeated the warning, and Frank, in turn, passed along the word to the man behind him.

As they drew closer to the area that Toby had called Blind Alley Valley, he slowed his pace, cocked his rifle, and held it across his pommel, ready for instant use. His senses were alert, and he felt the tingling of excitement that came with the knowledge that serious danger threatened.

Without being told, Mr. Blake moved ahead of his master now, and he, too, proceeded cautiously, stopping now and again to raise his head, cock his ears, and sniff. All at once the dog stiffened, and the hair on his body rose.

"What is it, Mr. Blake?" Toby called softly. "What have you discovered?"

A faint, barely audible growl sounded in the shepherd's throat.

That was the only warning Toby needed. He halted, threw his reins to Rob, and proceeded on foot, taking care to remain close to the huge boulders that lined the inside of the narrow trail.

Suddenly he realized he was not alone. Frank Woods had dismounted, too, and had crept forward with a quiet that was unusual for a man of his bulk.

Mr. Blake remained in the lead and seemed to slink now, rather than walk. He was showing the influence of the time he had spent with the wolf pack, Toby knew, and he was glad that the animal had acquired this valuable characteristic. Certainly no foes waiting at the head of the valley that opened beyond the double hairpin turn directly ahead would have any idea that the dog was approaching them.

As they drew near to the second of the turns, Toby gestured silently, and the dog obeyed him instantly, dropping back and remaining at his heels. Glancing back over his shoulder, Toby saw that Rob had reacted with his usual efficiency and had organized the volunteers for a surprise attack. A half-dozen of the men had dismounted and were following on Frank Woods's heels. The others remained mounted and were handling all the horses. But they, too, were prepared for an emergency and had their rifles ready for immediate use.

Toby halted, held up a hand for silence, and peered with extreme caution around the boulder on the inside of the final turn into Blind Alley Valley. He was in no way surprised when he saw at least a dozen roughly dressed men fanned out so they covered the trail completely. All of them had their rifles in their hands, prepared to open fire the moment their pursuers appeared.

Unfortunately for them, however, they did not take Toby Holt into their calculations. They were expecting to see mounted men, and Toby and his volunteers were on foot. Even more important, the pursuers saw their foes and were able to study their formation before Harrison's men realized that they were under enemy scrutiny.

Patting the shepherd dog in order to quiet the animal and prevent him from springing forward onto the foe, Toby quickly analyzed the situation. His major question now was whether to fire each of the weapons under his command in sequence or whether to discharge a volley. After considering the problem briefly, he concluded that the volley would be far more effective if the fire was accurate, because it would do a great deal toward demoralizing Harrison's supporters. He was not for a moment forgetting that, in all, he and his band of volunteers were outnumbered by four or five to one, odds that had to be overcome if he was to succeed in his mission. Beckoning to his men to get into position for firing, Toby took careful aim at a burly lumberjack, who appeared directly in his sights. He had to take the slight risk of speaking in order to achieve his end, so he called softly, "Ready . . . aim . . . fire!"

Eight rifles sounded almost as one, and the results were all that Toby could have wished. His own bullet drilled into the head of the enemy, who slumped to the ground and died without making a sound.

Frank Woods was equally successful. He shot another man, who threw his hands high in the air and screamed in pain and terror as he pitched forward onto the ground to die.

The volunteers succeeded in wounding several other of the men who had set an ambush for them. Toby at no time was certain of the results, and they did not matter, for Harrison's cohorts took to their heels and fled, the wounded dragging themselves to safety behind their companions, and the bodies of their two dead left in the open.

Toby was tempted to order his men to open fire and shoot down their fleeing would-be attackers, but he refrained. He had no quarrel with these misguided lumberjacks and others, who, through favors of financial assistance and fear, had become followers of Tom Harrison. He felt that if he did not press them too hard and anger them into making a last-ditch stand, perhaps they would desert Harrison.

Toby was disappointed that he had not actually encountered Tom Harrison himself, but he counseled himself to be patient. He had drawn first blood and had emerged victorious from the struggle, with his own supporters suffering no casualties. Certainly Harrison would think twice before trying to set another ambush, and his followers would be reluctant to participate in such a venture.

The tide, Toby thought, was beginning to turn in his favor, and he hoped he was right, that he wasn't merely indulging in wishful thinking.

"I'm sorry that Cindy couldn't join me at supper this evening," Eulalia Holt said, "but she has an exam tomorrow, and we agreed she'd be better off using her time studying for it." She smiled down the length of the mahogany dining room table in Lee Blake's house at Fort Vancouver.

Lee Blake, trim in his uniform of blue and gold, grinned in return. "Next time, we'll be sure to have you over on a weekend when Cindy can come with you." He turned to his daughter. "You'll entertain her, won't you, Beth?"

The girl nodded dully, and her reply was lethargic. "If you say so, Papa," she replied dutifully but without enthusiasm.

"That's kind of you, Beth—Lee," Eulalia said, "and I appreciate it—for Cindy's sake. She's at such an impressionable age, and I'm delighted she has Beth to look up to."

The general smiled. "I must warn you that there are many young lieutenants at the fort who are bound to turn Cindy's head. They certainly did with Beth when she was in her mid-teens."

Eulalia replied with a light in her eyes. "I know of no better way to get Cindy's mind off the recent tragedy than to return her thoughts to normal channels. Meaning—boys."

Lee joined in her laugh. Beth, however, remained somber and did not even smile.

Her father glanced at her curiously. "Are you feeling ill, Beth?"

She shook her head. "No, I'm fine," she answered, and there was a hint of curtness in her tone.

Her father and their guest finished their coffee, and then Lee suggested, "If you'd like, Eulalia, I'd recommend a walk up to the artillery batteries that overlook the Columbia. The view of the river is rather spectacular there, and if you haven't seen it, it's well worth the effort of the climb."

"By all means," she answered cheerfully.

"You want to come with us, Beth?" Lee asked.

The young woman shook her head. "No, thanks. I've seen the view of the river from there many times. Besides, I wouldn't want to intrude."

Lee blinked in surprise. Eulalia, however, immediately understood the full implications of the remark and refused to allow it to pass unchallenged. "You're never intruding when you go somewhere with your father and me," she said firmly. "We have nothing to hide, and we're not looking for privacy."

Lee was embarrassed by her candor.

Beth, however, gave no sign that she had even heard her remark. "If you'll excuse me, I think I'll go to my room," she said. "I have a headache." She left the dining room without a backward glance.

General Blake and his guest went to the front hall where he kept his dress hat and his sword, and as he was donning them, he said, "You may want to help yourself to a short cloak. It's quite windy up on the promontory, and at this time of year it's often a bit chilly."

Eulalia looked at the cloak hanging from a wall peg and hesitated very briefly. "You're sure you won't mind?"

"Why should I mind?" Lee's bewilderment was genuine.

"This cloak was one of Cathy's," she said. "I distinctly recall her wearing it on several occasions."

"It will still protect you from the wind," Lee told her lightly, "and that, as I understand it, is the purpose of a cloak."

Eulalia was silent as they left the house and started up to the hill that overlooked the river. "It's just as well that Beth didn't come with us," she said at last.

"How so?" he asked.

Eulalia again hesitated and then decided to face the issue squarely. "I feel quite certain," she said, "that Beth is piqued because you and I have been seeing each other rather frequently of late."

Lee was shocked. "But that's absurd," he replied. "We've been good friends for years, and we've gone through all kinds of trials together. Now we're linked together in a mutual tragedy. It's only natural we should see something of each other."

"That," Eulalia replied slowly, "is spoken from your viewpoint—and, if you will, from mine. But that isn't the way Beth sees us."

"I honestly don't understand," he murmured, and leaned on the rail that had been built around the heights on which the guns were located.

Eulalia joined him at the rail and, standing beside him, stared down at the mighty Columbia River below. Precisely as Lee had said, the view was extraordinary, and for the moment she forgot everything else. "You're quite right when you say the climb is well worth the effort," she said. "I thought I knew the Columbia River from every angle, but this sight is new to me, and it's breathtaking. It's like having a bird's-eye view."

"I'm glad you like it," Lee replied.

The issue between them was not yet resolved, and Eulalia braced herself. "In a nutshell, Lee, Beth resents our friendship. She sees us both as being disloyal. You to your late wife, and me to my late husband, not to mention my disloyalty to Cathy, my close friend."

"But that's ridiculous," he said indignantly.

Eulalia spread her hands on the rail. "Absurd or realistic, that's the way she feels," she said. "Beth has taken her mother's passing quite hard. It's foolish to indulge in comparisons, I know, but Cindy is a far more practical girl, who lacks Beth's imagination and, I daresay, is less sensitive. Well, Cindy has accepted the loss of her father quite well. She knows that no matter how hard she grieves, he won't come back to life, and she's trying to rebuild her own life."

Lee nodded and seemed lost in thought.

"I'm sorry, my dear," Eulalia said, placing a hand on his arm. "I certainly didn't mean to upset you. That was my last intention."

"I'm upset for a very private reason that I feel I must explain to you. Forgive me, Eulalia, for being premature, but I'd do you a disservice if I were less than honest with you."

"Of course," she murmured, and as she stood close to him, looking up to him, she was reminded of the many days they had spent together on the long wagon train journey across the country to Oregon. There had been many tensions and hardships along the way, but they had survived them and come out intact. She hoped that she and Lee retained enough of that resilience and endurance to see them through this present embarrassment.

"It's quite true," he began, "that we've seen a great deal of each other since the tragedy."

"Yes," Eulalia replied, interrupting him, "but that's been only natural, at least in my opinion. We've been leaning on each other for support."

"That's the way I've looked at it," he said. "Certainly romance has been farthest from my mind."

"From mine, too," she added, laughing.

"But I've got to be completely honest with you," Lee said. "Just in the last day or two, I've detected a change in my attitude. I've been aware of you as an exceptionally handsome woman, and I've been conscious of myself as a man who isn't quite ready to go into a home for aged veterans of the Grand Army of the Republic. We share so much in the way of backgrounds that I couldn't help wondering, frankly, whether you'd be too shocked if I suddenly proposed marriage to you."

Eulalia met his steady gaze without flinching, neither moving farther from him nor inching closer. The subject was too important for subterfuge of any kind. "I can't say I'd be shocked," she replied slowly. "I'd think it rather normal and natural to be asked."

"And what would you reply?"

She looked at him, and her eyes became mischievous when she shook her head. "That, sir, is a question that can be answered in only one way. When you actually propose, you'll be given an appropriate answer."

Lee knew she was not being coquettish and that he deserved the good-natured rebuke. "I stand corrected," he said, "and I shall certainly keep your words of wisdom in mind for future reference."

"Good," she said emphatically but demurely.

He reached out, touched her hand on the rail, and then covered it with his own. "I don't want to be insensitive, Eulalia," he said. "I know it's too soon after the tragedy to be thinking in such terms. For the sake of the proprieties as well as our own peace of mind, I think we should take a longer period of time and devote some serious thought to the matter."

"I shall," she said, "and if you want the absolute truth, Lee, the idea of our getting together has occurred to me lately, just as it has to you. It's obvious to me that whether we admit it or not, we've been drawn toward each other."

He nodded. "It's a hopeful sign, I think. It seems to point down a road toward the future."

Eulalia shrugged. "Perhaps it does, and perhaps it doesn't. There may be too many obstacles in our joint path. I must say one thing for Beth: I give her credit for being far more sensitive to the moods and feelings of others than I have ever before given her credit for being. She saw something in our relationship that we ourselves failed to see."

"That's quite true," Lee murmured, and then added far more forcibly, "but it's no excuse for her to mope about as though we're defiling the memories of Cathy and Whip."

"She's young," Eulalia said. "Very young. But I refuse to worry about her attitude toward us now, or about what Toby might think. It's a mistake to jump ahead. We'll go one step at a time, and if ultimately we reach a point where we decide we want to live our lives together, then we'll face the issue of how to deal with our children."

Toby Holt knew his imagination was playing tricks on him; nevertheless, he could have sworn that he was being guided by the spirit of his father as he led his volunteers on the second day of his hunt for Tom Harrison and his cohorts.

Ascending steadily onto higher and higher

ground, Toby seemed to pick the best routes and paths as though Whip were really whispering at his shoulder. When he had a choice of two routes, he invariably chose the easier, the one that imposed less strain on the men and the horses. He seemed to sense every locale that could have been used for an ambush, and repeatedly he sat alone on his mount, peering off into space, and then choosing his next move.

Harrison knew he was being followed, and he used evasive tactics. But Toby proved impossible to shake. No matter what Harrison tried, Toby clung to him and continued to follow.

One encouraging sign was the attrition that took place in Harrison's ranks. Many of his men found the demands being made too much for them, and any number were unable to maintain the blistering pace. Neither fear nor the promise of greater rewards influenced them, and they dropped by the wayside to return to Tumwater as best they were able.

Several of these men were intercepted by Toby's volunteers, and questioning them closely, he was relieved to learn that Lucy was still alive and well. Those who had served Harrison were unanimous in their insistence that the child was well fed and that she rode a horse all day and was never forced to exert herself physically. Toby, however, would not be satisfied until the child was safely in his own possession.

Climbing above the timberline, the pursuers arrived in a region of natural citadels. Every individual height was protected by its own walls of stone and by heavy boulders that rendered it difficult, if not impossible, to storm.

When a hail of sniper fire was directed at the column, Toby promptly called a halt and ordered his men to take cover. The task he had set for himself had been difficult, and now it was rapidly becoming almost impossible to carry off successfully.

Three of the volunteers came to Toby at the point where he sat his mount behind a high boulder. "Cap'n Holt," the leader of the trio said without preamble, "we reckon we've had enough, and we want to get us back to Tumwater. When we volunteered for this here job, we didn't know we'd be climbing around in the wilderness like mountain goats."

Toby could afford to lose no followers, but he met the challenge with seeming calm. "You lads will have to do what you think best," he said. "There's no way I can force you to stay on with me, and I sure wouldn't try."

The trio exchanged uncertain looks. "What about you, Cap'n? If you know what's good for you, you'll turn back, too."

Toby smiled and shook his head. "No, boys, I'm going to keep going until I rescue that little girl and come home with Tom Harrison's scalp hanging from my belt. I'm not a quitter!" By implication, he was accusing them of being cowards, and their uneasiness increased.

"I ain't never been one to walk out in the middle of a job, myself," a burly lumberjack muttered. "I reckon you can count on me to stick around as long as you want."

"Me, too," the second of the trio muttered.

The leader, finding himself deserted, hastily abandoned his stand. "I left Tumwater with you, and I'll stick around until I can go back with you," he said.

Toby thanked them calmly, as though nothing

out of the ordinary had happened, and then he was forced to think in earnest. He had overcome one crisis, but he knew human nature well enough to realize that others soon would follow. His entire band soon would become discouraged, and there would be defections that he could ill afford.

He realized that in one way or another, he had to force the issue and confront Tom Harrison at once. The plan that came to his mind occurred to him full-blown, and he thought of it so easily and quickly that once again he had the feeling his father's spirit was guiding him. He weighed the scheme, and unable to find any fault with it, he moved forward to the position that Rob and Frank were holding at the boulders nearest the trail. Outlining his plan to them, Toby told them, "Cover me while I go forward, and keep an eye on Mr. Blake for me. I don't want him getting involved, much less hurt."

His friends stared at him. "You'd be mad to take such risks," Frank said fiercely.

"Stay put, Toby," Rob said. "You've already shown your courage, and you don't have to go to such lengths. We'll think of something."

"Just do as I've asked you," Toby replied firmly. "Cover me for sniper fire, and if anybody tries to shoot me, take care of him in a hurry. And, Rob, look after Mr. Blake."

Rob knew it was useless to argue with Toby when his mind was made up, so he went up to Mr. Blake, looped a length of rope around the dog's collar, and tied the end to his horse's reins. "Sorry to do this to you, Mr. Blake," he said. "I feel as bad about it as you do, but we're up against it, both of us. We've got to do what we're told."

Their expressions bleak, Rob and Frank watched Toby ride into the open, a white handkerchief flying from his upraised rifle as a flag of truce.

The shepherd dog made strenuous attempts to join him, trying to leap forward and break the hold of the leash that held him back. Unable to break the bond, he whimpered in frustration.

Toby rode forward boldly about fifteen or twenty paces and then drew to a halt. There was no sound, no sign of the enemy, but he knew that Harrison and his men were there hiding behind boulders and waiting to overwhelm him and his band. All at once a rifle sounded, and a bullet sang out, passing about three feet above Toby's head to his left. A sniper had ignored his flag of truce.

But Rob Martin obeyed his close friend's instructions to the letter. His own rifle spoke an instant later, and a rider toppled to the ground within sight of Toby and lay still in the dust.

"Honor this white flag," Toby called clearly, "and there will be no more random killing. We don't believe in it, and I imagine you boys value your lives too much to stick your necks out."

The silence that followed was profound.

"Are you there, Harrison?" Toby called. "Do you hear me?"

There was no reply.

Toby regarded the silence as encouraging. Had Harrison been elsewhere, one of his lieutenants undoubtedly would have responded. The failure to answer meant, in all probability, that Harrison indeed was there.

"You've been running away from me for days, Harrison," he called. "You even had to kidnap a little girl in the hope of protecting your own hide. You like to think of yourself as master of Tumwater, but you don't act like the master of anything. Either you accept my challenge of man-to-man combat, or I'll drive you out of town for all time, and the men who've been following you will pitch in and help me. What do you say to that?"

There was no sound from the boulders and heights beyond, but Toby could sense the uneasiness in the air. No man who ruled by fear as Tom Harrison did could refuse the challenge that had been issued to him.

Toby was not bluffing, and he hoped that Harrison knew it. Harrison's kingdom, built on corruption, crime, and fear, was bound to crumble when the personal courage of the ruling individual was at stake. This was the way of the West, a country that had its own strict, inviolable codes of behavior. Newcomers here soon learned to abide by these laws or to perish.

Tom Harrison had survived for a long time as the head of his fiefdom because no one had seen fit to challenge him. His bulk, his personal strength, and his ruthlessness had seen to that. Now, at last, someone who was not afraid of him had challenged him to personal combat, and if Harrison refused or ignored the challenge, his world would crumble away. To Toby's gratification, he recognized Harrison's harsh voice. "What you got in mind, Holt?"

"First off," Toby replied promptly, "ride out in the open where I can see you—if you dare."

Even some of the enemy laughed.

His face red, Tom Harrison rode into the open. His clothes were rumpled, and he looked as though he had not rested since the pursuit had begun.

Toby felt very confident as he called, "Here are my terms. We use neither rifles nor handguns. I happen to have heard that you're pretty good with throwing knives, and I suggest we use those. Each of us will carry only six knives, and no other weapons will be permitted. If we miss each other with the knives, we'll fight with our bare fists until one or the other is vanquished." He knew, as did his auditors, that he was proposing an unusual fight to the death. No personal enmity that had progressed this far could be settled unless one or the other of the combatants was killed.

Harrison absorbed the terms in silence. "What about our horses?" he demanded at last. "Do we ride them, or must we fight on foot?"

Toby shrugged. "I'll leave that strictly up to you."

"Then I choose to ride," Harrison replied promptly.

"Do I gather that you accept my other terms?" Toby demanded. Harrison hesitated. "Either you accept," Toby told him harshly, "or you'll be disowned by every last person in Tumwater for your lack of manhood."

Harrison's face glowed a beet red. "I accept," he said quickly.

Toby was elated. "Good. We'll both return to this spot in exactly fifteen minutes." Turning, he rode back to his own followers, disappearing behind the boulders. Rob and Frank could not hide their consternation as they stared at him. "Now I know you're crazy," Rob said flatly.

"No man can win a fight on the terms you've outlined," Frank said. "You're sure to die."

Toby looked at each of his friends in turn,

grinned, and shook his head. "Sorry to disappoint you boys, but I'm going to take care of Tom Harrison once and for all."

"You're going to face that brute without firearms when he's carrying six throwing knives," Frank said. "That's suicidal."

"It is not," Toby replied emphatically. "I expect you're both familiar with throwing knives?"

His companions nodded their heads. It was not uncommon for men of the West to know how to use knives as well as guns.

"Well, then, you know they're not easy to use," he said. "They require a special knack and a special skill that takes years to acquire. Most people assume that all you've got to do is pick up a knife, aim it, and throw it. I assure you that not one shot in a thousand will find its target when thrown by an amateur."

"Do I gather that you don't consider yourself an amateur?" Rob demanded.

Toby smiled thoughtfully. "I was no older than little Lucy Snow when my father started to give me instructions in the art of knife throwing. We practiced for many years, long after he started to teach me to use firearms. I don't want to brag, but I think I can hold my own with just about anybody who wields a knife."

"If I'd known all this," Rob said, relieved, "I wouldn't have worried."

"I don't mind telling you that I'm plenty worried," Frank Woods muttered. "You're going into personal combat with Tom Harrison, and just because such combat is honorable doesn't mean that he's going to behave honorably. In fact, I'd be mighty surprised if he abides by the rules. He sees a chance to get rid of somebody who's been nagging at him for a long time, and he's not going to miss his chance."

"If he succeeds in tricking me," Toby said quietly, "I'll leave it up to you to retrieve my honor for me, Frank. Just remember that you're not going to rescue Lucy until Harrison has been disposed of."

"I'm not forgetting it. Not for one minute," Frank assured him.

Toby handed his firearms to Rob, then unwrapped his saddle roll and removed his throwing knives. These bone-handled weapons, with exceptionally sharp blades of the finest English steel, had been made a generation and more earlier for Whip Holt, who had given them to his son. Their balance was perfect, and Toby smiled grimly as he weighed each in his hand, testing it before carefully placing it in his belt. Then Toby rode out again into the flat, open space beyond the boulders. He raised one hand in a final salute to his friends, then sat his stallion, quietly waiting for Tom Harrison to appear.

The quarter of an hour that Toby had specified elapsed, but there was no sign of the other man. After waiting another five minutes, Toby was on the verge of announcing that the match had been forfeited and that Tom Harrison was a coward. Before he could call out, however, Harrison rode rapidly into the open, relying on the tactics of surprise to unnerve his opponent.

Toby, however, remained steady and unmoving. He noted instantly that contrary to the rules to which he had agreed, Harrison was carrying a cocked Colt six-shooter. If he killed his opponent, it was obvious that he would brag to his subordinates that he had outsmarted a naive foe. As he raised his gun, intending to shoot the defenseless Toby in cold blood, the younger man swiftly reached into his belt and plucked a throwing knife from it.

The revolver was being lowered and was aimed at him as he let fly with the knife. His aim proved true, and the blade sliced into Harrison's hand between his thumb and forefinger, forcing him to release his grip on the trigger. His moan of pain broke the silence, and as his now-useless gun fell to the ground, blood spurted from his wound.

He ignored his injury, not taking the time to retreat and bind it in order to stop the flow of blood. He lost his temper, and an animallike roar echoed across the mountains. Tom Harrison was determined to kill his foe as rapidly as he could.

The duel that followed was so incredible that it was remembered by the witnesses as long as they lived. Both of the horsemen resorted to unorthodox riding tactics, galloping, halting abruptly, sending their mounts first in one direction and then in another.

Toby had spent his whole life in the saddle and was completely at home in combat of this sort. He was forced to admit, however, that Harrison was his match. The man might rely on bluster and bravado to have his way, but in riding he knew few peers. He hurled a knife at the younger man, and only Toby's quick reflexes allowed him to escape being hit.

Now it was Toby's turn, and he flipped another blade at Harrison, lofting it into the air so that it rose gracefully and then plummeted like an arrow. Unfortunately, however, his stallion started to plunge just as he released the blade, and the jarring movement spoiled his aim, sending the knife harmlessly into the ground, a foot or two from the place where Harrison was sitting his mount.

As the spectators on both sides watched breathlessly, the strange duel went on. Toby was by far the more expert at knife throwing, but Harrison seemed to enjoy an almost magically protected existence. Each time his opponent hurled a knife, his horse caused him to shift his position, and thus Toby's aim was spoiled.

Harrison was wild in his use of the knife blades, and soon he, like Toby, had exhausted his supply. Now, according to the rules that Toby had outlined and to which Harrison had agreed, they would fight with their bare hands.

Toby was eager to bring the fight to an end, and consequently he dismounted. He knew from the gleam in his foe's dark eyes that Harrison intended to ride him down and trample him to death beneath his horse's hooves.

But Toby was prepared for precisely such a trick. Having grown up on a ranch where horses were raised, he understood the animals and, even more important, had no fear of them.

It was this intimate knowledge that he was relying on now as a surprise tactic in this grim battle to the death. Bracing himself, he waited, a half-smile on his face.

Now Harrison dug his spurs into his stallion's flanks and sent the mount shooting forward. Rob Martin cried out a warning, and Frank Woods cursed loudly and bitterly, thinking that his friend had been tricked.

But Toby held his ground quietly as the great beast thundered toward him. He remained completely calm, and his tranquillity was not feigned. He knew what no one else present, including Tom Harrison, even suspected: the man's horse, having been subjected to rigorous training, would not overrun or crash into a human being unless he felt menaced. Therefore, Toby realized that as long as he stood very still and made no move that the stallion might regard as threatening, the animal would avoid him. There was nothing more he needed to do in order to avert a disastrous collision.

Harrison, indifferent to the fact that he had broken the agreed rules of the combat, could think only that his hated rival was about to be eliminated for all time. His eyes gleamed, and his lips were parted in a half-sneer, half-smile as he urged his stallion to even greater speed. The thundering of hooves echoed and reechoed across the mountain wastelands.

Toby continued to stand very still, his expression confident. The stallion bore down on him, and Frank Woods, unable to tolerate the suspense, averted his gaze. Suddenly, however, Rob Martin grasped his arm. "Look, Frank," he gasped in utter disbelief.

When only a hairbreadth from the man who stood in his path, the stallion suddenly swerved and passed so close to Toby that he actually grazed the man. But there was no collision, and Toby was unhurt.

Toby now took advantage of the opportunity that presented itself to him. Realizing that the most astonished person on the field was his opponent, he reached up, caught hold of Harrison's leg, and pulled with all his might. The gesture was so unexpected that Harrison slipped, losing his balance, and reached out an arm to steady himself.

This gesture, too, Toby had anticipated, and catching hold of the man's arm, he hauled him out of the saddle as the stallion thundered on alone down the field, finally being halted by one of the volunteers, who grabbed his reins.

As Harrison tumbled to the ground, his momentum carried Toby with him, and he, too, fell. They rolled over and over, their arms and legs entangled, and Toby immediately launched the fistfight that he had anticipated as the next phase of the struggle. He lashed out repeatedly, his blows catching his enemy on the face and the upper portions of his body.

Although taken unaware, Harrison had a natural advantage. He was so big, so solidly built that his capacity for absorbing punishment was limitless, and the blows of his opponent, although delivered with considerable force, seemed to have no effect.

Toby's mind continued to function clearly, and he soon recognized the extent of his predicament. He was inflicting little or no damage on Harrison, but he knew that one or two blows from the larger man's hamlike fists were certain to jar him. He quickly abandoned any idea he may have harbored of standing toe to toe and engaging in a slugfest.

Having accomplished his original objective, he did not push for a further advantage and, scrambling to his feet, retreated a safe distance out of range of Harrison's long reach.

Tom Harrison hauled himself to his feet more slowly, and he and his wiry foe stood facing each other. At least, Toby reflected, they were meeting now on equal terms. Neither was armed, neither was mounted, and what happened from this point on in the fight depended on the courage, abilities, and stamina of the combatants.

Toby instantly recognized the need to develop special tactics, since his physical strength was no match for that of his burly opponent. What he had to do, he reflected, was to inflict punishment as best he could while staying out of range of Harrison's murderous reach. He acted accordingly, and weaving, bobbing, and sidestepping so that he did not present a stationary target, he darted in, his fists flailing. He caught Harrison with a left jab to the cheekbone that jarred the giant, and he followed it with a hard, short left that caught Harrison in the eye and caused him to wince.

Retreating instantly, Toby danced out of reach. He was encouraged to note that his foe's left eye was swollen and was closing. Taking full advantage of this small break in his favor, he darted toward his opponent again and made Harrison's left eye his primary target. He struck it with a long left and hard jabbing right and knew he had caused sufficient distress to prevent Harrison from pursuing him too rapidly as he again retreated.

Toby never allowed himself to forget what Whip had taught him: when you employ tactics that succeed, keep using them until they are no longer effective. That rule was basic. So Toby moved in for the third time, well aware of the fact that his opponent had not landed a single blow, while the damage he himself had inflicted was considerable.

He quickly sensed from Harrison's defense that the man was favoring his left eye. Therefore, Toby chose a new target and began to concentrate on his foe's right cheekbone. He delivered his blows quickly and sharply, his feet always on the move, and he was gratified when he landed four smashes in succession. His knuckles stung, but he saw that he had opened a cut on Harrison's face that was bleeding profusely. This time, as Toby started to weave backward again out of range, Harrison's frustration and anger got the better of him, and he suddenly launched a hard kick at his foe, aiming his heavy boot at Toby's groin.

Had the kick found its target, Toby would have been severely injured. But instinctively he leaped out of the way and at the same time reached for the offending foot. Toby's fingers closed around the bigger man's ankle, and Toby jerked his arm upward, causing Harrison to lose his balance. He crashed to the ground, his head striking the edge of a boulder, and he lay where he had fallen.

Toby did not move too close to him, suspecting that Harrison was trying to trick him again by feigning injury. The big man groaned, then sat up slowly and pulled himself to his feet. There was no longer any doubt that he had suffered a major injury when he had struck his head.

"He's groggy, Toby!" Frank Woods shouted.

"Finish him off!" Rob Martin added.

The cries of encouragement to Toby infuriated the bull-like Harrison all the more, and bellowing inarticulately, his face puffy and bleeding, he charged toward his foe, his shoulders hunched, his fists flailing.

Toby knew better than to face such an onslaught and to absorb the fury of Harrison's attack. He backed cautiously from his foe, occasionally glancing over his shoulder to make certain he did not approach too close to the precipice behind him. There was a drop of two or three thousand feet from the cliff to

the rocks and boulders of the canyon below, and a
tumble, as he well knew, would prove fatal.

Infuriated by his inability to land a single blow,
Harrison called, "Stand still and fight, damn you!"

Toby paid no attention to the challenge. As Harrison lumbered toward him, he sidestepped once
again. His patience exhausted, Harrison cursed his opponent volubly and at length.

Ever aware of his proximity to the lip of the
precipice, Toby circled warily on the balls of his
feet, waiting for an opportune moment to strike again.
But Harrison had no intention of waiting, and he insisted on carrying the struggle to his opponent. He
well realized that young Holt, living up to his great
name, was making a fool of him in the presence of his
supporters. Lowering his head, his shoulders hunched,
Harrison lunged forward like a mad bull. Certainly he
had lost his reason and was consumed by only one
thought, the idea of crushing this foe who had dared
to defeat him in every form of combat in which they
had yet engaged.

Toby sidestepped deftly. Harrison's momentum
continued to carry him forward, toward the edge of
the cliff.

"Watch out!" Toby cried involuntarily.

Tom Harrison could not halt, however. He had
thrown himself forward with such vigor that it was
impossible for him to slow his pace or to turn aside.
Before he quite realized what was happening to him,
he ran right off the lip of the precipice.

His scream of terror sounded inhuman as it
echoed through the mountains. Within a moment or
two it died away, and Tom Harrison fell to his death

more than two thousand feet below the place where he had engaged in combat for the last time.

There was a stunned silence on both sides of the high boulders. Harrison's foes and friends alike were astonished by the sudden, tragic end to the fight. Toby was too dazed to think clearly.

Then one of Harrison's supporters, still unseen, expressed the sentiments of virtually everyone present when he cried out, "Nobody ever beats a Holt!" That comment firmly established for all time the myth of Toby Holt's invincibility.

Suddenly a bedraggled figure appeared from behind the boulders where Harrison's supporters were still concealed. Lucy Snow, her long hair wild, her dress torn, walked uncertainly into the open. Her wrists and ankles had been bound, but the thongs that had held them had just been cut by one of the men and were dragging behind her. She halted and stared uncertainly at Toby, only half recognizing him.

Frank Woods dismounted and bounded forward into the open, his arms extended as he shouted, "Lucy!"

The child flew to him, and Toby was uncertain whether she was laughing or crying. Frank swept her off her feet, and they hugged fiercely, with the little girl burying her face in the man's broad shoulder.

Feeling began to return to Toby. The knot, which had seemed a permanent part of him since it had formed in his stomach, dissolved, and he felt as though a great weight had been lifted from him. Tom Harrison had met the fate he had deserved, and there was no pity to be wasted on him. As for Lucy, she appeared none the worse for her grueling experience.

Frank held the child at arm's length and exam-

ined her carefully. "Are you all right, Lucy?" he asked
anxiously. "You're not hurt?"

"I—I'm all right," the child replied in a tiny voice,
"but I'm hungry, Uncle Frank."

He frowned and glared in the direction of the
boulders. "Did they give you anything to eat?" he demanded.

"Oh, yes," she said. "They gave me breakfast and
dinner and supper every day, but I was so scared I
couldn't eat much. Now, all of a sudden, I'm hungry."

Frank grinned at her. "I think we can do something about that," he told her. "What do you think,
Toby?"

Toby smiled at the little girl, too, as he approached. "Your mother is terribly worried about you,
Lucy, so we want to get you back down to her in
Tumwater as rapidly as we can, but I guess we'll be
unavoidably delayed for a couple of hours while we
hunt for some meat and have us a little feast. What
do you say to that?"

The child clasped her hands together. "I say it's
wonderful," she declared.

There was a sudden movement behind the boulders and rocks at the far end of the field, and then
Tom Harrison's supporters rode into the open. Trumbull, who led them, carried a white flag.

Rob Martin immediately led the still-armed volunteers onto the field.

Looking upset but in control of his emotions,
Trumbull approached Toby and dismounted. "We
surrender to you, Mr. Holt," he said, "and I can't say
any of us is too sorry for what happened to Tom. He
had that kind of an end coming to him, you might
say."

"You understand, I'm sure," Toby said, speaking loudly enough so the entire group could hear him, "that we intend to bring charges against you. There's going to be a new sheriff in Tumwater, and this time his jail is going to be full."

"That's fair enough," Trumbull replied meekly, "but I hope you understand that none of us had anything to do with the kidnapping of this little girl. That was strictly Tom's idea and was all his doing."

"That's right," Lucy said. "He was a bad man, and he wouldn't listen when the others told him to let me go home."

"For the sake of all of you," Toby said, "I'm relieved to hear that you're not too severely implicated in the abduction of Lucy Snow. As for the other charges that will be brought against you, you'll have an opportunity to prove your innocence or to suffer if you're guilty. The one thing I can promise you is that there's a new day ahead for all of the Washington Territory, and that includes Tumwater. The laws of the United States and of the territory are going to be obeyed, and any man who breaks them will suffer the consequences. Anybody who demonstrates that he's not a criminal and that he intends to live decently will have the right to do so."

On his instructions, the members of Harrison's group surrendered their weapons, and having been rendered harmless, they joined the victors at supper later that day, after an antelope had been killed and cooked.

After the meal Lucy fell asleep in Frank's arms, and at his suggestion the ride down to Tumwater was begun at once.

The men rode until the small hours of the morning before they finally halted to enjoy a brief respite. Lucy was blissfully unaware of all that went on around her, and safe in Frank's embrace, she slept soundly.

When the march was resumed, Toby maintained a lively pace, wasting no time as he hurried back to town. When they reached the outskirts of Tumwater, he called Frank Woods to the head of the column.

"I think we'll part company here for the present, Frank," he said. "Rob and I want to prefer charges against these friends of Harrison's, and that will take us time. I think you have something else to occupy you."

"I reckon I do," Frank replied, grinning broadly, and cantered off, one arm firmly encircling the little girl who clung to him.

Clarissa had been keeping Bettina Snow company during her ordeal and answered the summons when Frank tapped at the door of Bettina's apartment.

She saw Lucy, and, her face wreathed in smiles, she called over her shoulder, "Bettina! Come quickly!"

Bettina, still in her nightdress and robe after a sleepless night, came into the living room, and when she saw her daughter, silent tears of relief and joy streamed down her face. She dropped to her knees, and she and Lucy kissed and hugged repeatedly. Clarissa vanished discreetly and silently into the kitchen.

At last Bettina looked up at Frank, whose eyes were suspiciously damp as he watched the reunion. She questioned him silently.

"Lucy is fine," he said, "and Harrison won't be committing any more crimes."

She nodded.

Speaking succinctly, Frank told her how Toby had fought Harrison but did not have the man's death staining his hands or his conscience. "He actually killed himself," Frank said. "If ever there's been a case of divine justice, this was it."

Clarissa, who could not help overhearing the conversation from the next room, shook her head. It was typical of Toby Holt, she thought, to risk his life, gambling wildly, by proposing conditions for a fight that no reasonable, sane man would have suggested. She was filled with emotion as she thought of him, and all she knew was that she couldn't wait to see him again.

Bettina, clasping her daughter's hand tightly, looked up at Frank, her eyes huge. "I can't tell you how grateful I am to you," she said. "There's no way I can repay my debt to you."

"There's where you're wrong," Frank replied. "There is a way to repay me, and if you're smart, you'll do it."

Perplexed, Bettina looked up at him, waiting for him to continue.

"You're the kind of woman," he said, "who naturally attracts trouble. Trouble you can't handle. You need somebody to take care of you and so does Lucy. So, the way I see it, you'll just have to marry me and let me look after both of you."

Clarissa smiled to herself as she tiptoed out of the apartment and returned to her own dwelling next door. She knew that neither Bettina nor Frank would miss her.

By the end of the day, one fact was very clear to

Toby Holt and Rob Martin: Tom Harrison's reign of terror in Tumwater had come to an end for all time. The relieved citizens of the town rejoiced, and the lumberjacks who had been intimidated by Harrison now eagerly sought other employment. For the first time since the three friends had begun lumbering operations on their property, manpower was no longer a problem.

Late in the afternoon, after Toby and Rob had made a quick visit to Olympia, a new sheriff, appointed by the governor to straighten out the affairs in Tumwater, arrived in the town. With Harrison out of the way, there was no question of the new man's falling under anyone's sway. All of Harrison's subordinates, including the former sheriff, suffered accordingly, and along with Mr. Trumbull, they were held without bail in the local jail.

As Toby and Rob rode out to the cabin on their own property, they felt that the community at last was on the right track and was capable of living up to its potential.

Toby intended to shave and change into clean clothes before calling on Clarissa Sinclair. But he was delayed because he and Rob found Frank Woods waiting for them. Neither was surprised when Frank told them that he had proposed to Bettina and had been accepted.

Accepting their congratulations, Frank appeared somewhat subdued. "I've got a problem," he said, "and I need you two to help me think of a solution."

"What's wrong?" Toby asked.

"Our labor problems are solved," Frank said. "We have all the lumberjacks we need, and we'll have no trouble getting the lumber to the sawmills either.

What bothers me, though, is a matter of plain and simple arithmetic. We're splitting the profits three ways, and I'm not rightly sure that my share is enough for me to support a wife and daughter."

Toby and Rob exchanged a quick glance, and both of them grinned. There was no need for a private exchange between them; they were of one mind.

"I don't think you have any problem that's going to keep you awake nights, Frank," Toby said. "As things are working out, Rob and I are going to have our hands full surveying in Montana for the new railroad."

"That's right," Rob said. "In fact, I've been wondering how to break the news to you, Frank, that in the future, we're not going to be able to spend any time on the property here. The surveying job is going to occupy our full time and attention for a good many months to come."

"As a matter of fact," Toby said slowly, "these so-called predicaments—yours and ours—are happening at a fortunate time for all of us. Rob and I went into the lumbering business to begin with because we owned this property and we weren't any too certain how we wanted to spend our lives once we got out of the army. The surveying for the building of a transcontinental railroad was especially right for us, and when we had the opportunity, we grabbed it."

"So it seems to me," Rob said, "that in order to be fair all around, we should leave the lumbering operation and the handling of the Tumwater property completely in your hands, Frank."

"And that means," Toby added, "that you should be compensated accordingly. Speaking for myself, without having consulted privately with Rob, I'll say

XI

Governor Pickering looked at each of his guests in turn, then rose to his feet behind his desk. "You lads," he said, "did more than set Tumwater free from a disease that was eating into the very heart of the community. You also saved the territory vast sums of money. Tom Harrison had created such a chaotic situation in Tumwater that I did indeed finally manage to persuade the legislature that the territory itself had to act in order to protect its citizens. Thus, a constabulary force will be established in Tumwater, and no one need ever again be afraid of going about his business."

As Toby and Rob watched, the governor picked up three heavy parchment envelopes from his desk.

"But even with the constabulary, clipping Harrison's wings and rendering him harmless would have been a major task that would have cost the territory many thousands of dollars," he said. "You lads, however, solved that problem yourselves very neatly."

"You might say that Harrison provided his own solution," Toby said. "He seemed to lose his perspective and perhaps his reason."

"Be that as it may," the governor said, "the legislature voted that Toby Holt, Robert Martin, and Frank Woods be awarded gifts from the grateful territory of Washington." He handed each of them an envelope, giving Toby the third envelope to bring to Frank.

Toby was astonished to discover that his share was the staggering sum of five thousand dollars. Rob was equally stunned when he found that he had been awarded the sum of one thousand dollars, Frank being given the same amount.

When Toby and Rob tried to express their thanks to the governor, Pickering silenced them with a wave of his hand. "We still have business—vastly important business—to conduct," he told them. "I have here a joint resolution passed by the United States Senate and House of Representatives and subsequently transformed into an executive order, which President Johnson has signed. Under its terms, you two are authorized to conduct any and all surveys that you find necessary for the proposed construction of a railroad across the Montana Territory, which will join with the western extension, here in Washington."

Toby was pleased, and so was Rob.

"I can't say that I envy you," Pickering told them. "You're going into some of the most rugged and inhospitable country on the entire continent of North America. Are you familiar with Montana?"

Rob shook his head. "No, sir, I've never been there," he replied.

"What about you, Holt?" the governor asked.

"I'm about as familiar with Montana as I am with Washington, sir," he said. "My father took me on a number of trips there. The mountains are mighty desolate."

Governor Pickering nodded somberly. "So is the grass plain region that lies to the east," he said. "The Sioux still travel there extensively because of the buffalo they shoot, and they're determined not to allow the white man to settle permanently in the territory."

A thin white line formed around Toby's lips. "I'm familiar with the Sioux," he said. "My father and I had several encounters with them, and I expect that Rob and I will be seeing a great deal more of them than we like."

"If I could," Governor Pickering said, "I'd write to the governor of the territory and ease your path for you. But I suppose you know that Sidney Edgerton, the first governor of Montana, has resigned, and the temporary governor, Meagher, died under mysterious circumstances. It's been claimed that he was murdered, but no one really knows. In any event, Montana has no governor at the moment, and there's no territorial legislature. The Indians grow increasingly hostile, bandit gangs roam the territory, plundering the countryside, and the infantry battalion already stationed there is hard pressed to maintain law and order."

"I knew that we were heading into a rough frontier area," Rob said, "but I'm afraid I didn't quite realize how very rough it would be."

"One way and another, we'll manage," Toby said quietly. "We believe it's America's destiny to have a railroad that joins our whole nation together by stretching from the Atlantic to the Pacific. It's important that the railroad be built—so important that neither the mountains, nor the Sioux, nor the bandit gangs can halt us."

Studying the documents that Governor Pickering gave them, Toby and Rob discovered that they were directed by President Andrew Johnson to begin work in the Montana Territory in six weeks, or as soon as the snows melted. At that time, they would begin their survey in the mountains dominating the western portion of the territory and then would go on to survey the great prairie lands in the eastern portion of the territory.

Having reached their agreement with Frank Woods, the pair no longer had any responsibility for the lumbering operations, so they planned to return to Oregon to pay their families a visit before starting their new assignment. They were still in Tumwater when Frank was married to Bettina Snow, and Rob stood up with the groom, while Toby, at Bettina's request, gave her away in marriage. Ted and Olga Woods came for the ceremony, and it was arranged that Toby and Rob would travel with them the following day.

Somewhat to Toby's surprise, he found himself inviting Clarissa Sinclair to accompany him on the visit to his mother, and he was further surprised when she accepted promptly. He had not intended to issue the invitation to her; in fact, the idea did not cross his mind until he was seated next to her at the modest reception that followed Frank and Bettina's wedding. He asked her without weighing the matter, and she replied in kind.

The construction of a new road through the wilderness that lay between Olympia and Fort Vancouver made it possible for the travelers to ride rapidly, safely, and without incident. When they reached the fort, Rob stopped off there to see Beth Blake before proceeding to the home of his parents across the river. In the meantime, Toby and Clarissa went to the south bank by ferry, and soon thereafter, they reached the Holt ranch.

Toby was relieved and gratified to find that his mother continued to hold up after her ordeal. As always, she kept herself busy with the ranch, and if she was grieving privately, she gave no sign to others that anything was amiss with her.

Eulalia revealed that she and Cindy were invited to dine that evening at the Blake house at Fort Vancouver, and she insisted that Toby and Clarissa were included in the invitation. This was confirmed by a military messenger, who arrived with a note from General Blake, making it very clear that Toby and the young lady also were expected.

When Eulalia left the parlor to change her dress for the evening, Toby turned to his sister. "Is there some special function at the Blake house tonight?"

Cindy shook her head and sounded bored as she answered in the condescending tones of a girl in her mid-teens, "No, it's just the usual. Either Mama and I go over there for supper or the general comes here, usually dragging Beth with him. I wouldn't be surprised if he and Mama end up getting married."

Toby was surprised. "I didn't realize that he and Ma were that serious."

Cindy shrugged, unconcerned by the doings of her elders. "They're thick as thieves," she said, and as far as she was concerned, that ended the subject.

Toby was still somewhat perplexed when he and Clarissa were alone, and he sought her advice. The situation was delicate, as she well knew, and she had no intention of saying too much, having no idea how Toby might feel about the prospect of his mother marrying the general.

"Your mother," she said cautiously, "is an exceptionally attractive woman. Any man would be delighted to have her as his wife."

"I suppose so," Toby replied, and frowned. The idea disturbed him, and he knew why. For many years he had thought of his parents as an indissoluble entity. Now that his father was dead, it was not logical or reasonable for him to expect his mother to spend the rest of her days alone on the ranch, but at the same time, the thought that she might be contemplating marriage to another man disturbed him deeply.

Realizing he was being selfish, however, he kept his thoughts to himself, and Clarissa, aware that he was perturbed, was glad to drop the subject.

That evening, Dr. and Mrs. Martin also were guests at the Blake house. Beth, in spite of her pleasure at being reunited with Rob, seemed tense and high-strung. Toby, who remembered the gay, laughing Beth Blake of the past, was distressed to see that she was still greatly troubled by the events of the past months.

After the meal, Lee Blake announced that he and Eulalia were going to climb to the artillery battery at the top of the hill to see the view of the river, which they appeared to make their regular practice. He invited the others to accompany them, but only the elder Martins accepted.

So Beth and Rob were left alone in the parlor with Toby, Clarissa, and young Cindy. No sooner had the two older couples departed on their walk, than Beth said, "I'm sorry, Toby, that you had to be subjected to a shock on your homecoming, but it couldn't be helped. Perhaps it's just as well that you know the truth. How do you like it?"

Toby blinked in bewilderment. Beth's sharp tone was totally unexpected.

"I tried to tell him this afternoon," Cindy said, yawning, "but he didn't listen to me either."

"Your mother," Beth said with asperity, "has set her cap for my father and is very busily chasing him."

"Oh, I think the opposite is true," Cindy interjected. "General Blake is sweet on Mama, and he's courting her like mad."

Rob, who had been apprised of the situation by Beth, said tactfully, "Let's just say that Mrs. Holt and General Blake are mutually attracted to each other, and we won't try to concern ourselves with which of them is the pursuer and which is the pursued. That's a fine point that I find rather irrelevant."

"Whatever the case," Beth snapped, "now that you've come home, Toby, I hope you can do something about it."

He swallowed hard, lifting an eyebrow. "What can I do?" he asked helplessly.

"Tell your mother to act her age," she said stridently.

Cindy giggled.

Toby weighed the suggestion, then shook his head. "I've never had that kind of relationship with my mother," he said. "My father put her on a pedestal, and I guess I did the same thing. I simply couldn't criticize her and tell her I disapprove of her remarrying." His mind continuing to revolve, he added, "Perhaps you could speak to your father?"

"I already have," Beth said, and appeared so disturbed that Rob took her hand.

"What happened?" Toby asked.

Cindy, who had already heard the story, giggled again. Beth glared at Cindy and replied succinctly, "He told me—in so many words—to mind my own business."

There was a long silence while Toby tried to absorb what he had learned. It was startling to discover that his mother was engaged in a romance with General Blake, and he was equally surprised to discover that Beth seemed to be relying on him to call a halt to the relationship.

"I find it hard to believe that this is really a serious involvement on either side," he said slowly.

Clarissa, who had kept her own counsel, felt the time had come for her to intervene. She had observed both General Blake and Mrs. Holt at the supper table and had formed her own conclusions. "Why do you think that?" she demanded.

"For one thing," he said, "I know how very much my mother and father loved each other. For another, I understood all my life that Lee and Cathy Blake felt the same way."

"They did!" Beth cried.

Clarissa nodded and fell silent.

Beth studied her. "You disagree?" she demanded.

Toby realized that Clarissa was holding her tongue. "Please," he said to her, "speak up."

"Very well," she replied, "but you won't like this, and Beth will dislike it even more. I don't deny that your parents loved each other and that yours did, too, Beth. It would be presumptuous of me to question their relationships. But I've lost both my parents, so perhaps I see the situation somewhat more clearly than either of you do. I'll put it to you this way. No matter how much Eulalia and Whip Holt may have loved each other, Whip has passed on. No matter how close Cathy and Lee Blake were, Cathy is no longer living. So the survivors face a radically altered situation."

"True," Toby said, nodding.

"Don't for a moment forget that Eulalia Holt is far more attractive than most women of her age. She's lovely! I just hope that I've kept a fraction of the looks that she's retained when I'm as old as she is. If General Blake is interested in her, I'm quite sure he isn't alone. Any mature man in his right mind is sure to want her."

Toby swallowed hard, impressed anew by Clarissa's forthright manner. Even Cindy no longer looked and acted bored. She stared openmouthed at the young woman who spoke with such confidence.

"Now," Clarissa said, "as to General Blake, I urge you, Beth, to look at him objectively, not as a daughter. He's a very handsome man, you know. He's vigorous and polished, and he has a quality that any woman would find fascinating—he's been accustomed to command, and he has an aura of genuine authority about him at all times."

Beth reluctantly agreed.

"I can't pretend to speak for Mrs. Holt," Clarissa said, "and frankly, I have no idea of what might be going through her mind. But I'll say this: if I were in her shoes, I'd be very flattered by the attentiveness that General Blake showed me."

Beth clenched her fists. "What you're saying," she cried, "is that my father and Aunt Eulalia should get married. You're approving of their romance."

"No," Clarissa said. "I have no right to speak for either of them. What I am saying, however, is that all of you should acclimate yourselves at least to the possibility that they're engaged in a serious romance. They've suffered terrible blows, both of them, and they've turned to old friends with whom they've shared many problems in the past. Because both of those old friends are uncommonly attractive people, the whole romantic process may be speeded up. I don't know, but I suggest that you brace yourselves."

As always, Toby was grateful for Clarissa's candor. "Assuming that you're right," he said, "I don't see that there's anything we can do about this matter. In all justice to my mother and to the general, I don't see how we could have the temerity to tell them how to act or what to do. Don't you agree, Clarissa?" he added, feeling the need for her support.

She smiled faintly. "I was being careful not to express my own opinion, but since you asked for it, Toby, here it is. Both of these people are adults. They've seen the world, and they've tasted both triumphs and defeats. I'd think you'd be going too far, presuming too much, if you dared to interfere in any way with their romance."

"That's easy for you to say!" Beth cried. "It isn't your father who's making an idiot of himself."

Toby was astonished to discover that he resented Beth's words. Even though he was badly disturbed by the possibility that his mother might be engaging in a romance with General Blake, he nevertheless could see the matter through the general's eyes and could understand how he could become infatuated with Eulalia Holt.

The older couples returned from their walk, and their reappearance terminated the conversation. General Blake suggested a nightcap, and Rob helped him serve it.

Beth withdrew into a shell and said very little. Toby was so shaken that he became self-conscious, and for that reason, he, too, was silent. Rob, however, tried to behave naturally, and to an extent, he succeeded. But the burden of acting as spokesperson for the younger generation fell on Clarissa's shoulders, and she handled herself with natural grace and good humor, acting as though nothing out of the ordinary had taken place.

A messenger arrived bearing a letter for Dr. Martin, which interrupted the talk. He read the communication and sighed. "I'm sorry," he said, "but I'm wanted at the hospital for an urgent consultation."

"I've never known it to fail," Tonie said as she stood up. "Every time we're enjoying ourselves, he's called to the hospital. Beth, take a word of advice from your future mother-in-law, and when you have sons, discourage them from being doctors."

Eulalia announced it was time for her to return home, too, so the party came to an end. Toby and Rob went out to the stable for the horses, and during their absence, Eulalia and Lee withdrew to the front hall, where they conversed in low tones. No one seemed to regard their behavior as anything other than normal. Then, when Toby and Rob reappeared, she repeated an invitation to the entire group to dine at her ranch house the following evening.

"I'll be there," Lee told her, smiling.

His reaction caused Beth to bridle, and after the guests had gone, she continued to seethe but concealed her feeling sufficiently, so that only Rob, who was staying for the night, was aware of it.

The general announced that he was sleepy and went upstairs. Beth waited until he was out of earshot. "Would you do me a very great favor, Rob?" she wanted to know. "Please be a dear and pour me a drink of that French brandy in the square, cut-glass bottle."

He was surprised but did as she had asked.

"I wanted this," she said, "because it will help me to simmer down. I have an important decision to make."

Rob put his hands on her shoulders. "I hate to interfere in something that's not my business, really, but I've got to tell you that I think Clarissa Sinclair is right. You have no call to interfere in your father's romance with Aunt Eulalia, and the same goes for Toby and for Cindy."

"I have no intention of interfering," she said, swirling the brandy in a bell-shaped glass and holding the amber fluid so that it caught the light of the fire still glowing in the hearth. "I quite agree with Clarissa, even though I think her reasons are wrong. If my father and Aunt Eulalia have so little regard for their own marriages of years and years that they're willing to desecrate the memories of Mama and Uncle Whip, that's indeed their business, and I don't intend to interfere in any way with them. It's my own future that concerns me." She raised the glass, inhaled the aroma, and took a small sip of the potent brandy.

Rob was alarmed. "To the best of my knowledge," he said, "you've decided to cast your future lot with me."

"Indeed I have, my dear," she replied, and smiling up at him, put a hand on the lapel of his jacket. "We had agreed to postpone our marriage for a time. Indefinitely, really, as we never did settle on a date."

Rob nodded.

"One of my greatest problems," she said, her voice becoming husky, "is that I was brought up to be a lady. I've been a lady all my life. I dress as I'm expected to dress, my manners are impeccable, and my behavior is exemplary, at least most of the time. Well, if I'm a lady, so be it. I intend to take advantage of that fact."

Rob looked at her quizzically.

Suddenly Beth giggled and curled her arms around his neck. "It's the privilege of a lady to change her mind," she said. "When Mama died, I asked you to postpone our wedding. I now reverse myself and ask you not to postpone it for one moment longer than is absolutely necessary."

Rob was elated, but at the same time, he could see complications. "I think your decision is wonderful," he said, "but keep in mind that I'm obligated to go off to Montana with Toby in less than six weeks."

"I see no reason we can't make arrangements and be married within a week," Beth told him. "That will give us almost five weeks together, at the very least, as man and wife."

"So it will," Rob replied, taking her into his arms.

"And maybe we can figure out some way," she

continued, "that I could go to Montana with you."

He protested at once. "I don't think that would be suitable," he said. "It's still a wild, rough frontier country."

Beth nestled close to him, her body pressing against his. "I'm no fragile flower," she said. "I grew up on army posts. I was taught to fire a gun when I was still a small child, and I learned the manual of arms from one of my father's sergeants when I was five. I had a box seat for the Mexican War when we were stationed in Texas, and I went through the San Francisco riots when we lived at the Presidio. If there's any way that I can possibly get to Montana with you, I want to go."

Wanting her badly, aroused by her proximity, Rob lost his ability to think clearly. "Maybe we could work out something," he said. "There are a couple of little towns in the territory, and although it wouldn't be easy for you, maybe we could arrange for you to stay in one of them while Toby and I are off on our surveying jaunts."

Beth hugged him fiercely. "I knew you'd find a way!" she cried, "I knew it!" Raising her face to his, she returned his kiss with such depth of passion that it left him shaken.

Afraid he would lose his self-control, Rob dropped his hands to his sides and took a backward step.

Beth stared at him anxiously. "You'll do it, darling? You agree to be married at once?"

"The—the sooner the better," he replied.

That was all she wanted to know, and she felt she had triumphed. Not until much later did it occur to her to wonder why she had been so insistent on an immediate marriage, reversing her whole approach. Was it because she was so disapproving of the romance of her father and Eulalia that she wanted to beat them to the punch and be married first? Or was it because she sensed Toby's compatibility with the tall, frank-spoken young woman with whom he was consorting, and realized that she would never enjoy such a relationship? Perhaps she was jealous.

For whatever her reasons, the die was cast.

Although the wedding was held in haste, no detail was overlooked, and thanks to the efficiency of Eulalia Holt, aided by Clarissa Sinclair, the entire affair went off smoothly.

The ceremony itself was held in the chapel at Fort Vancouver, and every pew was filled, most of the seats being taken by old friends of the Blakes, the Holts, and the Martins, who had traveled across the continent with them on the first wagon train to Oregon.

Sitting on the bride's side of the aisle were Andy and Susanna Brentwood, who would soon be giving birth. Taking his wife's hand, Andy smiled to think that his younger cousin, Beth, whom he had always loved to tease, was now a grown woman and getting married.

Lee Blake, gray-haired and distinguished, gave his daughter away in marriage, and as Clarissa Sinclair had indicated, every mature woman in the church stared at him as he came down the aisle in his full-dress major general's uniform.

Rob awaited his bride at the altar, nervous in a snug-fitting suit with a stiff collar that chafed his neck. Toby Holt, his best man, stood beside him and felt waves of envy as he looked at Beth as she entered the rear of the church with her father.

Everyone agreed that Beth was a spectacularly attractive bride. Her hair resembled spun gold, and her deep blue eyes, which could be so placid on occasion, sparkled with an intense inner sense of excitement. As every woman who saw her white gown agreed, it was beautiful, truly a labor of love on the part of her late mother, who had spent many hours making it in anticipation of this day. White lace frothed in the veil and swooped to the floor in her train as she made her dignified way down the aisle, a slight, triumphant smile on her lips as she looked at her waiting bridegroom.

Clarissa Sinclair, standing beside Eulalia Holt on the bride's side of the aisle, could not help reflecting that Beth was everything that she herself was not. She regarded herself as tall, ungainly, and clumsy, while Beth was the epitome of dainty, feminine grace and charm. At no time, and in no way, could she even faintly resemble this picture-book bride.

It was no wonder, Clarissa thought, that Toby still loved Beth. Not that he said anything, of course, but Clarissa knew it from the way that his eyes devoured Beth as he watched her move closer down the aisle.

Did Clarissa want Toby for herself, even though she knew he had not overcome his love for the woman whom he'd known all his life? Clarissa, as honest with herself as she was with others, could not answer that question. She didn't know, to be sure, whether Toby would be sufficiently interested to propose to her, but she was uncertain whether to use her own energies to elicit a proposal from him.

Ordinarily sure of herself and of the direction in which she was heading, Clarissa knew that this once she needed to exercise both patience and caution. If Toby married her while still loving Beth, she would be inviting insoluble problems, and their marriage would be doomed from the outset. Was she capable of causing him to forget Beth and to fall in love with her as he had given evidence that he was doing? She could not answer that question either, and told herself she would have to wait and let the future unfold itself.

Of all the women in the church, only one attracted as much attention as the bride. Eulalia Holt, resplendent in a gauzelike dress, her dark hair piled high on her head, was actually relieved when Beth appeared at the rear of the church and took the spotlight from her. She had been extremely uncomfortable and had felt that everyone present was staring at her.

There could be only one possible reason for their interest in her, and she assumed that her relationship with Lee Blake had become the talk of Oregon. Looking at Lee now, Eulalia couldn't help smiling. He was such a dear, such a thoughtful, generous, and considerate man. He was unlike Whip in so many ways, but in terms of unswerving dedication to honesty, the two men were remarkably similar.

Eulalia had given her heart to Whip many years earlier, and she still cherished his memory. He would remain part of her as long as she herself lived, occupying a special niche that no other man could occupy. At the same time, however, she was learning that she had the weaknesses, as well as the strengths, of the living. She craved love, and specifically she yearned for Lee Blake. At least she thought she did.

Beth had made her own attitude all too painfully clear, and Cindy, of course, was so immersed in her teenage self that she couldn't think in terms of her mother's problems. Eulalia wanted to discuss her future with Toby, but she hesitated, feeling it would be a disservice to Lee and a dishonor to Toby's memory of his father. Perhaps, she reflected, she could talk to Clarissa Sinclair. Clarissa was very young but had a sensible head on her shoulders, and as a widow, she would understand how the older woman felt. Perhaps, Eulalia thought, she would have an opportunity in the coming days to sit down with Clarissa and speak her mind.

There was a hollow feeling in the pit of Toby Holt's stomach as he stood in the yard outside the house of the commander of the Army of the West at Fort Vancouver. Unmindful of the laughing, joking crowd around him throwing rice and shouting jocular remarks to the bride and groom, he stood silently as he watched Beth and Rob Martin, who had changed from their wedding clothes into traveling attire, climb into the carriage that would take them off to a secret destination for a brief honeymoon.

This was not the end of the world, he knew, but he felt as if it were. Annoyed with himself, he nevertheless could not shake off his sense of lonely doom.

Rob lifted his bride into the carriage, mounted the seat beside her, and turning, waved to the wedding guests. He caught Toby's eye, grinned at him, and said something to Beth.

She, too, found Toby in the crowd and waved.

Suddenly they were gone, and he felt completely bereft. Wanting to be alone and in no mood for celebrations, he started off in the direction of the garden where the wedding reception had been held. Then, suddenly, he stopped.

Directly in front of him he saw his mother and Clarissa Sinclair deep in conversation. Pausing to look at them, it occurred to him for the first time how they were the same physical type. Although the younger woman was taller and larger-boned, she and Eulalia both had the same graceful build, the same easy freedom of movement.

Even more important, he realized, was a quality that would not be visible to a casual stranger. Eulalia and Clarissa were alike because they had the same fierce spirit of independence, the same burning desire to stand on their own feet and make their own way in the world. Yet, he realized, both were vulnerable. His mother had needed his father, and now it seemed she was floundering and reaching out for Lee Blake. By the same token, Clarissa was supporting herself through her real estate venture and enjoyed the feeling that she depended on no one. But Toby knew, nevertheless, that she leaned on him far more than she realized. It was possible, he thought, that he was attracted to Clarissa—drawn to her far more deeply than he had known—because of her similarity to his mother. He had heard it said that a young man who had a happy, solid relationship with his parents often fell in love with a woman because she reminded him of his mother. This was in no way true of Beth but apparently was the case with Clarissa.

As he stood, he felt a hand on his shoulder and was mildly irritated at the interruption of his solitude, but his mood softened when he saw General Lee Blake standing beside him.

"It was a fine wedding, Toby," Lee said. "Thanks for all your help."

Toby grinned a trifle sheepishly. "Don't thank me, General," he said. "I didn't do a thing."

"On the contrary," Lee assured him, a twinkle in his eye. "You kept Rob from disintegrating before our very eyes, and consequently, you performed a very valuable service."

Toby joined him in a laugh.

Lee sobered. "We've been so busy these past few days that I haven't had a chance to thank you for clearing up the nasty mess in Tumwater. Harrison was causing us great problems, and frankly, I was at a loss for what to do. But you saved me the need to do anything."

"I was lucky, I guess," Toby replied.

Lee grinned and shook his head. "Now," he said, "you sound exactly like your father. Every time Whip cleared up a totally impossible, messy situation, he invariably attributed his success to luck. All I can say is that you're Whip Holt's son, and I thank the Almighty for it. I thought Whip was unique in all the world, that there was no one quite like him, but you've come along and have stepped right into his shoes. That's wonderful, Toby. Wonderful for the country and for the people of the West in particular."

Toby was deeply touched, but he was also confused by Lee Blake's attitude. The general had been his father's close friend and associate, his partner in many ventures over the years, and his admiration for Whip Holt was obvious and genuine. Yet at the same time, it appeared he was courting Whip's widow.

Toby tried hard to convince himself that his mother's private life was her own business and that it was wrong of her son to try to make it his concern. Perhaps he was naive and consequently didn't understand human nature well enough to know how any man could admire a friend so much and yet yearn for the friend's widow. On the other hand, as Toby knew only too well, he himself was still desiring Beth, who was now the legal wife of his own best friend.

"I'm worried," Lee said, "that you and Rob are biting off far more than you can possibly chew in Montana. You're going into the wildest and most rugged country in all of North America. The Indian problem there is very serious. The Sioux are a clever, strong, and courageous people, and they are utterly determined not to give up one square inch of land to the United States. Outlaws are operating everywhere, terrorizing the settlers, and no one has been able to bring them under control. I was hoping that your railroad survey could be postponed until Andy Brentwood has at least the opportunity to pacify the region. But his regiment will just be arriving in Montana about the same time as you and Rob."

"Well, I appreciate your concern, General," Toby said, "but I can't afford to wait for conditions to improve. Our orders from President Johnson specify that we're to lose no time initiating our survey. We're told to begin work as soon as the snows melt in the mountains, and we're to complete our work as soon as feasible. The East is anxious to have the Northern Pacific Railroad built, and Lord knows the West is even more anxious. I feel a tremendous sense of responsibility, and I'm eager to get started."

Lee looked at him in admiration. "I know precisely how you feel, Toby, and I admire you for it. I know you'll do superbly and that you'll produce ex-

★ WAGONS WEST ★

A series of unforgettable books that trace the lives of a dauntless band of pioneering men, women, and children as they brave the hazards of an untamed land in their trek across America. This legendary caravan of people forge a new link in the wilderness. They are Americans from the North and the South, alongside immigrants, Blacks, and Indians, who wage fierce daily battles for survival on this uncompromising journey—each to their private destinies as they fulfill their greatest dreams.

☐	26822	INDEPENDENCE! #1	$4.50
☐	26162	NEBRASKA! #2	$4.50
☐	26242	WYOMING! #3	$4.50
☐	26072	OREGON! #4	$4.50
☐	26070	TEXAS! #5	$4.50
☐	26377	CALIFORNIA! #6	$4.50
☐	26546	COLORADO! #7	$4.50
☐	26069	NEVADA! #8	$4.50
☐	26163	WASHINGTON! #9	$4.50
☐	26073	MONTANA! #10	$4.50
☐	26183	DAKOTA! #11	$4.50
☐	26521	UTAH! #12	$4.50
☐	26071	IDAHO! #13	$4.50
☐	26367	MISSOURI! #14	$4.50
☐	27141	MISSISSIPPI! #15	$4.50
☐	25247	LOUISIANA! #16	$4.50
☐	25622	TENNESSEE! #17	$4.50
☐	26022	ILLINOIS! #18	$4.50
☐	26533	WISCONSIN! #19	$4.50
☐	26849	KENTUCKY! #20	$4.50

Prices and availability subject to change without notice.

Special Offer
Buy a Bantam Book
for only 50¢.

Now you can have Bantam's catalog filled with hundreds of titles plus take advantage of our unique and exciting bonus book offer. A special offer which gives you the opportunity to purchase a Bantam book for only 50¢. Here's how!

By ordering any five books at the regular price per order, you can also choose any other single book listed (up to a $5.95 value) for just 50¢. Some restrictions do apply, but for further details why not send for Bantam's catalog of titles today!

Just send us your name and address and we will send you a catalog!